A G
BEST
FRIEND

A GIRL'S BEST FRIEND

LOUISE MARLEY

POOLBEG

This novel is entirely a work of fiction. The names, characters and incidents portrayed in it are the work of the author's imagination. Any resemblance to actual persons, living or dead, events or localities is entirely coincidental.

Published 2004
Poolbeg Press Ltd.
123 Grange Hill, Baldoyle,
Dublin 13, Ireland
Email: poolbeg@poolbeg.com

1 3 5 7 9 10 8 6 4 2

A catalogue record for this book is available from the British Library.

ISBN 1-84223-172-3

Typeset by Patricia Hope in Palatino 10/14
Printed by
Litografia Rosés S.A., Spain

www.poolbeg.com

About the Author

Louise Marley was born in Southampton and worked as a civilian administrator for the police before becoming a full-time writer. Her previous novels include the bestselling *Smoke Gets In Your Eyes* and *Why Do Fools Fall In Love?* She also writes short stories and articles, which have been published in both Ireland and the UK.

Louise recently moved to North Wales with her husband and two children, and is having a wonderful time scrambling up mountains and going to beach barbeques when she really ought to be working on her fourth book . . .

For more information about Louise Marley visit her website www.louisemarley.co.uk

Also by Louise Marley

Smoke Gets In Your Eyes

Why Do Fools Fall In Love

Acknowledgements

Thanks to all at Poolbeg for their support, especially: Paula Campbell, Brona Looby, Sarah Conroy and Georgina Wilson.

And a special mention for Gaye Shortland, for her brilliant editing and ability to translate my creative punctuation!

This book is dedicated to:
Sue Dawson, Roxanne Molloy,
Tracey Golding and Sue Dickens –
who are always there for me.

And also to:
Andy, Jodie and Luke
with love

(From The Calahurst Echo)

FAMOUS DIAMOND LOST FOREVER

by
Jemma Stortford

The priceless Ashlyn Diamond has been stolen from a jeweller's workshop.

Last night, its 92-year-old owner, Mary, Lady Alverstoke, the grand-daughter of adventurer Harry Ashlyn, pleaded for the diamond's safe return. "I am afraid it will be cut into smaller stones," she said, "which would make it easier to dispose of. The Ashlyn Diamond will be lost forever."

A total of £6 million in diamonds were stolen when four men entered the local workshop at 8.00 am, shortly after staff opened up. Wearing smart suits, with balaclavas hiding their faces, they threatened staff with handguns, forcing them to empty the safe.

Within 5 minutes the men had loaded precious stones and complete works of jewellery into a black Nike holdall and escaped.

It is not clear how the robbers were able to evade a sophisticated alarm system – which included sensors and infrared beams. Police also refused to speculate if this raid is connected with a similar break-in at a jeweller in Dorset last week.

It is thought the Ashlyn Diamond was at the workshop to be cleaned, prior to its exhibition in the British Museum as part of the display entitled Heroes of the Empire.

To read the incredible story of how Harry Ashlyn came to own the diamond – turn to page 4.

Chapter One

SEPTEMBER

Jemma Stortford opened her eyes and wondered where the hell she was. Blearily she gazed up at the painting of Aphrodite, romping across the ceiling with Adonis in glorious Technicolor. No one else had Greek gods gambolling through their apartment. For once, she had fallen asleep in her own bed.

She sank back beneath the sheets and closed her eyes, pulling the duvet up around her ears. Bliss, perfect bliss. The panic only set in, ten seconds later, as she became aware of someone else's deep, rhythmic breathing. Tentatively she lifted the bed-sheet – and found a man asleep beside her.

He had flawless olive skin, an unremarkable straight nose, a square jaw and short, softly spiked, dark-brown hair. Totally relaxed in sleep, he looked untroubled, curiously vulnerable, but devastatingly handsome.

And Jemma was pretty confident she had never seen him before in her life.

As she attempted to remember what she had got up to last night, Jemma began to feel a lot like Dr Jekyll, the morning after. At least she was still wearing her T-shirt, jeans and ankle-boots (she had gone to bed in her *boots*?). She might be able to throw off her clothes in wild, drunken abandon, but she doubted very much that she would be able to throw them back on again.

The subject of her scrutiny suddenly yawned widely and opened eyes the colour of maple syrup. It took a while for him to focus on her and when he did, he abruptly pushed away the bedcovers, sat up and said: "Who the hell are you?"

"More to the point," grumbled Jemma, tugging the bed-sheets protectively back up to her chin, "who the hell are *you*?"

He looked around her bedroom with growing disbelief, taking in the turquoise walls, silver drapes and magnificent painted ceiling – which looked as though it had been scraped off the Sistine Chapel – and ran his hand through his hair, unwittingly making it stand on end.

"This is not my house. What am I doing here?"

"Maybe you were abducted by aliens?" suggested Jemma, burrowing back beneath the duvet. Having woken up in strange beds many times, she could relate to his embarrassment. Although, at the moment, he didn't appear in the slightest bit embarrassed. She could see he was fully dressed too – casually, in jeans and sweater. So they hadn't had sex . . . Jemma wondered why – and began to feel piqued. Hadn't he found her attractive?

He was first to interrupt the resulting awkward pause. "So," he began, smiling beguilingly. "Are you gonna introduce yourself?"

Even better, she thought sourly. He didn't want her for sex; he just wanted to be friends. More to the point, he probably wanted breakfast – though a glance at the clock showed it was closer to tea-time. Men! She thumped the pillow into a more comfortable shape, wishing it was his head. Why didn't he just get lost? Except all indications pointed to the unassailable fact that he already was . . .

She begrudgingly stuck her hand out from under the duvet – but without turning her head to look at him. "Hi," she grunted. "I'm Jemma. I live here."

He caught her hand in a warm, firm grasp. She attempted to pull it back into the warmth of the bed, but found he wasn't letting go so easily. She was forced to make eye contact.

"Hello, Jemma."

His voice was deep, amused and faintly accented. As she raised her head to look at him once more, it occurred to her that he bore more than a passing resemblance to Antonio Banderas. If she had met him anywhere else she would have been delighted to have got off with such a hunk – but, at the back of her mind, lurked the worrying thought that he could be a mad axe-man. He was certainly mad – dressed from head to foot in black like a character from an Anne Rice novel –

wait 'til Isabel found out she had got off with a Goth!

As Jemma appraised him, she felt a slight twinge of recognition – although that was impossible. She had never met him before, had she? She sincerely hoped he wasn't one of her girlfriends' boyfriends. She'd been in trouble for that before . . . Best-case scenario: they had met at The Parson's Collar wine bar on the quayside last night. Maybe. And maybe he was the Tooth Fairy.

Jemma had another attempt at retrieving her hand. "Do you know The Parson's Collar?"

"Sorry, I'm not a great fan of boy bands," he replied, still keeping a firm grip on her fingers.

She tugged ineffectively at them for a few moments. If he didn't let go soon, she would have to resort to all-out arm-wrestling. And he needn't think she wouldn't.

So, they didn't meet at the pub. Best brazen it out . . .

"Look," she began, looking at him directly so as to appear sincere. "This is a bit awkward for me. I mean, it's not as though I make a habit of this sort of thing . . ." *Much* . . . Oh well, she might as well come straight out with it – *casually*: "Um, so tell me, where did we meet?"

There seemed to be the slightest hint of laughter hovering around his lips, yet he remained remarkably straight-faced as he said, "I haven't the slightest idea. Is it important?" He raised her hand, not taking those dark, seductive eyes from her own, then gently kissed her fingertips, one by one.

Jemma felt the thrill of reciprocated lust hit home. Not so much Banderas as Valentino wannabe. Was the guy this full-on *all* the time? Not that she was complaining. Although it was starting to bug her that she couldn't remember picking him up . . .

"We didn't meet at the wine bar down the road?" she persisted.

He shrugged apologetically. "Maybe . . ."

"I didn't order pizza, so you can't be the pizza delivery guy." Aware how silly her conversation was becoming, she attempted to joke her way out of it. "And if you've come to read the meter, you're seriously lost!"

"Dr Livingstone, I presume?" he smiled and his mouth unexpectedly landed on hers.

Either he was in denial or he had grown tired of being interrogated. Jemma knew an evasion tactic when she saw one. She still kissed him back. After all, she had never pretended to be perfect . . .

It was a full five minutes before she remembered that he might be a mad axe-man – he was certainly a Goth – black daywear? So 1980s!

She pushed him away. "I don't know your name . . ."

"Nico."

"Short for Nicholas?"

"Long for Nic." He bent his head again, covering her face with butterfly kisses.

Jemma turned her face away and his tongue slipped into her ear by mistake. "That still doesn't tell me who you are."

He paused, faintly exasperated. "Who would you like me to be?"

"Someone I know!"

He leant back on his elbow and laughed, his breath

fanning her cheek, his free hand tenderly stroking her cheek. "And not some crazy stalker who broke in here while you were asleep?"

"I didn't say that." Oh no, *she* had been thinking more along the lines of the Vampire Lestat . . .

"OK," he said, settling himself back against the pillows, "life history coming up. I'm an impoverished writer – the inky fingers are probably a dead giveaway. I'm twenty-six years old. I adore 70s New Wave, takeout pizza and Quentin Tarentino movies. I can't see the point of sushi, hate nine-to-five routine and despise boy bands, as you know. My star sign, so I am reliably informed, is Scorpio."

"How weird," said Jemma, "so is mine. We have something in common."

"Not as much as I'd like," he said, leaning over her again. "Now, quit with the chat. I'm not at my best when performing to a running commentary."

* * *

So they spent the rest of the day in bed, except for the bit where Nico had to nip down to the local Indian takeaway when Jemma's rumbling tummy was drowning out the sound of her orgasm. And Jemma was feeling like heaven really was a place on earth when she noticed the sky outside was growing darker and the digital figures on her alarm-clock were relentlessly flickering around until they reached eight thirty.

Time's up, she thought. The whole sorry business of 'When will I see you again?', 'I'll call you' – *yeah, right*!

Nico, who had been contentedly occupying himself by counting off each of her ribs, suddenly realised she wasn't as enthusiastic as she might have been.

"What's up?" he asked.

"I've got to go to a party," said Jemma. "It was supposed to start at eight thirty. I'm late."

Nico didn't seem to think that an earth-shattering problem. "So cancel."

"I *can't*," muttered Jemma, ignoring the little voice in her head chirping: *you can, you can!* "It's my best friend's birthday. It wouldn't be fair to cry off."

Nico let out a huge sigh, flopped onto his back and stared moodily at the ceiling. "I see."

No, she thought, he didn't see. All *he* could see was her giving him the brush-off. She opened her mouth to try to explain, but by now he was climbing out of bed and looking around for his clothes. Or maybe he was just looking for an excuse to brush *her* off?

Nico prodded her shoulder. For some reason he was showing her his sweater. Nice bit of cashmere. He couldn't be that 'impoverished' – unless he had a wealthy girlfriend / wife in the background . . .

"Do you think it'll be all right for me to wear this?" he asked.

Jemma regarded him blankly. "Sorry?" So now she had become his style consultant?

"To the party."

"You're coming too?"

"Yeah, sure, no problem." He gave her a quick sideways glance. "If that's what you want?"

Chapter Two

The party was being held at Stortford House, a Georgian folly in the heart of the King's Forest. It had been built from honey-coloured stone, had three stories and was perfectly square, like a giant sugar-cube. There were rows of Ionic columns embellishing the walls, a balustrade edging the roof and a decorative pediment across the front. Even to Nico's untrained eye, the best of ancient Greece appeared to have been wantonly plundered and cemented onto an otherwise insignificant Georgian house.

By the time Jemma and Nico made it to the party, the cars outside were parked three deep. With careful manoeuvring, Nico was able to squeeze his rusting, black Fiesta into the gap left between a gleaming Ferrari and a top-of-the-range Aston Martin. As he switched off the engine, he noticed a security camera, wedged into the fork of an old oak-tree, following his every move.

Apparently the theme of the party was Arabian Nights. Jemma was resplendent in purple harem pants and matching sequinned bikini top, bells on her ankles and rings on her toes. The harem pants were made from a silky, diaphanous material, which became transparent when the light fell a certain way. Nico admired her bottom as he followed her up the worn stone steps and into the hall, hitching up the white cotton bed-sheets he wore over his clothes, which were moonlighting as a Lawrence of Arabia costume.

Finding the hall deserted, they followed the loud dance music along the corridor and into a ballroom. It was decorated like a 1970s advert for Turkish Delight. Swathes of red fabric were gathered across the ceiling to recreate a Bedouin tent; elegant gilt chairs and chaises longues, almost obscured by richly embroidered cushions, lined the walls. Antique looking-glasses, in tarnished gilt frames, were hung, one after the other down the length of the ballroom. Crystal chandeliers were suspended before every mirror, reflecting the light into infinity.

Nico caught sight of his reflection in one of the mirrors. Jemma's white cotton bed-sheet did not go with black cashmere and jeans. He looked like a Hell's Angel who'd got drunk and decided to go trick or treating.

He tugged the sheet off over his head and stuffed it behind a sofa, then realised Jemma was watching him in amusement.

"Hot?" she teased, her eyes crinkling at the corners, her lips widening into a broad smile.

"Costume parties are not really my thing," he admitted, but was unwilling to debate the matter further. To distract her he said, "This is some house. Who are these guys? Lottery millionaires?"

Jemma seemed to find this funny. "Isaac van der Straatan owns Vanders – a chain of up-market jewellery shops. He has two daughters, my friend Isabel and the very frosty Danielle – who's coming this way right now." Jemma grabbed a couple of champagne flutes from a passing waiter and handed one to Nico. "Smile and look as though you're enjoying yourself," she advised in an undertone. "And if she asks where Isabel is, deny all knowledge."

Nico glanced towards the beautiful girl making her way towards them. She didn't have to force her way through the crowds on the dance-floor; they parted before her. Dressed in black harem pants and a gold-sequinned cropped top, she wore her red-gold hair piled up on her head, flickering different shades of fire in the light from the chandeliers. She looked like a younger, sexier, Nicole Kidman, decided Nico. But when her cool grey eyes settled back on him, he realised he had been staring.

"Hi," said Danielle, in a low, husky voice. Her eyes flickered suspiciously in his direction, then back to Jemma. "Glad you could make it."

"Danielle, this is Nico," said Jemma. "He's a writer. Nico, this is Danielle van der Straatan. She sells jewellery."

Understatement of the year, thought Nico, his

attention drawn to the fortune in diamonds she was wearing around her neck.

"Hi, Nico," she said, taking in his V-neck sweater and black jeans. "Interesting costume. Tom Jones, right?"

He grinned. "What's new, pussycat?"

"You're a friend of Jemma's . . ."

It was easy assumption to make, as Jemma was currently digging her considerable fingernails into his wrist, threatening to sever a main artery. Maybe she thought he was going to do an about turn and hightail it out of there.

"Uh huh," he agreed, hoping Danielle wasn't going to get funny because he didn't have his own invite.

"Where did you two meet?"

Nico looked helplessly at Jemma, who began to giggle.

Danielle, glancing at the half-empty champagne glasses, evidently decided they were both the worse for drink and tactfully changed the subject. "Have you seen Isabel?"

"Nope," said Nico, remembering Jemma's warning.

His easy insouciance did not go down well with his hostess who muttered, "Christ!" under her breath.

"I'm sure she'll arrive soon," Jemma said quickly. "Isabel is always late for everything."

Danielle's mouth was set in a firm, scarlet line. "I didn't think she'd have the affront to be late for her own birthday party!"

"That's Isabel," sighed Jemma. "Gotta lotta front."

"You shouldn't encourage her!"

Jemma's face took on a rosy hue.

He would hate to get on the wrong side of this girl, decided Nico, sliding his arm around Jemma protectively. An awkward silence descended. Jemma helped herself to another glass of champagne as soon as a waiter offered it, and Nico had no intention of keeping the conversation going with small talk. The sooner Danielle went, the better he'd like it.

However, Danielle, oblivious to any bad vibes, stuck close beside them and surveyed the people crowded into the ballroom. Nico noticed the way her fingers were tapping against her thigh, the way she constantly licked her lips until the scarlet lipstick had melted away. Generally, she was doing an excellent impression of someone suffering inner turmoil.

The main lights were abruptly switched on, leaving them all blinking; the DJ stuck 'She's The One' on the deck and everyone stopped dancing.

"Oh *brilliant*!" muttered Danielle, as everyone turned to look at her. "Perfect timing. Look," she said to Jemma, "I'm going to have to blow out candles – if you see Isabel, tell her – no, forget it. It'll only lose in the translation." She glanced briefly back at Nico, half-formed a comment, then stalked off towards the stage set up at the end of the ballroom.

Nico watched her go. She could have been walking the green mile. If this was the girl who had everything, why was she so miserable?

"Is she always like this?" he asked Jemma.

"You caught her on a good day," was the frank retort.

As Danielle stepped up onto the stage, there was a man already waiting there, who greeted her with a kiss. Not a lover's kiss, decided Nico; perhaps he was her father. He was attractive enough, in a rugged sort of way, in his late forties or early fifties – well preserved so it was difficult to tell. The kind of man who played tennis and jogged, but still enjoyed his cigars and brandy.

As Danielle stepped back, Nico could see the man's pale eyes, dark eyebrows, square forehead – enough of a family resemblance for Nico to have his theory confirmed, even if Jemma hadn't stood on tiptoe up to whisper helpfully in his ear:

"That's Isaac van der Straatan. The one I was telling you about."

"So where's Isabel?"

Jemma grimaced. "I have no idea."

"But this is her birthday party!"

"Isabel can be a little eccentric," conceded Jemma, "but I'm sure she'll turn up sometime."

"Maybe in time for the next one."

Dutifully, they all sang 'Happy Birthday' and after Danielle had blown out the twenty-five candles on her pink iced cake, Isaac presented her with a beautifully wrapped present – all shiny gold paper and white satin ribbons. Danielle carefully peeled back the paper and pulled out a black velvet box. She flipped open the catch and held up an exquisite gold watch, glittering with diamonds.

"Speech!" cried someone. "Speech!"

Nico almost laughed out loud at the look of absolute horror on Danielle's face. Anyone would have thought she'd been asked to take all her clothes off.

Isaac, taking pity on his daughter, held up his hand for silence. "It's great to see you all here tonight," he said, turning his charm on the crowd. "We don't seem to get together to celebrate the good things as often as we should. In fact, these days we only seem to meet at weddings, christenings and funerals. As neither of my girls is likely to be getting married in the near future, I think tonight would be the perfect time to make an important announcement."

Danielle looked anxiously at him and he took her hand, squeezing it reassuringly.

Birthday surprise number two coming up, decided Nico cynically. Sports car? Racehorse? What *do* you give the girl who has everything? Oh yes, *a jewellery empire . . .*

As he watched Danielle for her reaction, he could see the same idea crossing her mind. Her fingers were twisting themselves nervously, but her face was flushed with pleasure. Certainly she looked the most cheerful he'd seen her all evening.

"I have come to the conclusion that I am growing too old for the cut and thrust of high-powered business," Isaac was saying, tongue firmly in cheek. "I've made more money than is decent for one person in their lifetime, so I've decided to take early retirement and sell up. I'll be giving some of the proceeds to the girls so they won't starve!" He laughed heartily and patted Danielle on the head as though she was still a six-year-old with gap teeth and ringlets. "As for the rest – I'll be signing it over to charity."

The room erupted with a roar of approval. Isaac kissed his daughter again and stepped down from the stage. Waving away the congratulations of his friends and relations, he scooped up a glass of champagne and walked out of the ballroom, urging everyone to 'get on down' and enjoy the party. The DJ stuck on 'Love Don't Cost A Thing', which to Nico, his eyes still on Danielle, seemed dreadfully ironic.

For a brief moment Danielle stood alone on the stage, unnoticed by the guests at her own party, her face pale, her eyes blank. Only her clenched hands gave the hint of that barely suppressed emotion. Then her eyes met Nico's.

For a split second they stared at each other. As he half-smiled in sympathy, she abruptly turned away, jumping down from the stage and running out through the door.

"Well," said Jemma, knocking back her third glass of champagne in one go. "That was unexpected. I wonder how much Danielle and Isabel will get? Lucky cows! I wish Dad would give me a couple of million."

Nico wasn't really paying attention. "Danielle doesn't seem too thrilled."

"Vanders was her life," shrugged Jemma. "What's she going to do now? Sign up for job retraining?"

Nico saw Jemma's glass was empty, which gave him

the perfect excuse to ask: "Shall I get you another drink?"

She handed him her glass. "Thanks!" And, as she turned her attention back to the dancing, she failed to notice Nico dump their empty glasses on a waiter's tray before swiftly exiting the door beside the stage.

* * *

Nico could hear the argument as soon as he left the ballroom. Checking no one else was about to witness his next move, he walked silently down the corridor until he came to the door he judged the row was emanating from, then pressed his ear against it.

The voices were muffled so he gently turned the handle and let the door swing slightly ajar, praying that it wouldn't squeak. As the gap widened, he caught a glimpse of thousands of dusty brown volumes locked away behind glass cabinet doors. Some kind of library? The door swung open another inch. Sitting behind a desk, tapping his fingers irritably on the arm of his chair, was Isaac van der Straatan. He was arguing, albeit good-humouredly, with someone on the other side of the room who was standing just out of Nico's range of vision.

There was no way Nico could risk opening the door any further, but as he was calculating his next move he heard a woman's voice, clearer now, saying: "I can't believe you just said that! Why on earth are you giving up now? Vanders is doing so well. We've never been so successful. I've planned a whole new range for the next two years, to appeal to the younger customers. We could move even more up-market, give those London stores a run for their money!"

"I'm getting too old." Isaac slumped back in his chair, studying his hands, twisting his wedding ring around on his finger, seemingly anything to avoid looking at his daughter directly. "I want to retire, relax, enjoy life while I still can, not have to worry about keeping one step ahead of the Inland Revenue."

"You mean that diamond robbery last month has got you running scared!"

"That too," he admitted, glancing up. "I'm not too proud to admit it. Why slog your guts out for the best part of twenty-five years, only to have your head blown off for the sake of a few carbonised crystals."

"Fair enough," said Danielle. "So why don't you give *me* the business?"

"And what am I supposed to live on for the next thirty years? A state pension? Please!"

"OK, sell the rest of Vanders, but keep the branch at Calahurst and Port Rell, and the workshop, and give them to me in lieu of my inheritance."

"For you to play at shops? I don't think so."

"Excuse me? What do you think I've been doing for the past two years? I've been running those branches almost single-handedly."

"But what good is the workshop to you?"

"It keeps Vanders exclusive if we can create our own pieces."

"Buried down here in the King's Forest? You need

an outlet in London for that kind of venture. The tourists in Calahurst want postcards of deer and cute little squirrels, not oak-leaves dipped in gold."

"You had to bring that up."

Isaac chuckled. "OK, that was below the belt. But you can't sell designer stuff here. No one will pay the prices."

"So give me the Norchester shop too!"

"Swap you Mayfair for Park Lane and a hotel? We're not playing Monopoly."

"Stop prevaricating and tell me why you won't let me keep Vanders! I've been your assistant for the past two years; I've increased business, made useful contacts – got our jewellery at film premieres, even in *Vogue* magazine once. Vanders is hot."

"It's fashionable, I grant you," agreed Isaac. "But fashions change. Don't waste your life on an empty dream, Danielle. Look at the alternative. If I sell Vanders you won't have to work for a living – you won't have to work ever again. Aren't you tempted, even for a minute? With the money I'm offering, you can do whatever you want."

"That is *not* what I want! I *want* to make a success of something on my own terms. Gain respect on my own merit."

"Why? You have nothing to prove."

"No matter where I go, what I do, I'll always be known as the daughter of 'the wealthy Isaac van der Straatan'. I want to show everyone I have more to offer."

He smiled wryly. "Is being my daughter so bad?"

"That's not what I meant and you know it."

"What makes you think you'll be respected on your own terms if you take on Vanders? It's a family business created by me. You'll be carrying on a tradition – treading water, if you like."

"If Vanders goes down the pan, you'll be proved right. But if I make a success of it, everyone will realise it was down to me. I'll be the name behind Vanders."

"Next stop, world domination." Isaac sadly shook his head. "Why don't you find some nice man and settle down? Have babies. I'm sure it'd calm you down, make you more mellow, less – less *feisty*."

Danielle refused to bite. "What's wrong with being feisty?"

"All men want a nice, friendly, non-threatening girl that they can take home to mother. Trust me, I know. I'm Joe Average."

"Perhaps I'd better stay single. I wouldn't want to inflict my freaky feisty disposition on some unsuspecting man."

Isaac seemed genuinely hurt. "I would like grandchildren."

Pause.

"There's always Isabel," said Danielle.

"Let's not go there." Isaac sounded pained. "You're the sensible one. You're the one I expected great things from."

"Then give me this chance and I'll prove you right."

Isaac wasn't going to give in that easily. "Wouldn't

you rather have the money and buy some nice trendy boutique?"

"Boutiques are for girls. I want to run Vanders."

Isaac put his hand up to his head. "I feel as though we're travelling in circles here. You used to do this to me as a child. Keep on and on, hoping to wear me down. Well, it won't work. I'm selling Vanders and that's the end of it. Take the money and run. I don't care what you do with it. Fritter it away on frivolities."

"What if I refuse to take the money?"

"Give it to charity, I really don't give a damn. Then maybe you'll find out what it means to actually work for a living, to start something up from nothing, make a success of it – then sell up and enjoy your new prosperity, which is exactly what I intend to do. Just hope to God you never give birth to such ungrateful children as I did."

"I'm not ungrateful," explained Danielle patiently, "I just want – "

Isaac held up his hand. "It's OK, you can stop there, I know this bit, we've been here before. I think it would do you good to have some leisure time. You work too hard – it's starting to affect your common sense. I mean, look at you – you're twenty-five years old and still single."

"Practically on the shelf! Bloody hell, Dad, I don't think Bridget Jones need worry she's got competition yet. You sound like a Jewish momma."

"With good reason! There's some people around here are convinced you're a lesbian." He paused. "You're not, are you?"

"Would it matter to you if I were?"

"You know it wouldn't." But Isaac's voice was uneasy.

"You really don't understand me."

"Women have always been a complete mystery to me."

"Don't come out with that crap. Spinning out chauvinistic blarney might work on your lady friends, but not me. I'm your *daughter*. If *you* don't understand me what hope in hell chance does any other person – any other man have?"

"You've got me there," admitted her father, with a smile. "Although I always thought you got on well with Josh. Why not give him a call, for old times' sake. I'm sure he'd like to take you out."

Danielle made a noise that sounded like a cry of strangulated exasperation. "If I was a man we wouldn't be having this conversation!"

"Of course not," agreed Isaac. "We'd be getting in a pint down the pub and discussing last night's footie."

A sudden crash and Nico guessed Danielle's fist had just made contact with the table.

"That's it! I've had it! Sell the business – see if I care! I'll start up by myself, become twice as big as Vanders!"

"Go ahead," said her father. "How about an estate agency? Or an employment agency? Give up on jewellery retail, there's no money in it and too many villains waiting to take your hard-won profit off you. And I'm not talking about the ones in the balaclavas."

"I do give up – you're quite patently not listening to me." Her footsteps clattered across the floorboards.

On other side of the wall, Nico swiftly ducked into the shadows and out of sight.

As Danielle stormed through the open door, she paused only long enough to take her frustration out on a suit of armour standing in the corner of the hall. It hit the deck, disintegrated, and bounced across the polished floor, the left gauntlet spinning against Nico's feet.

He held his breath, but Danielle did not even turn her head, just stalked down the corridor, through the dining-room and out into the garden.

Back in the library, Nico could plainly hear Isaac laughing.

This was one seriously dysfunctional family.

Chapter Three

Taz Taylor forced a path through the crowded ballroom towards the dining-room – a cinch when you're six foot four, built like a Sherman tank, play bass with Australia's foremost rock band and have a reputation for being a hellraiser.

Ignoring the long trestle tables, decorated with so many exotic flowers there was hardly any room for the cous-cous, he made straight for the booze. Swiping a bottle of Bollinger and two glasses from beneath the nose of a bemused waiter, he muttered, "Cheers, mate," and sauntered out the door into the garden.

He was grabbed by a tall redhead, wearing a skin-tight pink sheath dress, who simultaneously plastered a passionate kiss on his surprised mouth and relieved him of the Bollinger.

"You're a sweetie," she grinned. "I need some alcohol

to warm me up. I'm so cold my nipples are sticking out like doorknobs."

"Oh, yeah?" said Taz, and made to close one hand over her breast.

Isabel van der Straatan slapped his hand away, giggling.

Taz produced a couple of champagne glasses from the pocket of his leather jacket as Isabel clamped the champagne bottle between her knees, pulled out the cork to a loud 'pop' and quickly poured the fizzing alcohol into the glasses before too much disappeared between the flagstones.

"Cheers!" she said, helping herself to a glass and crashing it against Taz's. She downed it in one go.

"Way to go!" said Taz, seriously impressed.

"Have another?" she asked, topping up both glasses again.

He noticed her hand was shaking, goose-pimples covered her arms and shoulders and her teeth were chattering. "God, girl, you're freezing." He slipped off his jacket and slung it over her shoulders, almost taking out her eye with the zip.

"Careful, you'll ruin your reputation," she said, sipping at her second glass of champagne with a little more decorum. "Go and bite the heads off a few bats."

"Nah, they taste like old boots. Gimme a hamster any day – tender underbelly. Why are you hiding out here? It's your party, go strut your funky stuff."

"Please," grimaced Isabel. "With that bunch of losers?

I think Danielle must have hired a job-lot of guests from Tossers Inc."

"She hired me and the guys to play a set." Taz pretended to look affronted. "I hope I come up to expectations."

"If you don't, I'll get Danielle to ask for her money back!"

"Couldn't I just have sex with her?"

"You want frostbite? You'd need a whole crate of de-icer just to thaw that girl out! Sorry, I shouldn't have said that. I'm a complete cow. Ignore me, it's the alcohol talking. Which, incidentally, I wouldn't need to drink so much of if it hadn't been for Dani's bloody fancy-dress party stressing me out." She clapped her hand over her mouth. "Oops, I did it again!"

Taz gave her a reassuring hug. "Let me take you away from all this. It's a short trip to the airport. We could charter a flight to the South of France. It's still summer there."

"Don't tempt me. Come on; let's get away from the house. Maybe I'll calm down – start behaving like a normal, rational person."

"God forbid!"

Taking his hand, she led him down the two shallow steps into the terrace garden. For a few moments they walked in silence, away from the noise of the party, around a small fountain, bubbling from an old millstone. They took the path through the topiary hedge into the garden beyond and sat on an old stone seat set beneath a huge Lebanon cedar. In daylight they would have been able to glimpse the village of Calahurst over the top of the woods below. In the pitch black of the midnight hour they could barely see the nearest hybrid tea blossoming in the rose garden.

"While I was waiting for you to fetch the drinks, I almost bolted off to the nearest pub," Isabel admitted unexpectedly.

As a man who played bass for a living, Taz did not have a particular flair with the English language. But he made a sympathetic grunt, squeezed Isabel's hand reassuringly and let her rattle on.

"I really don't want to be here. I feel like a stranger at my own party. Danielle arranged it, Dad paid for it – they just told me who I was allowed to invite, when to turn up and what to wear – some horrible palazzo pants and a bra that looked like a sequinned parachute harness, *trés chic*! I could have been playing panto in Basingstoke. Luckily I had this tucked away at the back of my wardrobe."

"You'd look sexy wearing a bin-liner and you know it," said Taz. (Flattery he could do.) "Stop whinging and sit on my lap."

Isabel eyed him askance. "You just want to get into my knickers."

"Too right – I'm starting to get excited thinking about that bin-liner."

To wind him up, Isabel hitched up her skirt, sat astride his lap and linked her hands behind his neck. But because he was wearing leather trousers she kept sliding off. Taz laughed, wrapped his arms firmly around her waist and pulled her towards him. She pressed her nose into the hollows of his neck to keep warm. His T-shirt was sleeveless, she noticed, and advertising his next tour.

"Are you cold?" she asked, feeling guilty. "Would you like your jacket back?"

She heard him chuckle, a warm rumbling sound that seemed to start somewhere around his boots and gurgle up through his barrel-like chest. "Are you kidding? I'm in severe danger of going up in flames!"

"You are so predictable," she said, kissing his forehead affectionately.

He shrugged. "I'm a rock star. Having women throw themselves at me because I'm famous means I don't need an original line in chat-up."

"You bang them over the head with your guitar, then drag them by the hair to your hotel room for a night of free love?"

"Works for me," nodded Taz. He slid his hands along the sides of Isabel's thighs, beneath her diamanté-encrusted gown and encountered her bare bottom. "Christ!"

"I hate VPL," said Isabel blithely.

"Me too," said Taz. "Fancy a quickie?"

Isabel grinned. "I thought you'd never ask," she said and pressed her mouth against his.

A sudden crash made them both jump apart.

Taz stared at her. "What was that?"

"You must have left the door open. I think it slammed in the breeze."

They heard the door give another definite creak, then the heavy clump of footsteps across the terrace.

"Bloody hell," grumbled Isabel, tugging her dress back over her thighs. "It's impossible to have quick fuck these days without everyone wanting to join in."

* * *

Nico followed Danielle through the door to the garden. Slightly disorientated, he paused, taking a good look around, calculating the route she would have taken.

He was standing on a deserted terrace. The moon, emerging from behind a cloud, cast a cool, pale light, turning everything into a romantic Hollywood movie set. He could see the gaps between flagstones were overgrown with sweet-scented thyme, the herbaceous borders around the edge still crammed with the last of the summer's flowers.

Directly in front of him was a shallow fountain, the water bubbling up through an ancient millstone, cascading over an array of multi-coloured pebbles. He walked around it, hoping this was the route Danielle had taken, not having the time or inclination to try any other way. He could feel the chill breeze through his sweater as he moved further away from the house.

Separating the terrace from the remainder of the garden was a topiary hedge with a row of stone seats in front. Nico, not a great fan of unnecessary exercise, sat on the one nearest the fountain.

Fumbling for his cigarettes, he realised they were still in his jacket, abandoned on the back seat of his car. "Damn!"

Another rustle from the next seat along revealed he was not alone. Reluctant to discover a courting couple, Nico squinted into the darkness and found a pale, tear-stained face squinting back at him. The moon had transformed the gold of her hair to silver. It was Danielle van der Straatan.

"Sorry," said Nico. "I didn't mean to interrupt. Do you want me to go?" There was no reply so, calling her bluff, he walked over to sit beside her. His foot knocked something, which in turn clinked against the stone seat. He bent and groped along the ground.

"It's a champagne bottle," sighed Danielle. "I brought it out here to drown my sorrows." She paused. "Unfortunately I can't get the cork out."

Nico laughed. As though on cue, a nightingale began to romantically sing from branches of the cedar behind them. At least, he thought it might be a nightingale. It was certainly not a sparrow.

"Shall I open it for you? Maybe it will cheer you up."

"Ha! Finish me off altogether I should think! I've drunk far too much already."

"You're entitled to get pissed on your birthday. And you don't have to worry about driving home."

As she giggled, Nico decided that perhaps she did have a sense of humour after all. He uncorked the bottle while he was ahead on points. The cork exploded into the garden and the champagne fizzed frantically over the neck of the bottle, showering the grass and soaking his shoes.

Nico licked his dripping fingers to get rid of the

stickiness. "Tastes good," he commented. "But you forgot to bring out any glasses."

"I'm not too posh to drink straight from the bottle!"

A *dry* sense of humour, he decided. And probably a sharp tongue if crossed. He wondered why she had been reduced to hiding out in the garden at her own birthday party. Surely she wasn't sulking after the row with her father?

"This party is for your birthday, isn't it?" he said, purely to keep the conversation going. He handed her the bottle and watched her take a large swig, wiping away any possible residue on her top lip with the back of her hand.

"Yes – but it wasn't my idea. I would have been happy for it to have passed in complete anonymity."

"Your twenty-fifth?"

"It's not such a big deal. Except my father seems to think I should be married with 2.4 kids by now, hence the reason for this party. I'm supposed to chose a husband from the crowd of Hooray Henrys he invited tonight. Cinderella in reverse. Subtle, eh? As far as Dad's concerned, I'm not just on the shelf, I'm bargain basement."

"You got one hell of a birthday present." Nico was unable to resist the dig. "Wasn't that worth the ritual humiliation?"

Danielle drank some more champagne. "Money isn't everything."

"Something rich guys say to make the poor feel cool about poverty. If you don't have any, believe me, money *is* everything. Be grateful you're not stuck in a trailer park in Texas."

"Are you?"

"No, thank Christ."

"Then stop trying to sound like one of those crusading journalists that write for *The Guardian,*" she grumbled, then glanced up. "You're not, are you?"

He smiled. "No – I write techno-thrillers. Except lately they've not been very thrilling."

"Take my life," muttered Danielle. "More than enough thrills for anyone. All I want is to be left alone to get on with my career without interference. Fat chance. My father would give Machiavelli a run for his money."

"Perhaps he needs a hobby, to keep his mind occupied. Golf's the usual thing for a guy his age, isn't it? Or maybe tennis."

"Vanders is his life," Danielle said sadly, "which is why I cannot understand why he is giving it up."

Father and daughter had more in common than perhaps they realised. Nico, feeling he wasn't getting a result fast enough, decided on a change of subject. "What about your mother? Does she have any influence over him?"

"My mother died a long time ago. I never knew her. But Dad has never lacked female company." She gave him a sideways glance. "The latest is your friend Jemma."

"You don't like Jemma, do you?"

"She's only after Dad's money."

Maybe it was the alcohol causing her to talk so freely,

but Nico, finally feeling he was getting somewhere, took advantage of it. "Her surname is 'Stortford' – the same as this house. What's the connection?"

"Jemma's father was the 11th Earl of Stortford – and this was their family seat. He died and left no money, so she and her brother, Josh, had to move into Home Farm and rent the house to us. First she made friends with Isabel, so that she could keep being invited back – then she moved in on our father."

Nico could see several flaws in this theory. Firstly, if Jemma was madly in love with another man, would she have been so willing to sleep with him? Secondly, "She must be thirty years younger than him. It's a huge gap."

"She has a title, my father has money, they're perfect for each other."

Nico was not so certain. "And they're up-front about it?"

"Of course not! She says he's her 'mentor'," Danielle almost spat out the word. "He got her the job at *The Calahurst Echo,* which he part owns, and he advanced her the deposit for that apartment at the quayside. Funny how people having an affair think no one else notices. My worse nightmare is that one day they'll announce their engagement. Dad lives in such a Neverland he thinks we're all going to be one big happy family." Pause. "I think I'm going to throw up."

Nico, thinking she was serious, hastily confiscated the bottle. "Take deep breaths," he advised. "Shall I take you back to the house?"

"Are you kidding? If I never see any of my bloody family again I'll die happy."

"Maybe you need to lie down."

Danielle eyed him suspiciously. "Oh yes?"

He grinned. "Sorry, that came out wrong. I only thought you might want to . . . lie down!"

"Pity." Danielle stood up, swaying slightly. "I thought my luck was in. Lead the way, Sir Galahad!"

Nico watched her stumble, grabbing hold of his arm to prevent herself from falling over. Christ, how much had she had to drink?

"I don't know the way," he pointed out. "I've never been here before."

Which was not *strictly* true . . .

Danielle laughed. "Then I suppose you'd better follow me." And turning abruptly on her heel, she walked straight into the hedge.

Nico caught her as she collapsed into his arms – out cold.

* * *

A benefit to being tall and beefy was that Nico was quite capable of literally sweeping women off their feet. Most women of his acquaintance tended to be less than 5′5″ – skinny little things that looked as though their idea of a binge was two lettuce leaves and a stick of celery. And carrying them, usually giggling, up a short flight of stairs and throwing them onto a bed in a display of Latin machismo was not difficult and always guaranteed results.

Danielle van der Straatan was at least 5'10" and, while not at all fat, was still fairly hefty. He had only the vaguest idea where her bedroom was and could just imagine her father's reaction if he stumbled back past the library with her over his shoulder like Captain Caveman.

Luckily, at that moment Danielle opened her eyes, stood up straight and picked the bits of yew-tree out of her hair as though nothing had happened.

"It's this way," she said blithely and took hold of his hand to lead him across the terrace.

* * *

Danielle had her own suite on the second floor, decorated completely in white. White walls, white curtains, white leather furniture. Nico had never seen such an uncluttered room. The girls he knew collected hoards of ornaments and fluffy toys, which they refused to store or throw away, not to mention piles of ancient *Cosmopolitan* and *Marie-Claire* magazines waiting to trip up the unwary. Either Danielle had had a blitz before the party or she was the tidiest woman alive – even allowing for her being born a Virgo.

On a low table in the centre of the room was a fish tank, stocked with a shoal of silver fish, which flitted from side to side as though they were one. Nico paused to watch; it was oddly hypnotic. The fish shared their water with silver weed, a miniature crystal palace and an inch of glittering stones scattered across the bottom. For a brief moment Nico wondered if they were real diamonds, then laughed at his naivety. The van der Straatans were provincial jewellers, not the Oppenheimers.

Danielle had poured herself a Baileys and handed Nico a cold beer from a little fridge in the corner of the sitting-room. She sat down on the settee, out of place in her gaudy sequins and harem pants. Nico joined her, careful not to sit too close. He didn't want to scare her off, not when everything was going so much better than he'd hoped.

"Whose idea was it to hold a costume party?" he asked.

"Mine. I thought it would liven things up a bit. Except half the women turned up in little black dresses and my sister, Isabel, doesn't even bother to show. I think she does it deliberately to wind me up."

Nico suppressed a smile.

Now it was Danielle's turn to change the subject. "Are you going back to the party?"

"I don't think so. It's getting late. I think I'll make my way home."

Danielle swilled her drink around in its glass to prevent the sediment settling on the bottom. "If you're worried about drinking and driving, you can stay here the night," she said, without looking at him.

Home base, thought Nico in surprise. In less than thirty minutes. She didn't seem the type.

"You can sleep on my couch," she added. "Because of the party, all the guest rooms are full."

"That would be . . . er, great," he said, trying not to think of Jemma's nice warm bed waiting for him back at Calahurst Quay. "I have to let my flatmate know, else he'll leave the door on the latch all night. Could I use a phone? I left my cellphone in the car."

"There's a guest telephone down the hall, in a little alcove at the top of the stairs. Help yourself."

* * *

Isabel, deprived of a comfort-bonk and irritated with Danielle beyond measure, and Taz, stiff in all the wrong places, decided to reconvene in the relative privacy of Isabel's suite. It should be a whole lot warmer too. Taz, as the advance party, went on ahead and Isabel sneaked into the kitchen for a plate of leftovers. Apart from music, the other thing she had in common with Taz was that sex, even the mere anticipation of it, made her feel hungry.

As she tiptoed back along the corridor she tripped over Jemma, who was sitting cross-legged on the floor, weeping into a bottle of Bollinger.

"What's the matter?" asked Isabel, sitting beside her and confiscating the bottle before she diluted good champagne further.

Jemma grunted and attempted to wrestle back the bottle. Isabel handed it over; it wasn't worth falling out over. She stared at her friend, totally nonplussed. She had never seen Jemma so much as whimper and had always had her down for a bit of a tough nut.

"What's up?" she asked. "Do you want to talk about it?" – hoping she didn't. Taz, left to his own devices, was liable to get bored and wander off in search of an amenable groupie.

"My bastard boyfriend has buggered off with your bitch of a sister!"

Isabel felt her mouth actually drop open. "*Danielle*? Pinched your boyfriend? Are you *sure*?"

Jemma took another swig of Bollinger. "He said he was going off for drinks and I never saw him again. I searched the whole ground floor and eventually spotted the two of them chatting intimately on the terrace. The next thing, she's pretending to faint in his arms and whisks him off upstairs. She's probably shagging him right now!"

Isabel, remembering the conversation she had overheard earlier, doubted it. So Danielle's new admirer had arrived with Jemma . . . curiouser and curiouser.

"Kind of ironic," she said out loud. "Considering you pinched Max off Dani."

"Little Miss Tactful!" Jemma staggered to her feet "This has been the crappiest party of my entire life. Where can I throw up?"

"Maybe things aren't as bad as they seem," said Isabel helplessly, as Jemma tipped the flowers out of a beautiful blue vase and stuck her head in it.

Jemma wiped her mouth on the tablecloth and replaced the flowers, arranging the more delicate blossoms at the front. "I fail to see how they could possibly be worse," she said and, pointedly turning her back on Isabel, she headed off in the direction of the front door, occasionally bouncing off the furniture.

Isabel's eyes dropped to the champagne bottle now

rolling around on the rug. "At least tell me you're not going to drive home?" she called after her friend.

"I'll call a cab," sniffed Jemma. "Seeing as this place is all out of knights on white chargers."

Isabel watched her leave, feeling she would only make things worse if she intervened. It would be better to discuss this rationally, tomorrow, when Jemma had sobered up.

Although she felt genuinely sorry for Jemma, Isabel had to admit this was an amazing development. Danielle, who never seemed to bother with men, appeared to have swiped some hunk from beneath Jemma's nose. Was she getting her own back after Jemma lured Max away the month before? With Dani, anything was possible.

Forgetting all about her illicit snack, Isabel began to climb a little wrought-iron staircase to her suite. Originally the servants' access, the staircase from the kitchens was narrow and curled around several times before it reached the landing. As Isabel neared the top, she could hear someone talking but, because of the design of the stairs, could see nothing. From the sound of it, an American appeared to be using the guest telephone. Bloody cheek! He'd better not be calling the USA!

Isabel paused, a couple of steps from the top – all the better to eavesdrop.

"That stuff we talked about? I need it e-mailed first thing tomorrow." His voice echoed down the corridor. "Attach anything you can lay your hands on about the van der Straatans, particularly the Ice Queen, Danielle. OK?"

Isabel, feeling herself bristle on her sister's behalf, was just striding forwards to get a better look at this creep when she heard the phone rattle back into its cradle. If she didn't get a move on the guy would be long gone. So she sprinted up the last few steps, forgot she was wearing a tight gown, and stumbled on the last tread. She was sent sprawling onto the red carpet, which stretched the length of the first floor.

A pair of smart black shoes stepped into her line of vision and a hand appeared two inches from her nose. Isabel took it – she wasn't proud – and stood, tugging her skirt down over her bottom.

Instead of meeting the intruder eye-to-eye, as she usually did with the male population, she found herself looking directly at a stubbly chin, and had to tilt her head to look into his toffee-coloured eyes. So this was the guy Jemma had been weeping over earlier? Boy, did he get around!

Isabel quickly composed her features, assuming a suitably haughty expression.

It was nothing compared to the look of horror on Nico's face. "Danielle!"

She laughed at the shock on his face. "No, I'm *Isabel.*" It was fun watching him squirm. *Suffer a bit more, you rat!* "Didn't Jemma tell you?" she goaded. "Danielle and I, we're identical twins!"

Chapter Four

Jemma Stortford lived in a large Georgian town house, which had been converted into smart apartments and overlooked Calahurst Quay. The house was painted an anonymous cream, identical to the ones on either side. It had no front garden, only a couple of feet of paving slabs and black railings bordering the pavement. Surrounded by fashionable boutiques, coffee shops and gift shops, a few doors down was The Parson's Collar wine bar, where Jemma was on first-name terms with all the staff.

Jemma's immediate neighbours consisted of assorted media and PR folk who wined and dined and then forgot which flat they lived in. They were young and beautiful, had money to spend and someone always had a party going on. They got on very well with Jemma.

Having failed to hack it as an author/illustrator of children's books, Jemma was now a journalist with the local newspaper, but would rather spend her time painting extravagant, Michelangelo-inspired murals for her friends. Occasionally she fantasised about chucking in her job, selling up and backpacking around the world – purely for the hell of it. But she never did anything about it. The truth was that, despite her love of adventure, Jemma was rather too fond of life's little luxuries to go roughing it.

The day after the twins' birthday party, Isabel clumped up the three flights of stairs to Jemma's flat, too impatient to take the lift. Turning the handle, she made to step over the threshold, but instead banged her nose on the door, which had refused to budge. She looked at the door in surprise and rubbed her nose. Jemma never locked her door during the day; it was open house to all her friends and neighbours. Isabel would often find perfect strangers slumped on the beanbags, watching the Disney Channel and munching their way through Jemma's Rice Krispies.

Now what was she going to do? Was Jemma out? Isabel stuck her ear against one of the brightly painted wooden panels. She could hear the faint sound of pop music so she knocked and waited. And waited. And waited some more. What *was* the girl doing in there?

Eventually Isabel got fed up and delivered a hefty thump to the panel beside the lock – something she'd seen Jemma do when she'd locked herself out. Hey presto! The door swung open.

"Shit, it's a raid!" exclaimed a voice from the next room.

A man's voice, realised Isabel, taken aback. She had

thought Jemma would be alone. He had an accent – American? She wasn't sure . . . was it Nico?

"You must lead a very exciting life if every time someone knocks on your front door you think it's the police." Jemma sounded her usual insouciant self.

Isabel grinned and closed the front door behind her, wandering into the sitting-room. The decor was quite restrained for Jemma. Red walls, red carpet, gold curtains. Except the huge, gilt-framed family portraits on the walls were fakes – carefully painted trompe l'oeil.

Even through it was almost midday the curtains were still drawn, adding to the general gloom. Isabel could see the place was empty. Jemma and her male admirer must be in the bedroom. Isabel padded across the red shag-pile carpet, neatly side-stepping the huge beanbags and sequinned cushions Jemma preferred to a three-piece suite.

The voices were louder now.

"Where can I hide?"

"Why would you want to hide?" Jemma was sounding more and more perplexed. "It could be someone you've never met before. Brazen it out."

An image of a rumpled Latin sex-god sidled uninvited into Isabel's sub-conscious and was abruptly booted out. But if the man wasn't Nico, who was he? Max? He was American too – yet she was sure Jemma had left the party alone . . .

"You won't be able to hide in there, you know," Jemma was saying. "Too much junk."

"So help me here?"

"The fire escape?"

"I'll freeze my balls off!"

"The bathroom? Considering your macho image, you are such a wimp!"

"Call it self-preservation, babe."

Isabel knocked before opening the door and found Jemma lying on her tummy in the bed; the floor littered with empty beer bottles and discarded pizza packaging. Some of the boxes still had congealed pizza in them. Isabel wrinkled her nose, and then noticed the pair of pink fluffy handcuffs still swinging from the other end of the bed. The door opposite, which led to the bathroom, was just closing.

Isabel hid a smile. It had taken Jemma a very short time to get over her broken heart.

"Hi, Jem. Am I interrupting something?"

"Hullo, Is." Jemma was wearing an over-sized Elvis T-shirt instead of a nightdress. Her toffee-streaked, blonde hair was standing up on end, last night's eyeliner ringed her grey eyes like a panda. She still looked as gloriously sexy as ever.

Yawning widely, Jemma sat up, swinging her legs over the side of the rumpled bed and reached for her dressing-gown. "You know, it's not frightfully convenient for you to be barging in on me right now," she scolded, in her soft, smoky voice, although the reproach was cancelled out by a wink.

"Sorry." Isabel, unable to resist the temptation, flicked one finger against the fluffy handcuffs, setting them swinging again. Both girls giggled.

"One day you're going to get stuck," said Isabel, intentionally loud enough for the man in the bathroom to hear, "and you'll have to call out the fire brigade. They'll break down the door and find you butt-naked, handcuffed to the end of the bed."

"Oh heaven," sighed Jemma. "I do love a man in uniform . . ."

There was a crash, followed by loud cursing, from the bathroom.

Both girls collapsed in laughter. Jemma leant across to her bedside table for her cigarettes. Calmly she lit one, deftly flicking the match halfway across the room to the bin. She took a deep drag on the cigarette, the tip glowing orange in the dim light.

"Poor darling," she reflected, "I think he's squashed himself in the cupboard under the sink."

"Is there room?"

"Darling, there's room enough for two!"

"You're incorrigible, Jemma!"

Jemma slid off the bed, jamming her feet in her Simpsons slippers. Wandering into the sitting-room, leaving a trail of cigarette smoke behind her, she dragged back the curtains, knocking over several dried and shrivelled houseplants. Jemma was the type that either over-watered or completely ignored plants. She treated her boyfriends in much the same way.

"Can I get you a drink?" Jemma asked, blithely sloshing a measure of blackcurrant vodka into a glass.

Isabel picked up a bent cactus and gingerly straightened it although she could do little about the crumbs of compost burying into the shag-pile. "Ugh, it's not even lunch-time, Jemma!"

"To me, it's still last night. Why are you here anyway? Were we supposed to be meeting up?"

"I wanted to interrogate you about your boyfriend, Nico."

"Got off with your sister, did he?" Jemma took another swig of vodka.

Isabel nodded, faintly embarrassed, but she had known Jemma too long to be able to lie.

"Bastard," Jemma muttered into the bottom of the glass. "He's also now my ex-boyfriend. With a capital X. That's if two and a half shags count as a relationship."

Isabel hastily moved the conversation on. "Where did you two meet? Had you known him long?"

Jemma shrugged. "Parson's Collar, the night before last."

"Are you sure? I don't remember seeing him there – and let's face it – he's not the sort of guy one would forget!"

Jemma poured herself another glass. "I'm doing my best!"

Isabel began to feel as though she was tightening the metaphoric screw. "So, if you didn't meet Nico at The Parson's Collar on Friday night, you must have met him sometime on Saturday?"

"Sounds logical."

"Where did you go on Saturday? The sailing club? A bit of retail therapy in Port Rell?"

"I spent the whole day in bed, not waking up 'til tea-time, and there he was – in bed beside me."

Isabel regarded her silently for a moment. "And you have no idea how he got there? My God, Jemma, he could have broken into the flat, the same way as me, and climbed into bed while you slept! You'd have been none the wiser!"

"In my dreams!" scoffed Jemma. "Perhaps I'll wake up next to Robbie Williams tonight."

"Be serious!"

"I am serious! Isabel – I would have noticed!"

Isabel was not convinced. "I doubt it! *I've* just broken in. All I had to do was thump the door and it opened."

"I keep meaning to get that lock fixed . . ." Jemma's tan seemed a shade paler. "You know, you could be right. Nico was behaving a bit strangely. He could have been an axe-murderer or anything. I'm going to call out a locksmith right now and get a deadlock put on the door."

"I think a deadlock on the drinks cabinet would be more effective."

"Don't be a cow, Isabel. You've proved your point."

"Sorry." Isabel searched for a less emotive subject and failed. The whole Nico thing was really preying on her mind. And let's face it, with the vacuous life she led, there wasn't a lot else to think about. "You really haven't a clue how he got there?"

"No!" snapped Jemma. "Don't keep harping on about it!"

"Sorry," repeated Isabel. "But as the scheming bastard's just moved in with my sister, I intend to find out everything I can about him."

"He's a Scorpio."

"Thanks, Jemma, that helps a lot."

* * *

Nico had woken up that morning feeling incredibly guilty. In two days he had conned two women into bed and his conscience was just about catching up with him. He did not usually behave this way. He had not intended to behave this way. What had started as another job was now becoming a whole lot more involved.

Partly because he felt ashamed, Nico suggested to Danielle that he take her out and they spend the day together. She was quite happy to agree – provided they dropped into Vanders before they left Calahurst, so she could check up on a few things.

Vanders was located on Quay Street, a few doors down from Jemma's apartment. A Georgian building, the showroom was decorated in blue and gold with lots of glass and gilt, and relics that would have been more at home in the tomb of a pharaoh.

Danielle's office was on the first floor, overlooking the street. She abandoned her briefcase beside the mahogany desk and opened her small wall safe. Nico, trailing behind, sat on the edge of the desk to wait. She took out a small tray, containing about ten tiny cut diamonds carelessly scattered across the black velvet lining and placed it casually next to Nico. Reaching into the back of the safe, she brought out a sapphire-blue jewellery case, marked with the outline of a tulip in gold – Vanders trademark.

"You don't have much in the way of security," said Nico, idly stirring the diamonds with his index finger, wondering how much they were worth.

"You mean, apart from the locks, bolts, modern alarms, security men," Danielle ticked the list off on her fingers, "security cameras in the shop and trained on the big safe downstairs, panic alarms throughout, linked to the local police station – which, incidentally, is located a couple of hundred yards around the corner."

It was the wrong thing to have said. "Relax, I wasn't thinking of turning the place over."

Danielle gave a ghost of a smile. Nico found her coldness disconcerting. It also made him more determined to crack that icy exterior. But why did she have to make it such damn hard work?

Danielle flicked back the clasp that held down the lid of the jewellery box. He could not help but stare, open-mouthed, at the string of glittering stones she held up to the light.

"They're beautiful!" he said.

"You think so? I thought they were a bit over the top."

"Are they pink diamonds?"

"Yes, a customer commissioned the necklace and eventually she'll have a bracelet and earrings to match."

"Someone famous?"

"The actress, Paige Lorraine. She's about to marry the director of her last film. The diamonds are a wedding present to herself – her poor fiancé only merits a pair of gold cufflinks."

Nico examined the necklace more closely. It was made from interlocking platinum links and set with eight pale-pink diamonds of graduating size.

"Did this take long to make?" he asked. "I imagine it wasn't a factory-line job?"

She smiled witheringly. "It took months to re-cut and polish the stones. Miss Lorraine postponed the wedding because she was so determined to wear her pink diamonds down the aisle."

"Actresses!"

"Unfortunately, in today's economic climate, film stars and foreign royalty are the only people who can afford to buy the larger diamonds. We bend over backwards to keep them sweet. It was lucky that I had this range half-planned, else it would have taken longer. We were terrified Miss Lorraine would go somewhere else, perhaps to one of the more famous jeweller's in London.

Nico dangled the necklace in front of the window, admiring the way the light sank deep into the very heart of the diamonds, then exploded out like a rose-coloured firework. "How do you get the stones to sparkle like that?"

"With difficulty." Danielle held out her hand and reluctantly he handed the necklace back. She carefully put the necklace back into its box and closed the lid.

"Pink diamonds can evaporate when subject to the heat of a cutting wheel."

"Expensive mistake."

"Exactly."

"If pink diamonds are so rare, where did you get these?"

"Flynn, the dealer we use, bought them from a little old lady in America. She had been a Broadway star in the 1950s and they had been given to her by wealthy admirers. She was selling off jewellery to keep her in comfort in her old age."

"Sad."

"Yes, but he gave her a good price – we don't cheat little old ladies. It was an opportunity we couldn't pass up. Pink diamonds are rarely mined; the only way to get them is through auctions of second-hand jewellery."

Nico wasn't really paying attention. His eye had caught a large portrait of Isaac van der Straatan, painted in oils, hung high on the opposite wall. It seemed to be watching his every move. Nico deliberately averted his gaze. What kind of a man commissioned an oil painting of himself?

"Will you have another go at convincing your father to give you this place?" queried Nico, before he could help himself.

"Of course."

"Do you think you'll be able to run the business on your own?"

Danielle's eyes darkened. "I've been his assistant for years. Yes, everyone humoured me at first, but anyone who underestimates me now is a fool. I've worked my guts out for this and I'm not about to give it up.

Nico tactfully backtracked. "And your sister, Isabel? Will she want to work here with you too?"

Danielle was still seething. "You must be joking! She doesn't care about the business, provided she has something sparkly to wear to a party!"

She picked up the jewellery box and almost threw it back in the safe. Quickly scribbling 'OK, clean and despatch' on a post-it note, she stuck it on the lid of the box and turned to collect the tray of diamonds.

Nico watched her. Her passion had melted the ice in her eyes and they blazed like the precious stones she loved so much. He was sure that beneath that diamond-hard exterior was a marshmallow softie struggling to get out.

He leant forward and kissed her.

Danielle, at first taken aback, did not resist. Encouraged, Nico began to undo the front of her dress.

She pushed him away. "What are you *doing*?"

Hell, she hadn't complained when he had crept into her bed last night. What was with the vestal-virgin act? Was it the thought of Papa-dearest glowering down from his portrait, watching their every move? Or maybe there was a security camera in here too?

"What would you *like* me to do?" he parried calmly.

"What if someone comes in?"

"I locked the door," he admitted, sliding his arms around her waist, drawing her towards him until the front of her thighs knocked against the edge of the desk. She was so tall, she only had to tilt her head slightly to gaze up at him. Beneath the frost of those silver-grey eyes, he could swear he caught of glimpse of amusement bubbling beneath the surface.

"You planned this!" she accused him.

"No, I couldn't help acting on impulse."

"Hmm." She didn't sound convinced.

He gently ran his knuckles over her cheek. "Mr Impulsive, that's me." He flipped his hand over, his thumb moving closer to the edge of her mouth with every stroke. As she turned her head slightly, expecting to take it into her mouth, he dropped his hand back to his side. He saw her eyes darken with disappointment and felt cheered.

"I guess," he said softly, "when we don't go back downstairs, the sales staff will figure something is . . . er . . . up."

"And is it?" said Danielle, her fingers suddenly closing over the buckle on his belt.

Nico hoped the shock didn't show on his face. He was not expecting her to call his bluff. Expecting to have his face slapped at any moment, yes, but not this. Danielle was no longer looking into his eyes, but at his mouth. He quickly closed his hands over hers and pulled them firmly away, sliding them behind her back while he kissed her. This was his seduction, he was in charge; determined that this was one area in which she wasn't going to be in control.

He watched her eyes close, but as his tongue attempted to part her lips to explore her mouth, it met hers trying to probe his. Nico felt slightly exasperated. Their lovemaking was like an old-fashioned dance – where the partners were fighting over who was going to lead.

Firmly taking the initiative, before he was beaten to it, Nico slid her dress from her shoulders, and then lifted her up beside him. As Danielle made a grab for her in-tray, which wobbled dangerously close to the edge, Nico snapped open her bra and stuck it in 'pending', then pushed her back against the blotting-pad. He seized a handful of diamonds from the tray and sprinkled them liberally over her bare skin.

"Nico!"

"Yes, honey?" he said, and quickly bent to kiss her again before she could reply. It really was the only way to shut her up.

"I know exactly how many diamonds were in that tray. . ."

"Good – because it's going to be hell finding them all . . ."

Chapter Five

As the sun set over Calahurst, Isaac van der Straatan stood alone in St Peter's churchyard, clutching an expensive bouquet of red roses and a bottle of mineral water. There was a gentle breeze sweeping up from the river, ruffling his blond hair and causing his grey eyes to sting. He blinked quickly, to prevent tears forming.

He was not entirely oblivious to the attention he was attracting. There seemed to be a non-stop parade of people passing by the church, staggering back from the shops with bags of groceries, intrigued at the middle-aged man in the suit becoming emotional in a graveyard. Yet somehow he couldn't tear himself away from the white marble headstone in front of him.

Helena van der Straatan, it said. And that was it. Because Isaac had been extremely pissed off with his wife when she died and had not felt like adding anything else. And now, twenty-five years later, he was beginning to think he might have made a terrible mistake.

Fumbling in his jacket pocket for a handkerchief, he became aware of a young man standing nearby, watching him intently. He was dark-haired, with a tanned complexion and was dressed completely in black, his trench coat swirling theatrically in the breeze, as though he'd stepped out of some hip horror-flick. Isaac thought he looked familiar and wondered if he was one of those new popstars he ought to have heard of. Perhaps the one that was dating Isabel?

He began to feel faintly ridiculous, standing there, sniffing like a schoolboy, and still clutching these ostentatious roses. Quickly he stuck them into the little stone vase beneath the headstone, removing the dead ones first, then topping the vase up with water. He then found he had nowhere to put the dead flowers. Usually he discarded them over the wall and into the ditch – but it was a bit awkward to do this when one had an audience. The dead flowers started to drip stagnant water onto his handmade shoes.

The young man, oblivious to Isaac's hostile vibes, came to stand next to him. He glanced at the gravestone and then back at Isaac.

"Was she your wife?" he asked. He had the faintest hint of an American accent.

What was it to him? "Yes," replied Isaac shortly, wishing he would go away.

"She died young."

Stating the obvious. "Yes."

"It must have been devastating."

Isaac, impotently clenching the fist that didn't have the flowers in, was sorely tempted to turn round and snap, 'No – because I was fucking someone else at the time', but didn't.

"Was it cancer?"

For Christ's sake! "Childbirth," muttered Isaac.

For a moment the young man studied him, his dark eyes softening sympathetically. "You know, you shouldn't blame yourself . . ."

For a moment Isaac stared at him in shock. Were his feelings that transparent? How could the man have realised that he had always blamed himself? That if he hadn't been playing around, the delicate Helena would never have risked childbirth – because she was desperate to win back her husband.

Now thoroughly spooked, Isaac attempted to fathom where he had seen this young man before. Those amber eyes, they were so familiar it was beginning to bother him. An actor? A TV presenter? Hell, the man could work behind the bar at The Parson's Collar – what did it matter?

Isaac finally noticed the water staining his shoes, giving him the perfect escape opportunity. "I'd better go and find a bin to put these into," he said, turning away. "Goodbye, it was nice meeting you."

"Sure, see you around."

Isaac walked off and did not look back. Which was a pity. For, if he had, he would have seen the young man take out a notebook.

* * *

A few days later, Nico sat at the desk in Danielle's suite, slid a CD into his Discman, switched on his laptop computer, keyed in his password and began to work. Danielle had just disappeared off to Vanders, spraying Paris scent in a thick cloud around her body, dictating memos into a mini tape-recorder and frantically hunting lost paperwork. He had watched her fondly, marvelling at her ability to do several things at once.

Danielle, on the other hand, had not quite adjusted to having him live with her and almost forgot to say goodbye before she left. As Nico made kissing noises in the air, she turned to plant her lips on his forehead, before peering disinterestedly at the screen and politely ask what he was working on.

"An exposé of the nouveaux riches," he had replied, quickly closing the file before she could read anything.

Danielle had laughed at his secrecy, accused him of being a perfectionist and then left, leaving him feeling more than a twinge of guilt.

He had moved his belongings into Danielle's apartment the day before: a few clothes (black) and assorted toiletries (expensive). Danielle, worried that he might bolt at any moment, had been reassured by the appearance of his computer. What writer could operate without one?

Nico felt uncomfortable in this museum-like house and didn't dare light a cigarette in case he burnt a hole in some two-hundred-year-old rug. It was not a family home. The main part of the building didn't look as though it had been redecorated for over a hundred years, yet Danielle's apartment resembled something from *Homes and Gardens*. He remembered Jemma's flat; although built at the same time, it was definitely a 'home' where she had incorporated her own tastes, even if they were wildly eccentric.

Danielle never mentioned Jemma. Thankfully the two girls were not friends. Nico had no wish to meet Jemma again, certain he could never bring himself to look her in the eye. She had been so friendly, affectionate, trusting. Danielle was a different prospect altogether. Danielle could take care of herself. And Isabel? Isabel was seriously weird.

Towards lunch-time, Isabel had crept silently into Danielle's sitting-room, right up behind Nico, and yelled "Boo!" Nico had to be virtually scraped off the ceiling. He had untangled himself from his Discman, cursing her for her warped sense of humour before he remembered to hit the escape button on the laptop.

Not that she had seemed the slightest bit interested in his work – she was too busy killing herself with laughter. When she had calmed down sufficiently, she had offered to take him out to lunch, to 'keep him company' while Danielle was at work. Although deeply suspicious of her motives, he accepted her invitation. He couldn't afford to miss the opportunity to learn something new.

Taking one disdainful look at Nico's rusting black Fiesta, Isabel offered to drive them in her Mercedes SLK. After a hair-raising drive through Calahurst and along the clifftop road to Port Rell, they arrived at La Dolce Vita – an Italian bistro in a glorified beach-hut adjacent to the sand. Isabel was greeted like a long-lost friend. Nico watched all the kissing and hand-waving with amusement. Despite her weirdness, Isabel appeared to have plenty of friends.

They sat on green wooden seats pulled up around a table with a green and white checked tablecloth. Instead of sitting opposite him, Isabel sat beside him, ordering lasagne for herself, and teasing Nico for wanting a pizza.

"How boring, I should have taken you to Pizza Hut. It would have been cheaper!"

Nico refused to rise. "I like pizza."

"I should hope you do. With a name like Nico you must have some Latin blood."

Nico regarded her thoughtfully. "My given name is Nicolas, but you're right; my mother was American, although her family originated from Puerto Rico."

"I knew it!"

He took pleasure in correcting her. "My father is Irish though."

"A veritable mongrel – and you write books too?"

"Yes . . ." Nico wondered where this was leading.

She picked up the bottle of complimentary house wine and sloshed it into both their glasses without asking. "Thrillers and stuff?"

Finding her blatant interrogation wearing, he attempted humour to deflect her interest. "What is this? *Twenty Questions*?"

She looked up at him, her large grey eyes the very picture of innocence. "I've never heard of you."

"Maybe you don't read the kind of books I write."

"Now don't get in a huff! I'm only making polite conversation." She took a sip of her wine, her eyes never leaving his. For a split second Nico wondered if she was flirting with him, attempting to woo him away from her sister, but then she said blithely, "We can talk about me if you like, but I know men like to talk about themselves."

Ouch! He remembered the night he had first met Isabel, after he had made his telephone call. How long had she been there? How much did she really know about him? So he remained silent. He had got this far, he had no intention of tripping himself up with an indiscreet revelation.

The food arrived and conversation ceased until Isabel said dreamily, "You know, you've got the sexiest eyes. Like runny honey."

Nico, who had just taken a huge bite of pizza, choked.

Isabel had to thump him on the back. "Sorry!"

As her eyes were now alight with mischief, Nico doubted her sincerity. Putting down his fork, before he was tempted to stick it in her jugular vein, he asked, "Why did you ask me to lunch?"

"Because I'm madly in love with you. Can't you tell?"

"Yeah, right!" He pushed his pizza aside, his appetite completely gone. The cheese was congealing and it looked as though the chef had sprinkled it with grass cuttings. He took out his cigarettes to calm his nerves and lit one, without asking Isabel if she minded. "Tell me the real reason."

"Because I'm nosy?"

He nodded, taking a deep drag on his cigarette, feeling the calming effect of the nicotine, and ignoring the glares of the customers at the nearest tables. "That sounds more like it. Why are you so interested in me? Do all your sister's boyfriends get this cross-examination? Or is it a 'twin thing'?" he mocked, making imaginary quote marks in the air.

Isabel smiled enigmatically. As Nico debated his next move, she plucked the cigarette out of his hand, dropped it into his drink, then leant over and kissed him.

Nico was taken completely by surprise. Isabel wore a different scent, but she was such an exact replica of her sister it was scary. As he closed his eyes, going along with her, to see how far she would take it, he felt her hand drop onto his thigh, hesitate, then began to creep slowly upward. He could tell she was losing her nerve, that she was about to withdraw in embarrassment.

As she stared to pull back, Nico yanked her onto his lap, holding his hand against the back of her head, his fingers buried in her hair, forcing her lips to remain against his as, this time, he kissed her. Two could play at that game, he thought smugly, feeling her go rigid with shock.

"*Nico*!"

Oh *shit*! He would have recognised that husky voice anywhere. Abruptly he pushed Isabel away from him and looked up to see Danielle glowering at him.

"You – you – womaniser!" cried Danielle.

Isabel burst out laughing, her confidence returning in spades. "Danielle, *please*! You sound like a Barbara Cartland novel!" She leant towards Nico. "She'll be calling you a 'cad' next," she confided. "Poor girl doesn't get out much."

Danielle rounded on her. "And you can shut up! How could you do this to me? I'm your sister, for goodness sake! I only met him a few days ago and already you're moving in on the poor sap. Does it give you some kind of evil little thrill? Why do you always want what I want? Get a life, Isabel! Get a life of your own and stop trying to take over mine." She picked up Isabel's lasagne and turned it upside down over her head. Unfortunately, it had become so congealed it refused to be parted from its dish.

Isabel howled with laughter, the tears pouring down her cheeks. Not for the first time did Nico wonder if the whole family were deranged. The waiters were huddled nervously in the kitchen doors, perhaps plucking up the courage to chuck them out. The people at the next table had left long ago.

The sight of Isabel laughing hysterically was the last straw for Danielle. She picked up Nico's pizza and slapped it into her sister's face. For a moment it stuck there, before gently sliding off and plopping onto Isabel's lap. The laughter stopped as Isabel found she had a mouth, eyes, and nose full of mozzarella.

Nico couldn't help but cringe back as Danielle rounded on him. He half expected a china plate to come freewheeling in his direction, like Odd-job's bowler hat in one of those old James Bond movies.

Danielle's assault on him, however, was verbal. "And as for you, you – "

"Womaniser," supplied Isabel helpful. "Oh sorry, you've used that one. How about 'blackguard' or 'bastard'. 'Bastard' is good."

Danielle ignored her, saving her venom for Nico, lowering her voice until it was the merest icy whisper, emphasising each and every word. "I never want to see you again!" She swivelled on her high heels and marched proudly from the restaurant.

Nico half expected the enrapt waiters to burst into applause. Instead they hurried over with damp cloths, hoping to limit the damage to their tablecloth.

"Is Madam all right?" asked the headwaiter solicitously.

Isabel peeled bits of pizza from her face. "I've never enjoyed a meal so much in ages. How about you, Nico? Almost as good as the Jerry Springer show, eh?"

Nico, who had just seen all his carefully laid plans disintegrate, was not so sanguine. "Fuck off!"

Isabel smirked. "You wish!"

Chapter Six

The next morning Isabel wasn't feeling so smug. After her lunch date with Nico, she had gone to confess all to Jemma and the pair of them had spent the evening celebrating his comeuppance, giggling over Jemma's *Friends* videos and scoffing more pizza, washed down with a crate of Stella Artois. So now Isabel was suffering a monumental hangover, on top of horrible squirmy guilt for splitting up her sister's new romance. And, to top it all, she was woken up at six thirty by Britney Spears singing what Danielle always referred to as 'Isabel's theme song': 'Oops, I Did It Again . . .'

Isabel grabbed her Rugrats alarm-clock and, holding it two inches from her nose, squinted. *Six thirty in the morning!* Just because Dani had to get up early she thought everyone else should be up and about too. It was like living with Bagpuss.

Isabel banged forcefully on the wall. "Shut up! Shut up! *Shut up!* Some of us are trying to *sleep*!"

But Britney carried on into the following verse and a large lump of plaster fell from the wall, showering liberally over Isabel's white bed-sheets.

"Great!"

As it was impossible to try to get back to sleep, Isabel got out of bed and quickly dressed in a black T-shirt, customised Levi's and leather jacket. (Since she had started dating Taz, she had dumped her usual 1950s Riviera look in favour of being a rock chick). Disregarding the cleanse, tone and moisturise business, she paused only to collect her kitbag, then slammed the door behind her.

Another lump of plaster dropped lethargically onto the bed.

* * *

Isabel's retreat was a gym named Granger's, overlooking the quay, a few doors down from Jemma's flat. A nondescript Victorian building, it had previously been a nightclub, a cinema and a Methodist church. A blue neon sign proclaimed its name and beside the entrance was a large black and white poster of matinee idol Stewart Granger.

Isabel pushed against one of the blue double doors and walked through the lobby, decorated in 1950s kitsch. "Morning, Kimmie," she said, acknowledging the receptionist, who looked as though she'd be more at home on a TV show about Californian lifeguards.

The beautiful blonde Kimmie, who had been

engrossed on the telephone, broke off long enough to waggle frosted pink fingernails: "Hi, Isabel!"

There were only two other people sweatily working out in the gym. Isabel was able to have her usual workout without too much trouble. Three circuits took an hour and by the time she was relaxing in the jacuzzi she felt a lot calmer; her headache had completely disappeared. Isabel closed her eyes and let the warm jets of water buffet the tensions away.

In fact she was practically asleep when a voice said cheerfully, "Hi, babe!" and she was almost washed out with the resultant tidal wave of 6′4″ Taz clambering in beside her.

Isabel blinked the chlorinated water out of her eyes. "Hi, Taz," she smiled. "You know, you need to ask the management for your money back. This is a health club and you look terrible."

"I haven't had any kip!" Taz groaned. "I've been up all night rehearsing for next week's gig in Cardiff. Beano couldn't get the riffs right. I nearly wrapped the Strat around his bloody neck!"

Aware that Talisman's enigmatic lead guitarist practically slept with his beloved guitar underneath his pillow, Isabel winced. "I hope you didn't."

"Nah – I went back to the dressing-room and stamped on his jellybeans."

"Tuh, rock stars!"

Taz rested his arm on the side of the jacuzzi and began to stroke her shoulder. "Truth is, I'm feeling neglected."

Isabel waited for a punchline that never came. How could a pampered rock star, with hot and cold running groupies, ever feel neglected?

"Tell me about this Nico guy?" Taz added, before she could formulate a reply.

Isabel was even more perplexed. "What do you want to talk about him for?"

"Carson saw you with him at La Dolce Vita yesterday."

Carson was Talisman's lead singer. A flamboyant gay misogynist (despite his legion of female admirers), he had never liked Isabel and was convinced she was going to do a Yoko on Taz.

The water seemed suddenly colder. Isabel glanced up at Taz, trying to gauge his emotions, but his usual friendly, open face appeared to have an unfriendly, closed look about it. Isabel decided to concentrate on the bubbles instead, and work on a plausible defence.

It appeared she had two options. (1) The Truth – which had the disadvantage of revealing her true personality to be that of a complete cow or, (2) A Barefaced Lie. The problem with this solution was that she couldn't actually think of one.

"Well?" prompted Taz.

He wasn't happy, this she could tell. Any minute now he was going to say, 'You are the weakest link, goodbye' and she had no one to blame but herself.

"It's like this," she began, hoping that, if she started talking, a brilliant excuse might actually come out of her mouth by itself. It didn't; she felt herself become more flustered and pink-faced by the moment – and it couldn't all be attributed to the heat of the jacuzzi.

"Yes?"

"Nico was feeling depressed because Danielle was neglecting him – and you know how that feels, Taz – so I thought I'd take him to lunch to cheer him up, only he took it the wrong way and jumped on me."

"He *did*?"

Isabel felt a twinge of panic at his apparent surprise and decided not to push her luck, adding lamely, "Or he could have seen Danielle coming in and kissed me to make her feel jealous."

"He *kissed* you!"

"Only a small kiss!" Bugger! Rule number one for the barefaced lie – Under No Circumstances Volunteer Additional Information. "Only the slightest brush against my cheek. In fact, I'm not sure his mouth actually made contact with my skin at all. It was more of an air kiss. You know, *mwah, mwah,* like that. Anyway, he only did it to make Danielle jealous because she had been neglecting him – like I've been neglecting you, haven't I? And I'm *soooo* sorry!" A sudden thought popped into her head. "I hope you haven't been snuggling up to any groupies to get your own back? Although I appreciate that I deserve it," she added humbly.

Despite having to listen to such rubbish, Taz now had a smile on his face.

Yippee! thought Isabel, *I'm in the clear . . .*

"Cut the crap, Isabel. You deliberately set Nico up to sabotage his relationship with your sister."

"*What*? How did – "

His smile now had a certain self-satisfied quality. "Jemma told me."

"*Jemma*? I mean – "

"About half an hour ago," he explained, "when she came to cadge a packet of painkillers for her hangover. We had quite a nice little chat – well, I talked, she grunted."

"Then why did you – "

The smug smile broadened into a smug grin. "It's kinda fun seeing you twist yourself up in knots! It's sweet you've only got Danielle's best interests at heart, but I think she's old enough to make up her own mind without interference. Besides, this Nico bloke is nice enough. I know you want to be loyal to Jemma, but I think you're worrying about nothing."

"*Nice*!" spluttered Isabel. "He shagged my best friend *and* my twin sister in one evening and *you think he's nice*? What planet are you on?"

"Come on babe, I don't want to fight over someone else's problem."

"You started it," muttered Isabel.

"So let me finish it," he said and kissed her.

Isabel, not one for sulking, kissed him back. Taz was right. What was the point in getting all stressed out over someone else's problem? Nico was out of her sister's life now, so the 'problem' had gone bye-bye – *yes*!

"OK," she said, "I forgive you."

"Excellent," said Taz. "Fancy a quickie?"

* * *

Amidst a lot of giggling and splashing, they jumped out of the jacuzzi and raced each other to the changing rooms, leaving a trail of puddles in their wake. (Even Isabel drew the line at having sex in front of Kimmie).

The changing rooms were empty. Taz jammed the door shut with a black plastic wedge; no way was he going to risk coitus interruptus again. He ripped Isabel's jazzy swimsuit off, lifted her onto the vanity unit, sweeping the bottles of complimentary shampoo onto the floor. Isabel wrapped her legs around his back, her right heel fitting snugly against his buttocks, and Taz was just about to plunge manfully inside her when they both heard the door rattle.

Isabel dug her fingernails into his shoulders and almost fell into the sink in shock.

"*Shit*!" said Taz. "I don't believe it!"

"*Shh!*" Isabel placed a finger against his lips. "Keep quiet – maybe they'll go away."

"Is anyone inside?" bleated a reedy male voice.

"No, but I'm working on it," muttered Taz.

Isabel tried to stifle her giggles.

"Kimmie, I think the door is stuck!" said the same voice again.

"Hang on!"Kimmie's voice wafted down the corridor. "I'll get the spare key. Maybe Mrs Granger locked the door for security as not many people are in."

Isabel stared at the door in horror, suddenly realising the extent of her predicament. The changing rooms were not unisex; one of them was in the wrong place – and she had the feeling it was probably her . . .

"Bloody hell," muttered Taz, pulling his shorts up.

"I couldn't have put it better myself." She glared at him. "You got me into this mess, now get me out!"

"We'll have to brazen it out."

Typical Australian. "No, *thank* you. You might get up to these sort of hi-jinks all the time, but I assure you, I don't. You're famous; it'll get in the papers and I'll be known forever as the girl who shagged Taz Taylor in the men's bogs."

"Changing rooms," said Taz.

"Think like the editor of a tabloid."

Their situation didn't seem funny any more. Falling into silence, they looked around for an alternative plan, an alternative exit, an alternative *anything*!

"Climb through the window in the dunny," suggested Taz. "The fire escape runs right along the side of the building. You can jump onto that, a quick sprint and you're outside the ladies' and then you can climb back."

Taz was clearly used to shagging female groupies – expert at shinning up drainpipes, squeezing through small windows, leaping over security guards with one bound – generally up for all kinds of shenanigans. Isabel, however, was beginning to feel tired and fed up.

"I don't know what kind of girls you usually date, Taz, but I can assure you – "

"It looks as though the door's stuck again, Caitlin," Kimmie was saying to her boss. "Do you want to get Marc to break it down or shall I call out the fire brigade? Someone could be trapped in there."

"Eek!" said Isabel and, hopping off the sink she ran across the changing rooms to the toilet cubicles.

For once Taz failed to admire the view. "Don't forget this!" he hissed, chucking her swimming-costume after her.

As it was impossible to run and haul on a wet swimsuit at the same time, Isabel had to stop to make herself decent; she shut the cubicle door first. When she was clothed, she climbed clumsily onto the toilet seat and knelt on the wobbly cistern to undo the catch of the window. It swung back and thumped against the outside wall.

Gingerly, she put one foot through the open window and levered herself across the cistern and window ledge. Her leg scraped against the rough brickwork on the other side as her foot felt for the fire escape. It was further down than she had thought. She had to hold onto the sides of the window frame for support until her toes finally touched the rusting metal grillwork of the fire escape. Now she had to hop about on one leg, the latticed surface digging painfully into the ball of her foot as she tried to retrieve her other leg from inside the window.

"Bugger, bugger, bugger," she muttered under her breath, wishing she had the double-jointed limbs of her old Barbie doll.

There was probably an easier way of climbing through windows, she concluded, as she landed on her bottom but, as she did not break and exit on a regular basis, any apparent knack eluded her.

The fire escape was filthy and had stamped a rusty criss-cross pattern across her swimsuit. Below her, she could see a road. Luckily, it was a service road and not Quay Street – so there was no one to witness her humiliation. She moved across the fire escape; the cold metal dug painfully into her bare feet, but the frosted window of the ladies' toilets was just a few feet away. And it was open! Now all she had to do was climb in. Simple.

From the inside the building, Isabel could hear Caitlin Granger patiently asking Taz, "But why did you jam the door shut, Mr Taylor? You know that we would always respect your privacy. The press aren't allowed in here."

"I didn't *mean* to lock myself in," Taz was turning on his full antipodean charm. "I guess I kicked this wedge thing in the way."

A dubious silence, then, "So why did you take so long to answer?"

"I was in the dunny!"

"You could have shouted a reply. We thought you might be stuck."

"Poor old Taz, stuck in the lavatory?" He was laughing now. "Caitlin, if I ever get trapped in a dunny, I'll sing 'Rescue Me' in a three-part harmony with myself – so you'll know I'm stuck and not just constipated."

What Caitlin Granger said to that was unclear, but for the moment it had gone quiet. Isabel rested her elbows on the narrow window ledge of the ladies' toilets and levered herself up onto the sill, crawling through the gap until she was once more balanced precariously on the cistern.

She realised she was facing the wrong way for an easy descent and so attempted to turn round. Her knee skidded across the slippery ceramic lid and she fell through the window, bounced off the toilet seat and hit the deck with a crash.

As she sat up, somewhat dazed, she was not surprised to hear: "What the heck was that?"

She slid the bolt across the door just as the handle rattled.

"Is anyone in there?" asked the same female voice.

Isabel scrambled to her feet, flushed the loo, shut the window, adjusted her swimming-costume, now decidedly the worse for wear, and opened the door.

On the other side stood a chubby, middle-aged woman with flushed cheeks and an anxious expression. "Are you all right?" she enquired nervously. "Only I heard this awful clatter . . ." She peered past Isabel and was relieved to see the toilet cubicle looked much the same as usual.

"I'm fine, thanks. I think the noise came from outside," lied Isabel, her heart still thumping.

The woman appeared unconvinced and stared meaningfully at the floor. On the pale tiles were some distinctly black footprints.

From the corridor Kimmie could be heard to say, "What was that crash? Did you hear it, Caitlin?"

"We'd better check it out," replied Caitlin's voice. "Perhaps someone's slipped up. Those tiles can be treacherous for anyone with wet feet."

Taz (nervously): "I'm sure it's nothing."

Oh bloody hell! thought Isabel. Her life was turning into a *Carry On* film. She shoved the woman out of the way, darting into the integral sauna as the door opened.

The first thing Caitlin saw was a perplexed chubby woman standing alone in the middle of the changing rooms. "Is everything all right, Madam?"

"I think so . . ." replied the woman doubtfully.

The two of them eyed the black footprints leading from the toilet cubicle to the sauna.

"Jolly good," said Caitlin, in a voice that sounded as though it plainly wasn't. "I'll leave you to it then."

Isabel, leaning against the inside of the sauna door, the better to catch every word, sank back against one of the benches as the door closed and there was silence. Peeling off her swimming costume, she used it as a pillow and lay back, closing her eyes. At *last* – peace, perfect peace!

Isabel fell asleep.

* * *

She awoke with a start, burning hot. Someone must have turned the heat up. She wriggled into her swimming-costume, now bone dry, and pushed at the door.

It would not open.

Must be stuck, she decided, and tried again. The door didn't move. Isabel felt a tight knot of anxiety expanding through her stomach.

She hammered on the door. "Help! Let me out! I'm stuck!"

Someone would hear her. Someone would come and let her out. She mustn't panic. The door was only stuck. It could not be locked because it didn't have a lock.

Isabel banged on the door with her fists. "Help! Let me out! Help! I'm stuck in the sauna!" She began kicking at the door.

No one came.

The door had a tiny window at the top, which had steamed up. She rubbed it clear and tried to see into the changing room. It appeared to be empty. Perhaps everyone had gone home? She had no idea how long she had been asleep, though surely it was only just gone lunch-time?

Her normally pale, translucent skin was burnt fiery red. Sweat dripped from every pore, only to evaporate on contact with the skin. As she stared around in despair, she suddenly remembered the water bucket. If she sloshed it over the coals the large amount of water would short the element beneath and cut out the power.

The water bucket had vanished.

Isabel began to panic. It was impossible! There must be a water bucket – it had been here when she had come in . . .

"Kimmie!" she screamed, thumping the door. *"Kimmie, let me out!"*

She began to feel dizzy and sick. She slid onto the floor, trying to focus on the bench opposite, praying she wouldn't pass out. There, lying beneath, was the wooden ladle used to pour water onto the hot coals.

Isabel grabbed it, smashing it against the glass.

Nothing happened. She tried again; the ladle just bounced straight off.

Savagely she beat the door. *"Let me out!"* she screamed. *"For God's sake, let me out!"* A snap and the head of the ladle broke off. Isabel was left holding the stick. She burst into tears and slid onto her knees. This wasn't happening, it couldn't be happening to *her*.

The door opened.

Isabel fell onto the freezing cold tiles and found herself nose to nose with a pair of strappy sandals. Looking up, she could see Caitlin Granger, wearing a pretty lilac dress as though she was off to a garden party.

"What the hell is going on?" demanded Caitlin.

Isabel sat up. "The door . . . the door was stuck . . ." The cool, fresh air stung her lungs. She coughed.

"I thought you'd gone home," said Kimmie, helping her to her feet.

Isabel swayed as the changing room did a couple of laps without her. She caught hold of Kimmie for support. "Someone locked me in!"

Caitlin was shocked at her accusation. "The sauna hasn't got a lock."

Isabel was not in the mood for a debate. Recovering her legs long enough to weave over to her kitbag, she dragged out her jeans and pulled them on over her swimming-costume.

Kimmie bent and picked up a small black plastic wedge. "Maybe this got stuck beneath the door. That would stop you getting out. It's used by the cleaners to hold open the door when they mop the floors."

Caitlin took the door-wedge from Kimmie. She appeared genuinely upset. "I'm so sorry, Miss van der Straatan. It must have been a freak accident. I promise it won't happen again. Perhaps we can make amends for your inconvenience? Would you be interested in free beauty treatments?"

Isabel hugged her kitbag close to her chest, still dangerously close to tears. "Firstly, I don't need a beautician – I need counselling. And secondly, if you think I'm setting foot in this place again you're *crazy*!"

Chapter Seven

Isabel sat in her car, still trembling with shock. Where the hell was Taz?

She wrenched back the zip of her kitbag, tossed the crumpled bundle of sweaty clothes onto the floor and unearthed her mobile phone from where it had become lodged in one of her Reeboks. Her hands were shaking so much she dialled the Tandoori Indian Takeaway before she got Taz.

"Hi, babe," he said.

Strangely, his calm voice just agitated her further. "Where the fuck are you?"

Taz, perhaps too stunned by her apparent fury, failed to make a response.

Aware she had lost control completely, Isabel burst into tears and, in her frustration, tossed the mobile phone out of the car window. It sailed over the railings that divided the pavement from the road and plopped into the churning water below. Realising what she'd done, Isabel collapsed across the steering wheel and had complete hysterics.

It was some time before she realised Taz was tapping nervously on the car window. "Are you OK?" he muttered, keeping a safe distance in case she turned nasty.

Isabel, overcome with shame, opened the car door and threw herself into his arms. "I'm sor . . . or . . . ry," she wailed, her voice coming out in gulps. "I'm a selfish cow and I don't deserve you!"

"*Babe,*" he said, crushing her against his chest. "What happened?"

He had changed into baggy T-shirt and joggers, his dark hair was still wet from the shower and he was not wearing his usual tatty trainers. He must have run all the way here in bare feet, realised Isabel fondly. How sweet!

"Someone tried to kill me," she said and began to feel the first twinges of embarrassment. Her fears sounded silly when put into words. She was turning into exactly the kind of neurotic woman she had always despised.

"*What*?"

Isabel shifted uncomfortably. Perhaps she *had* over-reacted a teensy bit, she decided. *No – really?* her conscious mocked by way of return. "I fell asleep in the sauna," she explained to Taz. "When I woke up, the door was jammed."

"How can it jam? The doors open outwards."

"One of those plastic wedges had become stuck beneath the door."

"It sounds like it could have been an accident?" Taz suggested tentatively.

Isabel had to admit it that this did seem likely. Oh hell, she was never going to be able to show her face in Granger's again.

"Do you want to call the police?" he asked.

"I can't," said Isabel, and to her great shame she realised tears were trickling down her cheeks again. "I chucked my mobile phone in the river."

"Oh," said Taz. *"Right!"* He began to laugh.

Isabel found herself smiling too. "Take me home," she pleaded. "I think that would be best for everyone. I'm not safe to be let out in public."

He ruffled her hair affectionately. "You could come back to my apartment? We could chill, have a few beers, you could phone the police from there if you still want to?"

"OK," said Isabel. Anything to get away from the gym. She imagined Caitlin and Kimmie watching her from the window, worried she was going to sue, assuming she was some crazy, mixed-up bitch who had nothing better to do than accuse perfect strangers of trying to kill her. A sorry case, who had so much spare time on her hands she spent her life trying to make life hell for everyone else, just because she wanted the attention.

"Good on you." Taz took hold of her hand and led her along the pavement towards the beautiful Georgian house at the far end of the quay where he had a penthouse. "A couple of Fosters will make it OK, you'll see."

* * *

They spent the afternoon entwined on his settee, drinking beer and working their way through his collection of Buffy DVDs.

Isabel was left feeling more depressed. Was this how the rest of her life was going to pan out? Beers and videos of American TV shows into infinity? Like Danielle was always nagging, she needed to get a life before it was too late.

So when Taz suggested they went out for dinner she jumped at the opportunity. Taz, not one for standing on ceremony, actually had the local Indian in mind – but Isabel phoned up and booked them a table at the smartest restaurant in the area: Jacob's, situated on the seafront at Port Rell.

Isabel sauntered through the door, still wearing her jeans and leather jacket, daring the staff to refuse her entry, because she was spoiling for a fight and wanted to inject a little excitement in her life. Unfortunately, because Taz was with her, the maîtr d' didn't bat an eyelid.

Following the maîtr d' across the crowded restaurant, Isabel paused to talk to some friends, wave to others, and then she froze. On the very edge of the restaurant, at a secluded table, sat Danielle and Nico, holding hands, gazing into each other's eyes. *Shit!*

As Isabel stopped dead in her tracks, Taz, who never looked where he was going, cannoned into the back of her.

"Wassup?" he grumbled, rubbing his chin, which had just made contact with the top of her head.

"We can't eat here," muttered Isabel, ducking behind him before Danielle saw her.

"Why not?" Taz watched their waiter disappearing into the distance and then caught sight of Danielle's bright red hair. "Hey look, it's your sister! *Dani*!" he yelled. "Over here!"

Taz had a carrying voice, used to making himself heard across US football stadiums. Half the restaurant turned disapprovingly to see who was making all the noise. On seeing it was their own local celebrity, they smiled indulgently. Surprisingly rock stars did count for something in Port Rell – even Australian ones.

Isabel, however, cringed and tried to blend into a nearby floral arrangement. "Taz!" she muttered furiously. "What are you doing? They'll see us."

"That was the idea." Taz waved. More people turned to locate the source of the sudden commotion.

She tried to tug his arm down. "I really don't want them to see us."

"I'm not surprised – after what Jemma told me about how you've been trying to split them up. Why do you dislike the guy so much? He's cool."

Bloody Jemma talked too much! Isabel squirmed. Taz was so straightforward she hated lying to him. "I have this feeling. You know, women's intuition."

"Bollocks. Don't you want your sister to be happy?"

"Yes, and that's why – "

"Oh come *on*!" Taz grew tired of her prevarication and, grabbing her hand, he began pulling her between the tables.

Nico and Danielle did not look particularly pleased to see them, but Danielle's good manners got the better of her.

"Taz, this is Nico Morales," she sighed. "He's a famous writer. Nico, meet Taz Taylor, he plays bass with a rock band called Talisman."

"Yeah, I think I've heard of them," said Nico, grinning widely as the two men shook hands.

Taz appeared about to comment further, but Danielle cut in.

"How did your rehearsals go, Taz?" she asked, still in Royal-Family-making-polite-conversation-to-the-plebs mode.

Taz didn't do small talk. "Don't ask, babe," he said, rolling his eyes. Oblivious to any undercurrents, he pulled up a chair and sat the wrong way round, resting his arms across the back.

Isabel glared at him meaningfully, but he failed to take the hint, so she was forced to sit on the only remaining seat – right next to Nico – or else look a complete idiot. Aware Nico was finding her embarrassment highly amusing, she studied her fingernails instead and tried not to look as though she was sulking.

A waiter was trying to get Danielle's attention.

"Excuse me, Miss van der Straatan, there is a telephone call for you."

"Tell them I'll call back."

"The caller said it was urgent."

Danielle glanced across at Nico. "That's odd. I switched my mobile phone off so that no one would be able to bother us. How did they know I was here."

Her sister looked secretly pleased, all the same, thought Isabel uncharitably. It proved Vanders couldn't operate without her.

"Perhaps the call is for me?" suggested Isabel. "Well, it *could* be . . . I've, um, lost my mobile phone."

Taz, who knew exactly where her mobile phone was, snorted loudly.

The waiter glanced towards him and did a double take.

"The call is more likely to be for me," said Danielle coldly. "After all, I have a business to run."

"And I have a social life to maintain," retorted Isabel.

They glared at each other in mutual dislike.

"Do you think I could possibly have your autograph, sir?" the waiter was asking Taz. "For my . . . er, cousin."

Taz obediently scribbled on a menu. "There you go, mate. Now, put the girls out of their misery and tell them who's asking for 'Miss van der Straatan', or we'll be arguing about this all night and I'm starving."

"Lady Jemma Stortford, sir," replied the waiter, folding the menu into four and tucking it into his breast pocket. "In connection with Mr Isaac van der Straatan."

He bowed his head, turned on his heel and walked back through the restaurant.

Isabel frowned. "Why on earth would Jemma phone me up to talk about Dad?"

Danielle was already on her feet. "Christ, she's run off with him!"

"As if!" Isabel thought this was funny. "You know Jemma doesn't see him in that way. He's her 'mentor'."

"Rubbish!" Danielle's voice rose hysterically. "He's asked her to marry him and now she's phoning up to gloat!"

Isabel watched Danielle run after the waiter and then rolled her eyes. "That girl has a real problem! I suppose I'd better sort it out. Don't want her blowing her stack at poor Jem."

As Isabel left, Nico glanced across at Taz. "Do you think they'll need a referee?"

"Nah." Taz abandoned his chair in favour of Danielle's. "They'll be OK. When they fight it's best to stay out of the fall-out zone." He picked up the bottle of champagne and twisted it around to read the label. "Do you think this place has got any beer?"

"I haven't a clue," Nico shrugged. "Champagne isn't really my thing, but Dani beat me to the wine list."

"I guess alcohol is alcohol." Taz poured himself a glass, then, as an afterthought, poured one for Nico too. "Drink up. You know women and telephones. They'll be ages yet." He studied the menu. "What shall we order? I fancy a burger – or do they only do posh crap?"

* * *

By judicious use of her elbows, Isabel reached the phone first. "Hi, Jem, what's up?"

"Isabel?" Jemma's voice sounded strained. "Is that you? I've been trying to reach you all afternoon. Is Dani with you?"

"Yeah, she's here," replied Isabel. She knew her sister was standing directly behind her because she could feel those cold grey eyes boring holes directly into her back. "What do you want to speak to her for?"

"I don't!"

Jemma's voice was so vehement, for a split second Isabel worried that she really had run off with Isaac.

"Look," began Jemma, "I hate to tell you this over the phone – but the police are doing a crap job of tracking you and Danielle down and there's a couple of reporters from this paper heading your way right now. I don't want them blurting it out first."

"Police? Reporters?" Isabel felt a chill of fear. "What the hell's going on?"

There is nothing more frustrating than only hearing half a telephone conversation. Danielle fidgeted beside her. "What's she saying?" she hissed. "Let me talk to the gold-digging bitch!"

Isabel was not listening. She replaced the receiver and stared at Danielle in shock. She was having trouble breathing.

"Jemma's run off with him, hasn't she?" said Danielle triumphantly. I knew I was right! Well, she's not getting her hands on Vanders – "

"Dad's dead!"

"Dead? Don't be ridiculous. He was fine last night."

"He's been in a car accident. It happened last night, but the police didn't find the car until this morning. It was completely burnt out. They haven't released his name to the press because they couldn't find us to tell first. But everyone knows it's him. Jemma says there are reporters on their way over here now, to ask us how we feel. Fuck, how do they think we feel?"

"For goodness sake, girl, get a grip and tell me which hospital Dad's been taken to, so we can get over there and be with him. And if Jemma thinks she's going to be playing at Florence Nightingale she can – "

"Bloody hell, Dani, why do you never listen? It's too late! *He's dead*!"

(From The Calahurst Echo)

MILLIONAIRE KILLED IN MYSTERY CRASH

by
Jemma Stortford

Local jeweller, Isaac van der Straatan (51), has been found dead after a mysterious road accident in the King's Forest. His car went out of control, left the road and plunged down a steep bank. It is not thought that any other vehicle was involved – although the police are refusing to speculate until the accident investigation unit has completed its report.

The burnt-out wreckage was discovered yesterday lunch-time, after another motorist reported seeing smoke in remote woodland.

Mr van der Straatan owned a chain of exclusive jewellery stores along the south coast. He was a popular man, who did a great deal for charity and had recently announced his intention to give much of his fortune away on his retirement. He had been a widower for many years but leaves twin daughters, Isabel and Danielle van der Straatan, who recently celebrated their 25th birthday with a lavish costume party.

Isaac van der Straatan – self-made millionaire ***(see page 4).***

Chapter Eight

OCTOBER

The wind whipped around the churchyard, bending the trees standing sentinel over ancient headstones, as Danielle waited for the final curtain to drop on her father's life. The long, wet grass was slowly soaking through the hems of her trousers and she had to step from foot to foot to prevent her high heels from sinking irremediably into the soggy ground. She could not quite bring herself to stand on the carpet of green plastic grass, draped artistically around the newly dug earth of her father's grave. She wasn't sure that the carpet was intended to be stood on – or if it was only to improve the look of what was basically a muddy hole in the ground. The hole she had managed to avoid looking at until now.

She watched the pallbearers lower the coffin onto the turf – a coffin so shiny and new it seemed almost a pity to be burying it. Why had her father wanted to be buried in this windswept place? There was a lovely modern church on the outskirts of Norchester, with a nice lady vicar, but he'd written it into his will that he wanted to be buried next to his wife. A good enough reason for anyone else – except Isaac had admitted to Danielle, long ago, that he had cheated on her mother throughout their married life – and she was certain he'd never visited her grave after her death. Isaac had been the world's biggest hypocrite. He had lived his life deceiving himself as much as everyone around him, and she had gone along with it.

From the corner of her eye, she saw Jemma picking her way through the crooked headstones – not the easiest thing to do in short skirt, sheer tights and high heels – and inwardly groaned. What was she doing here? She wasn't family – and she certainly wasn't a friend. Deliberately Danielle moved to the opposite side of the grave.

Jemma was accompanied by her elder brother Josh, the Earl of Stortford. They were not alike. Whereas Jemma was small, blonde and snappy, like a bad-tempered whippet, Josh was more a good-natured labrador – tall and broad with dark wavy hair, which curled when damp. You wouldn't find him propping up a bar until closing time, waking up in strange beds and shagging his way through the best-looking of the tourists who descended on Calahurst every summer.

Josh smiled at Danielle and walked over, taking her hands in his. "You're having a rotten time of it, aren't you? If you need any help, or just a chat, you will call me?"

Danielle nodded, a lump in her throat preventing her from replying. His kindness made her want to burst into tears on the spot. She took a couple of deep breaths, to steady her voice.

"Thank you for the flowers," she mumbled. He'd sent an old-fashioned posy, tied with white ribbon and signed from himself and Jemma – although she doubted Jemma had had much to do with it. "Dad used to love freesias, because of their beautiful scent."

"I grew them in my father's old hothouses," he said. "It's a new line for me. I'm doing a roaring trade at the market! I didn't realise people were prepared to pay so much for fresh flowers."

Danielle could imagine what a stir he must cause at the market, with his good looks and cut-glass accent.

"Josh!" hissed Jemma.

Realising he was holding up the proceedings, Josh quickly kissed Danielle on the cheek, murmured, "Talk to you later," and returned to stand beside his sister.

The vicar had started reading from his bible when a tall blond man sauntered into their midst, casually dropping a bunch of cerise chrysanthemums on top of the flowers carefully arranged around the grave. He had dark circles under his eyes and gingery stubble peppering his chin, but still looked as though he ought to be posing for a photo shoot in *GQ*.

"Sorry, Dani," murmured Max Falkenhayn, squinting tiredly across the grave. "I got held up at work. Paige

Lorraine's damn pink diamonds." Then he smiled; the slow, lazy smile of someone confident of their attraction to the opposite sex, certain he would be forgiven for any misdemeanour.

Despite herself, Danielle felt her cheeks glow. When Max had lolloped into Vanders about eighteen months ago in search of lucrative employment, Danielle really thought she had found her soul mate. Apart from her father, there was no one else who enthused about diamonds as much as he did. She and Max had enjoyed an intense, passionate affair – until Jemma sauntered into his life, all tight T-shirts and streaky blonde hair. How could Danielle compete? There had been no explanatory phone call, no 'Dear Dani' letter; Max had abruptly traded her in for Jemma. *Bastard*!

He had had his hair cut shorter since she had last seen him, but the diamond watch she had given him for Christmas still glinted on his wrist. The diamonds in his ears were a new addition, however.

Although she kept her eyes lowered, she knew he was watching her intently. Maybe he did still desire her and was already regretting his impulsive fling with Jemma. More likely he had realised that, now her father was dead, he was looking at his new boss.

The last thing Danielle wanted was for Max to think she was still moping after him, so she pretended she was scanning the crowd milling outside the church for a familiar face. The entire village had turned out to pay its respects. Yet Isabel . . . Danielle frowned. Isabel was nowhere to be seen . . .

The sky darkened and the first raindrops began to splash against the brass plate on the lid of the coffin. Danielle shivered, wishing she'd worn a coat over her trouser suit. The vicar finished speaking; the coffin was jerkily lowered into the grave. Danielle turned away, unable to watch, blinking determinedly to prevent the tears from sliding down her cheeks.

Jemma stepped forward. Tugging a crimson silk tulip (the Vanders trademark) from the buttonhole of her black jacket, she lightly dropped it onto Isaac's coffin, muttered a few unintelligible words, then promptly burst into tears. Max put his arm around her and she buried her face in his shoulder, as he whispered against her hair.

Max had never been that attentive when he'd been with her, thought Danielle bitterly. Perhaps she wasn't the sort of girl to inspire that kind of protectiveness?

Jemma's sobs were becoming noisier. The vicar looked over the top of his spectacles in concern. Danielle found her fingers tapping irritably against her thigh. Was this nightmare ever going to end?

Jemma, realising that the vicar had paused, looked up. "I'm all right," she said bravely. "Ignore me. It's just, well, I loved him so much . . ."

This was all too much for Danielle to bear. "Who the *hell* do you think you *are*?" she hissed. "This is my father's funeral, you weren't invited, I don't know why you're here, but as you *are* here, will you quit with the attention-seeking and *shut the fuck up*?"

There was an awkward silence, as though no one

could quite believe what they had heard. Perhaps they were waiting for her to take back the remark, to apologise – relying on her sensibilities not to make a scene?

Oh fuck the lot of them! By her reckoning she was just about due for a mental breakdown. Perhaps then *she'd* get some sympathy, *she'd* get the shoulder to cry on and someone to hold *her* close and tell her everything was going to be all right . . .

These last few months she had put up with more grief than anyone could take: Jemma sleeping with her father and blatantly seducing Max. Isabel trying to seduce Nico – and Nico allowing himself to be so easily seduced. Her father – not realising how much Vanders meant to her. Her father – trying to sell Vanders from under her. Her father – getting himself *fucking killed* . . .

How could he abandon her this way?

"Tell me why you're here, Jemma?" she continued. "I'd really like to know the reason. I know Max is here because my father was his boss, and he feels it is vital that appearances are kept up. Appearances are important to Max. Josh is here because my father was his tenant and, because he's a good person, he considers it the honourable thing to do. But you? You're not family, you're not a friend. You have absolutely no right to be here – "

"I'm here to pay my respects," Jemma said, in a quiet, dignified voice. "Your father was very kind to Josh and me when our father died. We'd have ended up on the Oaks Estate if it hadn't been for his financial advice."

"Which would have been a complete tragedy!" mocked Danielle. "Lady Jemma Stortford living in a council house? You must think I'm stupid! Do you really think I didn't know exactly what was going on between you and my father? All this 'mentor' crap! You were his mistress and I can't see why you don't come right out and admit it!"

Her eyes met Jemma's, who stared back, equally boldly.

"OK, I admit it." Jemma smiled. A small, self-satisfied smile, of triumph and victory. "How do you feel now? Knowing he loved me more than he loved you. That's what this is all about, isn't it? You're jealous of me, you always have been; because I've got what you were so desperate to have – the love and respect of your father!"

At which point Danielle was all for launching herself onto Jemma for a good old-fashioned cat-fight, but was hindered by Max leaping into action and pinning her arms to her sides before she'd taken two steps around the grave.

Danielle glared up at him. "This is the bit where you tell me I'm a sad, unhinged bitch?"

Max sighed. "I'm sorry your father's dead, Danielle, but you can't go through life treating people like this."

"Ha! Like you're the expert! What about the way you treated me?"

Max, unable to meet her accusing stare, looked off into the middle distance instead. "Our relationship wasn't working out. I'm sorry, I should have said something at the time, but it seemed easier this way."

Max, Danielle remembered, had never been very keen on confrontations.

By now Jemma had sauntered off through the lychgate and Max, judging that Danielle had cooled off sufficiently, tentatively released her arm. He glanced towards Josh and said to him, as though Danielle wasn't there: "Will you be OK?"

Josh nodded. "You can leave her with me."

Like she was an unwanted child, thought Danielle miserably, the fight all gone. Passed from one uncaring relative to another.

Exit Max, greatly relieved, without even a backward glance.

"Danielle – " began Josh.

"Save the lecture," she said tiredly. "I know I'm behaving badly, but after what's happened over the last few months I don't think I care anymore.

"I understand."

He kept glancing over her shoulder, so she turned to see what he was looking at and spied Jemma patiently waiting for him by the gate, clearly testing where his loyalties lay. She was his sister after all.

"You know you can always talk to me," Josh was saying. "Your father's death, being landed with the business and feeling responsible for a wayward younger sister – I don't think you realise the enormity of it all. I've been there; I know what it's like. You think it's bad now? It's going to get worse."

She smiled weakly, not trusting herself to speak. Dear Josh – if only she could have fallen in love with him instead of Max, how much more simple her life would have been.

"I'll take you home," he said. "I've got the Land Rover parked – "

"No, I'm all right now. I'd rather be alone."

"If you're sure?"

His dark blue eyes stared deep into her own until Danielle felt she could bottle up the overwhelming misery no longer. She was about to throw herself into his arms and sob her heart out when Josh broke eye contact to glance towards his frantically waving sister.

"I don't know where you draw your reserve of strength from," he sighed, patting her shoulder absent-mindedly. "You're so courageous." And then he left her, standing beside her father's open grave, becoming slowly soaked by the relentless rain.

No, come back! she wanted to yell after him. *I just want someone to hold me, to look after me. I'm not really brave at all . . .*

But Josh met up with Jemma and Max at the gate and companionably they walked off down the road; Max and Jemma towards his flashy sports car – and Josh to his battered old Land Rover.

At least with the raindrops streaming down her face no one could see her crying, she thought irrelevantly, and wondered if it really would make her feel better if she wept hysterically – giving into her anguish rather than having it fester away inside her?

There wasn't anything to be gained from remaining here. It was cold, bleak and lonely, and she wanted to go home. So she took one last look back at her father's final resting place, then made her way back to her car.

The road was deserted now, save for the funeral car, which was drawing up beside her. The line of parked cars had gone and there was no sign of a rusting black Fiesta . . .

Where the fuck was Nico?

* * *

Nico, feeling he had done his duty, had sneaked out of the church, intending to take a quick cigarette before joining Danielle at the graveside. Funerals made him feel uncomfortable, reminding him of his own mortality, but he had felt obliged to accompany Danielle to provide moral support. Except she seemed to be coping remarkably well with the shock of her father's death, making all the arrangements for the funeral in her usual inimitable style. Nico felt totally superfluous to requirements.

He loosened his tie, lit up a cigarette and leant over the churchyard wall. A sudden movement below caught his eye and, as he looked down, he saw Isabel sitting on the wet pavement, curled up against the other side of the wall, her head tucked into the crook of one elbow.

"Hello, Isabel," he said, hoping he was not setting himself up for another row. "Are you OK?"

Isabel reluctantly raised her head. "It was seeing the coffin. I was all right until I saw the coffin. It was as though he wasn't dead at all; just somewhere else . . . and then I saw the coffin. I'm sorry . . . I thought no one would see me here. You don't have to stay, you know. I'll be all right."

Despite himself, Nico felt a twinge of pity. Her huge grey eyes were filled with tears; her red-gold hair had escaped from its French pleat and hung limply about her little pointed face. Even her nose was pink. She looked young and vulnerable and Nico felt the white knight in him come charging out.

He leant over the wall and helped her to her feet, handing her a clean tissue. Sitting on the floor had made her dress muddy and she had an enormous ladder in her tights.

Fat raindrops began to splatter the pavement. "You can't stay here. Why don't we sit in my car until you feel better?" Hell, had he really said that? Talk about masochistic . . .

But she nodded and he climbed over the wall, leading the way along the row of parked cars. The pavement only ran the length of the churchyard and most cars had been abandoned on the grass verge to avoid obstructing the road.

The car wasn't locked. Isabel waded through the long grass at the edge of the ditch and climbed into the passenger seat. Nico got in the driver's side and there they sat, in relative quiet, apart from Isabel's sniffs. Usually he would have put on some music but, knowing Isabel, anything he chose would be wrong and he was tired of fighting.

"I guess the service is over," said Nico, to kill the awkward silence.

The mourners, who had been standing around in little groups of three and four, were walking off through the lychgate, climbing into their cars and driving away. Isabel slunk down in the front seat, so no one could see her, and twisted Nico's handkerchief between her fingers.

He attempted a joke, anything to provoke a reaction. "Are you worried Danielle will see you? She already thinks you have the hots for me."

"Ha! My sister is not as daft as you think she is."

Nico did not know whether to be amused or offended. "I take it you haven't?"

"I despise you. The sooner you're out of Dani's life the better!"

Nico was unsure whether he had heard her correctly. "Sorry?"

"I don't trust you. Who are you anyway? You say you're a writer, but I phoned up WH Smith to order one of your books – *any* one of your books – and their computer has never heard of you. Where did you come from? You told Jemma you met her at The Parson's Collar but, as she can't remember, we only have your word for it. I took your photo from Dani's wallet and showed it to Harris Roberts who works behind the bar. He's never seen you there either."

"You have a real problem with obsession."

"Stay away from my sister, Nico No Morals. She's been hurt enough."

Nico was unsure what his next reaction should be. He was taken aback. He also felt incensed. What had he done to deserve such venom? This girl really hated him – she hardly knew him – she *didn't* know him. She hadn't the slightest idea of what motivated him and yet she was judging him on perceived behaviour.

There was also something in the way she avoided looking at him directly that told him there was more to this. "Who's fault is that?" he prevaricated. "You came on pretty strongly at La Dolce Vita."

"Don't flatter yourself! It was a means to an end. It worked brilliantly too – for about ten minutes! What did you do to get her to forgive you so easily? Boy, did I underestimate you."

Nico caught her hand. "*What* did you say?"

"Ow!" cried Isabel, as the many rings she wore dug into her fingers. "You're hurting me!" She struggled to pull her hand away.

"You *expected* Danielle to turn up?"

"I invited her!" Isabel was now revelling in his impotent rage. "She thought she was meeting me there for lunch – the poor trusting soul."

For a moment he could hardly comprehend the extent of her insidious scheming. "You *bitch*!"

Still Isabel remained unruffled. "Only to you, darling."

"Get out of my car!" He released her, staring through the windscreen, unable to look at her any longer.

Isabel, taking one look at his furious expression, knew when to quit and quickly got out. Almost before she was standing on the verge, Nico started the engine, put his foot down on the accelerator and sped off down the lane.

Isabel allowed herself a small smile of triumph.

"Bye, bye, Mr Morales!" she muttered beneath her breath – and raised her hand to cheekily wave and wind him up further.

It was at that point she realised that, as she appeared to be the last person left at the church, she was going to have to walk home.

Or ride in the funeral car with Danielle . . .

* * *

The thought of being stuck in a confined space with her sister was enough to make her turn abruptly on her heel and walk down the hill to the wine bar on the quay.

When she arrived back at Stortford House, about three hours later, she found Danielle sitting alone in the dining-room, dejectedly pulling the petals off a white chrysanthemum, chanting: *"I'm a bitch, I'm a cow, I hate myself. I'm a bitch, I'm a cow, I hate myself,"* only pausing to take large swigs of sherry, straight from the bottle.

"Funeral went well then?" said Isabel, confiscating the bottle. She looked at the tables, spilling over with untouched food. Where was everyone? The house should have been packed – free food, free drink, and Isaac had been very popular. She looked back at her sister, suspicion mounting. Had Danielle had upset everyone *again*? Honestly, she couldn't be left on her own for five minutes.

Danielle continued shredding flowers across the table. "Where were you?" she was grumbling. "'Daddy's little princess' – and you couldn't even be bothered to turn up?"

"I'm sorry," said Isabel honestly. "I couldn't face it."

Instead of launching into her usual lecture on 'dereliction of duty' and 'lack of responsibility', Danielle buried her head in her arms and began to cry.

Great, thought Isabel, picking up a bottle of sherry for herself and walking off towards the staircase with it. Aliens had abducted her anal-retentive sister and left her with a clone of Woody Allen.

Chapter Nine

Isabel stared at the solicitor in disbelief. "Danielle gets *everything*?"

The solicitor regarded Isabel calmly. "If Danielle van der Straatan is the eldest child of the late Mr Isaac van der Straatan, then yes, that is correct. Stortford House is leased from the estate of the Earl of Stortford, but there is still the apartment in Monte Carlo, recently bought by Mr van der Straatan; a 51 per cent share in the business known as Vanders; his collection of sports cars; a few pieces of good furniture; a couple of valuable paintings and various personal effects."

Danielle, not bothering to hide her impatience, wandered restlessly over to the window. A small tingle of euphoria was beginning to burn through her and it surely couldn't all be due to the effect of the anti-depressants. It was not the money. All her life she had felt her father cared only for Isabel. She had tried everything to gain his approval, even becoming involved in the family business. And now, after his death, Isaac had left the sign that she had been waiting for. If only it had not come too late.

Isabel had slumped back in her chair. "I can't believe it," she said, more to herself than anyone else. "I can't believe Dad would do this to me. Had I upset him in some way?"

"Perhaps you should have displayed more of an interest in the business," said Danielle, then felt ashamed of herself. Of course she would split her inheritance with her sister – but let Isabel sweat it out just a little bit longer.

"Sorry," snapped Isabel "but diamonds never really turned me on. They're so unutterably *boring*. Cold, hard, transparent lumps of crystal, cut into pretty shapes to fool the punters that they're interesting really. You have to scrabble around in the dirt to find them; you need no talent to sell them – just tell the gullible public that they're rare, beautiful and forever. Where's the creativity in that? It's not like making a film, cutting a record, painting a picture. Mother Nature has done all the hard work for you."

"Our designer is *very* creative. He makes beautiful jewellery – and not only from diamonds. He uses all manner of precious and semi-precious stones – as you would know if you ever came into one of our shops. You can be so pretentious, Isabel. Who are you to criticise? The only creativity *you've* ever shown is in spending money. Where do you think your money comes from?"

"I no longer have any money! I've been left penniless. I have no career, no trust fund, no savings, nothing much to sell. Sit back and enjoy watching me starve, Danielle, and then you can say: 'I told you so!'"

"I won't let you starve." Danielle had meant this to be a jokey, throwaway remark, but, somehow it came out wrong – scornful, arrogant, *patronising*.

"And I don't want your charity!" Without even looking at Danielle as she said those final words, Isabel stood up and shook the solicitor's hand. "Bye, Mr Smith. Thank you for all your help."

"Isabel," pleaded Danielle. "Don't go like this. We'll share the money. I don't need it all. I was only ever interested in taking over the business; you know how much work I've put into it."

Isabel paused, one hand on the door. "Now you have it all to yourself, as you've always wanted. This is not about money. It was never about money. I can go and get a job behind the bar at The Parson's Collar; Harris Roberts is always looking for staff."

"Bar work! You can't work in a bar, you're a van der Straatan!"

Isabel laughed. "Like we're a royal dynasty! Give the money to Jemma if your conscience is giving you grief. She only needs a few more thousand to pay off her bank loan for the apartment."

"Over my dead body." Why the hell should she give money to Jemma? Was Isabel deliberately trying to wind her up?

"And if she slings a palimony suit your way?"

"*Palimony suit*?" Danielle paled. Up until now she'd rather hoped the little scene at the funeral had been Jemma's idea of a joke. "You mean she was telling the *truth*? She *was* our father's lover? And you can stand there and – "

Isabel was smirking. "Can't you tell when I'm taking the piss? You haven't heard from her because she doesn't want to upset you further. No one ever wants to upset you. You go through life like a malevolent tornado, happily causing havoc to all and sundry, only thinking of yourself – and no one's allowed to stand up to you in case they hurt *your* feelings!"

"I'm not like that . . ."

"I don't think anyone's had the guts to say it to your face before – "

"Isabel – "

"Why do you think Max left you? Because of Jemma? No, because you were an utter bitch and you treated him like shit. You treat everyone like shit and wonder why you have no friends. Well, now you have no family either. Jemma has been more of a sister to me that you've ever been. I'm going to move in with her."

"You're going to leave me on my own?"

"With your diamonds. Just how you like it."

Isabel stalked through the door, slamming it behind her.

* * *

Danielle drove through the King's Forest to an industrial estate just on the edge of Norchester. It was here, in a small, insignificant building, that the Vanders' workshop was located. Built in the 1970s, of unimaginative concrete and glass, it was plain and anonymous. There wasn't even a nameplate over the door.

Isaac had always said that he set up his workshop for sentimental reasons rather than profit – and because, like his eldest daughter, he liked to be in control. The jewellery was made in the traditional way. The methods used to cut diamonds had been general practice for centuries and were time-consuming. It could take all day to saw through a one-carat diamond. Danielle had wanted to drag the workshop into the twenty-first century and install the latest computer and laser technology. Now she had no one to stop her, to tell her it would be an unnecessary expense. Vanders was all hers. She could do whatever she wanted.

Isaac's office was on the first floor, overlooking the area where the gemstones were cut and polished. Danielle stood for a moment, her nose pressed up against the window, watching 'her' staff working, then she sat in Isaac's high-backed leather chair, swinging round to put her feet up on the desk.

Her first priority would be to redecorate the office. A bright, stinging yellow for the walls, take out all this awful leather and chrome furniture, replace it with a few pieces from Stortford House and that Tissot painting her father had bought last year. She ran a finger over the top of the desk. Her finger left a shiny trail through the thin layer of dust. It looked as though no one had entered the office since Isaac had died. Their reverence was understandable, but she thought someone would have come in to clean.

Tugging at the desk drawers, she found the one at the bottom was locked. It had been an old trick of her father's, because of his habit of perpetually losing keys, to hide them by taping them to the underside of desks. Feeling beneath the table's edge, she discovered a small key embedded in a blob of Blue-Tack. Inserting the key in the lock, she turned it and the drawer opened.

There was nothing much inside – a few scribbled notes and a couple of leaky biros. Her father did not use this office very often, preferring his study back at Stortford House. Groping around at the back, she discovered a well-rotten apple and a screwed-up paper bag. Distastefully she dropped them into the bin. The apple 'plopped', the paper bag 'clunked'. Hastily she fished the bag out of the bin and unfurled it. As she upended it over the desk, a cushion-shaped, brilliant-cut diamond rolled out.

Danielle stared, not daring to believe her eyes. The stone caught the dull office light and transformed into a myriad of rainbows. Carefully she picked it up. It must have weighed at least fifty carats, possibly more.

She twisted it, reflecting the light onto the desk. It ought to be a fake, yet her instinct told her otherwise. But if her father had purchased a diamond of this size surely she would have heard – if not from him then from someone else. A diamond as beautiful as this could not be kept a secret.

The diamond had a slight blue tinge and was cut in the old style. Danielle examined it though the loupe, which all jewellers carried as habit. There were what appeared to be two very fine lines trapped inside the diamond, but she would need a magnification stronger than x 10 to be sure.

Why would such a lovely diamond be wrapped up in a paper bag and thrown carelessly in the back of a drawer as though it was rubbish? It ought to be in a museum, or at least a bank vault.

Unless it was stolen.

She picked up her loupe again. A stone this big would be well known. With her training she should recognise it. She unravelled the paper it had been wrapped in, thinking it might be an authenticity certificate. It was a plain paper bag.

Not daring to put the diamond down, Danielle went over to her father's bookcase and pulled out a well-thumbed book. It was a guide to the most famous diamonds in the world. It did not take her long to find what she sought – a large black and white photograph of a glamorous 1930s socialite, wearing a heavy, glittering tiara. Danielle compared the magnificent diamond in the centre with the large jewel in her hand. It did not need an expert to see they were identical.

"Shit," said Danielle – and dialled the number of Isabel's new mobile phone.

* * *

When Isabel left the solicitor's office she jumped into

her Mercedes SLK with the intention of putting as much distance between her and Danielle as possible. Jamming her foot on the accelerator, she hadn't a clue where she was going, only feeling a desperate need to get out of Calahurst. She had reckoned without the traffic freezing everything up. Now the tourist season had drawn to a close, the council had decided to dig up all the roads. After a couple of fruitless shortcuts and a close encounter with a juggernaut, she found herself stalled in the fast lane of the dual carriageway.

"You gotta death wish?" howled the driver of the juggernaut.

Hundreds of car horns echoed the same sentiments as they screamed for vengeance. Isabel rested her burning forehead on the steering wheel. Had she got a death wish? Was she going mad? She eventually became aware of a tapping at the window. A couple of young men were smiling earnestly at her. Deciding they looked more like college students than serial killers, Isabel wound the window down an inch.

"Yes?" she said haughtily.

"Are you all right?" enquired the first man. He had to raise his voice over the car horns.

"Fine, thanks," lied Isabel stiffly.

"You were going awfully fast," he added. "We really thought that lorry was about to hit you."

Isabel shuddered.

"We wondered if you needed a bump start," said the first man.

Would she! "That would be great."

The two youths scurried round to the back and began to push.

"Thanks!" called Isabel, revving the engine so that the car did not stall again.

"That's OK," replied the first man, wiping the sweat from his brow.

"Mind how you go!" called the second. "Better too late in this world than too soon in the next!"

Isabel's smile turned distinctly frosty and she abruptly wound up the window.

The second youth turned in bewilderment to his friend. "What did I say?"

"How to make friends and influence people," mocked his companion. "You do it every time. Don't worry about it. She probably had PMT."

Too late. The words of the young man burned into Isabel's mind as she left the traffic jam behind her. It was the story of her life – and now fate was having the last laugh. Instead of a university degree and a career in the family business like Danielle, she had dropped out of college, talked big about how she was going to be a singer, and then done absolutely nothing to achieve that ambition. She had carried on partying at her father's expense – now he was gone and she could see how empty her existence was. What hope was there for a woman with no education, no job and no income? What the hell was she going to do with her life – not that she had 'a life' in the first place . . .

Her new mobile phone rang, playing the theme from *Buffy the Vampire Slayer* – it had been a present from Taz.

The window on the phone told her it was her sister on the line. She took a couple of deep breaths to ensure her voice was steady. "Yes?"

"Isabel? It's me," said Danielle. "I need your help."

"My help? Huh, phone me because you want something, why don't you? Of course, it never occurred to you to apologise first."

"For what?"

"If you can't work it out, I'm not going to tell you." Isabel cut her off.

The phone rang again, almost immediately.

"OK, I apologise, now can we talk?"

"After the things you said to me? You're kidding. Sometimes, an apology isn't enough." As Isabel hit the off button she grinned, imagining Dani going purple at the other end.

Her telephone instantly started up a tinny impression of a thrashing guitar solo. She was going to have to get that ring tone changed before it drove her crazy.

"Hey, babe," said Taz, calling from Cardiff International Arena, where he was doing a sound check for a big gig that evening. "Did you miss me?"

"Yes, darling, but can you get off the line? I'm expecting Danielle to call with a grovelling apology."

Taz accepted this snub with his usual insouciance. "Sure, babe, text me later when you can talk. I'm due on stage at eight."

Isabel had to wait a full five minutes before the telephone rang again.

"OK, I'm really sorry. I should never have said those

things to you. I take them all back. I accept that I'm a horrible person and deserve to go straight to hell for treating people so badly. Can you ever forgive me?"

Isabel grinned. Her sister's one saving grace was that she did have a sense of humour and was not above taking the piss out of herself. "Apology accepted. Well done, I knew you could do it. Now all you have to do is phone up Jemma and – "

"I'm not a saint, Isabel."

"I'm sure you can apologise nicely, if you put your mind to it. Now, what can I do for you?"

"I can't tell you over the phone. Can you meet me at the workshop?"

"Is it to do with diamonds?"

"Yes –"

"You know I know nothing about diamonds."

"Well, now's your chance to learn!" snapped Danielle.

Isabel counted to ten.

"Please, Isabel?" said Danielle, in a meeker tone. "Please, please, please! I really need your advice." Pause. "Now Dad's dead, you're the only person I can trust."

Which didn't say much for her relationship with Nico, thought Isabel, cheering up. And later, as she drove towards the workshop, she reflected on how desperate her sister must be – if she had to resort to being nice . . .

* * *

By the time Isabel made it to Vanders' workshop, Danielle had two cups of coffee, a dial-out pizza and a pile of textbooks spread out on the desk.

"Come in and shut the door," said Danielle, not looking up. "I don't want anyone to overhear our conversation."

Isabel did as she was bid, but could not resist saying, "Do you want me to check for bugs too?"

"Sit down and don't be so ridiculous."

Isabel found another chair, sat down and helped herself to pizza. "Mmm, Hawaiian, my favourite. How did you know?"

"We're twins, identical in every way."

Not *every* way . . . Isabel bit into the pizza. "It's no good trying to argue with me because I shan't take any notice. What's this terrible problem?"

"This," replied Danielle, carelessly tossing the diamond across to her.

Isabel gasped as the diamond spun in a glittering arc across the desk. "It's huge! Where did it come from?"

"I don't know."

"You *don't know*?"

Danielle turned one of the textbooks around to face her sister and pointed to a black and white photograph styled by Cecil Beaton. It was of a beautiful woman wearing a wedding gown.

"Who is she?"

"Mary Ashlyn, granddaughter of the famous adventurer, Major Harry Ashlyn. This photograph was taken on the day of her marriage to Lord Alverstoke."

"Very interesting," lied Isabel. "But what's it got to do with us?"

"Look at her tiara. See the huge diamond in the centre? It's the same stone." Danielle turned a couple of pages. "Here it is in close up."

Isabel was silent for a moment. "So what are we doing with it?"

"I told you, I don't know."

"Weird," said Isabel, turning the diamond over in her hand, fascinated by the flashes of fire reflected in its many facets. "Are you *sure* it's the same diamond?"

"The descriptions are identical – right down to the two, tiny, almost invisible flaws."

"Has it got a name?"

"The Ashlyn Diamond."

"Figures!"

"It even has a story attached," added Danielle.

Isabel recognised the same, almost fanatical, tone her father used and prepared to become bored.

"Apparently, the diamond was stolen from a remote Indian temple by Major Harry Ashlyn, who seems to have been the template for Indiana Jones. There was supposed to have been a curse on all who touched it yet, the weird thing is, this diamond brought the Ashlyn family nothing but good luck."

"Excellent," said Isabel. "We could do with a bit of luck." She held the stone up to the light. It glittered innocently. "Do *you* think it's cursed?"

"You're thinking of The Hope Diamond, which was blue, and its curse was only invented to push up the price."

"I did tell you I didn't know anything about diamonds." Isabel handed the stone back to Danielle.

"You didn't have that this afternoon or you would have mentioned it. Did you find it here?"

"Yes, I was clearing out Dad's desk. I thought it was rubbish and almost threw it away. Luckily it went 'clonk' as it hit the bin."

"Perhaps some dustman would have found it and retired to the Bahamas." Isabel smiled dreamily into the distance. "Perhaps we could retire to the Bahamas."

"And give up Vanders?"

Isabel sighed. "How much do you think it's worth?"

"Millions – purely because of its history."

"It would be a pity to chop it up for some media tart's necklace."

Danielle put her head in her hands. "Sometimes I despair of you. I really do! Firstly, this diamond is already cut. Secondly, taking a cleave to this stone would be like taking a hacksaw to the *Mona Lisa.* Thirdly, any jeweller would recognise this stone as the Ashlyn Diamond."

"You know, every time you say 'Ashlyn Diamond' I get this really strange, déjà-vu type feeling. I know this is going to sound silly, coming from me, but have I heard of it before?"

"It was reported stolen nearly two months ago. Jemma did a story in the local paper. Remember? You told me she was hoping it would be her ticket to the nationals."

Isabel nodded. "But why would Dad buy a stolen diamond? I would have thought he was too savvy for that."

"Interesting thought. It didn't occur to you that our father might have stolen it himself?"

Chapter Ten

Nico awoke with a start. For a moment he lay in the dark, wondering what had disturbed him. He glanced across to the alarm-clock – it was half past one. He rolled over, sliding one arm across the mattress, his fingers searching for Danielle's soft, warm body, intending to draw her back against him. But her side of the bed was cold and empty.

This was not unusual. Danielle, whilst not exactly ignoring him, spent most of her time at Vanders. Their social life was zilch. Their sex life was minus zilch. For a man used to having women running after him this cavalier treatment was quite a shock. No wonder Jemma found it so easy to steal Danielle's boyfriends. Nico was beginning to get perilously close to wishing someone would have a go at stealing him.

He flopped onto his back, feeling more than a twinge

of irritation, and saw a light under the door leading to the sitting-room. Perhaps Danielle had been unable to sleep; she had had a lot on her mind – her father's death, taking over Vanders – anyone else would be a nervous wreck . . . Except Danielle; she got herself a prescription for anti-depressants and carried right on like the Duracell bunny.

He slid out of bed, giving up all attempts at sleep. He found her sitting cross-legged on the floor in the sitting-room, surrounded by a sea of paperwork – ancient authenticity certificates mingling with sketches of gemstones on yellowing paper. Her long marmalade hair curled her over shoulders, hiding her face, and she was still wearing her pyjamas. She looked so gloriously rumpled and sexy he wanted to throw her over his shoulder and carry her right back into the bedroom. He knew better – Danielle was not the spontaneous type. Besides, she had hardly bothered to look up or even acknowledge his presence.

"Hullo, sweetheart, couldn't you sleep?" He crouched next to her and ruffled her hair.

Danielle pushed him away. "I've got work to do."

"What do the people at Vanders do all day?" Nico joked to mask his annoyance. "File their nails? Why don't you delegate?"

Danielle gave him a look which clearly said: 'What do you know about it?' and other inanities died on his lips.

"I can't delegate this," she muttered. "It's too important."

"What about Isabel? Can't she help?"

"Isabel? It would be like putting Billy Bunter in charge of Cadbury's!"

Nico picked up one of the sketches. "What are you doing?"

"Looking for some paperwork that's been lost. I've got to go back through all the company records, detailing the purchase and selling of important diamonds – and they go back to 1978."

Nico whistled. "Some job!" He examined the paper he had picked up. It looked more like a mathematical problem than a gemstone. Realising that he was holding it upside down, he discovered that it was a diagram depicting the proposed cutting of a diamond. "Do you understand these drawings?"

"Yes!" Danielle snatched the paper back from him and placed it on the floor. "Do you mind? You're messing up my system!"

"Sorry! I'll go back to bed and get out of your way." He waited for her to protest, to ask him to keep her company, to show some sign of affection, damn it! To be honest, she appeared to have forgotten his presence. "Don't stay up too late. It's Jemma's birthday party tomorrow night."

"I know. I'm not going."

He was not really surprised. "Why not?"

Danielle glanced up at him. "Is it important? I thought you didn't like Jemma?"

Nico was so desperate for some excitement in his life he'd have gone to a political fundraiser. "As Taz would say, a party is a party. Even if you don't want to go, let's do something – catch a movie, eat out – "

"Bored with me already? You can do whatever you like. I'm going to sort through Dad's study."

"I could help?" he suggested. The thought of Danielle miserably sorting through the souvenirs and relics of her father's life made his heart crack.

"I'm sure you could, but this is something I have to do on my own." Danielle did not sound remotely miserable. "There's nothing to stop you going to Jemma's party on your own."

"You're kidding me, right?"

"Isabel will be there. And I know how well you two get along."

"Danielle!"

"And Jemma and Taz . . . plenty of people for you to talk to."

"I'd rather stay here with you."

"And I'd rather be on my own!"

Sometimes she could be such a bitch he wondered why he stuck around. "OK, have it your own way. I can see I'm wasting my breath. What am I gonna do in the meantime? Wait around here and twiddle my thumbs?"

"You can twiddle whatever you like! Why not do some writing? You are, after all, supposed to be a writer."

For one long moment Nico stared down at her then, not trusting himself to speak, he walked back into the bedroom and shut the door behind him.

* * *

When Danielle finally came to bed, Nico was asleep, or perhaps he was pretending to be, she didn't really care. When she woke up the following morning he was gone – although she was surprised to see he'd left his laptop behind so he must be coming back. The man had tenacity, she had to admire that. Treat 'em mean, keep 'em keen, she thought to herself, but didn't smile. It wasn't funny.

As she showered and dressed in old jeans and a jersey, she tried to work out her feelings for Nico. Sometimes she felt he got in her way – he was high maintenance, wanting attention all the time – to go places, see people. All she wanted to do, after a hard day's work, was chill in front of the TV. Nico didn't understand her, not that she blamed him – sometimes she didn't understand herself.

If they were going to become serious about this relationship, they really needed to sit down and talk – on neutral territory. Perhaps Jemma's party could provide the perfect opportunity. It would be difficult to row in front of lots of people.

After gulping down a slice of cold toast and carrying a mug of coffee up to the first floor, Danielle let herself into her father's study. The furniture, although protected by covers, was smothered in a thin layer of dust. The housekeeper had thoughtfully arranged for packing cases to be left outside the door. Danielle carried one through to the study and began to methodically search through, then pack, Isaac's files and paperwork.

After two hours she had found no clue as to where

the Ashlyn Diamond had originated. Her head ached and her vision was blurred from squinting at cutting diagrams. She decided to take Nico's advice and get out. A drive towards the coast perhaps, take in a pub lunch at The Smuggler's Inn? She remembered to go upstairs to ask if he wanted to join her – but her suite was still empty and this time he had taken the laptop with him.

She was going to have to face it – she and Nico were going nowhere. It had been fun pinching him off Jemma – getting her own back for when Jemma had pinched Max from her during the summer. But the novelty was wearing thin, she wanted her suite back to herself and she was tired of tiptoeing around someone else's hurt feelings, and feigning headaches when she couldn't be bothered to have sex.

Without leaving a note, Danielle picked up her bag and left.

* * *

She drove along the clifftop road to Port Rell. It took longer, but the view was more attractive. Besides, she couldn't bear to take the alternative route, through the forest, which went right past the site of her father's accident.

She parked the car in the main carpark next to The Smuggler's Inn, but a quick look at the menu pasted up in the window told her she would have to wait another thirty minutes for lunch to be served. So she decided to take a walk – up along the cliff, to avoid the dog-walkers scrunching along the beach.

The weather was quite pleasant for October. The sky was a cloudless blue and she soon began to feel warm in her Barbour jacket so she took it off and slung it over her shoulder, as she climbed higher, above the roof tops of Port Rell, even above the seagulls wheeling over the riverbank below.

A determined breeze soon demolished her elegant hairstyle, so she pulled out the pins that held it in place and stuffed them into the pocket of her jeans. She had always loved autumn – the cool after summer, the beauty of the countryside as the leaves turned to gold. Now it seemed that everything smelt of decay. Trying not to feel depressed, she walked into the comparative darkness of the woods, scuffling up the fallen leaves like a child. Ahead was the derelict Rell Manor, half hidden by its overgrown garden, where it was rumoured a smuggler had met a bloody death over two hundred years ago, after being pursued by the King's soldiers.

Rell Manor was a beautiful Elizabethan house – the oldest in the area – hence its haunted reputation. It had been built by a seafaring ancestor of Jemma's, and then used as a dower house before being taken over by the army during the Second World War. They had used the King's Forest for their manoeuvres and the beach at Port Rell to practise the Normandy Landings. When the house was handed back, after the war, it was a wreck. Jemma's grandfather had tried to sell it, but no one was interested and then it couldn't be demolished because it was a listed building. So the house was allowed to fall down instead.

It had once been surrounded by a large park, like Stortford House. Gradually the land to the west had become absorbed into the forest; the gardens behind eroding over the centuries, crumbling into the ever-expanding creek, until little more than a walled kitchen garden remained.

What had once been an elegant driveway leading up to the massive oak doors, had long since integrated with the soil, becoming choked with weeds; only the slightest dip in the ground marked where it had lain. Without realising quite what she was doing, Danielle walked through the crumbling stone gateposts and down the wandering drive until she stood in front of the boarded-up windows. Josh must have had it done to prevent squatters.

The house was built from redbrick and Portland stone, with large bay windows and ancient wisteria climbing up the side. The only windows unshuttered were those in the watchtower. Even the most hardened squatter would balk at having to climb all the way up there to gain entry.

She could see why no one had bought the house; the cost of renovation would be astronomical and the building did radiate a kind of sinister omnipresence, not helped by the sun abruptly disappearing behind the only cloud in the sky.

The local kids had sprayed yellow graffiti across the boards, leaving their cans amongst the weeds. Danielle had just bent to pick them up when a large black Labrador charged out of the bushes. As he jumped up, placing two muddy paws on her stomach, he sent her staggering back against the wall.

"Off, Lewis!" she commanded and the dog obediently dropped back to the ground, sitting lopsidedly, scratching its back.

Lewis belonged to Josh Stortford, had been rescued from an animal shelter and was absolutely useless as a gun dog, forever leading Josh's pedigree retrievers astray. If Lewis was here, Josh could not be too far away, perhaps in the woods beyond the front gate, which also belonged to his estate.

Remembering what she had said to his sister the last time they met – words which she still had not apologised for, she decided to take the path around to the back of the house. That way she could escape across the walled garden behind and through the rear gate, which led directly to the path along the clifftop.

As she waded around the long grass to the courtyard, she could hear Josh's familiar tuneless whistling and to her horror, saw him striding towards her.

Shit! It was too late to go back around the front and the stables and outbuildings had rotted so completely they would be a totally inadequate hiding-place. She seized the kitchen door handle and rattled it urgently. At first she thought it was locked but, as it suddenly scraped open, she realised it was only stuck due to lack of use.

Danielle stepped inside, leaving Lewis on the doorstep, closing the door behind her. The quarry tiles of the entrance hall were caked in dust, although there was a trail of mud detouring into the enormous kitchen. Someone else had been here recently. Must be Josh, Danielle told herself firmly – so why did she remain unconvinced?

Rell Manor had not been furnished since the end of the Second World War. Wallpaper curled due to the damp and parts of the floor had rotted away, leaving gaping holes. Cobwebs were catching in her hair, very disconcerting, but the spiders appeared to have died of old age.

She climbed the rather grand staircase to the next floor. The steps creaked violently and, worried that she might put her foot through a rotten one at any moment, she held firmly onto the rickety banister. As she reached the landing her nose began to twitch and she scrabbled in her jeans pocket for a handkerchief. She found it just in time.

"Atchoo!" she sneezed. Then paused as a faint sound reverberated back to her. An echo? What else could it be?

Danielle ignored her brain's persistent message to panic. She was far too practical to believe in ghosts and besides, old houses often emitted strange sounds. But still she found herself tiptoeing along the landing and peering cautiously into the first room. It was the master bedroom.

To her considerable relief it was empty. It had once housed an enormous four-poster bed, which had remained until very recently, as it would not fit through the door. She hoped Josh had not hacked it up for firewood. This room had always been Danielle's favourite. Not only did it have a beautiful view of the sea, the walls were covered with oak panels carved with flowers and woodland animals.

A small staircase to the little watchtower above had been cleverly hidden as a sliding section within the panelling so that it did not spoil the carving. This 'secret' door had always fascinated her and Isabel when they were children, and they had almost worn out the old mechanism by constantly playing with it.

Forgetting that she was supposed to be hiding from Josh, Danielle began to poke the carved panelling to find the switch. It was located in the centre of a large sunflower. A whirr and a click and the ancient mechanism rattled into lethargic action. Grating slightly, the whole of one panel from floor to ceiling began to slide back into a cavity but stuck halfway.

She stepped through the hole into the blackness within. There was a light-switch on the other side of the wall, but the electricity had been cut off for many years. The only light came from the shuttered bedroom. The air inside was warm and musty and Danielle began to feel claustrophobic. The little staircase had lost the appeal of her childhood and the walls felt as though they were closing in on her. In a panic she almost fell through the open panel, scrambling to get out as fast as possible.

She fell into the arms of a man.

Danielle screamed. A swift kick to his ankle released her from his grasp, but as she looked up into his face she paused.

"Sorry, Josh! I didn't realise it was you!"

"Obviously!" groaned Josh, rubbing his ankle. "What were you doing in that cupboard anyway? Trying to get to Narnia?"

Danielle smiled weakly. "No, just visiting the scenes of my misspent youth. You frightened the life out of me. I thought you were a squatter."

"I thought you were the ghost! Walking through the wall like that!"

Danielle grimaced. "The sliding panel became stuck."

Josh bent to examine the panelling then pressed the release button again. The panel grated shut.

"It only needs a touch of oil," he said. "After all, it is over three hundred years old. What are you doing here?"

Danielle merely looked at him. 'Hiding from you,' was the correct answer, but somehow her mouth wouldn't utter the words. She must be growing tactful in her old age.

"I'm sorry I said those things to Jemma at the funeral," she said, feeling her face burn despite her efforts to remain calm and in control. "It was uncalled for, I don't know what came over me. I didn't really mean it." *You did, you did,* her conscious mocked her. "I've been trying to get in touch with Jemma to apologise personally . . ." *Liar, liar . . .*

"It was understandable. Your father had just died."

"But – "

"It's OK, you don't have to explain."

But she did! Craving absolution, she wanted to get everything out into the open. Her bad behaviour, her emotions, his feelings – talk it all out until there was nothing left. Then maybe she'd be able to sleep at nights. Josh's forgiveness certainly banished some of the uncomfortable atmosphere, but she felt there was a barrier between them.

"Josh – "

"It's good to see you out and about," said Josh, deliberately speaking over her. "Sometimes I think you work too hard."

She gave up. Confessions, it seemed, were only for chat shows. "I came for a walk along the beach, but there were too many tourists. I needed to get out of the house. I've been packing up the things in Dad's study." Seeing Josh's navy-blue eyes soften sympathetically, she abruptly changed the subject. She wanted him to understand her – not feel sorry for her. "Why have you had the windows boarded up?"

"We had a break-in a few weeks ago. Now whenever I walk the dogs I check the place over. It should have been done years ago – it might have stopped the deterioration. I can't think why anyone would want to break in though. You would have thought that word would have spread amongst the criminal fraternity that I haven't got a bean!"

"Perhaps it was squatters?" suggested Danielle. "Someone wanting a roof over their head. It's a lovely house. I mean, I know it's a wreck, but it would be nice for someone to live here again."

"Funny you should say that – I've found a buyer – Elsa Tallant – the TV decorator. Her production company are stumping up the cash – she's planning an entire TV series and a range of books on the restoration of the house."

"What a great idea! It's a pity you couldn't have done that," she added, without thinking. "Jemma could have written the book about it!"

He laughed, not taking her seriously. "How could I afford to do that? It would cost millions!"

"I could have lent you the money – and cheaper than any bank."

"I don't want your money."

"Thanks!" said Danielle, bitterly hurt. She turned away, stalked off through the bedroom door and along the landing.

By the time Josh caught up with her, she was halfway down the stairs. He caught hold of her arm and she had to stop in case she over-balanced and fell all the way to the bottom. She tried to glare up at him, but as he was standing on the step above her she barely reached the V of his jacket.

"I'm sorry," he said gently, still not letting her go. "I didn't mean it to come out so tactlessly."

Danielle could identify with that. She couldn't do tactful either. "You sound like Isabel," she said resentfully. "I can't spend all this money by myself."

"Perhaps Isabel only wants to be independent. You were always telling her she should get a life!"

"And perhaps she wants to be awkward!" Danielle wrenched her arm away from him and stomped down the remainder of the staircase. "Honestly, I can't see what the problem is?" she muttered, partly to herself. "Why should I be the one to feel guilt? I'm rich, the rest of you are poor and you're going to have to deal with it. When I offer to give or loan people money I only want to help. I'm not interfering, or being patronising. Why can't anyone understand this?"

Josh smiled. "It's a mystery," he agreed. "I'm past redemption, but perhaps you can help Isabel in other ways?"

"How? Donate old clothing?"

"Only you know the answer to that."

Thank you, Josh, *very* helpful . . .

Josh locked the kitchen door and, as they walked across the courtyard and away from the house, Danielle glanced back at the watchtower. The old mismatched curtains hung limply against the dirty glass. One was so tattered it was virtually in ribbons.

It was strange how, at this distance, the threadbare material resembled a face.

* * *

By the time she returned to The Smuggler's Inn, it was packed with the usual lunchtime crowd, so Danielle bought a baguette from the bakery and ate it in her car instead. On returning home, she went directly to her father's study. As she looked restlessly around the room, her eyes alighted on an old theatre programme, casually shoved under chair. She picked it up, sat at his desk and began to thumb through it.

The programme was for a performance of *The Nutcracker* by the English National Ballet. She had seen it almost a year ago at the theatre in Norchester. Just herself and her father – as though Isabel would be seen dead at the ballet! As Danielle kept all her theatre programmes filed in alphabetical order in her sitting-room, this one must have been his copy.

A crumpled piece of paper fell out from the centre pages and fluttered to the floor. Danielle picked it up, more because she hated a room to look untidy rather than any curiosity. Idly, she smoothed it out on the flat surface of the programme.

Scribbled in pencil were notes and a diagram detailing the proposed re-cutting of the Ashlyn Diamond.

Chapter Eleven

Jemma had been born on the 31st of October. All Hallow's Eve. It was a lot to live down, but it could have been worse. She could have been born on the 1st of April.

For the past few years it had become a tradition for her to throw a Halloween Party in a suitably gothic setting. Last year it had been the dungeons of Norchester Castle. This time she had been able to hire an abandoned seventeenth century church, complete with graveyard, which was situated right on top of the crumbling cliffs at Port Rell. Very *Hammer House of Horror*.

By coincidence, the little church had recently been used as a film set for a tongue-in-cheek slasher movie, which convinced Jemma that her theme should be *Fright Night* – camp Hollywood horror. The weather was on her side, bursts of torrential rain thundering onto the patched-up roof, the occasional streak of jagged lightning glimpsed through cracked stained-glass windows. And, just before ten, even the generators had failed, momentarily plunging them into darkness, relieved only by the spasmodic candlelight.

Jemma had paid a fortune to the local florist to deck the little church in garlands of ivy, and vast arrangements of lilies were arrayed on all the windows. Fake cobwebs glittered in the candlelight, fake bats whizzed around on strings suspended from the ceiling – this time Jemma felt she had really excelled herself.

She meandered through her guests, chatting, joking, generally being scintillating, aware of the admiring glances she was receiving from the men and the envious stares from the women – all due to this wonderfully sexy red dress that clung to every inch of her body – and the watercress soup she had existed on for the whole of last week. It was a pity Max wasn't here to admire it, but he was working late *again*. Never mind, she was sure she could find someone else to appreciate her.

It was then she had glimpsed Nico, leaning against the stone pillar closest to the exit, perhaps hoping to make a quick getaway as soon as it stopped raining. He was the only guest not in costume – wearing his usual black cashmere sweater and trousers – with the addition of a strange leather coat, which swirled towards his ankles and made him look as though he was auditioning for a heavy metal tribute band.

"Hello," she said, smiling seductively.

"Hi there." His eyes flicked across the red dress, but he didn't comment further.

She felt her cheeks flush and a pleasurable tingle of desire shoot through her. Did he still find her attractive? Maybe her luck was in. However, there was a cloud on the horizon . . ."Where's Danielle?"

"I'm not sure. I was gonna meet her here. Maybe she got stuck at work?"

Brilliant! thought Jemma and pressed her elbows together to deepen her cleavage. He didn't even notice. In fact, he seemed more interested in what was going on over on the dance floor.

"Would you like to dance?" she asked, desperate to hold his attention. She could imagine his hands around her waist, his hips pressing against hers . . . With Danielle out of the way, who knows what opportunity might arise?

"I don't dance," he said flatly.

It was like a slap in the face. She stared at him in disbelief. Surely she hadn't been that crap in bed? Yet he'd dumped her pretty quickly when he met Danielle. She should walk away right now . . . oh, *why* was he so damned attractive?

He was looking over her shoulder again. "I think the caterers want to talk to you."

Jemma glanced behind her and could see one of the waitresses waving anxiously at her. *Honestly*, what was the point of employing people when one had to do everything one's self! Jemma irritably gestured in the direction of the catering manager and pointedly turned her back on the woman, giving Nico her full attention.

"I hate to think of you on your own," she said, pitching her voice as deep and as husky as she could. "You don't know anyone here – except for me."

He smiled. "You don't need to worry about me. I'm pretty self-reliant."

"If you don't want to dance, why don't we sit down, have a glass of wine, talk?"

"I don't think so." His pleasant expression never wavered. "Danielle wouldn't like it."

The unspoken meaning was clear – feel free to drool over him, but definitely no touching. He was the exclusive property of Danielle van der Straatan. It was virtually stamped on his forehead. Jemma stared at him in disbelief. He'd choose the frigid, bad-tempered, control-freaky Danielle over *her*? How many chickens had the witch sacrificed to get such blatant devotion? They were practically in the realms of Stepford here.

"You're really under the thumb, aren't you?" she grumbled and she wasn't entirely joking. "I'm surprised she lets you out without an armed escort."

"She loves me," he said, his amusement plain in his voice. "She also trusts me. We're friends as well as lovers. Friends don't do that to each other."

Bastard! Who was he to lecture her on loyalty? Jemma, fuming fit to combust, decided a tactical retreat was the only way to keep her dignity intact. He was a man, he was fallible, she'd get her revenge on Danielle someday, although it might take longer than she had first thought.

She forced a smile to her lips. "I'm so *glad* you came; it's been *lovely* talking to you, but now I've got to circulate. Give my love to Danielle when she arrives and I hope you *both* enjoy yourselves." And she stalked off, squeezing between the crowds thronging the dance-floor in order to disappear from his view more quickly.

Not that he was paying her any attention, she realised, after she'd finally reached the other side of the church. Those beautiful amber eyes were firmly fixed on the door, waiting for the love of his life to arrive.

Jemma kicked the side of a tomb in frustration. The behaviour of this asshole was spoiling her entire evening. She'd never met a man that she couldn't have – and the fact that he appeared madly in love with another woman made her even more determined to get him. She was going make him beg on his knees for her to take him back.

A gleeful smirk appeared on Jemma's lips. Oh yes, one day, *very* soon, she was going to make Nico Morales truly *suffer*.

* * *

As the incessant rain lessened to a fine drizzle, Isabel wandered through the floodlit graveyard towards the church. She might have paused to read the inscriptions on the weathered headstones, but memories of her father's funeral were too close. Her feet dragged; she had no real desire to be here. If Jemma hadn't been her best friend she would never have considered attending a party so soon after his death.

In a trunk in the attic she'd found an old black lace and taffeta gown of her mother's. It was very 1980s 'New Romantic', but the dramatic colour was a perfect contrast with her red-gold hair – which she had piled on top of her head to add a touch of glamour. After the trauma of the past few weeks, her skin was pale enough not to require any white make-up, but she added black kohl around her eyes, dark lipstick and two little red dots to her neck with lip-liner – to look as though Count Dracula had been snacking.

She felt like one of the undead as she drifted down the church path, carefully avoiding the large puddles, not at all in the mood for a party. Loud dance music blasted across the graveyard, echoed by the thunder and the crashes of the waves on the beach far below. As she stepped through the carved entrance to the church, the gargoyles squatting on the roof above seemed to be mocking her recreant behaviour with their twisted, rictus grins.

She pushed open the heavy, iron-studded door and was almost knocked sideways by the smell of pot, stale wine and sweaty bodies, all squashed together in such a confined space. The combination of blazing candlelight and stunning laser effects took a moment to adjust to after the blackness outside, so she waited a moment, hoping there was someone she would recognise.

It was intimidating to see so many young, glamorous people, crammed shoulder to shoulder, bumping and grinding, laughing and shouting above the noise, all having a terrific time. There was no sign of Jemma –

merely what appeared to be a room full of strangers. This was not unusual – Jemma was always attracting new friends.

Tables, scattered with autumn leaves and rose petals, had been set up alongside each wall, but most people were frantically dancing to one of last summer's biggest club hits in the small space remaining in the centre. Others were slumped against the ivy-strewn pillars, balancing half-drunk goblets of wine on the elaborately carved tombs of the seventeenth-century gentry. It was this in particular which Isabel found tasteless. What on earth had possessed Jemma to hold such a wild party in a church?

For that matter, what was *she* doing here?

Isabel abruptly turned towards the door and collided with a tall, dark and handsome stranger. Or perhaps not such a stranger. Glancing up, she saw two familiar amber eyes, smiling down at her.

"You made it!" he said and planted a kiss on her surprised mouth.

Nico! Isabel stared uncomprehendingly at him. Had he gone *mad*?

His easy smile suddenly faltered. "You're not Danielle, are you?"

Isabel wondered why she felt disappointed. "I'm Isabel," she said warily. "I suppose with my hair up like this I look like Dani. It was an understandable mistake – you don't have to feel bad about it." *Please don't feel bad about it!*

Nico seemed more worried that she was about to knee him in the balls. Surely she wasn't *that* scary?

"Great gown," he said eventually.

He was attempting small talk? Now it was Isabel's turn to be confused. "I raided the attics at Stortford House," she said slowly. She was sure he wasn't really interested, but for some reason she wanted to keep the conversation going. "I found this in an old trunk. It belonged to my mother. I suppose my father couldn't bear to throw it away."

Which exhausted that topic. Isabel was wondering what else they were going to talk about (politics, religion, world peace?) when she noticed he was wearing his usual black.

"Are you supposed to be Tom Jones? That's not very frightening!"

He pretended to look hurt. "I'm Angel."

"Don't be silly, you don't look anything like an angel. Angels wear white and have wings and halos."

"Not *an* angel – *the* Angel. You know, *Buffy the Vampire Slayer*? It was Taz's idea – he lent me this coat. He reckons I look like the actor, David Boreanaz."

"Taz is a sad case," sighed Isabel. "He's got this real obsession with *Buffy* – you're lucky you didn't end up in drag!"

"I guess so!" He laughed. "Would you like to dance?"

"Dance?" she repeated stupidly. Why was he being nice to her? After all she'd done to him, all she'd *said*?

"Or pistols at dawn if you'd prefer?"

"Now you're taking the piss!"

"Yes," he agreed, "but I'm serious about the dance. I'm tired of fighting, aren't you?"

"Yes . . . I suppose I am . . ."

"If you don't dance with me I'll have to dance with Jemma – and you know how well that would go down with Danielle. The girl's been practically stalking me all evening. Only you can save me."

Isabel was not convinced as to this argument, but was unable to think of a valid excuse, even to her conscience. She didn't want to appear rude, not after he was trying so hard to make his peace. Besides, Danielle was old enough to make her own decisions. If the girl wanted to date a con-artist it was up to her.

Still, Isabel couldn't resist teasing: "Aren't you worried I might push you off the cliff?"

He smiled again, his eyes crinkling up at the corners. "No – because there's a fence around it – I checked!" Firmly taking her by the hand, he led her to the centre of the church, where everyone else was dancing to Screaming Jay Hawkins.

Nico was an excellent dancer, realised Isabel with some surprise. With the added realisation that every woman in the place was watching them with ill-concealed jealousy, it began to dawn on her how attractive he was. She'd been so wrapped up in wrecking his affair with her sister, it had almost passed her by. Almost . . .

He was tall – 6'1", maybe 6'2". He had glossy dark hair, cut short, spiked up at the front like Bart Simpson – with what looked suspiciously like hair gel. Then there were those gorgeous eyes – currently half-shut as he got carried away by the rhythms of the music – his sun-kissed skin, surprisingly full mouth – Isabel found herself wondering what it would be like to kiss him, properly this time, tongues and everything, and brought herself up short. This was her sister's boyfriend and, up until five minutes ago, her worst enemy! *Get a grip, girl!*

Deciding it must be the passive pot-smoking that was turning her brain, she concentrated on the words of the song to take her mind off her libido. Even that didn't help.

"I put a spell on you," she sang absent-mindedly.

Nico's eyes had flicked open and he was watching her with some amusement. "Trying to turn me into a frog?" he enquired.

Isabel felt her cheeks colour. That was the drawback to having Titian hair: when she became embarrassed she got Titian skin to match.

"It's the song," she stammered. "I – I was singing along."

"I know. You have a great singing voice. Sing to me some more."

A casual compliment, but Isabel was worried there was some other motive behind it. She searched his face for any sinister intentions – she didn't entirely trust him – and instead surprised an unmistakable flicker of desire.

Isabel dropped her eyes, confused. It's not so strange, she told herself. She and Danielle were identical twins; if he found Danielle sexy it would stand to reason he would fancy her too. *But there's more to it than that,* her conscious argued back. Was he hitting on her? *Sure he was!* But what to do? *Get the hell out of there!* screamed her conscience. *This is your sister's boyfriend, her One True Love and trespassers will be very much prosecuted.* (To be honest, she couldn't entirely rule out a stake through the heart and a ritual beheading, either).

Perhaps this was a joke to him. Another test; see how far she would go to protect her sister, like that day at La Dolce Vita. That seemed more likely. So much for his 'truce'. Well, sod him!

Isabel suddenly dived through the writhing bodies on the dance floor, fighting her way towards the exit.

"Isabel!" murmured a voice in her ear, as she reached the same stone pillar where they had met earlier. "Where are you going?"

"Away from you and your silly pranks."

"I don't get it. What have I said to hurt you?"

"Why are you being nice to me?" She was tired of fighting and she was tired of subterfuge. Why couldn't they be honest with each other for once – and admit they hated each other.

"I thought we'd agreed – "

"Keep away from me," she hissed. "I don't trust you. I never have."

"You know, I don't understand you. Why are you such a bitch? Are you like this with everyone?"

Only him, although she was not about to admit that. She didn't want to know why she hated him with such a passion, she was afraid to examine her motives too closely. So she said nothing and opened the door, walking straight out into a blast of icy rain. She certainly picked her moment to make a histrionic exit.

He caught her wrist. "Don't be crazy – you'll get soaked!" Then, when she didn't move, just stared at him mutinously, he added: "At least wait until the rain stops."

"OK – just leave me alone."

"What's up? What have I said to upset you? We were getting on so well." He let the door swing shut behind them and suddenly they were alone in the porch, becoming slowly soaked by the incessant squalls of rain.

Isabel shivered, huddling back against the wall, away from the draught. "That's important to you?"

"Yes. You're my girlfriend's sister. I want to get on with her family. You know, I think somehow we got off on the wrong foot. I understand that you want the best for Danielle, that you want to protect her – you're suspicious that I seemed to have turned up out of nowhere, think maybe I'm after her money?"

Isabel flushed. He seemed to have her pretty well sussed!

"If you don't want to dance, could I get you a drink? Something to eat? There's no sense in starving while we wait for Dani and Taz to turn up."

Taz! She hadn't given him a thought!

"Or maybe you just want to go home?" he suggested gently. "Is it all too much for you – so soon after your father died?"

She looked up at him gratefully, feeling tears dampening her lashes.

"Did you bring your car? Or do you need a lift home?"

"I came in a taxi because I thought I'd be drinking," she admitted, *my sorrows away* . . .

"I'll take you back to Stortford House if you like?"

And spend ten minutes alone with him in a car? After what had happened last time? Not bloody likely!

"Oh, I couldn't possibly ask – "

"It's no trouble," he smiled. "I live there too, remember?"

She felt her cheeks burn again. Lucky it was so dark out here.

But not that dark. "Are you cold?" he asked, noticing her shivers.

"No," she said firmly – but found his long coat draped around her shoulders anyway. *Taz's coat,* she reminded herself. And where the hell was *he*?

"I don't think this rain is ever going to let up," he said, walking to the entrance and peering out. "We'll just have to run for it, OK? My car is parked where the road starts to dip towards the village." He pointed out across the rain-lashed graveyard. "Can you see it?"

Isabel gave him a sideways glance. He was asking her to spot a black Fiesta, at midnight, in a raging thunderstorm? "Perfectly," she replied sardonically.

He didn't notice. He had suddenly grabbed her arm and pulled her out of the shelter of the porch and into the icy rain. Isabel gasped at the shock. He was mad! They could have stayed in the porch a little bit longer; hell, they could have stayed at the party.

She was drenched within seconds. Instead of sticking to the church path, he appeared to be attempting a short cut across the graveyard, weaving between the headstones. For a moment she felt genuinely frightened. Where was he taking her? Then she saw a break in the stone wall. Without pausing, he seized her waist and lifted her over the rubble. Not wishing to stay in his arms a moment longer than necessary, she stumbled against one of the parked cars and realised it was his. Alongside the BMWs and Mercs, it was pretty distinctive.

He leant across her and unlocked the passenger side; for a moment, his shoulder brushed against hers and she abruptly stepped back. He didn't appear to notice, just ran around to the driver's side, opened the door and jumped in.

Taffeta crinolines were not designed to be crammed into the front seat of a Ford Fiesta, but somehow Isabel was able to squash in all the petticoats and shut the door after her. She was unable to find the anchorage for the seat belt, but had no intention of asking for help, so she held it against her and hoped he wouldn't crash the car.

Her father had died in a car accident . . . Isabel closed her eyes before the tears began again.

"Pick a CD," he said, dumping a heavy case on her lap.

Forced to open her eyes, Isabel flicked on the overhead light, opened the catch on the case and began to flip through the CDs. His taste was wide-ranging to say the least. Everything from R & B, to hip-hop and the blandest pop. Weird. And why, if his car was a complete rust bucket, did he have a decent CD player installed?

Every time she thought she had another facet of his character mapped, a new side appeared. He didn't seem the type to be mad about music. He certainly didn't seem to be the type to listen to Aphrodite – a new girl band currently storming up the charts. Really, she didn't understand him at all. Maybe she'd misjudged him? Maybe he was a nice guy after all . . .

Finally Nico managed to start the engine. He switched the air-conditioning to maximum, to get rid of the rapidly steaming-up windows, and it began to rattle like a box of nails.

"What have you chosen?" he asked.

Realising he was waiting for her choice of CD, Isabel quickly thrust an old Destiny's Child album at him.

He took it out of its case, slid it into the player and pressed 'shuffle', nodding approvingly as 'Survivor' filtered out of the speakers, filling the car, drowning out both the air-conditioning and the storm outside.

He swung the car out onto the road and began driving down the hill into Port Rell. "Good choice," he said. "This is one of my favourites."

Ironic, thought Isabel silently, because the song summed up his character quite neatly too.

Was she *ever* going to be rid of him?

Chapter Twelve

Despite the storm Nico took the cliff road back to Calahurst. As he approached the sailing club he slowed down, parking outside a row of Victorian terrace houses overlooking the river.

Isabel glanced nervously at him. "Why are we stopping here?"

"This is my house," said Nico blithely, throwing open the car door, letting in a blast of freezing air. "I need to pick up some paperwork."

Now? In the middle of the night? Talk about keen! But she didn't put voice to any of this, merely snuggled further beneath the leather coat he had lent her, hoping to keep warm.

"I'll wait here," she said, closing her eyes in anticipation of a nap.

The passenger door was abruptly pulled open. "No, come on in! I insist! It's no trouble. I might take some time and it'd be rude of me to leave you out here in the cold." He smiled charmingly.

Isabel would have preferred to wait in the car, no matter how long he'd take. But with the door wide open and fat raindrops splattering the upholstery in anticipation of another heavy downpour, she didn't appear to have much choice. So she slid one foot out and onto the pavement, then the other, making sure she had all her petticoats out and under her control before she allowed him to slam the door.

As the heavens open, they sprinted up the narrow concrete path to the front door. Nico had it open in a matter of seconds and she stumbled into the hall, remembering to wipe her feet first – heaven knows what her shoes had picked up in the long grass of the churchyard.

Nico was disappearing up the staircase. "Stick the kettle on," he called back to her. "We need something to heat us up. I'll be back soon."

Stick the kettle on? Isabel watched his retreating back in outrage. What was she? His servant?

Picking up her skirts, she stomped down the corridor in search of a kitchen. Nico had waved vaguely towards the back of the house, so she thought she would try the door at the end first. She pushed open the door and there it was. The kitchen.

It was a bit of a dump, she decided, wrinkling her nose – then promptly told herself off for being a snob. Not everyone could live in a stately home. All it needed was a lick of paint.

The kitchen appeared to have been modernised sometime in the 1960s and not touched since. The walls were currently white, which had dulled with age and blistered in places. The cupboard doors had been painted a sunny yellow, to match the chequered lino. There was a free-standing fridge and cooker, which both looked new, although inexpensive, and sitting on one of the worktops was a bright yellow kettle.

So she rinsed the inside under the tap then filled it, plugged it in and switched it on. She had to open all the cupboard doors until she found a couple of coffee mugs, decorated in horrible brown and mustard flowers, and located a jar of Nescafe – luckily still within its sell-by date – in an old-fashioned, walk-in larder.

This house did not look like it belonged to Nico, decided Isabel. OK, he was a bit of a mystery man – and maybe he did wear black all the time because he didn't trust his taste. Looking at these coffee mugs he certainly had a point! But something wasn't right here . . .

Isabel opened a few more cupboards in search of a clue – but found more disgusting crockery instead. There was a corkboard hung on the wall, with a menu from the local Tandoori takeaway pinned to it and also a faded newspaper cutting. She moved closer to examine it, but it was only a report Jemma had written about the local jewellery robberies. Perhaps he was thinking of going back to her? It was none of her business now. Danielle could sort out her own problems.

Isabel had left the kitchen door open and, looking

along the corridor, she could see two other doors. One led to the cupboard under the stairs – but the other?

As Nico was still banging about upstairs, she opened it. The room was in darkness so she switched on the light. It was like walking into Del Boy's flat. Brown velour furniture (how lovely), a teak sideboard (yum), and matching dining-table and chairs. Taking up most of the corner was a gleaming wide-screen TV and DVD player. Isabel stared in astonishment. Could Nico be a burglar in his spare time?

Hearing the kettle boil, she quickly switched off the light and returned to the kitchen to make the coffee. There was no milk in the fridge – there was nothing in the fridge – so she made it black, without sugar, as she was unsure whether he took any. She supposed she could always phone Danielle and ask her.

Isabel giggled, imagining the conversation. "Hi, Danielle, I'm just about to make your boyfriend a cup of coffee. Does he take sugar? Yes, that's right, I'm here in his house, *alone* . . ." That would *definitely* wreck the relationship!

But that was the old Isabel. The *new*, improved Isabel, who did not go around breaking up her sister's relationships because she didn't approve of the man, knew she couldn't be that cruel.

Picking up Nico's coffee, she strode to the foot of the stairs and opened her mouth to yell: "Coffee's ready!" To her astonishment she heard the shower running.

He was having a *shower*? *Bastard*! While she was hanging around down here, soaking wet, catching her death of cold, *he* was having a shower and changing into dry clothes! Damn him!

If Nico had been standing in front of her she would have tipped the coffee over him. Instead she had to content herself with flinging it into the sink. As she stood there, blistering with rage, she had an idea. He could be busy for some time . . . which gave her the perfect opportunity to check out the rest of the house . . .

She didn't need time to mull it over. She tiptoed up the stairs, testing each one for creaking floorboards first. On the landing she had a choice of three doors. The nearest had a strip of light visible beneath it – the bathroom, right over the top of the kitchen. Why hadn't she heard the water running earlier?

Mentally berating herself for her lack of attention, she opened the next door along and groped for the light-switch. It was a small bedroom, furnished as a study. Blithely ignoring the effect curiosity tended to have on cats, Isabel walked in. Like the sitting-room below, there was not much to look at: two black bookcases (very Nico), a desk with a laptop squatting amongst the dust and beyond that, another of those horrible brown floral mugs, crammed with pens and pencils. Abandoned beside them was a shorthand notebook, a Discman and three CDs (The Stereophonics, The Clash and Elvis Presley – Elvis *Presley*?).

If Isabel had any idea about how computers worked, she would have opened up the laptop and rifled through Nico's files. Instead, she had to content herself with flipping through his notebook. At first she thought the mass of swirls, dashes and dots were Spanish – then she realised he'd written in shorthand. Isabel cursed out loud and threw it back onto the desk. How come detective work was so easy in the movies?

A large silver ornament caught her eye. She peered at the inscription below. *'Journalist Of The Year'* it said. 'Nicolas Kearney'.

Nicolas Kearney? Who the hell was Nicolas Kearney? She pulled open the drawers of the desk. *Empty*!

The bookcase! She should have looked there first. She spun round, running her finger along the spines of the tattered reference books. They were mostly writers' yearbooks and help books, dictionaries of idioms and quotations – no blockbusting thrillers written by any 'Nico Morales' – but plenty of big glossy hardbacks by Nicolas Kearney. The real story behind the rise of a popular boy band; the double-life of a well-known MP; corruption in the police force – she pulled that one out.

Isabel recognised the cover of one of last year's bestsellers. On the front was a black and white photograph of a distinguished, middle-aged man – a detective superintendent with the local police, who had been jailed last year for his part in a property scam. The book had caused a sensation when first published, the media loving stories of corrupt police officers.

But the superintendent – Paul de Havilland – had been a friend of her father's. The fraud had not been at his instigation, although he had allowed himself to become caught up with it. His own daughter had been murdered by one of the perpetrators. Despite helping to bring the men responsible to justice, he had lost his job and his home and was then finally ruined personally by this tawdry publication. This book written by Nicolas Kearney.

Isabel turned the book over to look at the back. There was a colour photograph of the author. The dark hair was longer and he wore wire-rimmed spectacles balanced on the end of his straight nose . . .

But the face that stared back at her was Nico's.

* * *

Isabel picked up the keys to Nico's car from the hall table, let herself out and ran down the garden path to the road. It took her several attempts to start the Fiesta – she almost wrenched the choke right out of the steering column – but eventually the engine roared into life, she took the handbrake off and the car lurched down the road.

Nico ran out into the road behind her, wearing only a towel around his hips, waving frantically at her to stop.

Isabel, catching sight of his vulnerable position, was sorely tempted to reverse over him. Several times. But she gritted her teeth, reeling around the corner into Church Lane, past the very police station where Paul de Havilland had worked, past the graveyard where her father was buried – narrowly missing the war memorial outside. Finally she swung up the hill and into the forest, where she was able to put her foot down hard on the accelerator, safe in the knowledge that there was no way Nico would be able to catch up with her.

* * *

Stortford House was dark and empty. Isabel let herself in and switched on the light. Nothing happened.

"Great!" she muttered. "That's absolutely fucking marvellous. A perfect end to a perfect day. What the *fuck* did I do to deserve this?" Maybe it was Friday the 13th and she hadn't noticed.

The storm had caused a power cut. Or alternatively it could be a blown fuse. Isabel had the vague idea that there was a fuse box down in the cellar, but she hadn't the slightest idea how to change a duff one. Her father had paid staff to do that sort of thing. However, the staff didn't live in, Danielle must be either at work or at Jemma's party and her father was dead.

Isabel swallowed and determinedly didn't think about her father.

The only thing to do was to go to bed and forget today ever happened. Write it off, start afresh tomorrow – her life would seem better in the morning. Except tomorrow Nico Morales would still be Nicolas Kearney . . .

"Well, that's not my problem!" she said out loud, hoping to make herself feel better. "Nico is Danielle's boyfriend, nothing to do with me!" She turned and bolted the door. That ought to keep the spooks, witches and goblins out. *And Nico*, said a derisive voice in her head. Even though he had his own key, there was no way he'd be able to force his way past the bolts. Feeling calmer, she stepped into the darkness of the house, her hands outstretched in case she fell or bumped into something, as the hall received no natural light.

She walked straight into a body, solid and reassuringly warm, with arms that enclosed her waist, a head that bent close towards her own, a voice that whispered hoarsely, "Where's the diamond, sweetheart?"

Isabel screamed, her heart diving through her ribcage. Using all the strength she could muster, she shoved the man backwards, causing him to stumble against the staircase. She ran back to the front door, scrabbling to slide back the bolts – but she had dropped the key and had no idea where to find it.

"Come *here*," said the voice again. A low, abrasive, growl, it sounded almost inhuman.

Clutching her hand over her mouth to stop herself from crying hysterically, thus drawing attention to herself, Isabel ducked out of his reach, running down the corridor, blundering into small items of furniture. A small bust of the 9th Earl was sent crashing to the floor as she mistook it for the carved banister. Occasional tables, a valuable captain's chair, all were overturned in her desperation to get away from the intruder. He only had to follow the noise to know where she was – but, as he was as blind as her, they at least slowed down his pursuit.

More through luck than any skill on her part, she eventually fell into the dining-room overlooking the terrace. There were no locks on these doors. The moon had slid from behind the clouds and was high in the sky, the rain had stopped and she could see the garden – and freedom beyond.

But as she jammed a chair beneath the handle of the

dining-room door to prevent the intruder following her, she realised someone had reached the room before her. Another shadow was blended with her own against the wall. She turned. A tall, broad-shouldered man was silhouetted against the moonlit sky, his shadow falling right across the room.

Instinctively Isabel picked up one of her father's precious Cartier clocks from the oak sideboard and hurled it towards him. A childhood spent bowling cricket balls to her father ensured she scored a direct hit. The man gave a small moan of pain then crumpled to the floor.

Amazed that it had been so easy, Isabel sneaked forward to get a better look at him. He was wearing a leather jacket over jeans, his hair appeared to be dark, but his arm had fallen over his eyes, obscuring the remainder of his face.

Slowly, she reached out, tentatively drawing his arm away from his face.

A hand closed over her wrist, the fingers cruelly digging into her skin, as it wrenched her onto her feet, and again, against the very solid body of the man she had met in the hall.

The breath knocked out of her, all Isabel could do was look up, hoping to recognise him, as he evidently recognised her. All she could see was a firmly jutting chin and his teeth, gleaming pearly white in the moonlight.

"I'm not going to ask you again," he rasped, as he slapped his free hand across her face. "*Where's the fucking diamond*?"

Chapter Thirteen

NOVEMBER

Nico woke up feeling as though someone was attempting to hammer a six-inch nail into his skull without using the pointed end.

He was vaguely aware of lying flat on his back, on an uncomfortable cold, hard surface, with voices muttering softly all around. They seemed to be discussing him, but no matter how hard he tried he couldn't summon the energy to open his eyes, let alone defend himself.

"Mr Kearney? Can you hear me, Mr Kearney?" A male voice, louder than the others, pervaded the sleep that threatened to engulf him. It sounded educated and unequivocally English.

Nico failed to respond. It would require effort he didn't feel inclined to exert.

"Mr Kearney? Please, it's important that you remain conscious."

He felt his eyelids being peeled back – a searing white pain bouncing off his retinas . . .

He cursed profusely and sat up. Mistake! Nausea overwhelmed him and there was an excruciating pain across the side of his head. Opening his eyes to bright electric lights exacerbated it.

He shoved away all offers of help. "What the *fuck* happened?"

"Take it easy, Mr Kearney," advised the same voice.

By slightly turning his head, Nico could just make out a bespectacled, anxious-looking man, squatting by his side. His scalp, gleaming in the overhead light, was visible through thinning blond hair. And, as he blinked pale-blue eyes, he appeared to metamorphose into the white rabbit Nico had owned as a child.

Christ! Now he was hallucinating!

"It's all right, I'm a doctor," soothed the man. "You've received a nasty injury. It may require stitches. We're going to get you to hospital as soon as possible."

Nico lightly touched his fingertips against his temple to assess the damage, feeling across to where his skin was raised into a painful lump, faintly sticky, trickling fluid into his right eye, causing his vision to blur. He was about to wipe his sleeve over his forehead to eradicate the problem, when the doctor quickly produced a dressing pad from a black case open on the floor and gently placed it over the wound.

"Hold that there for a moment," he said. "It should stop the bleeding."

"Thanks."

It gradually dawned on Nico that he and the doctor were not alone. They were providing entertainment for a room full of people, some in police uniforms, some in suits, all standing around watching quizzically – all complete strangers. Slowly Nico realised the significance of the polished wooden floor; the beautiful antique sideboard and table large enough to seat twenty; the French windows along the side wall. He was in the dining-room at Stortford House.

"How did I get here?" His mind was momentarily blank.

"Maybe you were kidnapped by aliens?" a female voice taunted.

For a brief, horribly cold moment, he thought it was Jemma who had spoken, recalling the night of their meeting. But it was Isabel stepping from the shadows, still wearing her black gown and the long leather coat he had borrowed from Taz, but also sporting a colour-co-ordinated black eye.

"What the hell happened to you?"

She regarded him levelly. "You're denying that you were responsible?"

What planet was this girl on? "Of course. I would never hit you."

"If you can't remember how you came to be here, how can you be sure?"

"I don't hit women."

"OK, explain what you're doing here?"

Nico realised the police officers were watching him

intently. "I don't remember." *Pathetic,* his conscience mocked him.

Isabel smiled a smile of pure evil. "How about I remind you of your life to date?"

Please don't.

"Your name is Nicolas Kearney, you're twenty-six years old, you're a freelance journalist." Her tone was goading. "Which means you make your living inventing lies about decent people, ruining their lives."

He winced. "I wouldn't put it *quite* like that."

"So how would you put it?" One of the men in suits stepped forward.

A police officer, Nico reminded himself, before he spoke. And evidently the guy in charge, the way the others watched him with respect. He wondered about the man's rank. His suit was expensive, his shoes shining. Detective Superintendent, Nico decided, or maybe, if he was really unlucky, a hotshot Chief Inspector out to secure a promotion. The wealthy van der Straatans clearly warranted the best.

Nico ignored the police officer's question and concentrated his defence on destroying Isabel's credibility. "Why did you hit me, Isabel? Did you think I was a burglar? I live here, remember?"

The Detective Superintendent glanced back to Isabel, unable to hide his surprise. "He lives here?"

"He's my sister's boyfriend," muttered Isabel. "But they're estranged."

"You mean you'd like us to be." He was able to inject just the right note of hurt into his voice. Really, he should be in the movies. "Sibling rivalry," he explained to the by-now completely baffled Superintendent. "She always wants what her sister has. Girls and their toys, you know how it is . . ."

The Detective Superintendent was yet to be convinced. "Which doesn't explain why you deliberately cut the power to the house, leaving it in darkness."

"The power was cut?" Nico widened his eyes. *Mr Innocent, that's me!* "I thought it was because of the storm . . ."

"You're lying!" protested Isabel, belatedly catching on. She turned to the Superintendent. "Mr Hunter, can't you see he's lying? He's making it up as he goes along! Bloody hell, I thought you were trained to suss out this kind of thing? Call yourself a police officer?"

Dig your own grave, sweetheart! "There would be no reason for me to cut the power. Besides, I have no idea where the fuse-box is."

Detective Superintendent Hunter seemed suddenly unsure of his argument.

"Tonight I went to a friend's party," Nico explained. "Danielle couldn't make it – pressure of work – but I met up with Isabel instead. We got on well, we had a good time, and so I invited her back to my house for a drink." He paused. "Do you really want every last detail?"

Catching sight of a couple of uniformed officers exchanging amused and slightly envious glances, Isabel realised what he was implying. "Bastard! I would never sleep with you! You're my sister's boyfriend!"

"Isabel had an attack of conscience," Nico proceeded

blithely, "and borrowed my car to return home. I followed her on my motorbike, to make sure she was all right, to reassure her that I was equally to blame – "

"You followed me because you thought I was about to reveal your sleazy secret to Danielle!" Isabel glanced towards Superintendent Hunter. "Surely you don't believe this crap?"

"I don't know what to believe," said the Superintendent heavily, "but I'm starting to think I've been dragged out of my bed to deal with a domestic."

"So how did I get this black eye?" Isabel furiously jabbed her thumb towards her head. "Do you think I did it to myself, to set the guy up? What kind of sicko do you think I am?"

"Personally I'd like to know how I got this chunk knocked out of my head!" retorted Nico. "So I can sue for assault."

"See you in court! *I* threw the clock at you."

"*Clock*? What the fuck – "

"I thought you were an intruder! I thought you were going to *kill* me! It was you who cut the power!"

The doctor interrupted her. "Superintendent," he injected forcefully, "You've got to get this man to hospital. He shouldn't have to face an interrogation, look at the colour of him. The poor chap must be suffering severe pain."

"I am," agreed Nico, grateful for any respite from Isabel's accusations.

The Superintendent beckoned to one of the uniformed constables, waiting patiently at the side of the room. "Take Mr Kearney to Norchester General," he commanded. "Stay with him, make sure he's all right." He turned back to Nico. "Perhaps when you're feeling better we can have another talk about what happened tonight?"

Nico felt his smile slip. He wasn't out of trouble yet . . .

* * *

Danielle, driving at a leisurely pace down the drive of Stortford House, was alarmed to see three police cars belting towards her. Had there been an accident?

She pulled onto the verge to allow them to pass, which they did – in a blur of blue lights and fluorescent sponsorship logos. Watching their retreat, completely mystified, she expected at the very least for someone to stop and explain what was happening. Instead, the cars continued up the drive, slowing only as they reached the ornate stone gateway. It was then, as the last car swung out onto the road, she saw a man turn to stare through the rear window.

Nico.

For a brief moment, Danielle wondered whether she should follow. Then she decided to go up to the house first and discover what had happened. Parking beneath the oak-trees, she was surprised to see both Nico's car and motorbike parked there too.

She picked her briefcase up off the front seat and strode across the gravel to the front door. The butler opened it before she'd even reached the foot of the steps.

"Miss van der Straatan," he acknowledged, standing aside for her to enter.

Danielle walked into the hall, waited for him to close the door after her and then came straight to the point. "Why were the police here?"

"We had a break-in during the night. Nothing was stolen and the culprit has been apprehended."

Did he mean Nico? Danielle hesitated, for once uncertain as to her next move. "Is my sister in?" she asked at last, deciding she really couldn't be discussing her love life with the hired help.

"Miss Isabel is in her suite."

Danielle walked sedately up the stairs (although every instinct was urging her to run), as she was aware the butler was still lingering in the hall. Her mind, however, was churning. Nico had been arrested for breaking into Stortford House? How ridiculous!

She rapped smartly on the door to Isabel's apartment, hardly bothered to wait for a reply and marched in. Isabel was lying on her side on the settee, her arms wrapped around her ribs, still wearing last night's fancy dress – a badly creased, old-fashioned ball-gown, stinking of cigarette smoke and possibly body odour too.

What a slob! Danielle wrinkled her nose in distaste. One would hardly think they were related.

"Dani!" Isabel started guiltily and sat up. "What are you doing here?"

Danielle studied Isabel's heavy eye make-up, now smeared down her cheeks, and her bird's nest of a hairstyle, half-up, half-down, which had perhaps once been an elegant chignon. This girl seriously needed to get her act together.

"I live here," she said dryly.

"Well, yes, I know but – shouldn't you be at work?"

"At seven o'clock on a Sunday morning? I may be keen, but I'm not obsessed."

Isabel appeared distressed. "I didn't mean – "

Guilt asserted itself. Danielle dumped her briefcase on the floor and perched on the arm of the settee. If I really make an effort, she scolded herself, I'm sure I can be pleasant.

"Actually," she smiled kindly (and yes, it was an effort this early in the day), "I've already spent the night at the workshop. Dad's affairs are in a real mess."

She had over-estimated Isabel's interest in Vanders.

"So you didn't go to the party . . ." For some reason, Isabel appeared to be relieved.

"Party?" Danielle frowned, her mind momentarily blank. And then she realised that Isabel was still staring miserably at the floor and, what she had first taken to be black eye-shadow, plastered on in the style of Dusty Springfield was, in reality, the start of a nasty black eye.

"Bloody hell, Isabel! What happened to you?" Danielle's mind began to work overtime, calculating likely scenarios. It didn't take her long to come to the obvious conclusion. "*Nico*? My God, he – he attacked you?"

"Yes." Isabel's voice was the merest whisper. She couldn't even look Danielle in the eye as she spoke.

Danielle felt absolutely wretched. Nico had been her boyfriend, it was her fault Isabel had been hurt and, what was worse, Isabel seemed more worried about her reaction to Nico's perfidy than her own injury.

Danielle sat beside her, gently raising Isabel's face to the light so she could see the bruising more clearly. Her stomach churned. It was not attractive. "Have you seen a doctor?" she asked, concentrating on keeping her voice sounding calm.

Isabel, perhaps taken aback by this unexpected kindness – when she was actually expecting to be yelled at – promptly burst into tears. "Yes – it's only superficial bruising . . . nothing to worry about – honestly!"

Danielle may have appeared composed, but inside she was in turmoil. "I've just seen Nico being driven off in a police car. Did he . . . did he rape you?"

"Oh no, he didn't do anything like that!"

"I want the truth, Isabel. It's important to me. Don't give me one of your fanciful stories because you don't want to hurt my feelings, because you're worried about how I'm going to take it. You're the important one. If Nico has done anything to hurt you he deserves everything that's coming to him – and I'll make sure he receives it. Do you understand?"

Isabel nodded, taking a deep breath, perhaps to ensure her voice was going to be steady. "When I came home from Jemma's party I found the house in darkness. I thought it was just a power cut – and hadn't a clue how to fix it, so I decided to go to bed and let someone else worry about it."

Typical Isabel.

"I locked the door, turned around and walked straight into someone. And this voice . . ." Isabel's voice choked over the words, "this horrible voice said, 'Where's the diamond?'"

Danielle felt as though she was about to be sick. "The *Ashlyn* Diamond?"

"How the hell should I know!"

"How could he have discovered we have it?"

"Really Danielle, at that point I didn't give a shit! I just wanted to get away from him. I'd lost the key and couldn't find it in the dark, so I ran down the corridor to the dining-room. I was hoping to get out through the French windows and into the garden, but there was someone else already there, waiting for me. So I chucked one of Dad's Cartier clocks at him and knocked him out – then the first man reappeared and started punching me, saying over and over, 'Where's the fucking diamond?'"

"I *knew* it was stolen!"

"Luckily, the police turned up. Apparently, whenever the power is cut, an alarm goes off at the local station – because of that Tissot painting Dad bought last year. Did you know that?"

Danielle nodded. "The insurance company insisted on it."

"When the cops arrived, sirens blaring, wheels squealing, etc, etc, the intruder ran off through the French windows, leaving me in the dark with a body bleeding all over the floor. I honestly thought I'd killed him. Then the police walked in, with their torches half-blinding me, and we realised it was Nico I'd knocked out – fortunately he was still breathing."

"There were two men?" Danielle felt the relief wash over her. "Nico wasn't involved. He was in the wrong place at the wrong time. It was the other man who hit you. Contact the station and make sure they know the truth. Nico's been taken off in a patrol car. If you don't say something, he's liable to be charged with assault."

Consternation seemed to dawn on Isabel as she considered this version of events. "Yes," she said eventually. "OK. I'll do that. Um, right away."

"There's something you're not telling me . . ."

Isabel squirmed in her seat. "Uh – "

"The *facts*, Isabel."

"Nico isn't really Nico." Her words came out in a rush. "He's a journalist called Nicolas Kearney."

Danielle blanched. "The man who wrote the book about Paul de Havilland?"

"The police seemed really keen to arrest him."

"I'm not surprised! That book he wrote about Paul – it was also about corruption in the local police! *One Rotten Apple*. Don't you remember Dad ranting about it? It destroyed Paul. He lost everything." She paused. "Was Nico was doing an exposé on Dad?"

Isabel nodded reluctantly.

"And you knew this?"

"I – "

"How long have you known, Isabel?"

"Only since tonight. I was searching his house and I found his Journalist of the Year award – "

Danielle frowned. "Why were you at his house?"

"He was giving me a lift home from Jemma's party and said he needed to collect some paperwork . . ."

"You believed him? Honestly, men have been using that line since forever. I can't believe you could be that naive. You must have known what he was implying? It's one step removed from 'Come up and see my etchings'. What *is* it with you and Jemma? Can't you find men of your own? Why do you have to steal mine?"

"I didn't, I wouldn't! Oh why didn't you go to the party, Danielle? He was waiting for you – and kissed me thinking I was you."

It got better and better. Give Isabel enough rope and she was sure to hang herself with it. "You didn't bother to correct the misunderstanding?"

Danielle felt thoroughly exasperated. Time after time she was expected to bail out her younger sister, but now she really had gone too far. Danielle felt herself buckling under the strain of it all. Max's defection, her father's death, her inheritance turning out to be not so golden after all and finally her relationship with Nico biting the dust. She wasn't sure how much more she could take.

"Families are supposed to stick up for each other," she said bitterly. "Be there when the going gets tough. But while I'm out all hours trying to prove our father was no jewel thief, you're only interested in parties, parties, parties – and bugger the fact that our father was killed less than a month ago. And then, to add insult to injury, you make a move on my man!"

"You're getting it all wrong!" Isabel blinked away the tears hovering on her thickly mascaraed lashes.

Danielle's heart hardened. She'd been caught out like that before. Isabel had always had the ability to cry on demand. However, there was still something not quite right about Isabel's story.

"Did you throw yourself at Nico only for him to turn you down?" she asked. "And to regain face you needed to discredit him? You've been desperate to break us up from the start – I haven't forgotten the scene you created at La Dolce Vita. And perhaps when Plan 'A' failed, you called in the police and accused him of attacking you – thereby letting the real culprit escape to strike again. You really are the most *stupid* individual – "

"It wasn't *like* that! Why won't you listen to me? That's your trouble. You never listen to anyone's opinions except your own – "

"It was *exactly* like that! I *know* you Isabel, I know what you're capable of, to what lengths you'd go to make my life a misery. You've got no life of your own, so to relieve your boredom you wreck mine, without a thought of the pain you cause. You know something? This time, I've had enough! You can go. This is my house now, my money, and after your recent behaviour I really don't think I owe you anything. So get out, Isabel. Let's see how you cope when faced with the real world."

"You . . . you're kicking me out?"

It gave Danielle scant satisfaction to see Isabel's incredulous expression. "I'll send your stuff on to Jemma. No doubt you'll be moving in with her. Or perhaps Taz?

He's the one with the real money – he's also a man, so easy for you to manipulate. Just like our father."

Perhaps that was one dig too many.

"Danielle, what's the matter with you? Why are you saying this?"

She really didn't get it? Did she want pictures drawn too? "Because you've finally pushed me too far. I can't take any more of your bullshit. I've got enough trouble trying to keep the business afloat without you trying to sink me the moment my back's turned. I can't live with you any more. I can't stand having you around. You drive me crazy." Now she no longer cared how much her words would hurt. "Send someone else over the edge, give me a break. Of course, you could always do something *really* radical. You could get a job! Earn your *own* money, buy your *own* house, live your *own* fucking life. Like normal people do . . ."

Chapter Fourteen

So that was it, thought Isabel, thirty minutes later, as she manoeuvred her SLK through the gates of Stortford House. She was now officially homeless. No Fixed Abode. She would become one of those gangly scruffs, of indeterminate sex, that frequented Calahurst Quay during the summer months – all dreadlocks and beads, smoking joints and selling *The Big Issue*. Not that she'd ever bought a copy of *The Big Issue*, she realised guiltily. And now she never would. Because she was officially insolvent too.

At least she'd thought to change her clothes and pack a bag with a few essentials – she'd look pretty silly trailing around Calahurst in a ballgown! Danielle had been right, damn her, Jemma *was* going to be her first port of call. Isabel planned to crash out on one of her sequinned bean-bags for a few days, until Danielle calmed down and changed her mind. Which she would, Isabel was breezily confident of that. No way would Danielle cast her only sister out onto the street like a scene from a Dickens novel. Would she?

There was a strange gnawing feeling in her stomach, which Isabel had first taken to be hunger – she hadn't eaten breakfast after all. Now it seemed remarkably like fear. Danielle would come around, Isabel told herself firmly. She always had in the past – once she got beyond that white-hot rage. This was typical of Danielle. She'd explode, upset everyone, then, two hours later she'd be absolutely fine and unable to understand why no one liked her any more.

Isabel stuck a compilation CD in the music deck to keep her spirits up. It was unfortunate that the first track should be Britney Spears' 'Oops, I Did It Again' – her theme tune. Lately it seemed Britney was following her around. Maybe it was some kind of sign?

Isabel stabbed the eject button. It was a sign all right! It was a sign she needed to update her record collection!

Winding down the car window, she tossed the CD out of the window, where it briefly hovered, like a mini flying saucer, before slicing a path through the dry brown leaves that scuttled along the verge.

You could have sold that CD, a little voice inside her head scolded her.

And for what? A pound? Fifty pence? That wouldn't even buy a lipstick!

It would buy a cup of coffee.

Isabel had another vision of *The Big Issue* sellers on Calahurst Quay.

No, she told herself firmly, shoving another CD into the deck. *That's not going to happen to me.*

'Independent Women' blasted from the stereo.

Isabel grinned and turned up the volume. Now that was more like it!

* * *

It was almost eight o'clock when Isabel parked at the end of Quay Street, just a few yards away from the apartment building where Jemma lived. She couldn't get any closer because the street was pedestrianised. Not that she wanted to either. She didn't want Taz to look out of his bedroom window and spot her distinctive car parked outside.

She was still working on an excuse for not meeting up with him at Jemma's party last night, as she had promised. She felt an unaccustomed twinge of guilt. She hadn't seen the poor guy for days, except for when his concert had been televised on MTV. Even then she'd recorded it while she watched *Friends* on Sky One instead, promising herself she'd check it out later. Except she hadn't of course. For all she knew, he'd dedicated his latest record to her – not that Carson would ever agree to that!

She sat in her car for a few moments longer, staring across the street at the row of beautiful Georgian houses, wondering if Jemma was up yet. As Jemma was not a morning person, it wouldn't be in Isabel's best interest to wake her too early. Like Danielle, Jemma worked weekends too, although sometimes she just sent in her stuff in by e-mail – in which case she wouldn't get up 'til noon. And sometimes, of course, Jemma went out and about, interviewing the general public – who had no idea that the glamorous blonde reporter with the thirst for a hot story was the titled daughter of an aristocrat.

Jemma had been poor, Isabel reminded herself. Jemma would know what it was like. She had even gone to college – like a 'normal' person, as Danielle would have said. First to art school, then, when that didn't work out, to evening classes on a journalism course. Jemma was doing OK; she could afford to live here, in Calahurst's most exclusive apartment blocks, with a rock star (Taz) and a movie producer and his film-star wife for neighbours. Isabel felt her spirits lift. Perhaps she could become a journalist? Surely writing news wasn't that difficult – and on a slow day she could make it up!

Isabel recalled her English reports from school and cringed. But hey, everything was done on computers now. Computers had spell-check and grammar-checks; even Jemma would be the first to admit she'd be stuck without her thesaurus. Except Isabel couldn't work a computer either. She couldn't even type . . .

Isabel, tired of pointless introspection, got out of her car and slammed the door. She'd learn to type, perhaps enrol in evening classes – a million other people did it every day. Although how would she live until then?

Isabel's eye wandered along the buildings of Calahurst Quay. Jostling between the Georgian town houses were designer boutiques, coffee shops, Granger's Gym, The Parson's Collar . . . all these places would need staff to keep them running smoothly. She could get a job here – nice and convenient for Jemma's flat. She'd have to lower her standards of course – buy lipsticks from Superdrug instead of Chanel. She could make it a game; call it 'character building'. It'd be fun . . .

So why was she so depressed?

Deciding Jemma would cheer her up, even if it was a bit early in the morning for a social call, Isabel started to cross the road. As she reached the centre of the cobblestones, just as she could glimpse her reflection in the glass of the door opposite, it opened and Jemma walked through, smartly dressed in a black trouser suit and lilac blouse. Good grief, she was up and awake! It must be a 'get-out-and-meet-the public' day.

Grinning, Isabel raised her hand to wave – and then hesitated. Directly behind Jemma ambled Taz, yawning widely, wearing the black joggers he habitually slept in – and that was it. Bare chest, bare feet; his black hair standing on end, stubble darkening his chin. He looked as though he'd just got out of bed. He also looked beautiful, realised Isabel, chastising herself for neglecting him over these past few weeks – and even entertaining a crush on *Nico* of all people!

As she bounded forward, about to give him a puppy-like hug and beg for forgiveness, Taz bent forward and kissed Jemma on the mouth. Passionately, fervently, lustfully; smearing her frosted pink lipstick across her flushed cheeks, running his fingers through her choppy blonde bob, sliding his other hand into her waistband and stroking her bottom.

Isabel was outraged. It was the exact same way he always kissed her! So she could never doubt his enthusiasm for possessing her. But this time he was doing it to Jemma! *Jemma*!

Jemma calmly pulled Taz's hand out from her waistband and pushed him away, tucking her blouse back into her boot-cut trousers and smoothing down her hair.

Taz kissed her again and raised his hand to wave her goodbye. It was then that he saw Isabel.

"Oh *crap*!" muttered Isabel, realising she did not want to be seen – and certainly not standing in the middle of the street, her mouth open, a gormless expression on her face, looking less than beautiful in old clothes and old make-up. Less than *average*, really, if she was to be honest about it. And nothing in her bag that would make a remotely suitable weapon to castrate Taz and disembowel her ex-best friend.

"Isabel!" cried Taz.

He appeared distressed, Isabel noted, before she turned tail to flee back to her car, stumbling slightly over the blasted cobblestones. As well he might, the bastard! When she got through with him! But not here, not now, not when she was still feeling vulnerable after her less than sisterly encounter with Danielle. She would hate to do something really pathetic and forgive him.

"Isabel!" yelled Taz again, pushing past a surprised Jemma, attempting to sprint after her, hindered somewhat by his bare feet. "Come back!"

Isabel fumbled with the handle of her car door,

before she realised that, in her stupor, she'd not actually locked it. Jemma and *Taz*? The scene kept replaying in her head. It was surreal. Not in the slightest bit funny, as it had been when Jemma seduced Danielle's boyfriends. The way Dani treated her men they deserved to be stolen. But Isabel didn't deserve this. She and Jemma were supposed to be best friends, for heaven's sake! How could she do this?

"Isabel." Taz had arrived, breathless and panting, beside her car. "Honey. I can explain."

Isabel jumped into her car, slamming the door, nearly severing Taz's hand.

"Shit, Isabel, that was almost my strumming finger!"

Isabel wound down the window. "You're lucky it wasn't your strumming penis! Now get out of my way before I grind you both into the cobblestones."

Which were great words to make a sweeping exit on – except Isabel then had to execute a three-point turn, with Taz banging on the roof – pleading with her to stop, to open the door, let him make it up to her. He was practically in tears, but Isabel was too furious to stop. She had no intention of letting him confess, make *himself* feel better by unloading his guilt onto her. Their relationship was dead, it was not going to rise again. So what would a post-mortem, apportioning guilt and blame, prove to anyone?

Not particularly caring whether or not she ran over one of Australia's foremost rock stars, Isabel crunched the gears through the three-point turn, slammed her foot on the accelerator and shot back up the hill, through Calahurst, careering around the war memorial and into Mistletoe Lane.

It was only as she automatically pulled up outside the gates to Stortford House that she remembered she didn't actually live there anymore.

* * *

Danielle stared at herself in her bathroom mirror, her hands unconsciously clenching each side of the hand basin, as she carefully appraised her face.

Her red hair was piled up on top of her head in her usual style, the sculptured curls glinting with gold where they caught the light. Her pale grey eyes, sparkling with controlled fury, were huge under slim dark brows and naturally long dark lashes. A full mouth had narrowed to a thin, uncompromising line. Even allowing for vanity she was undoubtedly beautiful. So why did men always cheat on her? Did she have a neon sign flashing 'gullible fool' somewhere above her head? Did she sub-consciously choose men who would be unfaithful, in the way some women persistently married violent men? And why did her lovers always defect to either Isabel or Jemma?

Danielle scowled at her reflection. If it was not her looks then Isabel must be right – it was her personality. She knew she could be a bitch but hell, no one could be nice *all* the time.

She was surprised she did not feel more upset with Nico. Her anger was directed entirely at her sister, yet they were equally to blame. Perhaps she had been fooling herself all along and had never really loved him. It would explain why she was so offhand to him – to ensure he would tire of her first.

Her mobile telephone launched itself into a jangling 'Diamonds are a Girl's Best Friend' (one of her father's little jokes) and interrupted her introspection. She irritably plucked it from her jacket pocket, toying with the idea of dropping it down the loo and flushing. But she couldn't resist glancing at the screen, hoping to see her sister's name. The text blazoned across the window read *'Paige Lorraine'*. Danielle felt her blood pressure rising again. For fuck's sake, it was seven o'clock in the morning! Did her customers think she slept at Vanders?

"Danielle van der Straatan," she said politely.

"Danielle! Thank God! Look, I need the diamond earrings by the beginning of next month. Can you fix that for me?"

Earrings? The woman was phoning her at this ungodly hour to check up on an order for *earrings*?

"The pink diamond earrings that match the platinum necklace?" Paige rambled on. "My latest film is up for a royal command performance for The Prince's Trust on Christmas Eve. I'm going to meet Prince Charles!"

"Lovely!" said Danielle, but that was all. Butt-kissing was not one of her specialities.

Paige did not seem to feel Danielle was appropriately impressed. "My picture will be in all the papers."

Which was the most important thing.

"I've bought this beautiful, shimmering pink dress – low at the front, down to my ass at the back – and in your pink diamonds I'm gonna look stunning."

"You'll look out of this world," agreed Danielle. Straight out of *Barbarella*, in fact.

"So, can you hurry up the earrings for me?"

"Well, you've already got the tiara, and the necklace, and the bracelet," reeled off Danielle, unable to keep the note of doubt from her voice. "Won't that be enough?"

"A girl can never have enough diamonds," reproved Paige.

The woman was going to look like a Christmas tree. Prince Charles would need some kind of welding mask to protect his eyes from the glare.

Out loud she said, "I'm afraid it could be a bit tricky completing the order in such a short time-frame. You'll be pleased to learn we have finished one earring – but we discovered a small flaw in the second stone and we are having to polish it out on the wheel, bit by bit. It could take several months before it's completed, but we hope to still make our original date of February – ready for your wedding to Ross Whitney on Valentine's Day." Poor sucker.

"February!" shrieked Paige Lorraine, so that Danielle had to hold the phone several inches away from her ear. "But the premiere is on December 24th! I can't wear one earring!"

Danielle was tempted to point out that Paige could always wear it through her navel – after all, she was wearing diamonds everywhere else. "I'm sorry, Miss Lorraine, but there is little I can do. You still have the necklace, the bracelet and the brooch –"

"This is a royal premiere! The world's press will be there. Think of the publicity!"

Danielle was not sure that Paige Lorraine, practically naked and dripping from head to foot in pink diamonds, was going to provide the kind of publicity Vanders would want. Diplomatically (she was getting good at 'diplomatically') she held her tongue.

Paige's voice hinted of steel. "I'm not the kind of person to make threats, Miss Van der Straatan, but unless I can wear those earrings on Christmas Eve I'll cancel the order and take myself off to Theo Fennell. I should have gone there first."

Danielle managed to refrain from pointing out that any jeweller would have trouble producing a specialised order in such a short time. "But Miss Lorraine – "

The line had gone dead.

* * *

It was amazing how quickly a guy could get seen in casualty when he had a police escort, thought Nico cynically. He'd been in and out within the hour and had even been given a goody-bag of painkillers to take home with him. PC Wells was still by his side, driving the patrol car back to Calahurst. He was a pleasant enough lad, quiet, but a bit dim. Nico had the feeling that, should he make a break for freedom, PC Wells would just stand there with his mouth open, totally nonplussed.

After Nico had his x-rays taken and his wound bandaged by a pretty nurse, he had been surprised to find PC Wells still sitting in the waiting-room, leafing through a copy of *Bella* magazine. His very own ball and chain. But at least it would save on taxi fares back to Calahurst.

Apparently Superintendent Hunter had decided he wanted to interview him, radioing PC Wells to that effect – provided Nico got the all-clear from the hospital. Which was why, at nine o'clock that same Sunday morning, before most people had even woken up, Nico found himself in the interview room of Calahurst Police Station, his rumbling stomach threatening to obliterate the gentle but persistent questioning of Detective Superintendent Hunter.

Seb Hunter was aged somewhere between forty and fifty but, like Isaac van der Straatan, was remarkably well preserved. Undoubtedly a hit with a ladies too, decided Nico cynically, taking in the smart suit, expensive after-shave and fashionable haircut. There was not one grey hair on his dark head, barely a line on his handsome face. He was wasted in the police force. A dapper Cary Grant look-alike, he would have been more at home starring in some 1950s romcom with Sophia Loren.

Seb switched on the tape recorders, rattled off the legal necessities, then turned to Nico with a charming smile. "Mr Kearney. Tell me about yourself."

"In the hope that if I ramble on for long enough I'll incriminate myself?" mocked Nico. "Try again."

The smile disappeared. "OK. Your name is Nicolas Kearney, you're an investigative journalist and you specialise in unauthorised biographies of the rich and famous?"

"That's about it," nodded Nico. "I've even got my own website. Check it out."

"You came to Calahurst to research a book on Isaac van der Straatan and rented one of the houses in Riverside Terrace – although you've since moved into Stortford House with Danielle van der Straatan?"

"You stalking me?"

"Why Isaac van der Straatan? Why not Taz Taylor?"

"Give me some credit for originality. Besides, Isaac was rich, he was famous in his own field, diamonds are an exciting and glamorous subject – "

"But not enough to sell books in as large a quantity as you're used to, eh, Mr Kearney? For example, your last book, *One Rotten Apple* sold in excess of 60,000 copies?"

"In hardback," agreed Nico. "The paperback comes out next spring."

"And, let me see, this book, *One Rotten Apple,* it was about corruption in the police force?"

"Corruption in *this* police force," clarified Nico. Did the Superintendent think he would scare that easily? OK, so he was clearly not going to be Mr Popular with the local cops, but surely Seb didn't think he could get away with framing him for the break-in at Stortford House – purely because he had written a book he didn't like?

Nico fixed the Superintendent with a confident stare and promptly forgot his number one rule: Do Not Deliberately Antagonise The Police. "Would you like a signed copy?"

"How kind," said Seb. "But I'm still interested to know how you think you're going to shift 60,000 hardback copies of a book about Isaac van der Straatan, a provincial jeweller, who spent his days on the golf course (leaving his daughter to do all the work), his nights bedding a variety of grateful women and died in car crash after one too many brandies."

Nico perked up. "He was drunk then?"

"Slightly over the limit," conceded Seb.

"But not enough to impair his judgement." Nico slumped back in his chair, trying hard to conceal his frustration. There was something sinister behind Isaac's crash, he was certain. It was too much to expect the local cops to come up with a solution. Look how they'd made a complete crock of their last murder case – the source material for his much-maligned book.

Seb, meanwhile, had clicked off the tape recorder. "Look, I'm doing the interviewing here."

Nico waved his hand. "Carry on, I'm not stopping you."

"Why waste the tape?" Seb made a sound of pure exasperation. "Tell me, what do you know about Isaac van der Straatan that's worth a whole bloody book?"

"What do *you* know?" countered Nico fixing the police officer with his intense stare.

Seb blinked first. "What were you really doing at Stortford House? Surely you don't expect me to believe you're having it off with both his daughters?"

Nico grinned. "Not yet."

"I think there was more than one intruder."

"Is that what Isabel says?"

"No, but Isabel van der Straatan is lying her pretty little head off, purely to stitch you up – what did you do to her to make her hate you so much?"

"I wish I knew." That, at least, was the truth.

"Look, Nicolas, it's a waste of time your being here and we both know it. Take my advice, steer clear of the van der Straatans. These rich girls are more trouble than they're worth. Cut your losses, go back to London. Find another celebrity to dissect. Now that Isaac's dead, you have to admit your story has gone cold."

Nico allowed himself a tiny, mocking smile. "You reckon? I thought it was just hotting up."

"I'm not joking!"

"My life might just depend on it?"

Seb sighed heavily. "If you put it like that – yes!"

Chapter Fifteen

As soon as Danielle arrived at Vanders' workshop she went straight to see the designer, Simon Castle. Her father had hired him less than twelve months previously, so Danielle didn't know him that well. Although he had his own office on the first floor, right next to her own, they only seemed to meet around the coffee-machine.

She remembered to knock before she entered his office and found him bent over a pattern of Plasticene balls, which he was now carefully studding with diamonds. The room was painted the same neutral colour as the others; the only change he had made to assert his personality was the addition of several James Bond movie posters, featuring Sean Connery in the title role. He had a model of a gold-plated handgun on his desk too. Seriously weird.

He glanced up, a tiny diamond still held between a pair of tweezers. Instead of a suit, he wore a thick cable-knit sweater and jeans, which meant he looked as though he ought to be at home on the farm, rather than designing It Girls' jewellery (or saving the world from Dr No).

"Hi, Danielle," he grinned, genuinely pleased to see her. "How are you? Would you like a coffee? Decaff? Cappuccino?"

Danielle smiled; he should work in Starbucks. She couldn't blame him for trying to please her – and she knew it was not because she was now his employer. Danielle had realised long ago that Simon was attracted to her – hence those coincidental meetings next to the coffee-machine – but after the fiasco with Max Falkenhayn, the manager of the Port Rell store, she had sworn she would never date anyone from work again.

This was a shame because Simon seemed like a really nice person (apart from the spy fetish), with no secret agenda – unlike Max who'd wanted promotion to manager (and got it, because her father couldn't bear to see her date a mere shop-assistant), or Nico who had sought scandal for his book.

Simon was attractive too, in a safe, very average sort of way. She was surprised he *still* hadn't plucked up courage to ask her out – although Danielle had long ago come to the conclusion that, even if they were marooned on a desert island with no hope of rescue, she'd have to make the first move.

"I've got a problem, Simon." Danielle slid the tray of diamond-studded Plasticene across the desk and perched on the corner of his desk in a proprietary fashion, elegantly crossing her legs, sadistically aware of the effect her short skirt was likely to have on him. "Something's come up."

Simon manfully kept his gaze firmly on hers. "Paige Lorraine's pink diamonds?"

He must be psychic. "How did you know?"

"She telephoned me sometime after midnight. I told her to contact you!"

Not so Simple Simon. "Thanks!"

"You're welcome! I gather she wants to speed up production on her earrings?"

"Yes. Any suggestions?"

"I have the finished one here in the safe if you want to take a look at it. I'm certain Paige will be pleased with it. Then, if you like, we could go downstairs and speak to Bernard, find out how he's getting on with polishing the flaw out of the other."

The *flaw*. There was the rub. "How far is it from completion?"

"Could be any day now. Bernard is taking it very slowly, but he's almost finished." Simon got out of his chair, slid past Danielle without 'accidentally' brushing up against her, and opened his safe. After a few moments of fumbling, he brought out the familiar blue Vanders jewellery case, with the inlaid gold tulip design, and handed it to Danielle to open.

She took the solitary earring out. The large pink diamond was cut in a pear shape and had three marquise white diamonds arranged around it, designed to resemble leaves. The stones were set in platinum –

Paige Lorraine's trademark. It was breathtakingly beautiful. Even Paige, well-known for her fussiness, should have no cause for complaint. Once the pictures of the premiere were published, the orders would come pouring in.

Danielle wished her father could have seen this collection, created around the pink diamonds he had thought had been a mistake. *Her* pink diamonds. Who would have thought it! Danielle felt the warm glow of pride as she placed the earring gently back into the box.

"It's exquisite," she approved, "but you don't need me to tell you that."

Or maybe he did, she reflected, as he visibly relaxed. Was she that difficult to please?

"The setting for its twin is complete," he said. "The marquise diamonds are cut, we're simply waiting for the other pink diamond."

"So the order could be complete by Christmas?"

"Yes . . ."

He paused and Danielle glanced up at him, enquiringly.

"If we could get a couple of blue diamonds and repeat the design, they'd look fantastic on you," said Simon, the words coming out in a rush.

Dear boy! Even his cheeks had gone red with the embarrassment of his own audacity. She smiled gently. "Flattery will get you everywhere."

"Really? How about dinner tonight?"

She was tempted, really tempted. A light-hearted

affair with a nice, handsome man would erase all traces of Nico from her system. But what if it got heavy? If she got in too deep and everything went horribly wrong again? Honestly, she didn't think she could take the grief – and that was not even taking into consideration the fact that they had to work together.

"Sorry," she said gently. "I need to concentrate on Vanders right now. I want to build it up into an international business my father would have been proud of."

He was disappointed, but hid it well. "You can't blame a chap for trying."

They walked down the stairs to the cutting workshop where Bernard had established his own little corner. He was a small, beautifully dressed French-Canadian, who spoke English without a trace of accent. His eyes were small and dark like currants, his face round and cherubic and his bald head and full white beard gave him the air of a mischievous Father Christmas. Right now, however, he appeared very serious. The strain of working on these wretched earrings seemed to affect even the affable Bernard.

"Hi, Bernard, how are you?" asked Danielle, putting on her jolly, public-relations voice.

He looked up warily. "I was about to come and see you . . ."

"That's a coincidence, we've come to see the pink diamond. Where is it?" she couldn't help the note of paranoia slipping into her voice. "I thought you'd be working on it. Have you finished cutting it already?"

"There it is," said Bernard. His hand trembled as it pointed to the cutting wheel.

Danielle looked at the wheel. Instead of a large diamond clamped to it there was a smattering of chips. For a moment she did not realise the significance of what she was seeing. Then, when she eventually understood that all that was left of her precious pink diamond was a pile of dust, she gasped and found she was unable to say anything.

Simon took charge. "What happened?"

"I don't know," Bernard appeared to be in shock. "It sort of *exploded*."

Danielle ran her fingertips over the crumbs that were the only remains of the beautiful diamond and felt like screaming in frustration. "It's impossible," she murmured, almost to herself. "This can't have happened. Not now, not when it was almost finished . . ."

"The stone was flawed," said Simon, whose own voice wasn't exactly steady. "It was a risk. You know yourself this can happen to any gem, though it's more common with the fancy stones."

"It shouldn't have happened! Not here at Vanders." Her eye fell on the suitable sacrificial victim. "I thought Bernard is supposed to be the best?"

Bernard blanched and failed to meet her accusing stare.

"He is," protested Simon. "It wasn't his fault. You knew something like this might occur."

"But it took months to find a match!"

"So we'll start again." Simon placed a hand gently

on the small of her back and guided her away from the cutting wheel and the devastated Bernard. "I'm sure Flynn will find you another stone. I'll call him right away."

"What's the point? Paige will cancel her cheque. She was one of our best customers. We'll go bankrupt!"

"No, we won't. We'll find another pink diamond, make another earring and sell the set to someone else."

"And live happily ever after!" scorned Danielle, digging in her heels so that he was forced to stop too. "You're living in fairyland, Simon! Who do you know that can afford to buy a million pounds worth of bloody pink diamonds? Who in their right minds would *want* to buy pink diamonds? Only Paige Lorraine with her Barbie doll complex!" She took a deep breath, forcing herself to speak calmly, rationally – and keep the acute panic she felt inside well hidden. She didn't want to be written off as some hysterical, pre-menstrual female. "I want Bernard sacked. I'll pay him a month's severance pay, but he has to go now."

She saw Simon's mouth form an objection, saw in his eyes that he thought she was losing it, that she had already lost his respect by dismissing one of his staff with consulting him first. Why couldn't he understand? It wasn't a power thing, it was *business*.

"How can I trust him with another large stone after this?" she explained, ensuring her voice remained calm and steady. "What if it happens again? I can't afford to see my best diamonds turn into pixie dust."

"Aside from the obligatory employment legislation,"

Simon pointed out, somewhat coldly, "Bernard has worked for Vanders since your father started out. It wouldn't be fair – where would he find another job at his age? Please reconsider, Danielle, you can't do this to him!"

Danielle closed her eyes. When were people going to realise that she was no longer the heir apparent. Her father was dead – she was now in sole control of Vanders.

"This isn't a democracy, Simon," she said wearily. "I'm in charge. I can do anything I want." Her eyes flicked open and stared directly into his, so that there was no way he could misconstrue her meaning. "I can even fire you."

* * *

Isabel pulled away from the verge and drove off along Mistletoe Lane, without having a plan as to where she should go next. She drove slowly, aware that after a few miles the road petered out at a collection of farm buildings and that she ought to have worked out a destination before she got there and had to go through the rigmarole of another three-point turn.

Danielle didn't want her. Taz had been unfaithful. Jemma had betrayed their friendship. She had no cash on her, no clue what her balance was at the bank – but had a sneaky suspicion it was hovering around zero. Her last credit-card bill had not yet been paid – which meant pretty soon she was going to be in debt too. She could sell her car – but would only get a few thousand for it second-hand – and how would she get around without one? Trains did not come any further south than Norchester, the local bus service only ventured out twice a day. There was no need. The inhabitants of Calahurst were, in the majority, wealthy – apart from the council estate on the outskirts of the village and, come to think of it, the people that lived there all had cars too.

Isabel started to panic. She was never much good in a crisis – and it was ten times worse when that crisis was happening to her. She had dozens of friends, but had a nasty feeling that they would all melt away when she asked them for help. Basically, she needed somewhere to live and somewhere to work and the only friend who met that criteria was Harris Roberts, the Chris Evans look-alike who ran The Parson's Collar wine bar with his father.

Harris would help her! They'd dated briefly, decided they were too much alike, and promptly split up, remaining friends. He would give her a job, he might even be able to offer accommodation. The bar was on the ground floor of one of those Georgian town houses along the quay and they were huge. They were also a few doors down from Jemma and Taz, but Isabel tried not to think about that. This was an emergency.

Isabel did a 'U' turn and headed back towards Calahurst, trying to ignore Stortford House as she shot past but, as she approached the war memorial at the crossroads opposite the church, she had to hit the brakes to avoid hitting the car in front. A lorry had attempted to go all the way around the war memorial and got stuck, well and truly jammed between the stone cross and the wall around the churchyard.

Having neither the patience nor the inclination to sit in a traffic queue for the next twenty minutes, Isabel decided to do a 'U' turn and take the road through the forest, entering the quayside from the Port Rell side. It would mean driving past the scene of her father's accident but well, she had to go past there sometime.

The car behind had the same idea, as it copied her manoeuvre, then took the same turn-off. Soon the two vehicles were travelling through the cool green tunnel of oak-trees which gave the adjacent council estate its name. Isabel slowed, to let the other car overtake if it wished. She didn't want to get to The Parson's Collar before she had a chance to work out what she was going to say to Harris. The other car didn't appear to be in any hurry, so she kept at a steady 40 mph, concentrating on her driving, trying not to think about her father.

"Come on, you can do this," she muttered to herself, aware her fingers were gripping the steering wheel so tightly the bones beneath gleamed white through her skin. She hoped someone had moved the flower arrangement Danielle had left at the site of the accident. That way she might not recognise the place where it had happened.

She glanced in her rear-view mirror and wished the car behind would overtake. It was making her self-conscious of her speed and she had to keep checking herself, slowing down, to keep within the 40-mile limit in place throughout the forest. But every time she slowed down, the other car made no attempt to overtake but simply drew closer, forcing her to speed up to keep the distance between them.

Isabel began to get annoyed. There was a clear view for any oncoming traffic. Why didn't he overtake? She was blowed if she was going to be forced into racing along over the limit to please him. Knowing her luck, she'd meet a police car coming in the opposite direction and promptly get booked for speeding.

Deliberately Isabel turned on her left indicator and decelerated, watching her speedometer slip down to 35, expecting the car behind to pull out to overtake her. To her disbelief, she watched it decelerate and draw nearer.

Isabel began to feel frightened. What was up with this creep? Had she cut in front of him at some point? She didn't remember. As her tyres bumped against the verge, jolting her, she realised she had to keep her eyes on the road. She looked away from the mirror, concentrating on the road ahead. They would meet the cliff road soon, then it was a short journey down the hill, back into Calahurst and the police station. That's what she'd do, she resolved, speeding up again. She'd keep her doors locked and drive straight into the police-station yard. Let the boys in blue sort it out.

There was a dull thud. The other car had deliberately rammed her! Thoroughly frightened, Isabel risked another glance into her rear-view mirror as the car again smashed the back of her SLK. Bizarrely, all she could think of was the damage to her beautiful car. She hunched over the wheel and put her foot down hard on the accelerator, increasing the speed to 50.

She was so busy watching the white car behind her that she didn't see the bend in the road. It seemed that there were suddenly rhododendron bushes growing in the middle of the tarmac as she ploughed through them, the branches scraping against the sides of the car with an ear-piercing shriek. Then the foliage cleared, the car was plunging through mid-air, before walloping into the ground so hard Isabel felt her neck crack. She slammed her foot on the brake, but was far too late. A tree materialised in front of her, slicing easily through the car.

As though in slow-motion, Isabel became aware of three things:

The airbag failing to open.

Her skull smashing against the steering wheel.

Thick smoke pouring from beneath the bonnet.

Chapter Sixteen

Isabel opened her eyes and was surprised to find she was still alive. As she pulled herself upright, stretching out her limbs to assess any damage, she saw a thin trickle of blood staining the steering wheel. Her blood. She raised her fingertips to her forehead and they came away wet, sticky and red. Without really thinking about what she was doing, she wiped her hand on her jeans, undid her seat belt and clambered out of her car. Her legs ached and, glancing down, she could see a tear in her jeans and more blood staining the denim.

Ignoring that too, she hobbled around to examine the front of the car, which was completely wrapped around the tree. Even through a thick fog of pain she knew she was behaving irrationally – there was no way she was going to be able to get the SLK back onto the road and it was quite obviously a write-off. At least the smoke issuing from beneath the bonnet appeared to be steam hissing from a fractured radiator and not flames flickering around the engine.

She could have been killed, dying horribly like her father. She could have gone through the windscreen, the glass shredding her face, or had her ribcage crushed to pulp by the steering column. The fact that she had stepped out of this heap of junk relatively unscathed had hardly registered when she violently threw up. On and on she retched, yesterday's supper, lunch, breakfast splattering against the jewel-like autumn leaves, until her stomach muscles ached and the tears were streaming down her face in alternating waves of shock, pain and self-pity until she was all cried out.

It began to dawn on her how pathetic she was. How stupid she must look, crying over the fact that she *wasn't* dead. That she was perfectly all right, apart from a few bumps and scratches, and that she wasn't playing the lead in some chick flick and Prince Charming/Ben Affleck wasn't going to charge through the trees on a white charger/black Harley Davidson and take her away from all this. If she didn't get her act together, she was liable to wait here forever, paddling in her own vomit, wallowing in her own self-pity. In short, she was quite capable of getting the hell out of here by herself.

A quick search of the pocket of her jeans turned up half a packet of Polos, a lip balm, a couple of five pence pieces and a bit of screwed-up tissue she'd used to blot her lipstick the last time she'd worn these clothes. She wiped her eyes, nose and mouth the best she could with the tissue and discarded it in the bushes. She slicked on the lip balm and popped three Polos into her mouth in the hope of dispersing the disgusting taste of bile. Then she turned resolutely from the wreckage of her car and waded through the bracken, towards the road, where she came up against what seemed like an insurmountable wall of earth, brambles and stinging nettles. How the fuck was she going to get up there?

Isabel grabbed the nearest branch, got a foothold in some protruding roots and pulled herself up a few feet. That wasn't so difficult! She located another branch, seized hold of it, and scrambled a bit further, digging her feet and knees into the dirt.

It was curious how, at this moment of extreme stress, a primeval survivor's instinct seemed to take over, forcing her onwards and upwards, uncaring of the sharp branches ripping at her hair and clothes, the brambles tearing into her skin. Until, quite suddenly, she fell through the foliage and slid straight into a ditch, half-filled with stagnant water.

She squeezed the excess water from her T-shirt and hauled herself out, her hand catching on a sharp piece of wire. She cursed, and searched the long yellow grass to find what it was. Her fingers closed over what had once been a wreath of flowers, now decayed and rotten, the brown petals crumbling under her touch.

She stared at it in horror. Her father's wreath. The one Danielle had placed on the roadside, the day after his car had been found, a burnt-out shell.

She had crashed her car in exactly the same place.

Unable to even look at the wreath, she hurled it back

down the bank where it bounced off her car and vanished amongst the glossy leaves of the rhododendrons. She regretted it instantly. Finding the wreath could have been a positive sign, that her father was watching over her – instead she had cast away her one last tangible connection with him.

She had no idea how long she sat there, crying, soaking wet, shivering with cold, hoping someone would drive past and help her. No one came. It must have been the Good Samaritan's day off. She couldn't even use her mobile phone to dial 999 – her bag, along with her phone and all her money, was still on the front seat of her car. There was no way she was going back down there, even if she did have the energy. Which left the alternative of walking the rest of the way to Calahurst.

Nothing to it! she told herself, with fake gung-ho spirit. She'd survived a car crash, what was a short walk?

Short walk? It took ten minutes to reach the cliff road, then another twenty to reach civilisation in the form of a familiar line of terrace houses. At the bottom of the hill she could see the sailing club on the edge of the quay, the cables of the yachts clinking against the masts in the stiff wind that blew up from the river.

She limped down the garden path of the first house and tentatively knocked on the door. It was not everyone who would be thrilled to find a perfect stranger bleeding all over their doorstep. In fact, she would not blame the householders if they pretended to be out. Which they did seem to be doing. No one came to answer her knock despite the first-floor windows being open and jangling folk music blasting halfway down the street.

Isabel turned on her heel and returned to the road. Her shoes were not intended for long distances and were digging painfully into her feet. She paused, wriggling her toes, although she dared not take the shoes off. Her feet were so swollen that she'd never get them on again.

Dejectedly she walked on to the next house. This one appeared all closed up, as though the occupants had gone off to work. Isabel sat on the garden wall to get her breath back. Why didn't she give this up? A few doors down was Nico's house. A nice *warm* house, with a shower and hot drinks.

She recalled what she had said the last time they met . . .

Still, Nico was her only hope – if he was in. What if the local police were holding him in one of their cells?

It would bloody serve her right!

Isabel hauled herself up from the wall and walked slowly down the road to the house, second from the end, that she was sure belonged to Nico. She stood for a long time, staring up at the house, trying to pluck up courage to knock on the door. What if he told her to get lost? What if he got her arrested for wasting police time? What if . . .

She pushed open the gate with a confidence she did not feel, strode up the path and leant against Nico's doorbell.

It seemed to take forever for him to answer. She was about to give up when the door was thrown open and he stood there – intimidating, taller than she remembered, wearing jeans but no sweater, a towel around his neck and a crisp white bandage around his head. Which made him look sexier.

"You don't look very pleased to see me," mumbled Isabel, swaying from side to side.

"Are you stalking me?" snapped Nico. "Take your finger off that fucking bell – I have a headache!"

"Me too," said Isabel, feeling sick again and wondering about the best place to do it. When one felt really ill it was amazing how one's principles went right out the window.

Nico realised her clothes were liberally smeared in blood. "Who have you hit now?"

"A tree," muttered Isabel. "I've crashed my car – I ran off the road – but it wasn't my fault! Someone tried to run me off the road. I thought they were trying to kill me . . ."

"Can't think why." He regarded her without displaying any evident emotion. "Did you get his number?"

"No . . ." It dawned on Isabel that Nico did not believe a word she was saying.

"What make of car was it?"

Isabel put her hand up to soothe her throbbing head. "White, I think."

Unexpectedly he smiled. "Do you know how many white cars there are on the road?"

"Nico," pleaded Isabel. "Please shut up! I . . . I think I'm going to . . . going to . . ."

And she fainted inelegantly onto the doorstep.

* * *

Nico picked Isabel up and carried her into his house, hoping his neighbours were not watching through their inevitably twitching net curtains. For reasons he was unable to fathom, his neighbours found his life completely engrossing. It would be kinda awkward to explain away a young and beautiful girl fainting on his doorstep.

Isabel was heavier than she looked and it was difficult to manoeuvre both her and her platform mules through the narrow doorway. He was just able to heave her along the corridor and into his living-room, before dumping her clumsily onto the couch as his arms gave out.

After trying several times to ring Danielle's mobile, then Stortford House, without success, he telephoned for an ambulance. Isabel had not regained consciousness and was bleeding profusely onto the couch.

The ambulance made its usual discreet arrival – screaming sirens and flashing blue lights. The neighbours ran gleefully out into the street, not wishing to miss any of the drama. Nico realised too late that it was infinitely worse to have an unconscious girl carried out of his house than it was to have one carried in.

As soon as the ambulance rattled off, Nico called a taxi to take him round to Stortford House and let himself in with the keys no one had thought to take off him. He was worried that something might have happened to Danielle – he also wanted to claim his car and bike back.

The house was eerily silent, with no sign of any staff. Half-expecting to have a police officer leap out at him at any moment, Nico started up the long sweeping staircase to the first floor, then along to Danielle's suite. He didn't bother to knock, merely strode right in, and found Danielle sitting hunched over her desk in the corner, a pile of paperwork in front of her and a bottle of vodka beside her.

Without realising it, his face assumed a look of irritation. Didn't the girl ever let up? Work, work, work – she'd kill herself by the time she was thirty. The vodka bottle was a new character-trait though. When she'd been out with him, she'd hardly drunk alcohol at all. Could she actually be missing him?

"Hi there," he said.

Danielle eyed Nico balefully over the top of her glass. "What do you want?"

Then again, maybe not. He bit off the retort that came to his lips and said as gently as he could: "Isabel's been in a car accident."

"I don't see what business that is of mine."

Nico wondered if he'd heard her right. Maybe she didn't think it was serious. "Isabel's been taken to Norchester General in an ambulance. The paramedics think she's gonna be OK, but she has head injuries, concussion, that sort of thing."

"And your point is?"

Nico stared at her in utter shock. "Your sister, she's been hurt. Aren't you going to the hospital to be with her?"

"I'm busy."

"Too busy to even phone and check she's OK?"

Danielle's hand, still holding the glass began to shake, vodka splashing her precious paperwork. The paperwork that was apparently more important than any person. "She's not seriously hurt?"

The girl was joking, right? "After running off the road and hitting a tree? She has head injuries."

"But she's not going to die?"

"Would you care if she did?" he challenged. He was wasting his time and wished he had gone in the ambulance with Isabel as the paramedic had suggested. At least that way she'd have someone with her that gave a damn.

He turned away from Danielle, wondering if he had the energy to drive to the hospital himself or if he should find Jemma. As he opened the door, Danielle called him back.

"How do you know Isabel had an accident?" She regarded him with undisguised hostility. "Were you . . . were you with her when it happened?"

Her sister was being rushed to hospital in an ambulance and all Danielle was worried about was that Isabel might be having an affair with him! Since when did she care what he did anyway?

"The accident happened close to my house," he said, keeping his voice calm. "What does it matter? Your sister is the one who needs you."

Danielle uttered a rather dry laugh. "Isabel doesn't need anyone. Least of all me. She can take care of herself."

Nico abruptly left before he said something he knew he would regret later. Much as it pained him to admit it, he had to keep the lines of communication open between him and the van der Straatans or he'd never get his book finished. No book meant no money.

"Damn women," he grumbled, wrenching open his car door and throwing himself into the driver's seat. Why couldn't Isaac have had sons? Although that might have made the honey-trap he'd set for Danielle a little more difficult to carry through!

Nico lit a cigarette, inhaled deeply, feeling the calming influence of the nicotine flow through his body, then started the car. Not bothering with his seat belt, he reversed from beneath the trees, careful not to scrape Danielle's car as he passed – although it looked as though she'd already hit something with a wallop.

The Fiesta abruptly stalled. Danielle's car had been fine the last time he'd seen it. Two accidents? The most bizarre coincidence – or not?

He got out of the Fiesta and walked across to Danielle's car to examine it more closely. The front wing had a dent in it, quite substantial and located on the offside wing. Danielle must have hit something with considerable force to create that much damage.

Running through the dent was a deep scratch filled with contrasting paint. He scraped some off with his fingernail.

It was dark blue.

Chapter Seventeen

A couple of days later, Nico opened his front door to find Taz standing on the doorstep, clutching a large bunch of rather tattered red roses. The mauve paper wrapping was torn in places and some of the rosebuds were completely broken off. Taz didn't look so hot either. He had a black eye and a couple of nasty scratches across his cheek.

Taz thrust the flowers at Nico. "Here, have these."

"Thanks," said Nico. "I don't think a man's ever bought me flowers before. Or a woman, come to think of it."

"I bought them for Isabel, but it was a waste of time – she refuses to talk to me. Totally my own fault – she found out I'd been shagging Jemma."

"If you're hoping for sympathy, you've come to the wrong guy. I'm trying to work. I've a deadline looming, no material to fill a book of 100,000 words – and a splitting headache. So I'd be grateful if you'd just piss off to the nearest bar like you usually do when one of your indiscretions blows up in your face. Sort out your own shit. I'm not Patrick."

Taz, one of the few men tall enough to look Nico in the eye, ignored this tirade and peered over his shoulder into the hallway. "Interesting pad," he said. "Gonna show me around?"

"Oh for fuck's sake!"

"Thanks, mate!" Taz turned sideways to squeeze past him and into the house.

"Come on in," Nico didn't bother to hide his sarcasm. "Make yourself at home. I guess you want a drink too?"

Taz, strolling down the hall, his hands in his pockets, was apparently fascinated by the scuffed brown carpet, the little 1930s telephone table just inside the door, and the kitsch prints of forest wildlife hanging from the picture-rail.

Nico was forced to repeat the question: "Do you want a drink?"

"Got any beer?"

"No, just coffee. Black coffee."

Taz grimaced. "OK. If you insist."

Nico went into the kitchen, shoved the flowers into the sink, which was already overflowing with last night's washing-up, and switched on the kettle.

"I can't believe you're living here," Taz was saying, staring in disbelief at the yellow daisies a previous occupant had painstakingly painted on the doors of the kitchen cupboards. "Why didn't you get a place down at the quay like me?"

"She's *your* girlfriend, let her move in with you. Hey, you could give her a job as a backing singer with Talisman!"

Taz shuddered. "No way – Carson hates her. Please, I'm begging you on my knees. This rift Isabel's got going with Jemma is all my fault; I can't bear to think of her all on her own." His voice cracked. "You know, I love her to pieces."

Nico regarded him steadily. "You should have thought of that before you hit on Jemma."

* * *

Damn, I'm a soft touch!

Nico strode down the corridor of Norchester General in search of Isabel. After being forced to ask for directions, he was surprised to find she was not in a private room, but in a ward with three other women. This feud with Danielle must be serious, if Isabel was reduced to going NHS.

Walking breezily into the ward, not entirely oblivious to the admiring glances from the other patients, he sat down in the armchair beside Isabel's bed. Visiting time was well under way, and the others in the ward had two or three visitors each, the tables beside their beds laden with fruit, chocolates, large plastic vases of flowers. Isabel's was conspicuously empty; she didn't even have a get-well card.

Soon fix that, he thought, swinging the Tesco carrier-bag between his fingers. He had come bearing gifts – but not flowers. He had no wish to suffer the same indignity as Taz and risk having his face ripped open by a bouquet of roses.

"Hi there," he said, to the lump under the regulation white blanket. "How are you doing?"

"Piss off!"

"Charming as ever!" He helped himself to a drink of water from the jug beside the bed. Then, when that failed to provoke a reaction, rustled the carrier-bag enticingly. "I've bought you a present."

"I don't want your stinking flowers."

The man sitting beside the next bed glanced at Nico in concern.

"Pre-menstrual," mouthed Nico.

Isabel rolled over. "I heard that! My period's not due for another two – "

"Here you go," said Nico, dropping the carrier-bag into her lap. "Get well soon!"

Isabel looked at the bag as though it contained a severed head. "What's this?"

"Well, it's not flowers."

"I can see it's not sodding flowers."

"Why don't you take a look inside and find out for yourself?"

"Is it chocolates?"

"No."

"Bugger!" Isabel shuffled into a sitting position. "The hospital food is crap."

"Sorry, next time I'll bring along a pizza."

She poked the bag suspiciously. "Why don't you just tell me what's inside?"

"Because then it wouldn't be a surprise!"

"I hate surprises!"

He smiled wryly. "I remember."

She glanced up at the bandage around his head and her lips twisted. "We look like a couple of bookends!"

"You say the sweetest things."

Isabel gave an exaggerated sigh and peeked into the bag. "It'd better not be some kind of trick, something revolting," she warned – but even she was taken back by the small square box that fell out, wrapped in iridescent pink paper and tied with a white ribbon.

He searched her face for some kind of emotion but after the initial look of surprise there was none.

"I bet you didn't wrap this," was her only comment, as she tugged at the ribbon, the paper unfurling itself.

Nico wished he hadn't bothered. "Go on, say something nice."

"I think I'll wait and see what it is first." Isabel pulled away the last of the paper and stared at the blue and silver box inside. "It's a Discman," she said in surprise. And as she lifted turned it over to read the back, she noticed the CDs beneath. "Bloody hell!"

Nico felt himself relax. He hadn't a clue what sort of music she liked and had just picked up the latest chart compilations. But as her face split into a wide grin he found himself smiling too. She liked them! For once, he'd actually done the right thing.

"I don't know what to say . . ."

"Say 'thanks'."

"Thanks! It was a great idea. I'm really touched."

"I thought you might be bored."

"I am! Because I had concussion they're not letting me out until the end of the week. The other girls in here are very kind – they keep lending me their books and magazines, but I can't concentrate." She paused. "I . . . I keep seeing the accident happening over and over again. Except in my version, the car catches fire . . . and I . . . well, I'm sure you can work out the rest."

Nico indicated the little television beside the bed. "Why don't you watch a film, take your mind off it? They have all the movie channels . . ."

"I . . ." Isabel lowered her head and avoided looking directly at him. "I can't afford it. You have to pay extra."

"Is that all!" Nico reached inside his jacket for his wallet.

"No! I can't let you do that."

He shrugged. "You can pay me back if it makes you feel better."

"How?" she said bitterly. "With my first dole cheque?"

"I'm glad you brought that subject up." Nico flipped open his wallet, peeled a twenty from the back pocket and nonchalantly dropped it on the bedside table. "I think I've lined up the perfect job for you."

"Oh yes?" The suspicious look was back in her eyes. "What would that be?"

He hesitated. How was he going to put this? He'd already decided to make no mention of Taz's involvement – he had no wish to antagonise her further. The rehearsed speech went completely out of his head and he struggled to find the right words, the words which wouldn't make it look as though he was patronising her.

"You remember Jemma's party?" he said eventually.

She lay back down on the pillows. "How could I forget?"

"When we were dancing, you were singing along to Screaming Jay Hawkins. I thought you had a great voice."

"I don't think I've got it in me to be a cabaret singer."

"You should make a demo, send it in to a few record companies."

Isabel threw her head back and laughed. "Yeah, in my dreams!"

He took a deep breath. It was now or never. "I could get you an audition with an A & R guy."

"Meet many in your line of work?" The mocking note was back in her voice. "Don't tell me, some of your best friends are music executives?"

As this was pretty close to the truth Nico had to bite his lip to stop himself smiling. "It's like this," he began, "My father is Patrick Kearney . . ."

Although Nico hated telling people who his father was, it was almost worth confessing all to Isabel to see the stunned expression on her face. As an added extra, she was struck dumb for a full five seconds too.

"I bet you wish you'd been nicer to me now," he taunted her.

"You having me on, aren't you? This is some kind of wind-up, you've come here to torture me – "

He tossed his mobile onto the bed. "Call Taz if you

don't believe me. He's signed up to Patrick's record company. That's how we met."

"You knew Taz all along and pretended you didn't . . ." She looked up at him. "Why?"

"I was working undercover – remember?"

She handed back the mobile phone. "You're not supposed to use these things in a hospital. They interfere with the equipment."

Nico slid the phone back into his inside pocket. For a moment he thought he had her hooked – all he had to do was reel her in. But now she had a strange, set look about her face. Where had he gone wrong – oh yes: he'd mentioned the book he was writing about her father.

For a moment he was tempted to tell her he'd given up on Isaac's biography – but that would be one lie too many.

"So," he said. "Are you going to come up to Bath with me and meet Patrick?"

No response.

Maybe clarification was needed. "Patrick Kearney – the biggest rock star of the 1980s." Hell, he hoped he wasn't supposed to reel off all Patrick's number ones. He'd only been seven or eight at the peak of Patrick's success and, at that time, he'd considered house music to be the height of cool. Having a dinosaur of rock for a parent had been a major embarrassment.

Isabel began to manically pleat her blanket with thin white fingers, but still did not look at him or even say a word.

OK, try again. "Patrick Kearney – the guy who owns the largest independent record company in the UK . . ." Independent was right – *no one* told the maverick Patrick what to do. Not unless they wanted a job in the morning.

Isabel, running out of blanket, paused, realising the whole ward was totally engrossed in their conversation and eagerly waiting for her to reply. It was like a proposal scene from a Hollywood romcom.

"OK," she said. "If you like . . . "

Talk about anti-climax. Nico felt his shoulders slump. And he thought *he* was the one about to sell his soul . . .

Chapter Eighteen

The next afternoon, Isabel sat beside Nico as he drove his Ford Fiesta northbound on the A36 and wondered what the hell they were going to talk about for the next one hour, forty-five minutes – the exact time it would take them to journey from Calahurst to Bath, where Nico's father lived.

She had already sensed that he and his father did not get on. At the very least, he did not want to talk about him, which ruled out all the usual exchange of family information – brothers, sisters, parental divorces and 'What we did on our holidays when I was six'. She could talk about the weather, but it was November, this was England, and it was raining. She could ask him why he was suddenly so keen on helping her launch a career as a pop singer when, up until now, they'd never really hit it off – but she realised she didn't want to know the answer. She knew it already. He was still gathering material for his book.

Basically, they were using each other.

So instead of talking, Isabel slunk down in her seat, turning her head away from him to stare through the rain-splattered windows at the bare, blackened hedgerows and pretended to go to sleep.

She realised she actually had drifted off when Nico roughly shook her shoulder and called out, "Hey, Sleeping Beauty!" – which was followed by the sound of a car door being slammed.

Were they there already? She struggled to open her eyes. The combination of Nico's rattling yet efficient car-heater, plus his Sade CD, had lulled her into sleep. She had no time to check her lipstick was still intact and not smeared across her shoulder with drool as he suddenly opened the passenger door.

"Move your butt," he said. "I'm getting soaked out here."

Prince Charmless, thought Isabel darkly, sliding from the car seat.

They ran across a tarmac carpark, splashing through lake-like puddles, towards a glass door. Isabel dashed inside and realised that, instead of being in some rock star's mansion, she was standing inside a Little Chef, gently steaming.

"Table for two?" enquired a waitress politely, then led them off through the maze of tables to seats by the window, where they could admire the view of the rain-lashed carpark and the lorries hurtling at high speed along the dual carriageway. She waited until they were seated, then handed them each an enormous menu.

Isabel regarded it blankly. Nico, who had a father who could probably buy out Richard Branson several times over, had taken her to a Little Chef? Cheapskate!

"Whaddya fancy?" asked Nico, slinging his leather jacket over the back of his seat, before poring over the menu, practically salivating in anticipation of some juicy steak.

Isabel, making the effort to concentrate, glanced again at the menu. She could feel her cholesterol levels rising by the minute.

"Erm . . ."

"Spoilt for choice, eh?" he grinned. "I'm going to have a mixed grill. I didn't have time for lunch and I'm starving. Shall I order the same for you?"

"Ugh!"

He looked at her in surprise. So did everyone else. The pensioners on their mid-week special; the young families stopping off on their way to visit Granny; the clutch of businessmen, slurping coffee; and the chef, letting his burgers burn. All stared at Isabel.

Isabel squirmed. "Erm, that is, I'm not really hungry, maybe a small salad . . ." She flipped over the pages of the menu. "They do salads, don't they?"

"So now you're Bugs Bunny?" said Nico scornfully. "Come on, girl, you need feeding up! How about a cappuccino and a Danish?"

And a heart attack on the side, thought Isabel queasily. "OK," she said, not wanting to make a fuss. If she upset him, he was just as likely to abandon her here. "That's fine."

Nico placed their order with the waitress.

"Have we much further to go?" Isabel asked him.

"About forty-five minutes. My father lives on the north side of Bath. I thought we'd have a meal first – don't want to arrive too soon – "

"He does know we're coming?"

"Sure. I phoned him last night."

Isabel envisaged wild, rock-star parties that went on until dawn. "Do you think he might be still in bed?"

"Heck, no! He'll be blasting the hell out of the local wildlife. The fox-hunting season started this month and since he bought the place he's been enjoying life as a country gentleman."

Which didn't exactly conjure up a genial Santa Claus figure about to make all her dreams come true, worried Isabel. Later, watching Nico shovelling bacon and sausages into his mouth without a care in the world, she found she couldn't eat her Danish pastry – it stuck in her throat. What was she letting herself in for? Was it too late to return to Calahurst?

After Nico had paid the bill from another wad of tenners, they climbed back into the car to continue their journey. Nico swapped the Sade CD for the B52s and turned the volume up really loud to drown out the air-conditioning. The whole car began to vibrate to the beat of 'Rock Lobster'.

"That'll keep you awake!" he grinned, as he pulled out of the carpark.

And also prevented any possible conversation . . .

* * *

Due to a traffic snarl-up in the centre of Bath, they eventually arrived at Patrick Kearney's house at four o'clock. Ten minutes outside Bath, driving along a narrow winding lane, where the hedgerow growing on either side was too high to see over, Nico suddenly veered off to the left, practically colliding with a pair of huge wrought-iron gates. He wound down his window, keyed a number into a little black box beside the drive, then slowly, majestically even, the gates glided back.

Nico hardly waited for them to complete the manoeuvre before releasing the brake and shooting through. Isabel shut her eyes, convinced they were going to scrape the paintwork, but there was no bump, no shriek of metal, so she opened them again – to find the Fiesta was flying down a long tarmac road, between towering pines.

She glanced across at Nico, speculating on his apparent need for haste. They had taken nearly three hours to get to this point and stopped at the Little Chef so as not to arrive too early, or so he said – so what difference did an extra few minutes make at this point? One look at his hard, set, face precluded any attempt at asking him. Did he dislike his father that much? Or maybe his father disliked him . . .

After several minutes, when there was still no sign of any house, Isabel began to wonder if they had come to the right place. Then Nico careered around a corner, bumped along a dirt track for a matter of seconds and, almost before Isabel had time to register a medieval gatehouse, the car clattered onto a small bridge across a moat and straight through it.

Directly in front, in the shape of a lop-sided 'U', was a beautiful, sprawling manor house, built from red and yellow sandstone, with an array of oval, leaded windows and a roof of grey slate edged, in places, by crenellations. At one end there appeared to be a chapel, with a huge stained-glass window, and, in the gardens beyond, Isabel could just glimpse the ruin of some great hall, almost obliterated by the trees and a creeper that had entwined it.

"Good grief," said Isabel, as Nico parked the car right outside the front door of the manor, "it's a bloody castle!"

"It's an abbey," corrected Nico, throwing open his door and striding around to open up the boot and retrieve their bags. He possessed a smart Gucci suitcase; Isabel only had the battered Nike kitbag the police had been able to retrieve from the wreckage of her car. He slung her bag over his shoulder to leave his right hand free. "At least, it was an abbey until first Henry VIII, and then later Oliver Cromwell, tried to flatten it."

Which kind of knocked Stortford House into a cocked hat . . .

Isabel slid quickly out of the car and followed closely behind Nico, in case he disappeared into the house without her. The front door was not particularly large, but had highly decorative stonework surrounding it. There was no lock (not really needed when one had a gatehouse, drawbridge and moat to prevent marauders), only a large iron ring which Nico turned and the door opened.

The hall did not disappoint. Dark and gloomy, only relieved by the weak sunlight filtering through the windows, casting intricate shadows of the tracery across the flagstoned floor. The walls were adorned with tapestries and pennants, so tattered and worn they had to be genuine, and on either side of the hall were massive stone fireplaces, embellished by rampant lions holding shields.

As the fires were giving out some considerable heat – and rather sooty smoke – Isabel went to stand next to one while they waited for Patrick. She felt cold and damp, and was starting to wish she had access to her extensive wardrobe instead of one grubby kitbag. How was she going to impress Patrick Kearney wearing Gap jeans and one of Talisman's old tour T-shirts? What if Talisman were no longer signed to Patrick's company? Isabel quickly fastened the buttons on her denim jacket as an older man, casually dressed in an open-necked shirt and Gap jeans identical to her own, walked confidently into the hall.

"Hi, Nicolas!" he said, genuinely pleased to see them. "Shall I take your bags?"

Nico's father? Isabel started forward, her hand outstretched.

"No, thanks, Henry," grunted Nico. "I'm quite capable of managing by myself. Where's Patrick?"

OK, *not* Nico's father. Some kind of personal assistant perhaps?

The smile on Henry's face was becoming a trifle fixed. "Oh well, you know, busy old day!"

Nico's eyebrows drew together. "You mean, he couldn't be bothered to meet us?"

"Not at all, not at all. Mr Kearney has had his nose to the grindstone all week." Henry dropped his voice to a more confiding tone, although it still echoed loudly around the hall as though he was reading a lesson in church. "The Lost Boys' latest album is going rather badly . . ."

"He's in the recording studios?"

Recording studios? Here? Isabel perked up.

"Yes – but don't disturb him." Henry was now anxiously wringing his hands together. "He wouldn't be pleased."

"So we're expected to hang around until he deigns to put in an appearance?"

Henry attempted a bright smile, although it wobbled slightly at the edges. "Why don't I show you to the guest house? Then you can shower, relax, watch TV – Mr Kearney's had a new television and a whole DVD library installed since Talisman trashed it last summer."

Isabel folded her arms over her jacket.

"I can find my own way to the guest house. I used to live here, remember?" Nico hoisted Isabel's kitbag back onto his shoulder. "Come on," he instructed her, "there's no point waiting here. Let's go."

"Home?" In spite of her misgivings about the trip, Isabel felt a great whack of disappointment.

"No – to the guest house!" He kicked the door back with his foot, so that he could get himself and both bags through before it closed upon him. "I'm not that damned sensitive!"

Henry, trying to be helpful, made a grab for the door too late and was barged out of the way without so much as an apology.

Isabel trailed after Nico, her faith in his ability to arrange an audition with his father now more than a little shaken. "Why can't we stay here?" she grumbled. "Why have we been banished to a guest house?"

"The *gate*house," corrected Nico. "It's the opposite number to the one we've just driven through. Patrick hates having to share his house with strangers in case he wants to run round the house naked, or ravish the parlour maid on the billiard table."

Nico was conjuring up a very odd mental picture of Patrick Kearney. Or was he taking the piss? Looking up at his sour expression, Isabel decided he was probably not. Why did she get an overwhelming feeling that this was all going to be a horrible mistake?

To avoid antagonising him further, she remained silent as they followed a flagstoned path around the side of the house, CCTV cameras following their every move. All this security reminded her of Stortford House. Patrick would have got on very well with Danielle.

They walked past the ruin, which shielded a large outdoor pool from the worst of British summers and was incongruously covered by twenty-first century tarpaulin. Beyond were four leaf-strewn tennis courts. Nico took an abrupt right turn and stalked off across the lawn, between mature chestnut, walnut and mulberry trees. Isabel was wondering if they were going to have to walk much further, and whether they should have brought the car, when they emerged on the other side of the garden where, built into the surrounding wall, was the strangest looking, tower-cum-small-castle. It looked as though it had been airlifted in from Disneyland, Paris.

"Oh my God," she said, before she could stop herself.

"Patrick actually," said Nico, grinning, his black mood having apparently lifted. "He's into castles and forts in a big way. It was converted for my mother – a place for her to stay when she visited the UK after their divorce. That way she could visit me and avoid bumping into Patrick's current mistress."

It was the first time Nico had mentioned having a mother. While aware it would have been impossible for him to have started life without one, somehow Isabel had assumed she was long since dead, like her own mother. She wanted to ask him more – but decided she didn't have the courage. She'd save it for when they were a bit chummier.

"Now the gatehouse is used as guest accommodation," Nico was saying. "Talisman stayed here last year, when they were working on their 'Amulet of Thor' album."

"Which is when you met Taz," said Isabel. The pieces of the jigsaw puzzle that were Nicolas Kearney were slowly beginning to fit together.

"We're old friends. When Danielle introduced us at Jacob's restaurant, he nearly blew my cover!"

Isabel wished he had. It would have saved a lot of heartache.

The gatehouse was certainly an unusual building. It was square, built from the same stone as the abbey, but with a turret on each corner, possibly added recently to emphasise the appearance of a miniature castle. The entrance arch, that would have extended right through the centre as in the case of its twin, had been bricked up, leaving a much smaller door.

Nico held it open for her. "In you go," he muttered and flicked on an electric light so she could see where she was going.

Instead of the ubiquitous flagstones, there were polished oak floors with islands of antique rugs. The walls were plastered and painted pale tangerine, the furniture was of heavy wood and very old. It was all quite tasteful – the only clue that the room had been decorated by a rock star, rather than a hereditary peer, were the three squashy couches, covered in the softest leather, the colour of dark chocolate. The jarring note was what appeared to be a large, grey-green lizard, frozen in mid-scurry across the wall, above the fireplace. It gave Isabel the creeps.

"Is that real?" she demanded.

Nico dropped the bags on the floor and flexed his fingers to get the circulation moving. "I'm afraid so. But it's dead!"

Like that made it better? "I should hope so,"

muttered Isabel. "Seeing as somebody's nailed its feet to the wall!"

"Patrick got it from a sale of movie memorabilia years ago. He often picks up artefacts that way. I've forgotten which movie it was in. You'll have to ask him. He's mad about movies – always wanted to be in one. He thinks he's John Wayne reincarnated."

Isabel now had a mental picture of Patrick Kearney, Eccentric Rock Star, who hunted girls dressed up as French maids, wearing nothing more than a Stetson. Scary.

"Don't fret, you won't be on your own. I'm staying here too."

Isabel looked at him in shock. "You don't have your own room at the main house?"

"I'm twenty-six years old. I left home a long time ago."

"But – but . . ." Isabel was having trouble thinking exactly what to say. Whatever came out of her mouth at that moment was likely to make her sound like someone's maiden aunt. The days of the chaperone are over, she told herself firmly. Nico's not interested in you. *He's only interested in his book!*

Unfortunately at that moment Nico chose to make the situation worse. "Patrick is under the impression you're my girlfriend."

"*What*!"

He shrugged. "The only way I could figure on getting him to see you, was if you pretended to be my girlfriend, came here for one of his parties, and jammed along with the other musicians – let him discover you himself."

"There's no formal audition?"

"It's better this way," he smiled encouragingly. "Less pressure for you."

"You tricked me!"

Nico rolled his eyes. "You're going to meet Patrick Kearney, sing for him. I never promised you more than that."

"You *promised* me an *audition*! Your actual words were, and I quote, 'I can get you an audition'."

"You know how many other girls would kill for this opportunity?"

"Bollocks! You had no intention of getting me an audition with your father – you wanted to lure me up here, into this overgrown playhouse, to get me on my own, so you can – " Isabel suddenly realised what she was implying and stopped abruptly, her cheeks burning fiery red.

Nico finished the sentence for her. "Have my wicked way with you? Please! I could have had you in Calahurst, in the comfort of my own house – why did you think I took you back there after Jemma's party?"

Isabel felt as though she'd been struck dumb. He'd taken her back to his house to have *sex*? And she thought it was just so he could collect paperwork! Danielle was right. She *was* stupid! She was naïve, she was –

She was kidding herself. She'd seen the look he'd given her on the dance floor. She knew he wanted her. If she was going to be honest with herself, she'd wanted him too.

"So why would I go to all the trouble of dragging you up here?" Nico metaphorically put the boot in.

Why indeed? Isabel sank onto one of couches, unable to look him in the eye. She looked at all the silver rings on her fingers instead.

"Look," added Nico, with more kindness in his voice. "I'm going to have a shower. I'm tired, I just want to chill in front of the TV, watch a movie, until Patrick decides to put in an appearance. What you do is up to you. Call a cab if you want to go home. I'll pay. But remember what you're going back to. No job, no friends, no family, no home."

Well, thank *you,* Nicolas Kearney! Her life summed up in less than a sentence. At least he didn't add, 'no life' and 'no hope'.

As she failed to answer, Nico turned and walked away, disappearing up a winding staircase in the corner of the room, lugging the bags behind him.

Isabel remained on the couch, mindlessly twisting her silver rings around and around on her fingers, until they were swollen and painful, and the tears welling in her eyes finally began to drop onto the soft brown leather of the couch.

Chapter Nineteen

Pale sunshine filtered through a network of branches, creating a delicate fretwork shadow across the forest floor and dispelling the lingering mist. It was quiet too – no birds singing, no squirrels scurrying up into the ancient oaks, the only movement the gold and amber leaves scuffled up into the air as Isabel kicked her way through them, giving vent to her frustrations.

Nicolas Kearney! Thud – her boot kicked a horse chestnut with such venom it smashed into a tree and split open. *Irritating bastard!* Crack, as her heel crunched down hard on a decaying branch, rupturing it in two. *Self-satisfied, evil, son of a bitch!* Ping! Her toe caught on a stone, sending it flying across the clearing, where it hit a gleaming, cherry-red Jaguar.

Isabel stared in horror. The beautifully waxed and polished car now had a wide scratch scored into the immaculate paintwork – all the way along the side. Her first impulse was to run off. But, with Nico's taunts from last night still ringing in her ears, she approached the car, expecting at any moment for the irate owner to jump out, waving his fist and screaming obscenities. Or worse, some businessman, shagging his secretary, stumble out of one of the rear doors, zipping up his flies.

As nothing happened she had to deduce the car was empty. It was a strange place to park, though. Unless the car had been stolen? Isabel bent to peer through the windows, shielding her reflection with her hand against the glass, but all she could see was thick grey smoke.

She caught hold of the door handle to wrench it open, but the touch of the chrome burnt and she pulled her hand away.

Nico appeared beside her. "What's the matter?"

"The car's on fire," she could hear her voice rising, panic-stricken. "I can see smoke inside. Someone might be trapped – like my father . . ."

"Your father's dead." His voice was calm, detached.

Flames were now beginning to flicker from beneath the bonnet.

"But we must do *something*!"

"You can't do anything, Isabel. It's too late."

"Too late!" Tired of holding out for Nico-the-Hero, Isabel darted forward, intending to wrench open the door, regardless of any danger.

Nico's arms reached out and enfolded her, pulling her back against him, no matter how hard she struggled.

"Let me go!" She tried to kick out at him, but he held her firmly and she was forced to watch as the car was transformed into an empty blackened shell in a matter of minutes. "What if someone was in there?" she sobbed. "What if someone died and we did nothing?"

But Nico was shaking her abruptly. "Wake up, Isabel! Wake up!"

The forest evaporated like fine mist and Isabel was sitting up in bed, Nico perched on the edge of the mattress, his fingers digging into her shoulders.

"Wake up," he repeated. "You're having a bad dream."

Her heart thudding, she realised she was back in her bedroom at the gatehouse and tried to get her head around the idea that nothing she had seen was real.

"Are you OK?" Nico asked gently. His eyes were half-closed from sheer tiredness, blue stubble peppered his chin and his dark hair was sticking up in all directions.

Touched by his concern, she nodded, blinking away the easy tears. He still had his arm around her. It felt warm and comforting and it was so tempting to lean back against him, snuggle in and rest her cheek on his shoulder. So she did.

"I'm sure it's the painkillers I was given at the hospital," she said. "They're giving me the most bizarre dreams. Surreal. Like I stepped into a Dali painting."

"*That* bad, eh?"

"I'm walking through the forest when I come across a red car. I can see smoke on the other side of the windows yet the outside of the car is perfect. I start to think my father's inside – but I can't open the door because the handle is so hot I burn my hand. The car turns into a burnt-out wreck and all I can do is watch."

"Grim."

Isabel, cuddled into his shoulder, was unable to check on his expression; she could only view his mouth and chin. And what a beautiful mouth it was. A few inches closer and he'd be kissing her. All he had to do was turn his head towards her . . . and if she lifted her face to his, parting her lips invitingly . . .

Nico abruptly removed his shoulder from beneath her head and she fell back against the headboard with a clunk.

Isabel regarded him in surprise. Everything had been going so well and now he was standing on the opposite side of the room, his hands shoved into the pockets of his towelling robe, a wary look about him. Did he think his virtue was at stake here?

"Would you like me to make you a mug of cocoa?" he suggested, the slightest of smiles curving that seductive mouth. "To help you sleep?"

Actually, I'd rather you kept me awake all night, thought Isabel sulkily. Honestly, *cocoa*? The favoured beverage of little old ladies? Unless it was the name for some new, illicit substance she hadn't yet heard of? But would he be offering to serve it up in a mug?

"Thanks," she muttered ungraciously.

"No problem." He turned away and walked towards the door. "Come downstairs when you're ready."

Isabel waited until the door had closed behind him, then leapt out of bed and began yanking a hairbrush through her unruly curls, wincing when she caught on the stitches. A squirt of perfume where she hoped to be kissed – which was pretty much everywhere really, then she stuck one leg into her jeans and hopped around the room until she'd got her other leg in beside it, yanked the jeans up over her thighs, breathed in sharply and fastened the catch. She tugged her Talisman T-shirt over her head, first giving it a quick sniff to check it was OK. It had to be. She had only one other T-shirt – apart from the one she was using as a nightshirt – and she was saving that for tomorrow night.

Hardly daring to check out her reflection, she was gratified to see she looked respectable, if a trifle rumpled. (Rumpled was good. Rumpled was *sexy.*) Unfortunately she couldn't wear make-up because of the bruises around her eye, and the gash still livid on her forehead. But she cleaned her teeth again and slicked on some clear lip-gloss. Wearing lipstick would seem as though she was trying too hard and she didn't want to look desperate, just kissable.

As Isabel carefully descended the twisting and very worn stone staircase, clutching for dear life onto the fraying rope 'banister', she was surprised to hear loud rock music emanating from the sitting-room. She knew Nico well enough by now to know he never went far without his CD collection but, at two o'clock in the morning, she had expected something a little more soothing than Aerosmith.

"Hi," said Nico, emerging from the opposite staircase which led to the kitchen/diner in the cellar below. He was carrying two strawberry-pink mugs, the size of small goldfish bowls, filled to the brim with frothy hot chocolate. Carefully he placed them on the shiny surface of one of the little round Moroccan tables. "Hope you like this. It's made to my mother's special recipe."

Precisely the opener she needed, decided Isabel, seizing the opportunity to interrogate him about his own dysfunctional family. "Does your mother like cooking?"

He wagged a finger at her. "*You* are seriously nosy."

She pouted, giving him the full benefit of her glossed-up lips. "I'm a woman, we're allowed to be."

He smiled as he flopped onto one of the couches, but didn't answer. He spread his arms along the back, stretched his legs out in front of him and stared at her unwaveringly, with those dark fathomless eyes, as though daring her to ask another question.

Isabel took up her seat on the couch opposite him. If she extended her own legs towards him, there was always the opportunity for footy-footy over the rug. My, what sexy legs he had! And was he wearing anything beneath that robe?

"Well?" she demanded. "Did your mother bake or did she serve you up ready-meals from Marks & Spencer?"

He regarded her silently for a moment. "My father employed a chef," he said at last, "and still does. My mother had her own career – she had no interest in baking or any other 'home-making' skills – it didn't make her any less of a good person."

Career? That implied high profile. "What did she do? Was she a singer too?"

"No, she modelled. Now she acts, in little theatres off Broadway. She doesn't care much for the movies."

Broadway? "As in New York? Is she American?" This explained his accent. Isabel felt as though she was rapidly crossing off all the numbers on a winning lottery ticket.

"Second generation Puerto Rican born in New York City. Her family name is 'Morales' – I borrow it when I go undercover." He smiled wryly. "It suits me better than 'Kearney' – I'm aware I don't look remotely Irish."

Morales – it couldn't be . . .

"Are you telling me *Maria Morales* is your *mother*?" A rock-star father and a supermodel for a mother – one *hell* of a gene pool! No wonder he was so damn sexy!

Nico smiled that half-smile she was beginning to find so aggravating, picked up the remote control that lay on the table next to the drinks and pressed a button. Isabel thought he was going to switch on the TV, but instead the fire roared into life, like some kind of supernatural special effect, making her clutch the arms of the sofa in shock.

He abruptly switched it off. "Sorry, that was tactless. Guess I really freaked you out?"

"No – you just took me by surprise. I . . . er, thought it was a *real* log fire."

"It's a fake," he agreed. "But it heats the room and looks good in the style magazines." He switched the fire back on, this time on a lower setting. "Drink your chocolate – we're letting it get cold." He reached forward and took one of the mugs.

Isabel picked up the other and took a swig of chocolate. It was wonderful stuff. She relaxed into the sofa. "My father would have loved this place," she sighed. "He was a real gadgets freak. He had the most amazing collection of sports cars, all the latest models. I suppose Dani will sell them now . . ."

"You were dreaming about him . . ."

"The strangest thing was that the car he was driving when he died was a green Jag not a red one. Do you think it's a sign of some kind?"

"Who knows?" Nico picked up his cigarettes and lit one, closing his eyes and leaning back, blowing the smoke skywards. As he stretched out his leg, his foot accidentally brushed against hers. He moved it away without comment or apology.

Isabel frowned. He was deliberately misreading the signals she was sending out. He must really dislike spending time with her. He certainly wasn't bothering to pretend otherwise.

Feeling like being awkward she said, "Do you think you could play something other than Aerosmith?"

He opened one eye and feigned surprise. "You don't like Aerosmith? I thought everyone liked Aerosmith."

"Not at two thirty in the morning."

"You don't have to worry about the neighbours," he said, lowering his voice with mock menace. "Out here, no one can hear you scream."

He was winding her up again. Just when she thought she'd got him sussed as a nice person, he would do something that really pissed her off. So much for the amateur psychology.

"I would like to listen something quieter!" she said firmly.

"Hey, listen to us! We're arguing like a genuine couple."

And in a minute he was going to get a genuine mug of cocoa over his head! Isabel gritted her teeth and remembered why she'd gone to bed early in the first place. If Nico didn't provoke her so much, she could have fallen asleep at a more reasonable time and wouldn't feel so wide awake now. This was all his fault.

As Isabel failed to take the bait, Nico gathered his robe about him, stood up and padded over to the state-of-the-art music system. "What do you fancy?"

"I leave it up to you." *Not Talisman. Please not Talisman!*

He stuck on Whitney Houston's greatest hits, which wasn't quite what she had in mind either, but at least it wasn't Celine Dion which would have really finished her off.

He seemed reluctant to return to his seat and she watched him light up another cigarette and restlessly pace the room instead. The hot chocolate, instead of calming him down, appeared to be hyping him up.

"Are you nervous about meeting your father tomorrow?" she asked. *Lie on the couch and tell me about your unhappy childhood . . .*

Nico took a long drag on his cigarette. "No."

"You're pacing – it's a man thing. My father used to do it all the time. Something bothered him and he'd be walking around his study like one of those caged animals at the zoo. You know, the really psycho ones that go up and down, up and down, staring at you all the time with their mean little psycho eyes." And she made little eye-like shapes with her thumbs and forefingers.

Nico stopped directly behind her. "Thanks, that's a real insight. And helpful too."

"If you don't want to talk, shall I switch the TV on?"

"Hell, no!" he brutally stubbed out his half-smoked cigarette on the stone window-ledge behind him. "At this time of night it'll be porn or Judy Garland."

"And I don't know which is worse," deadpanned Isabel. She took another swig of cocoa; it was fabulous stuff. If he offered the recipe to Cadburys she was sure he'd make a fortune. "Who would have thought that a model could invent such a fattening drink?"

He leant over the back of the sofa. The spark of humour had left his eyes. "Don't you *ever* give up?"

Which was guaranteed to put her back on the defensive. "We're going to have to talk about *something*. So why can't we talk about *you*? You've already discovered all there is to know about me."

"So let's talk about movies, music, books – "

"Yes, let's talk about *your* book. Why did you choose my father out of all the possible victims you could have picked – or do you have a thing about Calahurst? After all, you liked it so much you rented a house there."

"*Rented?* How did – ?" He paused. "Was it that obvious?"

"All the brown and mustard décor? It wasn't really 'you'. Neither is that heap of scrap metal you call a car."

"The Bat Mobile?" Finally he smiled. "It belonged to my brother – he learned to drive in it and never got rid of it – he's soft-hearted like that. The motorbike is mine."

Isabel pounced. "You have a *brother*?"

"Yes, I have a brother."

Isabel scowled. "Making small talk with you is like interrogating James Bond. Perhaps I should threaten to feed you to some piranhas. Don't you 'do' polite conversation? I bet you're a real hit at parties. Or do you stay in the kitchen?"

That wry smile was back on his lips. "You shouldn't ask 'closed' questions – ones that just require a 'yes' or 'no' answer. You're setting yourself up for failure."

"I never actually wanted to work for the Spanish Inquisition."

"I'll make it easy for you. I have a brother, he's twenty-three, my father named him Lachlan after his Scottish grandfather. My mother wanted to call him Lazlo, after *her* grandfather – so I think he got off lightly."

"Do you have any sisters?"

"No."

Bugger, another closed question. As she looked up at his now wide smile, and itched to wipe it from his face, she decided to throw in a grenade to stir things up a bit. "Why don't you get on with your father?"

"No comment."

"Cheat!"

"You think this is truth or dare? You're invading my privacy here."

His privacy? Typical bloody journalist! "Why do you have so make such a big thing about not talking about your family? You know, I think you're attention-seeking."

"And you're blowing things out of proportion."

"Sod you, I'm going to bed!"

He smiled. Slowly and leisurely. "Running away again?"

"I am not! And what do you mean by 'again'?"

He settled himself onto the arm of the couch, where he could look down at her in a very condescending manner. "What happened when you discovered your boyfriend was sleeping with your best friend? Did you confront them? Threaten them? Drive over them in your little blue car? No, *you* ran away."

"Which is a grown-up thing to do! I don't know how it is Stateside, but in this country murder is illegal!"

"How about when you found out your father had left you nothing in his will? Did you call in your own lawyer? Contest it?"

"What would have been the point of that?"

"You'd rather let Danielle have everything?"

"She's always worked hard for the business. She deserved to inherit 'everything'."

"Heroic – but when she kicked you out of the family home, you didn't stand your ground and fight that either."

"I thought I'd let her calm down. You know how Danielle flies off the handle. She'd have apologised – eventually."

Nico shook his head. "I don't know how you ever think you're going to succeed in the music business. You have no killer instinct. You let people walk all over you."

"Excuse me? My new pop career was your idea, remember?"

"You'd rather be waiting tables?"

Why did he do that? One minute they were flirting nicely, the next he was on the defensive, then he was turning nasty. She decided on a little dig to recover some ground, get her own back.

"At the Little Chef? I can't believe you took me there. This is prime tourist country. There must have been dozens of smart restaurants."

"I think the Little Chef is great," he said slowly. "It's my favourite place to eat when I'm travelling. If I spent all my hard-earned money in fashionable restaurants I'd soon have none left. Which, when you start earning a wage, you'll find out soon enough."

"Your father is Patrick Kearney. He must be a billionaire? You don't need to work for a living."

"I certainly do. It's his money, not mine."

"Don't you have an allowance? A trust fund?"

"Don't you listen? I left home a long time ago. I make my own way in this world and I pay my own bills."

"Like I'm going to."

The mocking half-smile made a reappearance. "Sure you will."

Isabel stood up, her leg knocking against the table; it wobbled, slopping the hot chocolate across the table. "You really are the archetypal journalist. You ignore the facts and twist the lies around to suit yourself. I don't have to stay and listen to you condemn me like this. I can bugger off back to Calahurst."

"You can," he agreed, "but you should listen to what I'm saying. It's the truth – and I don't think people tell you the truth very often. Your fair-weather friends tell you what you want to hear and you're too stupid to tell the difference."

Stupid? "What did I ever do to you, that you have to be such a bastard to me?"

"It's not personal. I'm giving you a wake-up call. You don't want to reach sixty-five and find you've done nothing with your life. That everything has passed you by and all you've got to look forward to is dying in your sleep in 'Sunnydale Retirement Home'."

As 'Sunnydale' was the home of Taz's favourite vampire-slayer – Isabel found herself thinking – dying in her *sleep* would be the last thing she could look forward to.

Nico reached across the sofa for his packet of cigarettes and flipped out another. His shoulder brushed against her. This time it was Isabel who jerked away from him.

"Sorry," he said, not looking remotely apologetic. He took a cheap plastic lighter from his pocket.

Isabel snatched it from his hand and threw it across the room, smacking the lizard on the head. It wobbled violently, but unfortunately failed to fall off the wall.

"You haven't even got the courtesy to ask me if you can smoke!" she yelled at him. "Why should I have to breathe in your obnoxious fumes?"

He grinned, refusing to take her seriously. "You can always go back to Calahurst."

"I wouldn't give you the satisfaction!"

A dignified exit was spoilt somewhat by her skidding on one of the rugs as she strode off towards the spiral staircase. At every step she thought he might call her back, apologise, grovel for forgiveness. But there was silence. Could she be sure he was even watching her?

Determined not to cry (crying was for losers and Barbara Cartland heroines), Isabel caught hold of the rope banister and marched upstairs.

Nico watched her leave. Then he picked up their mugs and returned them to the kitchen. Tipping the rest of the hot chocolate away, he helped himself to a beer from the fridge and returned to the sitting-room.

And there he waited, a good ten minutes, for all the deliberate stomping about above his head to die down, before he took out his laptop, plugged it into the nearest electric socket, typed in his password and clicked on the file called *'Isabel.doc'*.

Chapter Twenty

"Morning, gorgeous!"

Isabel flipped open her eyes in shock. Nico? In her bedroom? What the hell had *she* got up to last night?

But she didn't recognise the man who was looming over her, so close he filled her entire vision and she could feel his breath on her cheek. Black, shaggy hair; blue, deep-set eyes that creased in the corners as he grinned down at her; and the ravaged complexion of someone who has spent their entire life having too much of a good thing.

"Hi there!" he rasped, in a deep, dark, oh-so-sexy voice.

Isabel opened her mouth and screamed.

He shot back from the bed as though he'd been scalded. "Jesus, Mary and Joseph! Are you trying to give me heart failure?"

Isabel screamed again. Long and loud, her mouth wide open, in true American horror-flick style.

"Shh, shh!" he flapped his hands, gesturing for her to shut up. "Why all the fuss? I'm not going to hurt you! Fuck, some girls would commit a mortal sin to get me into their bed!"

But Isabel carried on screaming; there was a loud crash from the floor above, then footsteps pounding down the turret steps. Nico's long legs appeared first, then he jumped the last couple of stone steps, landing heavily on bare feet as he half fell into Isabel's bedroom.

At the sight of him Isabel shut up. Who wouldn't? He was dripping wet, with traces of shampoo still in his hair and trailing across the smattering of curling black hairs on his chest. With one hand he was clutching a small, white towel around his hips, just about covering his important places. The other hand was pushing water and soap from his eyes.

"What the *fuck* is going on?" he roared. Then he saw the man standing beside Isabel's bed. "Jeez, Patrick! Why didn't you knock? You can't wander into other guys' bedrooms like this!"

Patrick? Isabel's lower jaw dropped. "But you can't be Patrick Kearney, you're too *young*!"

Patrick chuckled and ruffled her hair with a large, callused hand. "I love *you!* You're sure to go far. Hey, Nicolas! I'm sorry I missed you last night, this Lost Boys album is really dragging on. Why I ever thought I ought to move into the boy-band market I'll never know. You should have had me committed when I suggested it."

Nico wrapped the towel a little more firmly around

his waist. He was shivering, Isabel noticed, and his beautiful olive skin had gone all goose-pimply.

"I told you the idea stunk at the time," he said. "Boy bands are so last century. Since when do you listen to me?"

"Never," agreed Patrick cheerfully. "Look, I've brought you breakfast in bed. Aren't you impressed?"

Isabel finally noticed a large silver tray balanced on the dressing-table. What looked like a full English breakfast was congealing slowly on two large plates, with a large bottle of HP sauce wedged between two mugs. Her stomach turned over. Oh, for a muesli and yoghurt! No wonder rock stars died young if this was the sort of crap they ate.

"You mean you couldn't wait to check out my new girlfriend," derided Nico. "Who, incidentally, you terrified half-to-death." He made a point of dripping all way over to Isabel's bed to drop a kiss on her forehead.

Isabel felt her cheeks burn. Try to look natural, she told herself. Try to look as though he does this sort of thing all the time . . .

"Isabel, I want you to meet Patrick. My father."

"Pleased to meet you," she stammered.

Patrick winked. "Likewise."

Horribly self-conscious that Nico's bare chest was only a few inches away, Isabel croaked up at him: "You ought to put some clothes on . . . er, darling. You don't want to catch cold."

Patrick watched this little floor show speculatively. "At least I didn't catch you shagging!" he said blithely.

This time Isabel definitely felt her face colour and wished she could pull the white cotton sheet over her head. Oh, the embarrassment of it all . . . Meeting Patrick Kearney with bed-hair and wearing a T-shirt with 'I Love Britney' printed across the chest. Good grief, she could have been *naked*! Although that would have made her look more rock chick and less suburban wannabe.

"So," Patrick made himself comfortable on the other side of the bed, "what shall we do today?"

Isabel glanced at Nico, expecting him to mention the reason they were visiting. Something tactful about what a great voice she had and how Patrick really ought to hear her sing.

Instead Nico shrugged carelessly. "We're just here for some R and R. You don't have to lay on anything special."

Patrick appeared hurt. "I've taken the day off specially. Once you've had your breakfast, I can give you the tour – Isabel hasn't been here before, have you, my darling? She'd like to look around. Then we can take an early lunch in Bath, maybe ride this afternoon . . . Can you ride, Isabel?"

Isabel nodded. It wasn't quite a lie. She'd ridden a pony along the beach at Port Rell once. When she was eight . . .

"Are you having a party?" interrupted Nico.

Patrick looked hurt. "It's my birthday – to be sure I'm having a party! Usual crowd, plus whoever's booked in to use the studios – The Lost Boys are laying down a couple of tracks. Do you remember Ellis Jackson? He's got a few of the guys over, they're working on a new jazz album – you'll be able to hear them rehearsing in the long barn."

"Quite a celebration then."

"Too right! We've got £60,000 of fireworks to get rid of." Patrick laughed. "It fucking rained on bonfire night – and here was me, with half of Somerset to entertain and a box of damp squibs!"

Isabel involuntarily clutched at the bed-sheets. Fireworks, bonfires . . . oh God, no! How could she face seeing an effigy of Guy Fawkes when she had lost her father in a fire?

Nico's hand closed over hers and gave it a reassuring squeeze. It felt warm and reassuring and Isabel held on to it firmly in case he decided to take it back. Well, she had to go along with the act . . .

Patrick's blue eyes, although baggy and bloodshot, didn't miss a trick. "Are you scared of loud bangs, Isabel?"

How could she tell the truth? If he had any kind of conscience he would cancel the display, which would embarrass her and disappoint his guests. What if he cancelled the party altogether? No karaoke, no fabulous performance on her part, no great impression on Patrick and *zero recording contract*. But there was *no* way she was going to be watching a firework display . . .

Nico answered for her. "We thought we'd have an early night. It's the first chance we've had to be alone together for a long time. I've been working on my book and Isabel helps out in the family business . . ." He smiled lovingly at her, without even the slightest hint of his tongue being firmly in his cheek.

He was a far better actor than her, Isabel marvelled silently. He had deflected Patrick's attempt at family bonding brilliantly.

Patrick was visibly deflated. "Whatever you want," he shrugged, standing up. "You're still coming to the party? We're having a real jamming session tonight."

Was Isabel imagining it, or was there a look of pleading behind the nonchalance?

"Sure," said Nico, in his usual laconic fashion.

They both watched Patrick leave via the turret staircase, down to the sitting-room below, but didn't relax until they'd heard the front door shut behind him.

"Thanks, Nico," said Isabel quietly. "You understand there's no way on earth I'm going to be watching a firework display . . ."

"I'm not a complete bastard," he said firmly, scooping up her hand again, enfolding her cold fingers into his own. "I understand the way you feel. No one is going to make you do anything you don't want to do."

Perhaps he had forgotten he was sitting on her bed, naked from the waist up. For as he raised her hand towards his chest, giving it another reassuring squeeze, her knuckles brushed against his skin.

Isabel felt a strange jolt deep inside and found she was quite unable to look him in the eye. At the risk of appearing like a vestal virgin, social convention did dictate that she should pull her hand back. Curiously enough, she didn't want to. And, curiously enough, she would have quite liked to have spread her fingers right across his chest, feeling the warmth of his skin burn against her palm, and perhaps his heart beating beneath his ribcage, slide her fingers amongst those tiny curls of hair . . .

Nico dropped her hand back into her lap.

"I'd better go finish my shower," he said abruptly. "I've left the water running and there won't be any left for you."

Aching with disappointment, Isabel watched him leave: that wonderful, honey-toned skin, the broad shoulders, and finally his long muscular legs as they disappeared up the steps to the bathroom.

She flopped back against the pillows and harrumphed discontentedly. Who the hell needed a warming shower?

When she was burning up with lust already.

* * *

Neither of them touched the breakfast Patrick had brought over, which was a shame. By the time Nico had finished his shower the food was stone cold and Isabel knew she wouldn't be able to eat even a mouthful of the revolting, greasy, yucky, ucky stuff. So Nico offered to take her into Bath for brunch, and Isabel accepted with alacrity. If she couldn't seduce him on his own turf, perhaps an away match would be more successful. She also sensed that Nico had his own agenda for escaping the abbey. And it all centred around his father.

Isabel found the relationship between father and son quite fascinating. Patrick seemed ready to forgive and forget; Nico still harboured a grudge. *But what for*? The connotations were driving Isabel crazy. He couldn't be holding his father responsible for the divorce – that was years ago. And Nico was a little bit long in the tooth to be jealous of the many women passing through his father's life. Patrick didn't look like a mass murderer, or appear to have any unpleasant perversions which would alienate his son – even his womanising seemed relatively harmless in the amoral twenty-first century.

Whatever it was, Nico had been reluctant to come here – and now he couldn't wait to get away fast enough. Before he whisked Isabel off in the 'Bat Mobile', he left a telephone message with Henry, so brief it could almost be construed as rude, to the effect that he was taking Isabel 'shopping'.

Isabel felt rather disgruntled that she was being used as the excuse. Patrick had said he'd put aside a day from his busy schedule to be with them – and here they were, abandoning him at the first opportunity? Guilt, guilt, guilt. This wasn't the way for her to be making a favourable impression.

After a hair-raising ride into Bath – he really was a crap driver – Nico parked/abandoned the Fiesta in the carpark beneath Waitrose. Then they walked up to Waterstones in Milsom Street, where Nico bought an armful of books which were quickly stuffed into the distinctive black-and-gold carrier-bags so Isabel couldn't see what he'd bought. The amount going on his credit card was fairly astronomical, though. She wondered if they were reference material, to help with the book he was writing about her father – and began to feel depressed. So he was still writing the bloody thing . . .

Judas.

As he went in search of yet another item, she had an urge to stroll over to the biography section, and leaf through one of his other books, just so that she could read something else he'd written. The biographies were well away from where she was waiting, however, and it would not have appeared subtle. If he realised she was *that* interested in him, he would make her life unbearable with his smart-arse comments.

Even as she dithered, she found she was out of time. Nico had known exactly what he wanted, picked it up, paid for it and soon they were strolling back down the hill into the touristy part of town.

For once it wasn't raining, although the pavements and cobblestones were still gleaming wet from the previous showers. The town was starting to get busy and nowhere more so than the area around the Roman Baths, where a large queue was developing.

Nico drew her attention to it. "That's why we're not eating in the Pump Room," he said, before manoeuvring her into a little cafe. "And not because I'm too much a cheapskate for an uptown girl like you!"

She was about to protest at this character assassination when she saw he was laughing at her. Great, now her little personality traits made her a figure of fun. How was she ever going to get him to take her seriously?

They took a table by the window. Nico said he liked to watch the people go by; Isabel supposed it must be something to do with being a writer. Isabel finally got to eat museli and yoghurt, Nico ordered a jacket potato and salad. Her healthy eating must be rubbing off on him. He then spoilt it by lighting up another cigarette the moment they stepped outside.

Isabel glanced up at the sky, hoping it might rain and extinguish his cigarette, but the even the weather was on his side, the heavy grey clouds peeling back to reveal flashes of brilliant blue sky.

"Was there anything you particularly wanted to buy? Apart from books, that is?" she asked him, as they meandered down the little side roads, window-shopping, competing with each other on seeking out the most original displays.

"No."

Here we go again, thought Isabel wearily. Why was it every time she started up a conversation, she felt as though she was interrogating him?

She didn't pursue the point. She was enjoying spending the afternoon meandering in a very lazy way. She liked passing time with him, even if he wasn't the most chattiest of companions. It was enough for her to watch him, as he liked to watch everyone else.

"Have you got a dress to wear to the party, tonight?" he asked, suddenly stopping outside a little boutique. Posing languidly in the bow-window was an impossibly thin mannequin, wearing a tiny gold-sequinned dress.

For a moment Isabel was a little slow on the uptake.

"Why?" she asked mischievously. "Did you want to borrow one?"

She suddenly realised he looked a bit awkward. His shoulders were hunched, the hand which wasn't swinging the Waterstones' carrier-bag was shoved deep into his pockets, a sure sign of his uneasiness. In fact, the penny had just about dropped when he said: "I know how it is with women, you like to dress up for these sort of things . . . compete with each other . . ."

"I can't let you buy me a dress," she said firmly. "It wouldn't be right."

"How about I loan you the money?"

"Are you ashamed of me? You think your father's friends are going to wonder what you see in a scruff like me?"

"That's right, chuck it back in my face," he grumbled, brusquely turning his back on her and striding off down the street. Then he paused, glancing back over his shoulder and made another attempt to be conciliatory. "I'm just trying to be practical here. Every other girl is going to be barely dressed in Julien Macdonald and Dolce & Gabbana and you'll be wearing jeans and a Talisman T-shirt – well, I suppose it shows loyalty."

To whom? Isabel wondered, still reeling from this unexpected kindness. Taz or Patrick's record company?

"I do have more than one T-shirt," she protested. It wasn't a fib – she had three – well, two and a nightshirt. "So don't worry about me."

He turned slowly, so that he was facing her. "I do worry about you," he said. "I worry about you a lot."

He was giving her that intense look again. The one which sent tingling sensations all down her spine and a strange, squirmy feeling of excitement in her tummy.

"Do you?" she said, taking one step in his direction, then pausing, uncertain. Maybe she was reading this all wrong? She would hate to make a fool of herself.

He held his hand out towards her. "Isabel – "

Tentatively she reached out to take it –

A large, frizzy-haired woman, pushing a screaming child in a buggy, barged between them with a terse "Excuse *me*!"

Isabel began to giggle and even Nico smiled.

"I think we ought to go back home," he said and, disappointingly, his hand flew back into the pocket of his trench coat. "And find out what entertainments Patrick has in store for us this afternoon."

So they returned to the car, Isabel walking beside him, a mere few inches away, but feeling far too inhibited to slide her arm through his as she so desperately wanted to do. Strange, she had never seen herself as the shy retiring type . . .

What on earth was the matter with her?

Chapter Twenty-one

For what seemed like the hundredth time, Isabel checked out her reflection in the full-length mirror in her bedroom. Her long red hair fell in shiny corkscrew curls over her shoulders; her only make-up – black kohl and dark-red lipstick. She wore her *other* T-shirt – black, sleeveless and clinging to every inch, a tiny denim skirt and knee-length boots. She looked great, no question. Taz would have proposed on the spot. But to celebrate the birthday of the legendary Patrick Kearney, at a star-studded party at his country estate? To be honest, she looked as though she ought to be parking the cars.

Isabel felt her ego deflate and regarded her mirrored image with ill humour. Was it too late to change? And into what? Not for the first time did she wish that, when she had stormed out of Stortford House after the row with Danielle, she had had the foresight to cram more clothes into her kitbag.

"Are you ready yet?" Nico's voice echoed up the stairs. It indicated more than a hint of irritation. "The party's been going for ever and if we don't hurry Patrick is quite capable of sending over Search and Rescue."

"I'm coming, I'm coming." Isabel flipped the top off her kohl pencil and applied another layer to her eyelids. She had closed her eyes to ensure universal coverage when she felt the pencil being plucked from her hand. She opened her eyes and saw Nico's reflection behind her.

"I mean like *now,* Isabel!" he grumbled, sliding the pencil into the top pocket of his black shirt.

"Hey, give that back!"

"And have to wait another two hours before you decide you're ready? No chance."

"That's the only one I've got!"

"You can have it back after the party," he replied calmly, taking hold of her hand and dragging her towards the staircase.

Still she prevaricated. "Do I look OK to you?"

"Fine."

"You haven't even looked at me!"

Nico gave an exasperated sigh, stopped, gave her a very cursory once over, said: "You look terrific," and started down the staircase, pulling her behind him.

Isabel yelped and grabbed hold of the rope banister. "Not so fast! I can't walk in these boots."

"Then why wear – no, I'm not even going there. It must be a girl thing."

Tripping down a spiral stone staircase proved to be a doddle compared with a trek across the lawn in the pitch black of a November evening. All the lights were around the other side of the Abbey and there was no path to the gatehouse – only spongy, marshy lawn, a swimming pool and a ruined hall to negotiate before they reached the front. The only way to stop herself sinking into the grass was to walk on tiptoe but, even so, Isabel stumbled along, clutching at Nico's arm, jacket, shirt – anything that came to hand.

"I could give you a piggyback?" suggested Nico, as he was almost yanked into the mud for the third time.

Isabel promptly quashed a little thrill of delight. "No, thanks. I'm OK, really. I always walk like this."

After the dark of the garden, the bright spotlights set up in front of the Abbey hurt Isabel's eyes and it took a moment for them to adjust.

"Bloody hell!" she hissed, as she watched a particularly glamorous couple walk through into the hall. "That's David Bowie."

"Great guy," nodded Nico. "You should get him to tell you his joke about the lady vicar and – "

"Mick Jagger!"

"You've heard it."

She dug her fingernails into his arm. "Over there, look!"

"Isabel, do you think you could cultivate a little cool?"

"George Michael! Elton John! Oh my God, I'm going to die, I'm just going to *die*!"

The van der Straatens' social circles had spun in quite a different orbit from those of these rock luminaries (Taz didn't count), and Isabel was quite overcome.

"Fine," Nico excavated her fingernails from his wrist, one by one. "I'll leave you outside, then no one will trip over your decaying corpse."

"Nico!" She attempted to clip him around the ear, but only managed to reach up to his shoulder. Then she realised that Elton John and his party were waiting politely by the door to let her go in first.

Nico nodded an acknowledgement.

"Hi, Nicolas," beamed Elton. "How are you?"

As they walked into the entrance hall, Isabel dug her fingernails once more into Nico's forearm. "Elton said '*Hi*!'. Elton John *spoke*!"

A pretty girl dressed in a French maid's outfit – which looked as though it had come straight out of an Ann Summers catalogue – took Nico's leather jacket. Isabel, who wasn't wearing a coat, only her T-shirt accessorised with goose-pimples, tried hard not to think about billiard tables.

She jumped with a guilty conscience as Patrick loomed up out of the shadows, one arm wrapping its way around her bare shoulders to give her a quick squeeze, the other pressing a glass of chilled champagne into her even colder hands. She quickly gulped it down to fortify her nerves.

"Great to see you again, Isabel," he murmured. "Do you like my house?"

Isabel nodded, feeling slightly distracted by the touch

of his hand gently stroking the back of her neck, his beautiful cobalt eyes staring intently into her own. She felt like a chestnut being gently roasted over an open fire.

"The place was a bit of a wreck when I bought it back in the 1980s," Patrick was saying. "The guy who'd owned it before me had let it fall down around his ears because he begrudged leaving his children an inheritance he didn't think they deserved. When they sold it to me, they still reaped several million after tax, so they didn't do too badly." For a moment his eyes met Nico's and he smiled wryly. "I think there's a moral in there somewhere."

"Yeah, never rely on your parents," was Nico's dry reply.

"Patrick!" Elton John was walking across the hall.

Patrick had to retrieve his hand from Isabel's neck to greet him. At once Nico's arm had snaked around her waist and was pulling her away, towards the corridor behind them.

Patrick winked conspiratorially at Isabel. "You guys go ahead and enjoy yourselves!"

Nico grunted. Isabel waved Patrick goodbye, feeling that at least one of them should keep up appearances. She was about to chastise Nico for not wishing his father a happy birthday – when she caught a glimpse of his thunderous expression and thought better of it. Must be really bizarre, she thought, having your father make a play for your girlfriend right under your nose.

Nico needn't get outraged on her account. While being groped by Patrick Kearney was not in *quite* the same league as being groped by a sad, middle-aged loser in The Parson's Collar on Friday night, she was quite capable of taking care of herself.

Nico still held her hand as they walked in silence along a chilly, vaulted passageway, emerging into a medieval banqueting hall. Isabel could hardly stop herself gaping at the splendour. The hall was huge – at least 120 feet long, with large mullioned windows along each side and twin rows of pillars supporting what appeared to be a modern glass ceiling.

Isabel flinched as they passed a great flaming torch, fixed to a wrought-iron bracket on the stone wall.

"Relax," muttered Nico, squeezing her hand. "It's a fake. Patrick's had a thing about pyrotechnics since his glory days at Wembley Arena. You think he'd be able to get insurance on this folly otherwise?"

Isabel smiled weakly. Thank goodness she wouldn't have to sit through the firework display.

The rest of the hall appeared authentic enough – brightly coloured tapestries, a ferocious display of medieval weaponry, waitresses dressed as serving wenches, waiters as knaves . . . Isabel hid a smile; Patrick had a serious King Arthur complex.

Two long tables had been set up on each side of the hall and were scattered with white rose petals, thick white candles flickering at intervals along the middle. Nico pushed her into a high-backed, wooden chair, boldly emblazoned with Patrick's coat of arms.

"Sit down," he said. "and try not to look as though you've fallen down a rabbit hole."

All very well for him to say – he had grown up at Camelot. But Isabel did as she was told, entertaining herself by taking a good look around to try and commit everything to memory so she could tell her friends about it later and have a good laugh. Except, of course, she no longer had any friends . . .

Nico sat opposite and picked up an uncorked bottle, checking out the label before murmuring, "Mmm, good stuff – back catalogue must be selling well."

As he sloshed it into their glasses, Isabel watched the bubbles fizz up and over the glass. "What did you give Patrick for his birthday?"

Nico frowned. "I didn't. Do you think I should have done?"

Strange family. "It is traditional."

"I don't think there is anything he wants. The guy is a billionaire after all."

"Maybe you should have baked him cookies? As a token gesture . . ."

"You're taking the piss."

"What did you get him last year? Socks?"

"Er, nothing."

Isabel didn't ask why. She didn't have to – she already knew the answer. It looked as though she was going to spend the whole evening tiptoeing around Nico's sensitivities.

A petite blonde, her hair styled in a choppy bob, very similar to Jemma's, suddenly appeared behind Nico, sliding her hands over his shoulders and kissing his cheek.

"Hello, Nico!" she said warmly, smiling as he started. "I didn't expect to see you here! Who's your friend?"

For the first time since she'd met him, the usually self-assured Nico appeared ill at ease. Isabel smirked. This should be good. The girl was obviously an ex-girlfriend – so how was he going to talk his way out of it?

"Hi, Emily . . . this is Isabel. Isabel, meet Emily Cavendish – she sings with Aphrodite."

Like she didn't know? The girl's face had dominated advertising boards, magazines and even cereal packets since Aphrodite had blazed a trail through the music business four years ago: a girl band that wrote their own songs and could actually play instruments instead of having to rely on session musicians and backing tapes.

"Hello, Isabel!" Emily stretched out her hand and shook Isabel's with a surprisingly strong grip for such a fragile-looking creature. "Nico and I are old friends."

And you are *so* possessive of him, thought Isabel gleefully. What an excellent opportunity for mischief-making.

She smiled back. "Any friend of Nico's is a friend of mine. We're really *close.*"

Nico looked pained; Isabel winked at him. *You wait, lover-boy, I'm going to make you suffer!*

She had to admit Emily was stunning (albeit in a pocket-sized way) and exactly the sort of girlfriend she could imagine Nico having. Along with the obligatory blonde hair, Emily had flawless skin, knowing brown eyes and a naughty smile. She was beautifully dressed too, in a short, suede dress and pink cowboy boots. She made Isabel feel like a carthorse.

Emily had already cast her eyes over Isabel's sleeveless black T-shirt with such an amused expression that Isabel had fully expected her first words to be: 'Is it dress-down Friday?'

"May I sit down?" asked Emily. "It's getting really crowded in here. I haven't a clue who half these people are."

Then you're an idiot, thought Isabel, seeing as the three of them were the least famous people in the banqueting hall.

Emily slid into the seat next to Nico, but somehow managed to leave one hand on his shoulder in a proprietary way. "What have you been up to?" she asked him, smiling prettily in Isabel's direction, as though to prove she wasn't *deliberately* intending to exclude her from the conversation. It was merely happening that way . . .

Nico glanced again at Isabel. "Not much."

"He's writing a book about my father," said Isabel. "He came to Calahurst to interview him and fell in love with me." She gazed dreamily at Nico. "Romantic, eh?"

There was a flicker of interest in Emily's sultry brown eyes. "What does your father do?"

"He's a small-town jeweller," she replied, not bothering to explain about Isaac's car accident. She did not want to get into the 'so sorry, what a tragic loss, time is a great healer,' business from a total stranger.

"Successful, of course – you know, self-made millionaire, etc, etc, but really quite dull. I can't think why Nico would be interested in him."

Nico kicked her under the table.

"Maybe he moonlights as a jewel thief," said Emily blithely.

"Isabel," said Nico, suddenly standing, "would you like to dance?"

"Dance?" pouted Isabel. "But I was having a lovely chat with Emily."

"They're playing our song . . ."

As some fat little producer was currently singing 'Mack The Knife', egged on by his friends, Isabel raised her eyebrows. Yet, before she knew what was happening, Nico had steered her onto the dance floor and was swinging her around, his fingers holding tightly around her own, so that she couldn't escape.

"Our song, eh?" she mocked.

"Be quiet and enjoy yourself. You're here to have fun, remember?"

"I am having fun," she said acidly. "I can't wait to hear what little gem Emily is going to come out with next. I used to think *my* family were odd. This weekend is turning into *Meet The Parents* but without the sadism. Or is that saved up for later?"

"I admit Patrick can be a little eccentric – "

"Ha, he practically jumped me in the hall! With you standing right there beside him! There must be an easier way to get me a recording contract. Why can't I make an appointment with a secretary? Have an audition?"

"Patrick doesn't operate like that. He hates the manufactured side of the music industry and likes to 'discover' the next big thing himself. He *never* gives auditions. He runs an *independent* record label and he wants to keep it that way. He's the ultimate control freak."

Runs in the family, reflected Isabel. "And why is your ex-girlfriend here? Or doesn't she know she's ex?"

He smiled wryly. "Three years ago she threw me over for Patrick. She's his girlfriend – not mine."

Isabel stared at him in shock. Emily dumped Nico for Patrick? Bloody hell! No wonder they were estranged!

"I certainly wouldn't fancy *her* as a stepmother!"

"It's not gonna happen. Patrick swore he would never marry again after my mother divorced him. Girlfriends have come and gone for nearly twenty years now and he's shown no apparent haste to enter into the state of holy matrimony."

"How would you feel if he did marry her?"

Nico shrugged with his usual insouciance and said baldly: "They won't."

"But what if they *did*?"

Nico stopped dancing and looked down at her with exasperation. "Look, I don't want to talk about it. Don't you get it? OK, Emily was my girlfriend before she met Patrick – it's no big deal – I got over it."

Isabel's mouth was practically hanging open. His father pinched his teenage girlfriend and he 'got over it'?

"My relationship with Patrick is private," he said

firmly, "and it's going to stay that way." His eyes flickered away from her own, glancing over her shoulder, across the room. "If I promise to keep Emily off your back, can we go back to the table? I really need a drink."

Without waiting for her reply, Nico stalked back to the table.

Well, sod you! thought Isabel. Except now she had no one to dance with. She could dance by herself – that wouldn't faze her – but could she be bothered? She had just decided to go and look for a stiff drink, when a sinewy arm slid around her waist and hugged her close to a warm male body.

"Lover's tiff?" mocked Patrick.

Oh great, Ollie the Octopus. She firmly unwound his arm. "Look, you're going to have to stop doing that. It could be misinterpreted."

"By whom?"

"Emily for one. She *is* your girlfriend."

He laughed. "She's used to me. Do you fancy a dance?"

And have to subject herself to his pawing? Isabel shuddered. "Not a good idea. Nico is possessive and doesn't like to share me. It could get very nasty, you know. Once, when we were in this club in Brighton – "

"Humour me," he said softly, moving closer so that only she could hear. "I want to get to know you better."

That's what worried her . . .

Patrick was shorter than his son; his dark blue eyes were almost on a level with her own and he was standing so close she could see every curl of his black eyelashes. Those eyes were far too beautiful for a man . . . oddly hypnotic too . . .

His sensuous lips curved into a smile. "One dance wouldn't hurt."

"Do you love your son?"

"Eh?"

"Well, he loves me and you've already rotted up his life by swiping Emily from under his nose so don't you think you'd better cool it? Or you'll never see him again. Unless, of course, that's what you want? But if I were in your shoes, I'd think about building bridges."

"Eh?"

"How difficult would it be for you to say 'sorry'?"

"I only wanted a dance!"

"Let's hold that thought. Because you might be the most important man in the music business, but I'm quite capable of kneeing you in the balls if you touch me up again, OK?"

Patrick looked taken aback. "Er, OK."

"So long as we understand each other."

He slid his hands over her waist, his thumbs hooking into her belt loops and chuckled against her ear. "Does my poor son know what he's getting himself into, I wonder?"

They danced to a ballad, then some rock 'n' roll and as the third song finished, Isabel announced that she'd had enough and wanted to sit down. Patrick bent to kiss her cheek, but she saw that coming and swiftly ducked out of his reach, walking to her seat, Patrick trailing behind, still slightly shell-shocked.

Isabel sat down and smiled in what she hoped was a conciliatory way at Nico. "Your dad's a great dancer."

"You're pretty good yourself," said Patrick, ruffling her hair affectionately.

"My dad taught me. He loved loud rock music and used to dance around the dining-room. Once he hid in one of the suits of armour and started dancing Michael Jackson's 'Thriller' – which gave my sister and me the fright of our lives."

"Suits of armour?" queried Emily. "Where do you live? Buckingham Palace?"

Isabel ignored her, more irritated that Nico didn't stand up for her – perhaps he hadn't noticed the little digs. Men could sometimes be a little slow on the uptake. She wondered if Patrick would defend her instead, but without her realising, he had leapt onto the stage and in no time at all was belting out 'Livin' La Vida Loca'.

Bloody men, couldn't be relied upon for anything.

"Why aren't you up there with your father?" she goaded Nico. "You could duet."

He grimaced. "One diva in the family is quite enough."

"Are you going to have a go?" Emily asked her. "It's kind of a tradition at Patrick's parties, that everyone sings something. Of course, no one would mind if you didn't want to. It is rather nerve-racking – performing to a room full of strangers. You might make a complete fool of yourself . . ."

"Isabel's got an amazing voice," Nico said, before

Isabel could wrap her hands around Emily's throat and squeeze hard. "She can sing anything you like – blues, R&B, rock – she's like a young Tina Turner."

Isabel couldn't believe he'd said that. The way was now open for Emily to utter a great acidic put-down. Really, she was spoilt for choice . . .

Emily didn't disappoint. "When it's your turn, Isabel, you've got to sing 'Simply The Best'."

"Actually," said Isabel acidly, "I thought I'd do 'I'm Outta Love'."

Patrick suddenly appeared beside them, kissed Emily, then sat next to Isabel. This could have been because it was the only free seat, but his proximity did not help to make Isabel feel any more comfortable, especially when she was aware that Nico was watching them speculatively. So she turned her head to watch the boy band now on stage. The Lost Boys they were called apparently. Lost for a decent melody by the sound of it, as their lead singer consistently failed to reach the high notes.

"I hope you're not releasing this as a single," she heard Nico saying to Patrick. "It's dire."

"They're adamant that they want to. They wrote it themselves – and that means more royalties."

The Lost Boys finished to polite but decidedly lukewarm applause and were about to launch into an encore when Elton confiscated the lead singer's mike.

"That was great," he smiled, "but perhaps someone else would like a turn?"

Isabel was wondering whether this was her moment

when she saw Emily climbing up on stage, her blonde hair shimmering under the spotlight. She muttered a few words to the band and they obligingly launched into the intro.

Isabel had to admit she certainly had presence and a great voice – but it took a few lines before it dawned on her that the words Emily was singing were rather familiar. She was singing 'I'm Outta Love'.

Isabel stared at Nico in shock. "She's stolen my song! How could she do that?"

Nico looked blank and shrugged. Which was *extremely* helpful.

Despite the murderous rage building up inside her, Isabel had to admit Emily was brilliant – but then, she was already in a successful band so she would have to be. It was a different interpretation: Emily had a spectacular vocal range, soaring up and down, but she didn't really have the right personality for this particular song. Not that anyone else appeared to notice. Judging from the cheers and whistling which filled the hall, the other guests thought Emily was *great*!

Isabel felt the misery engulf her. This had been her last chance – and it had been wrecked by something she couldn't control. There was no way she could stand up there now and sing the same song.

Think of another song was the persistent message being sent out by her brain. Right now, Isabel had the feeling she wouldn't even remember the words to 'Baa Baa Black Sheep'.

After what seemed like an eternity, Emily finished,

to a rapturous applause. She stood for a moment, basking in the glory, and then she sauntered back to the table.

"That was a vile thing to do," Nico said in a low voice.

Emily ignored him. She gleefully placed the mike on the table in front of Isabel and said: "Your turn!"

Chapter Twenty-two

Isabel stared at the microphone lying on the table in front of her, horribly aware that everyone was expecting her to seize it, bounce up on stage and sing a rendition of 'My Heart Will Go On' – or something very much like it. After all, she wasn't one of *them,* she was an enthusiastic amateur – whose only experience of singing in public would be at the local pub after one too many Bacardi Breezers.

"You don't have to do this." Nico was watching her, concerned.

He was kidding, right? This had been his idea! To drag her all the way to Bath, to sing at his father's karaoke party, to impress him and be offered a recording contract – and *now* he was telling her she didn't have to do this? Was it some kind of reverse psychology?

"Of course you don't," agreed Emily happily. "It was unfair of me to put you on the spot like this. Let me take the mike back and – "

"No!" Isabel snatched up the microphone and held it tightly against her chest, almost as if she thought Emily was going to throw her on the ground and wrestle it from her.

Nico took her hands in his, squeezing her fingers reassuringly. "Isabel, perhaps you should think about this – "

His touch felt comforting and for a moment she was tempted to give in, let her dreams of becoming a singer wither and die. But something inside her, self-assurance she wasn't even aware she had, made her pull her hands away and she walked towards the stage with her head held high. She'd show 'em!

Emily patted her on the back as she passed and said: "Atta girl! One chorus of 'I Will Survive' and you'll have them eating out of your hand."

It was so tempting to swivel around and punch that smug smile off her pretty little face – Isabel could almost imagine herself doing it. What would it achieve? Apart from making her feel a whole lot better! The *best* revenge on Emily would be to put in a great performance . . .which brought Isabel right back to her original fear – looking a complete prat in front of half the rock gods of the late twentieth century . . .

The band on stage was made up from Patrick's friends – bona fide legends of the music business. When one got fed up, they would pass their guitar, or whatever, onto someone else and jump casually from the stage. The only constant was Elton John, who appeared to have taken up residence at the piano.

"Brave girl!" he said in admiration, as Isabel climbed the steps to the stage.

This did not do much to calm Isabel's nerves at all. Brave? Why did she have to be *brave*?

There was a little spotlight shining on her, creating a personal pool of stardust to stand in. The musicians watched her with humour, perhaps thinking she was psyching herself up, waiting for her to give them some clue as to the song she wanted to sing. But how could she tell them when she didn't know herself?

Eventually Elton leant over and stage-whispered: "What are you going to sing?"

Isabel opened her mouth. She was expecting to squeak: 'I don't know' in a pathetic little voice, then turn and run off stage. Strangely enough, her voice came out perfectly clearly.

Her choice didn't faze Elton in the slightest. He merely asked: "What key?"

Key? She looked sheepishly at him. "I haven't the slightest idea. Do you think you could aim for something in the middle? My voice is quite deep – I can't do high notes."

"Something in the middle," repeated Elton with a commendable straight face. "Don't worry; you'll be fine."

Isabel suddenly felt very alone on the stage, not helped by some wag saying quite audibly "Save us from amateur night!"

She felt that same surge of fury that had propelled her up here in the first place and the final remnants of nerves were blasted away as the drummer launched into a migraine-inducing rock beat. It was the most work he'd had all evening. He was then joined by the screeching crash of chords from three of the guitarists, which vibrated through the refectory with such ear-splitting intensity that the rest of Patrick's guests collectively jumped.

Isabel exchanged smirks with the lead guitarist. They had certainly woken everyone up. 'I Will Survive' indeed!

Secure in the knowledge of her own talent, Isabel began to sing: *"I want you to want me . . ."*

As the audience appeared totally stunned by the incredibly loud noise being created on stage, it was difficult to tell how they rated her. Isabel risked a glance towards Nico. He was sitting back in his chair, cigarette glowing between his fingers, his expression enigmatic. Emily, beside him, had a rather fixed smile, as she toyed with her wineglass. Patrick, however, was watching her intently, his only movement his fingers tapping against the table. Was that a good sign?

Isabel focused all her attention on him, positively chargrilling him with blatant sex appeal – she would worry about the consequences later. This was the first, last and only chance she was going to have to show what a huge talent she had and she was determined to make the most of it.

As the song drew to a close, she jumped from the stage and sashayed towards him as she repeated the final line. She had intended to plant a birthday kiss on

Patrick's forehead. She certainly wasn't going to risk going near his mouth – it would be about as safe as trying to snog a crocodile.

However, as she passed Nico he seized her by the waist, pulling her off-balance so that she landed roughly onto his lap, and plucked the microphone from her hand, whispering: "Quit while you're ahead, honey!"

She had to admit his suggestion was the best option, judging from the appreciative once-over Patrick was giving her. Business and pleasure never mixed – and what a total waste it would be if Patrick offered her a contract on the spot – only to be brow-beaten out of it later tonight by his jealous girlfriend.

Patrick leant over the table and, taking the microphone from Nico, stood up. "Let's hear it for Isabel!" he yelled and the room erupted into the loudest applause, cheers and whistling all evening. "You're going places, girl," he smiled, holding out his hand. "Come on, sing another! We could duet?"

She bet they could – but with Nico meaningfully digging his fingers into her ribs she didn't dare. Isabel shook her head. "Maybe next time."

"You're a lucky bastard," Patrick muttered to his son, before sliding the microphone down the table to another member of Aphrodite and heading off towards the bar.

Isabel tried to slither elegantly from Nico's lap. "You can let me go now," she muttered, as his arms remained tightly wound around her waist. "He's gone. We don't have to pretend any more."

"Who's pretending?" Nico chuckled, soft and low. "I'm not letting *you* go, sweetheart. You're stuck with me."

She turned her head, uncertain that she'd heard him correctly, and he dropped an unexpected kiss onto her lips – then laughed at her confusion.

Isabel checked the table for empty beer glasses, but amongst Patrick's cast-offs there was only one small whisky glass – with most of the contents remaining. So he hadn't been drinking? Maybe it was the cigarettes . . .

Nico, meanwhile, had finally managed to burrow one warm hand beneath her T-shirt and was stroking her ribcage with his thumb, gradually working his way towards the underside of her breast.

She had another attempt at sliding from his lap, but he was holding her too securely and appeared to be enjoying her fight to get away. So she clamped her arms against her chest and kicked his shin with her heel, which he merely ignored.

Emily, encouraging the last drops of a bottle of champagne into her glass (slapping the bottom as though it was a bottle of ketchup), watched these shenanigans with a resigned expression. "Get a room, guys, for heaven's sake!"

"Excellent idea!" said Nico, tipping Isabel off his knee, but keeping a tight hold of her hand. "Let's go, sweetheart. We can have an early night."

Early night! Isabel fumed as he led her through the tables and out into the corridor. She'd give him an early night! As soon as they were away from the noise of the party she opened her mouth to berate him, only to have it swamped by his own as he kissed her fiercely.

She stamped on his foot and was quickly released.

"Jesus, Isabel!" His eyes were watering as he bent to rub the top of his foot. His sock now had a distinct tear in it. "What the fuck did you do that for?"

"You needed a reality check!" she stormed. "What the hell are you on?"

"On?" As he stared up at her he did appear genuinely baffled. "I'm not 'on' anything. I haven't even had a drink!"

Isabel felt the steady ground of self-righteousness suddenly shift beneath her. "So why are you kissing me? We're alone. We don't have to put on an act anymore."

"I thought you liked it!"

"I . . . I . . ." As she saw his lips curl into a knowing smile, she realised a swift change of subject was called for. "You blow hot and cold! I don't know where I am with you. One minute we're fighting and you're saying the most horrible things to me – the next you're trying to get your leg over!"

"Leg over? What a quaint and so very English expression. Sounds like a cricket position, rather than a prelude to making love."

The conversation was getting seriously out of control. "I'm confused!" she hissed. "What do you want with me? Are you trying to get more material for your book? Am I a substitute for Danielle? Why did you really bring me here? Do you feel sorry for me? I don't want you to feel sorry for me, Nico."

The expression on his handsome face had now changed to pure exasperation. "What do *you* want?" he countered. "I don't think you even know yourself."

I want you to want me . . . The words popped, uninvited into her head, but there was no way she was saying them out loud. If she wasn't careful they could end up as a chapter heading in his book. The one subtitled 'How I seduced Isabel van der Straatan'.

Nico picked up her hand again and squeezed it reassuringly. "I think we need to talk," he said, his amber eyes boring into hers with an unsettling intensity. "There are some issues here that we really need to get out in the open."

Issues? How very American. But, hypnotised by those beautiful maple-syrup eyes, all Isabel could do was nod dumbly.

"Now, as your boots aren't made for walking, why don't I throw you over my shoulder and carry you back to the gatehouse?"

Chapter Twenty-three

If he didn't take the piss out of her quite so much, Isabel felt she wouldn't be confused as to his intentions. Clearly they weren't honourable, as he could hardly keep his hands off her all the way back to the gatehouse, sliding his arm around her waist and cuddling her close – 'to keep her warm', he had said. He had even draped his leather jacket around her shoulders. What had precipitated this total change of heart – the brief flirtation with his father? Was he *jealous*? From what she knew of Nico's blasé disposition, it didn't seem likely. He must have an ulterior motive.

On the other hand, they had barely walked into the sitting-room before he started kissing her again, sliding the jacket from her shoulders and throwing it casually onto one of the leather sofas. They stumbled against the wall; his body pressing so firmly against hers she was in no doubt his desire was genuine. Maybe he hadn't had sex for a long time?

He managed to wriggle one hand beneath the waistband of her skirt (she must have dropped a few pounds after the accident – she could have sworn it had been a tighter fit) and was soon groping around in a very disturbing manner. The other had caught her own hand, which had been half-heartedly fighting him off, and had it clamped to the wall like the rest of her.

After more downward probing, he finally located her knicker elastic and slid his fingers beneath it with triumph. For one unaccountable moment, Isabel was reminded of Taz and it brought her up short. Taz – how could she do this to him?

He did it to you.

And to Danielle – Nico was her boyfriend after all . . .

The sheer chill of the bare stone wall, seeping through her T-shirt, felt uncomfortable, bringing her back to the real world – and her left hand had gone numb where he had held her too tightly. She pushed him away – and meant it this time. It took a few moments for her breathing to return to normal.

He was frowning. "What's the *matter* with you?"

Good question. Was she searching for an excuse not to have sex with him or was she beating herself up for the fun of it?

"You're moving too quickly," she protested. "I've only recently split up with Taz. I don't want a one-night stand because you're feeling lonely. I'm not ready for another relationship. To be honest, my life can't take much more grief. I'm not sure how I feel about you – and I'm certainly not going to have sex with you on the rebound."

"Me neither," agreed Nico, reaching out for her again. "I was hoping for the couch."

She slapped his hands away. "Be serious, can't you?"

He moved away from her and switched on the light. They stared at each other. The aforementioned couch was now between them. Isabel tried to avoid looking at it. She couldn't quite meet Nico's eyes now the harsh white light filled the room, so she studied a painting on the wall instead. A Picasso print; a swirl of carnival colours. Although, from what she knew of Patrick, she wouldn't be surprised to learn it was the real thing.

Nico took a couple of steps around the couch and instinctively Isabel moved a couple of steps in the other direction. It was as though they were playing a bizarre game of musical chairs.

"Look," said Nico wearily, "I'm not going to play chase around the sitting-room so I suggest you make yourself comfortable. I'll go fetch us a hot drink and we can discuss this new development in our relationship like two rational adults." He disappeared off down the steps to the kitchen.

Relationship! Isabel quelled the desire to hurtle up the other stairway to her bedroom and lock and bolt the door. Except there was no lock and bolt. So she sat on one end of the sofa, as she had been instructed and, picking up a cushion, held it to her chest like a shield. Realising how silly this made her appear, she threw the cushion back onto the other side of the couch. Now totally insecure, she got up and hobbled over to the sound system to pick out a CD to play.

Her boots were killing her, so she bent and unzipped one and was just kicking it off when Nico walked back into the sitting-room and said, "Hey, you've started without me!"

Standing with the boot in her hand, Isabel felt like she could quite cheerfully clobber him with it.

"With you, everything is sexual innuendo," she complained.

His gaze flickered appreciatively over her body. "Sorry, guess it's uppermost in my mind."

"Where's the hot chocolate?" she asked, attempting to keep the conversation on neutral ground. "What have you been doing all this time?"

He shrugged. "I switched the kettle on, but it takes time to boil."

She deliberately turned away from him and sat on the floor to flick through the CD collection. Even though the discs were helpfully organised in alphabetical order, it was difficult to concentrate when she was very aware of Nico walking towards her.

She watched his shiny black shoes stop a few inches away. She could see the rip in his socks, the bare olive skin beneath and a small spot of congealed blood. She was flooded with guilt. What a cow she was!

He crouched beside her and said, conversationally: "What are you gonna pick?"

She tried not to look at him. "I don't know. There's so many here."

His hand reached out; long, square-tipped fingers hovered over the CDs, then slid one out. "Put this on," he said softly. "It's my favourite."

Isabel's hand was trembling so much she could hardly lever the disc out of the case. Nico seemed unconcerned. He had touched the power switch; an array of lights flickered on and the CD drawer slid out. Isabel dropped the CD inside and it disappeared into the machine. Seductive music poured into the room.

Nico helped her to stand. She still wore one boot, so now one leg was three inches shorter than the other, but she didn't notice. She was too aware of Nico to notice anything much. Leaning up against the sound system, there was nowhere to retreat to and no way she could continue avoiding his enquiring gaze unless she wanted to appear even more odd than she did already.

She looked up.

He was lowering his head and his lips touched hers, softly, insistently and then drew back, perhaps waiting for her to slap his face.

Isabel sighed and closed her eyes. Why was she fighting this? What was the big deal? Why not go with the flow, have sex, get it out of her system? A short, no-strings affair could be what she needed. They were both single and besides, after the way Danielle and Jemma and Taz had treated her, she owed *them* no loyalty. As long as she remained true to herself, her conscience was clear. She just had to make sure she didn't fall in love . . .

She felt his mouth touch hers again; he nibbled her

lower lip, then kissed the side of her jaw, her neck. This was all very nice, but he was going too *slowly*!

He was wearing a shirt tucked into black trousers. She began to systematically tug it out, but he caught her hands in his and chuckled. "Why the hurry? We've got all night."

Huh, he could talk! Or perhaps he thought it was different for men . . .

Unless . . . Oh hell . . . he thought she was a complete tart!

Nico rested his forehead against hers, his brown eyes staring deep into her own. He had a strangely troubled look on his face. Isabel felt a nasty cold lump drop in her stomach. Irony of ironies! After all this pent-up passion, he was now going to tell her he had changed his mind – that he didn't fancy her. Oh, the embarrassment!

"You know," he said in that deep, dark, sexy voice. "I think I love you."

Eek! She stared back at him, totally shocked. *That wasn't part of the plan!*

"Why are you saying this? You don't know me. You *can't* love me!"

"Crazy girl," Nico smiled affectionately. "Sure I can." In one quick movement he swept her off her feet and dropped her onto the couch. "And I'm damn well going to . . ."

* * *

Isabel woke up. She was lying in Nico's bed – at least,

she assumed it was Nico's bed; it certainly wasn't her own. She lay on her back, crimson bed-sheets rucked down to her waist, and realised she had woken because she felt cold – because she no longer wore any clothes. As this realisation hit, another was hot on its heels. Nico was curled up against her, legs entwined with hers, his head resting above her left breast. His huge powerful shoulders were hunched over her, as though to protect her from the chill November morning, one hairy arm lying casually across her ribcage. As he breathed, slowly and evenly, she could feel his breath tickling against her neck; a warm surge of love rushed through her, taking her by surprise with its intensity.

Love. That word again. He had said that he loved her. He had repeated it several times during the night, but Isabel couldn't quite bring herself to believe he spoke the truth. There was too much history between them. And those three little words, that could mean so much, were far too easy to say; they just tripped off the tongue and became meaningless.

She'd just have to hold her emotions in check awhile. Let him do all the running, go through the wringer. She couldn't face getting hurt again.

They had been due to return to Calahurst this afternoon. Exactly where in Calahurst had not been discussed. Perhaps, after last night, he'd ask her to move in with him? Yet, it was too soon – she wasn't ready to commit. Although as she was technically homeless, what choice did she have?

To be realistic: Danielle, Jemma or Taz. If she didn't

want to live with Nico she was going to have to be 'adult' and make it up with one of them.

Taz would now be preparing for Talisman's tour of the USA – and besides, their relationship was now kaput – there was no going back. Isabel didn't believe in second chances. Danielle? Perhaps she'd wait a little longer for the dust to settle on their last row. Danielle would not be overjoyed to discover her ex-boyfriend was now shagging her sister. And that left Jemma . . .

After several minutes of careful wriggling, Isabel was able to extract herself from beneath Nico's python-like embrace and slide out of bed without waking him up. She found the black shirt he'd worn last night and slipped it over her head – it smelt faintly of cigarette smoke – and him – and then slunk downstairs to her own room.

Her new mobile phone was buried in the depths of her kitbag. Isabel switched it on and was amazed to find she had several text messages and missed calls lined up on the screen, mainly from Jemma and Danielle.

She highlighted Danielle's name – then bottled out and cancelled it, flicking down to Jemma's most recent message, pressing return call without bothering to read what she'd written. It took forever to answer and Isabel was about to give up and head for the shower when Jemma finally picked up.

"Where the hell are you?" grumbled a husky voice, the by-product of a thirty-a-day habit. "And do you have any idea what time it is?"

"Hey, Jemma, what's up? What am I missing that you had to leave six messages for me?"

"Didn't you bloody read them?"

"Nice to hear from you too, Jemma."

"We've been out of our minds worrying about you – thinking you were lying murdered in a ditch – "

"And here I was thinking you didn't care." Isabel was not entirely joking.

Jemma, not one for confrontations, blithely changed the subject. "Taz said you'd run off with Nico, but he was joking, right?"

"Well, actually – "

"My God, you haven't? Danielle is going to kill you."

"Don't sound so disapproving," retorted Isabel. "What about you and Max?" As Jemma remained silent she filled the gap with: "Besides, Danielle threw *me* out. I had no where else to go."

Longer pause. "You could have come here, crashed on one of the beanbags."

"I did – and caught you with Taz! Bloody hell, you have a selective memory, Jemma! Danielle had thrown me out, you betrayed me with Taz, my father's dead – Nico was the only person I thought could trust. Do you know how that feels? To wake up one day and find your family, your friends, your lover – the people you thought cared the most about you in the world – really don't give a shit? That you're dependent on the charity of a stranger? I'm pretty sure anyone else would have driven their car off the nearest cliff!"

"I'm sorry . . ." The voice at the other end of the line

was wobbly and didn't sound at all like the usually confident Jemma. "I'm sorry I slept with Taz. I didn't mean to hurt you. Neither did Taz. He felt you were neglecting him – he's famous, he's not used to women treating him like that."

Which was a crap (and typically male) excuse. "And you? What's your defence?"

"Max keeps working late. He's so boring. I never see him any more."

"You mean he's trying to earn enough to make himself feel worthy of dating an earl's daughter."

"Rub it in, why don't you?" muttered Jemma. "You would never have found out about me and Taz if you hadn't turned up out of the blue like that. You could say it's partly your own fault . . ."

"Next time I'll hire a brass band to march in front of my car. And maybe a tickertape parade."

Jemma seemed to realise she had gone too far. "I was worried about you. I've been phoning the police, the hospitals – I thought perhaps you'd had another accident. You had disappeared off the face of the earth. If it was your idea of punishing me, I think it's sick."

"I didn't think anyone would miss me." Isabel was unable to stop the bitter note creeping into her voice. "No one came to visit me in hospital." No one except Nico . . .

"You didn't give us the chance! You discharged yourself and disappeared! Even the hospital didn't know where you'd gone." Pause. "So where are you?"

"With Nico," admitted Isabel. "We're staying with

his father in Bath. It's an incredible place. A bloody great castle! Makes Stortford House look provincial." Too late she realised she'd just criticised Jemma's childhood home. A home Jemma and her brother could no longer afford to live in.

"Lucky you." Jemma's voice was acerbic. "I hate to burst your bubble, but you've got to come home. Danielle needs you. I didn't want to tell you over the phone but, well, here goes . . ."

Isabel felt an icy hand twist her insides. "She's not . . . she's not . . ."

"She's fine," said Jemma hurriedly, "but the police have her under arrest and – get this – they think *she's* the one who stole the Ashlyn Diamond . . ."

(From The Calahurst Echo)

DIAMOND GIRL IN SHOCK ARREST

by
Jemma Stortford

The daughter of Isaac van der Straatan has been arrested in connection with the theft of the Ashlyn Diamond. This famous diamond was stolen as part of a £6 million raid on a local jewellery workshop. The police believe the four robbers involved were the same gang which have carried out armed robberies on a series of jewellers' along the South Coast.

Danielle van der Straatan (25) took over control of the family jewellery business, Vanders, following her father's death in a mystery car crash last month.

There has been speculation that Vanders is likely to make a substantial loss this year. At the time of his death, Mr van der Straatan had announced his intention to sell his share of Vanders and retire to the South of France.

Police this morning refused to comment on the arrest of Miss van der Straatan – issuing instead a statement to the effect that a local woman, aged 25, is helping them with their enquiries.

Diamonds are a Girl's Best Friend – the story behind the rise of Danielle van der Straatan as one of this country's most successful business-women – see page 4.

Chapter Twenty-four

How the fuck did I get myself into this mess?

Sitting on a hard plastic chair, drawn up against a coffee-ringed wooden table, Danielle was horribly aware that all eyes were on her. Sitting opposite was that smarmy Detective Superintendent, who wore wire-rimmed spectacles to make himself look more intelligent, then made the basic mistake of spending the whole time looking over the top of them. Beside him, a young DC in flashy dark-blue pinstripes laboriously took notes in careful, joined-up writing. Next to Danielle, sitting with her long legs crossed elegantly at the knee, was supposedly the hottest solicitor in the area – a sleek redhead in an expensive suit, who rejoiced in the name of Olivia Greenwich-Fitzpatrick.

Danielle let the three of them get on with business, arguing about her rights as though she wasn't there. She studied her nails instead, marvelling how they were perfect mini-barometers of her downfall. She used to have regular manicures, nails painted delicate shades of pink and lilac. Now the nails were bare, slightly yellow, chipped and flaking. But not bitten. She had not yet become such a nervous wreck that she was reduced to chomping on her nails as a stress-reliever. Swigging vodka was a far more mature alternative.

Vodka, however, clashed with the tranquillisers her doctor had prescribed – to enable her to sleep soundly and dreamlessly, keeping at bay the terrible nightmares that had plagued her since her father's funeral.

Instead of standing beside the grave, on the bright green plastic turf, Danielle would dream she was lying paralysed on top of the coffin as it was lowered into the earth. Then Max, Jemma and Isabel would appear with spades and gleefully fill in the hole. Danielle would feel the soft, crumbling soil showering her face and dropping into her mouth. If she was lucky, she would wake up screaming. If not, she would dream the whole thing over again.

Danielle found herself floating through life, in a mellow but increasingly detached state. She no longer had the embarrassing lapses into hysteria – but neither did she find much to smile about. She had forgotten what it felt like to be happy, as though someone had switched off an emotion chip in her brain. If only she had the courage to chuck the pills down the toilet – but that would mean facing the demons on her own.

"Miss van der Straatan, I asked you a question."

Detective Superintendent Hunter was again regarding her over the top of those steel-rimmed spectacles; the expression in his hazel eyes a mixture of irritation and sheer tiredness. He had been interrogating her for most of yesterday and had started again early this morning.

Danielle forced herself to smile politely. "Sorry, could you repeat the question? You've lost me."

The Superintendent was not deceived. "You don't seem to realise the seriousness of your situation." (Pause for enormity of seriousness to sink in.) "Since we last spoke, we have obtained videos of your father, filmed on security cameras, visiting all the workshops that were robbed. An unremarkable coincidence one might think – until one realises he is clearly watching the respective managers key in their security codes."

Say nothing, thought Danielle, hoping the shock of this latest revelation did not show on her face. The slightest slip could incriminate.

But saying nothing implied guilt . . .

"Is this all the evidence you've got?" She injected a scornful note into her voce. "My father often visited other workshops. We all helped each other out."

"Ridiculous!" An involuntary smile tweaked the corners of his mouth. "You're competing against each other!"

"To a certain extent," Danielle agreed, well aware she was digging herself in deeper, "but if one was looking for a particularly graded precious stone, to complete a necklace for example, another jeweller might be aware of where he could find it."

"All chums together. Sweet."

Danielle decided her pills were not as mind-numbing as she had assumed. She was quite clearly feeling a strong urge to punch the acerbic Superintendent in the face. The consternation that would cause! And blood; she could almost imagine it running in a crimson stream from his beaky nose.

"OK, you can go," said the Superintendent unexpectedly, jerking her so suddenly back to the present it was more of a shock to realise his appearance was normal. "Your young man is waiting for you in reception." Even then the Superintendent couldn't resist another jibe. "He must be quite taken with you – he's been there for hours."

Nico? Danielle felt an unexpected glow of pleasure. How kind; perhaps she had misjudged him. But after she was escorted through the maze of corridors in the police station, and passed the window that looked out onto the reception area, it was Josh she could see sitting hunched up on one of the blue plastic chairs, a black woollen hat worn low over his eyes, donkey jacket pulled protectively around him. The floor was covered in delicate swirls of mud and leaves, having dropped from his filthy boots, and the other people waiting in reception were giving him a wide berth. Josh appeared to have come straight from the farm – and could have easily been mistaken for a gentleman of the road, rather than a gentleman of quality.

"The Earl of Stortford himself," jeered the Superintendent. "What it must be to have friends in high places."

But Danielle was only aware of the sense of crashing disappointment that hit her stomach as Josh caught sight of her on the other side of the glass and it was his friendly face that grinned at her rather than Nico's.

* * *

"You look as though you need a drink," said Josh when they were safely outside in the carpark.

"You mean, I look terrible?" she replied with rare, albeit dry, humour. "Besides, I'm not supposed to drink alcohol with the . . . er, sedatives the doctor gave me." *Like vodka didn't count?*

"I was thinking more along the lines of a cappuccino at La Dolce Vita?" He gave her a sideways glance, as though gauging her reaction. Surely she wasn't that much of an ogre?

Danielle wondered how to get out of this one. Josh was only being kind, but really – after a night in the local police cells, lunch out at a trendy café was the last thing she wanted. What she *really* wanted was a long hot bath and a long dreamless sleep – possibly forever. She shuddered and tried to blank out that last thought.

Josh had brought along his ancient Land Rover, she noticed, and a weary sigh slipped out before she could stop it. Apart from the embarrassment factor, she was now going to get dog hairs all over her suit. *But it was the thought that counted*, she told herself firmly, wishing there was some magic spell she could utter to stop herself from being such an ungrateful cow.

Josh yanked open the door and she clambered into

the passenger seat. The Land Rover was so ancient there were no seat belts fitted, which didn't exactly inspire confidence. A brief image of her father's wrecked car flittered through her mind. And then there was Isabel's crash . . . Danielle gripped the seat and determinedly thought of something else.

Josh started up the engine, which fired on about the sixth or seventh attempt. Then the heavens opened and large drops of rain began to hammer on the grimy windscreen. He clicked on the wipers and, with a terrific screech, they swept over the glass, turning the dirt into a rainbow of varying shades of grey, before jamming solidly halfway across.

Josh smiled apologetically, in that typically helpless English aristocrat way, and said, "Best take you straight home, eh?"

Wonderful! That vision of a hot bath danced into her head once more – and she could change out of these horrible clothes, which somehow had started to smell of the same disinfectant prevalent throughout the cellblock of the police station. It would mean going back to an empty house – but she could always persuade Josh to stay the night – only for company – he'd sleep in the guest bedroom of course.

No, she was feeling vulnerable and likely to suggest that her own bed was far more comfortable than the guest room (remember Nico?). Was one night of comfort-sex worth ten years of a solid friendship hitting the deck?

Josh, blithely unaware of her inner turmoil, crunched

the gears and lurched out of the carpark, narrowly missing a patrol car coming in the other direction. He gave it an unwittingly arrogant wave and the Land Rover rattled off towards Mistletoe Lane.

"I suppose La Dolce Vita would be hell on earth," he added, which showed where his thoughts were. "Everyone watching, pointing, staring."

This hadn't actually occurred to Danielle. She had never been the most popular person in Calahurst, but now she was certainly going to be the most notorious. She had begun to feel the first twinges of panic, and that familiar craving for alcohol, and was about to suggest a quick detour to The Parson's Collar, when Josh slammed on the brakes. If she hadn't been clinging onto her seat for grim death, she would have shot through the windscreen.

"Whoa," he said, patting the steering wheel. "I nearly didn't see that one coming."

A gleaming Aston Martin, swinging around the war memorial outside the church, tooted at him furiously.

Danielle remained gripping tightly onto the seat as Josh had several attempts at putting the vehicle into first gear, gave up and took off in second. Chugging up the hill, painfully slowly, Danielle decided that at least by worrying about his appalling driving it prevented her from dwelling on her other problems.

"You've got to make it up with Isabel," said Josh suddenly, as they finally hit the straight and she felt confident enough to relax her grip.

So he was her relationship counsellor now? "I

would if I knew where she was! When I visited her in hospital she had already discharged herself. I've tried phoning her, texting her, to no avail. She doesn't want to forgive – it gives her power over me."

"Or maybe she chucked her phone in the river again?" suggested Josh with an amused glance. "There could be a simple explanation."

"The hospital said she was with a man," admitted Danielle. "Tall, dark, handsome – and 'foreign-looking'. All the nurses remembered him. They said he was dressed in black, like a rock star, and spoke with an American accent."

"Ah . . ." said Josh.

"She's with Nico."

Josh said nothing; he kept his eyes on the road and smiled sympathetically.

"You knew all the time!"

"Not *all* the time."

"*Most* of the time!" If she wasn't worried he might steer the Land Rover into a ditch she would have thumped him. He was supposed to be her friend – what was he doing fraternising with the enemy? On the other hand . . ."Jemma must have told you."

"She is my sister. We have been known to speak to each other on occasion."

"Why did no one think to tell *me*? I've been out of my mind with worry!" Surprisingly, it was true. In fact, Danielle had been taken aback by how much she had worried about her sister. Now their father was dead, would Isabel be able to take care of herself?

"She's with Nico," pointed out Josh, quite calmly. "He's not a murderer."

"We don't know that. We don't know anything about him."

"Well, actually . . ."

"Yes?"

"It turns out he's the son of Patrick Kearney." When Danielle didn't comment, he added, "You know, the 1980s rock star? He owns his own recording company now. Jemma says he's very successful – "

"I *know* who Patrick Kearney is."

"Nico has . . . ah . . . taken Isabel to meet his father, to try and get her a recording contract."

"So Isabel's still talking to *Jemma* then? In spite of her relationship with Taz, and our father? Un-fucking-believable."

Josh's face darkened. "Jemma has never had a sexual relationship with your father. She never saw Isaac in that way. She saw him as more . . . well, a mentor – a father-figure."

"Pah! Why do I seem to be the only one who can see what she's really like?"

Josh's fingers tightened on the steering wheel. "You will not talk that way about my sister."

It was on the tip of Danielle's tongue to blurt out: "Why not, it's true! She's a complete bitch and I hate her!" like some stroppy teenager. One glance at Josh's suddenly cold expression told her that this would be a serious mistake. She couldn't afford to alienate Josh. He was the only friend she had left.

"At least Isabel's fallen on her feet," she grumbled. "Once Patrick's heard her sing he'll give her a contract and make her famous. Which is what she's always wanted."

"Isn't it what you've always wanted? How often have you told Isabel that she needs to get a life? Now she'll be independent, out from under your feet. You won't have to worry about her any more. You can concentrate on Vanders."

Danielle didn't like to tell him that, actually, she quite liked having Isabel under her control. And that Vanders was proving to be too much trouble for her to cope with on her own – not the prize she had once thought it was. She'd always been able to run to her father for help – now she had no one.

Finally it hit her. She really was alone. Her parents were dead; Isabel – her only surviving family – had walked out of her life without a backward glance. Danielle had no friends – she had always been a loner, putting work first. There were no eager lovers on the horizon – Nico and Max had decamped into the nearest pair of open arms with almost indecent haste. Then there was Josh – what was she to him? An ex-girlfriend from nearly ten years past and an object of pity? The worse thing was, she had brought it all on herself.

Her eye fell on the delicate gold and diamond watch her father had given her for her birthday. *Diamonds are a girl's best friend*: he'd had the words inscribed on the inside. It had been an old family joke. Somehow the words had become ironic – and now prophetic.

The gates of Stortford House loomed up through the torrent of water rushing across the windscreen.

"You can drop me off here," she muttered, fumbling with the door handle.

Josh, already slowing to complete the manoeuvre into the driveway was forced to stop suddenly lest she fall out onto the road. "You can't get out here," he protested. "You'll get soaked walking down the drive."

"Good! A cold shower might wake me up to the stark realities of my life."

He never knew if she was merely being sarcastic, because the car door was slammed so abruptly he had no time to look into her face and see the truth.

Chapter Twenty-five

When Danielle finally reached the front door of Stortford House, totally drenched, she found it was locked. In disbelief, she gave it a hefty thump then rang the doorbell. Nothing.

She had no key, so she was forced to squelch around to the stables at the side of the house, which had been converted into an office for the security guards she had hired following the break-in. She found two of them cosily drinking coffee, with their feet up on the desk, watching Sky Sports and totally ignoring the bank of CCTV screens behind them.

As she threw open the door, sending it crashing against the wall, and stood there, silhouetted against the torrential rain, her clothes plastered to her skin, her hair plastered to her head, looking like a scene from *Carrie* (except with rainwater rather than blood), even they had the grace to look embarrassed. If one of them had made some smart comment like "Wet out there, is it?" she would have punched him.

Actually they made an effort to be kind, offering her a hot drink and a Chunky KitKat, and a coffee-stained tea-towel to dry her hair, all of which Danielle tartly declined. The three of them were then forced to make self-conscious small talk while one of them struggled to remove the duplicate keys from his belt, half-hidden beneath his paunch, and Danielle continued to drip puddles on the floor.

The old Danielle would have fired them on the spot for their blatant incompetence – and then sent them on their way with a string of expletives ringing in their ears. The new Danielle couldn't be bothered – the fight had been knocked out of her. She took the proffered keys without a word and strode out into the rain, hoping her dignity was still intact, and trying to pretend it was really a bright summer's day.

Rather than walk back to the front door, she let herself in through the French windows and into the dining-room. There was no sign of life, but when she walked into the hall she found resignation letters from both the butler and the cook, which explained why the door had been locked.

Beneath that was a letter from the board of Vanders, sarcastically quoting the latest share prices (as though she could possibly be unaware of it) and asking for an urgent meeting. They probably wanted to persuade her to step down and hand over control of the company to someone else. They could bloody well whistle!

There was a mass of other envelopes, mostly brown, waiting to be opened, but Danielle turned her back on them and was heading for the stairs when her foot slipped on something.

She glanced down, hoping she hadn't brought in fox doo-doo from the garden – which would *really* finish her off. Stark against the polished oak floor was a slip of paper. Although the thought of a steaming hot bath was urging her upstairs, curiosity got the better of her and she picked it up. One side was blank; the other held a hastily scribbled note from Simon. He must have written it before her arrest.

Dear Danielle

Just had a call from Flynn; he's finally found a pink diamond for Paige Lorraine's earrings – sounds great. Could you meet him at Jacob's for lunch on Monday? He's booked a table for twelve o'clock. If that's not OK, phone him. I'm off to my parents for the weekend as we agreed – so I'll see you Tuesday.

Regards

Simon

"Yes!" cried Danielle and, kissing the note, she did a little dance around the hall

She was back in the game.

* * *

If anyone had ever known Flynn's real name they had now forgotten it. He had been given the nickname after a series of dangerous pranks while still at college, culminating in a jump from the first floor landing of a hotel, onto a crystal chandelier, and swinging across a wedding party below, to land neatly on the opposite balcony. Now even his family called him 'Errol Flynn'.

He was twenty-five years old, of average height and chunky build. He had curly blond hair, which he cut short so that it did not look effeminate, a large squashed nose and deep-set eyes – but he had never had trouble attracting women – they found his rather battered appearance irresistible.

Flynn was never so happy as when he was up to his armpits in mud on a rugger field, but had dutifully followed his father into the family diamond-dealing business. Unfortunately, another prank, involving a fake sheikh, a suitcase of worthless gems and a representative from Harry Winston had gone horribly wrong. Eighteen months for fraud in Ford Open Prison had knocked the bounce right out of him and his father had died of shame. When he came out, Isaac had given him work when no one else would touch him. Slowly Flynn had built up the business again, although not to its previous dizzy heights and he had failed to inherit his father's sightholder status with De Beers.

Flynn idolised Isaac van der Straatan – but Danielle? Danielle was a bloody nightmare.

As Flynn waited impatiently in Jacob's restaurant, steadily working his way through a bowl of peanuts he had filched from the bar, it occurred to him that, for the first time in his life, he might have been stood up. He took a gulp of his dry martini and considered this unlikely scenario further. While he would not put it past Danielle to delight in humiliating him, surely she would not miss the opportunity to purchase this magnificent diamond?

Flynn looked at his watch. The bitch was now ten minutes late. As she usually arrived early and caught him on the hop, he had broken virtually every traffic regulation to arrive at the restaurant twenty minutes before their appointment.

He put his hand back in the peanut bowl, but found it empty. Irritably he picked up a breadstick, snapped it in two, and absent-mindedly crumbled the pieces in a three-foot radius around his seat, to the impotent fury of the nearby maîtr d'.

Ten minutes and six breadsticks later, Flynn decided to cut his losses and move in on the attractive brunette eyeing him up from the bar. Unfortunately Danielle chose that moment to finally make her entrance, accompanied by a hefty waft of Paris, rather than the cloud of red smoke and smell of sulphur he had begun to associate with her.

Flynn opened his mouth to point out that his invitation had been a lunch date, not a dinner date, when he caught sight of Danielle's cleavage, displayed to advantage in a tight black shirt, and was successfully distracted. She was wearing a burgundy trouser suit – she was a fine-looking woman; there was no doubt about that – and he'd always had a weakness for ball-breakers.

"Where's the diamond?" demanded Danielle, plonking herself down opposite him.

Although he would hate to be married to her. "Here." He fumbled in his breast pocket and pulled out an innocuous-looking piece of folded white paper. He gently shook it over the table and a single gemstone tumbled out. "Isn't it beautiful?" he breathed, hardly daring to take his eyes of it.

Danielle frowned. She didn't even need to dig her loupe out of her handbag, the stone was so obviously fake. Did Flynn think she was a complete moron – or was this another of his famous 'jokes'?

"It's very pretty," she agreed, aware she sounded sarcastic. "But not quite what I'm looking for."

"It's a *pink* diamond. That is what you wanted? You haven't even touched it, looked at it properly. How do you know you don't want it? Simon assured me that this was what you required and I've gone out of my way to get it for you. I'm out of pocket!"

Flynn's voice began to sound like a tape-recording played at high speed. Danielle was too exhausted to keep up the polite facade. The last few days had been spent in endless meetings with dealers, auction houses, fellow jewellers and, worst of all, an enforced stay at the bloody police station. Nowhere could she find a pink diamond even remotely similar to the one she possessed already. As the days went past, and Paige's deadline became imminent, she began to feel more desperate. She put a hand to her head as it began to thump uncomfortably.

The maîtr d' appeared at her elbow. "Is everything all right, madam?"

"Fine!" Danielle waved him away.

She fixed her gaze on Flynn.

"It's a fake, Flynn," she said wearily. "It's not an artificially coloured white diamond, it's not even paste. Your 'pink' diamond is glass – out of a Christmas cracker by the look of it. Honestly, Flynn! Why the hell are you wasting my time on crap? Pull another stunt like this and I'm never going to buy anything from you again – and neither will anyone else from around here because I'll spread the word. Do you understand? If there's one thing I hate, it's being made a fool of."

"Fucking bitch!" Flynn snatched up the diamond and crumpled the paper around it. "Who do you think you are? I got this direct from De Beers and if they hear you calling their stuff 'crap' they'll sue you. You're losing it, girl! If you can't tell a genuine diamond from a chunk of glass – "

Danielle abruptly stood up and walked out of the restaurant. She could not stand to hear Flynn's whining voice any longer.

The sun shone weakly through the rain clouds as Danielle stood on the pavement, staring across the sea. It was all so hopeless. She clenched her fists and felt as though she just wanted to scream. Her head was now pounding, blurring her vision. She scrabbled in her handbag for her Naratriptan, but all she could find were her bloody happy pills. With a howl of rage, she chucked them into the water. What was the point of taking something to numb her pain when they numbed every other reaction as well? She was turning into a zombie at the very time she needed all her wits about her.

A couple walking their terrier along the pavement were forced to step onto the road to avoid her as she stood in the centre of the pavement, staring out to sea, wondering if she ought to throw herself in after the pills and have done with it. She was oblivious to their mutterings.

"Taxi, miss?" enquired a voice by her ear.

He had to repeat his question twice before Danielle finally glanced round. Without realising it, she was standing by the taxi rank. The only vehicle, an old-fashioned black cab, was waiting there, engine running, and door open invitingly.

Danielle was too upset to even feign politeness. "I don't need a car," she said brusquely, "I have my own. It's parked right over – "

But as she turned to gesture towards the other end of the harbour, the taxi-driver unexpectedly gave her an almighty shove and she fell, sprawling, headfirst onto the back seat of the cab. Two men jumped in beside her. They were dressed in smart suits and, as Danielle looked up, she was just in time to see them pull black balaclavas over their heads, hiding their faces.

Danielle stared in disbelief. The drugs were addling her brain. Either that or she had wandered onto the set of a Guy Ritchie film.

"Dani-girl!" said one, grinning broadly. "We've got a present for you!" And he thrust a damp white cloth over her face. Danielle recoiled instinctively, but fell against the shoulder of the other man, who pushed her upright and held her face into the cloth.

It had been impregnated with a chemical and Danielle began to feel woozy. She attempted to struggle, using her teeth and her nails, like she had learnt in self-defence classes, kicking out with her feet, knees and elbows, knocking the cloth onto the floor.

She stabbed the second man with the metal heel of her stiletto shoe, causing him to curse. He thrust her away from him and she tumbled onto the floor. But his friend hauled her back by her hair, taking a perverse pleasure in causing her pain, yanking her head round until she cried out. Her elaborate hairstyle came tumbling down, the pins scattering across the floor. As one dug deeply into the man's hand, she was suddenly freed; it gave her long enough to bang once on the rear window, hoping to get attention, before she was dragged back onto the seat.

It was a waste of effort. The couple with the dog still walking arm-in-arm along the pavement, looked out across the water and heard nothing.

The second man caught hold of her more firmly and pinned her arms to her sides. Belatedly she screamed, more an instinctive reaction than a formulated plan, but the white cloth was again shoved over her mouth, the faint chemical smell making her gag. She frantically turned her head, right and left, trying to dislodge it before it choked her, but only succeeded in breathing more of the stuff in.

The chloroform rapidly took effect, making

everything appear as though she was watching it from the wrong end of a telescope. She could hear her heart beating, her own laboured breathing, and the men's voices through a fog.

"Hold it, hold it, we're nearly there."

The tunnel abruptly narrowed to a pinpoint of light and her world went black.

Danielle slumped unconscious onto the second man's shoulder. His friend held the cloth a while longer, to be certain, then slowly removed it, bending his head to listen to her slow, steady breathing.

"She's gone."

Chapter Twenty-six

The atmosphere during the drive back to Calahurst from Bath was as awkward as the outward trip had been. Despite having shared a bed, Isabel felt that she and Nico were still failing to communicate on the basest level. She was wracked with guilt that Danielle was having to deal with the police on her own, and worried that once Nico discovered she was as guilty as her sister, he would drop her immediately. What a wonderful scoop for his book! Chapter Ten – 'My Affair With Diamond Thief'.

The ninety-minute journey was mostly spent by Isabel staring out of the side window and muttering to herself: "I can't believe this is happening", "It's some kind of sick joke" and "Danielle would never do anything like this".

She knew she was rambling, she knew Nico was totally bored but too polite to interrupt, but somehow she was unable to stop. Eventually, as they hit Salisbury, he cracked, and shoved a Travis CD into the deck to drown her out. Not the most auspicious start to a brave new relationship.

They arrived at Calahurst police station just before midday. Nico struggled to find a space in the yard crammed with staff cars; in pure frustration he abandoned the Bat Mobile in a space painted with the words '*Det Supt only*'.

He'd hardly switched off the engine before Isabel had leapt out of the passenger side, running around the side of the building to the main entrance. Nico had lent her his trench coat, to keep her warm, and she could feel it flying out behind her like a superhero's cloak. How convenient it would be if she could snap the bars on Danielle's cell and fly them both to safety as though she was one of the Power Puff Girls. Except, on reflection, the Power Puff Girls didn't wear cloaks – they wore little pastel dresses and Mary Jane shoes, which wasn't her thing at all.

"Can I help you?" The sergeant behind the desk, a cup of coffee halfway to his lips, seemed surprised to see her. He frowned. "Weren't you here a moment ago?"

Isabel thumped the desk. "Where's my sister?"

"Sister?" The station sergeant's confused expression cleared. "Ah yes, *twin* sister. She's been released," he said calmly, and took another gulp of coffee as though that was the end of the matter.

"I should bloody well hope so – seeing as she's *innocent*!"

Nico appeared at her side. "Are you *looking* for a fight, Isabel?" he muttered under his breath, steering her towards the exit. "That is no way to talk to an officer of the law."

The sergeant, suspecting a hefty waft of sarcasm, looked up sharply, but the door was already swinging shut behind them.

Nico and Isabel squared up to each other in the carpark. Isabel's nerves were a frazzled mess, having spent the last ninety minutes imagining the worst had happened to her sister – which involved a lengthy spell in Holloway, with only a zonked out, heavily tattooed, shoplifter called Shazzer for company. It was rather an anti-climax to find Danielle had been released without charge – and had not implicated her in any way.

Isabel was starting to wish she hadn't rushed back from Bath. She should have known Dani was quite capable of sorting out her own problems. It was also starting to occur to her that walking out on Patrick, without so much as a 'thank-you' or 'good-bye', might have sabotaged any prospective career with Trick Records.

There was also her fledging relationship with Nico. They could have spent a few more days in the romantic splendour of the Abbey, taking their time to get to know each other – far away from Calahurst, where things were complicated by the death of her father and Nico's defunct relationship with Danielle. Then there was his book . . .

Last night it had been easy to forget that Nico was a

journalist, that he was actually in Calahurst to write a hard-hitting, muck-raking biography of her father. She appreciated that he had to earn a living. If she felt a little more at ease in his company she could broach the idea that maybe he'd like to pick another subject.

It was so unfair. For the first time in weeks, she really had felt her life was getting back on track. She should have known it was too good to last.

"Oh bloody hell," she said, and sat on the bonnet of the Bat Mobile. The suspension creaked ominously.

"Are you OK?"

For a moment Isabel thought he was talking to his car and couldn't help grinning at her mistake. She still hadn't got used to the way he was looking at her; that sensual brown gaze zipping straight through her heart and bouncing off her toes.

Nico appeared to translate her idiotic grin as a positive sign rather than abject hysteria. "You were panicking about nothing. Danielle is fine – I bet she made mincemeat of Superintendent Hunter."

Isabel frowned. "Dani is not as tough as you think."

"She's as tough as old boots and you know it." As Isabel was no longer smiling, Nico put his arm around her shoulder and gave her a reassuring hug. "Let's go home."

"I don't actually *have* a home . . ."

"My home – *our* home. You can phone Danielle from there."

"What if she doesn't want to talk to me? What if she puts the phone down? I think I'd feel happier if we drove round to Stortford House and checked on her personally." When Nico looked dubious at this suggestion, she added, "Even Danielle can't ignore me if I'm camped out on the front doorstep."

"Fine." Nico removed his arm from her shoulder and commenced a search through his pockets for his keys. "Whatever you like."

* * *

There was no reply at Stortford House, but a security guard, ambling around the corner, let them in and calmly informed Isabel that Danielle had gone out to lunch.

"Lunch?" echoed Isabel bitterly. "Sounds like she's really suffering."

Nico folded his arms and looked down at her. "So," he said stoically, "what do you want to do now?"

Isabel spoke without thinking. "I'm going to pack my stuff up so I've got some more clothes to wear – that's if Dani hasn't binned them! Then I'm going to wait for her to come back. You don't have to hang around," she added, unaware that her words sounded careless. "I can borrow one of Dad's cars."

"If Danielle's taken a working lunch, she could take forever."

"Then I'll wait forever. We have to talk to each other some time. We're sisters. We can't go on like this."

"I sure hope not," muttered Nico, but he briefly kissed her cheek before heading for the door.

Isabel began her trek up the curving wooden

staircase. As she reached the top, she remembered to look back and wave Nico good-bye.

Unfortunately he had gone.

* * *

Nico returned to his house; never had it seemed so lonely. There was a message from Patrick on the answering machine: "What's with the Cinderella complex – running out on me like that? You've got to get me the number of the gorgeous Isabel. I want to make her a star."

You want to make her, period, thought Nico, stabbing the erase button.

Just as he had made the connection with a beautiful, bright, funny girl, Patrick was going to snatch her away. Even if she did remain faithful, they would never see much of each other. It'd be work, work, work and the endless carousel of recording, performing and promotion. Nico had grown up in this industry – Isabel hadn't a clue what she was getting herself into.

Talking of work . . .

Amongst the pile of bills, junk mail and free samples that had been shoved through his letterbox, Nico discovered a gleaming white envelope from his publisher. He tore it open, knowing exactly what it was going to say.

Having paid an enormous advance for Nico's book about Isaac van der Straatan (who, until very recently, they had never heard of) his publishers were anxious to know how the project was going. As Isaac's mysterious death had even featured in a couple of the national newspapers, they were, understandably, concerned that Nico's pet project had literally gone up in smoke.

Now they were putting pressure on him to give it up. They had been approached by the management of a 'well-known girl-band called Aphrodite', who wanted to get a biography in the shops ready for next Christmas. It was expected to be an excellent money-spinner – and wasn't Emily Cavendish close to his father? It should be easy for Nico to gain exclusive access . . .

Nico crumpled the letter into a ball and tossed it into the bin. It would be so simple to write a biography about the rise of Aphrodite. He wouldn't have to do any research – and he had plenty of contacts – though he was sure it wouldn't be quite the sycophantic product Aphrodite's management had in mind . . .

Realising how little he had worked on his manuscript of late, Nico felt suddenly cold. The deadline for the completed work was next March. As it was now November, there was little chance of being finished by then.

He shoved the letter into the back pocket of his jeans, made himself a mug of coffee and went upstairs to the second bedroom, which served as his office. He found the blue envelope file, crammed with the cuttings he had collected on Isaac and, blowing the dust from the cover, opened it. He had so much background information, and had been working on the project for so long, it was horrifying to realise he had written so little.

He knew why, although he did not like to dwell on

it. First there had been his obsession with the cool, unobtainable Danielle – resulting in his suffering such a guilt complex he could hardly put laser printer to paper. Now he had fallen for Isabel – so hard that he found it impossible to feel anything other than an overwhelming need for her.

Nico leafed through the file, debating whether it was worth salvaging his stalling career, only to lose the girl – or to give everything up for true love – and *still* not get the girl. As besotted as he was, he had to admit Isabel (not exactly Ms Reliable) could be a bit flaky.

At the bottom of the file, badly crumpled, was *The Calahurst Echo's* profile on Isaac, published over a year ago, which had given him the idea for the book. It was a cleverly written, slightly flattering article, but Nico had to read it three times before he had worked out what was wrong. And, when the realisation hit him, he had triumphantly scrawled across Isaac's handsome features, '*How?*'

How could Isaac, who had clearly started out with nothing, make such a huge personal fortune from what amounted to a small chain of provincial jewellery shops, which were doing well, but not astoundingly so? Copies of the company's accounts proved the profit margin was comfortable – but not large by any means. Yet Vanders could turn out merchandise that would appear on the covers of magazines such as *Vogue* and *Tatler* – and Isaac could treat himself to Impressionist paintings.

Nico carefully put the cuttings back into the file and

replaced it on the shelf. He wished he could shelve his own book so easily – but there was the little matter of the mortgage on the apartment he had recently bought in London. It was Hobson's choice. Take the Aphrodite biography, get paid lots of money – and lose all the respect and credibility he had built up from his previous books. Or, finish the book on Isaac van der Straatan in a mad scramble to beat his deadline – and lose the love of Isaac's daughter forever.

Nico sat on the corner of the desk and picked up his coffee. It was now cold and skin had formed over the milk, puckering at the edges. He remembered that the milk had been in his fridge since last week sometime and firmly put the mug back on the desk. He didn't have time for food poisoning.

He lit a cigarette instead and stared out of the window, across the wild tangle of a garden, beyond the local school's playing fields, towards Calahurst Quay.

The Georgian houses, which looked so smart from the front, were an untidy mess of drainpipes at the back. Much like himself: a respected biographer with the soul of a sleazy tabloid journalist. Two months ago he'd crept across the same playing fields in the early hours of the morning, nipped over the wall of one of the smart Georgian houses, climbed up one of the fat drainpipes – and into bed with Lady Jemma Stortford. The silly bitch had assumed she had picked him up the evening before.

Jemma's hall window was open now. It was a miracle she hadn't been broken into previously. The window above was closed – but that was Taz's place and he was touring in America.

Nico stubbed out his cigarette on the table. How would Taz react when he found out Nico had moved in on his girlfriend? When he had asked Nico to look after Isabel, shagging her would not have been what he had had in mind.

Nico felt uncomfortable dwelling on this. Taz had been a friend – and he had treated him like shit. His thoughts turned instead to something Taz had said to him when they last met, about how unlucky Isabel was: a car crash, a break-in at Stortford House, suffering the indignity of becoming trapped in a sauna . . .

Nico's eye followed the line of Georgian houses, from residential to commercial, the stream of boutiques and businesses that lined the quayside – the most exclusive part of Calahurst – until he paused at a redbrick Victorian building. It had been a church originally, he remembered, and then a nightclub owned by a local villain – Paul de Havilland had been one of several police officers in his pay. The building was now a gym – a haven for the middle-class, middle-income population who abounded in Calahurst. What was it called?

Oh yes, *Granger's Gym.*

* * *

Kimmie stared at the man with the rock-star looks, who was waving a twenty-pound note in her face, and wondered where the hidden cameras were. Was Caitlin secretly testing her honesty – or was Graham Norton about to pop out of the jacuzzi?

"Are you *sure* you don't remember a woman being locked in your sauna?" asked Nico.

Kimmie glanced nervously behind her, to check the staff-room door was closed, before hissing, "Are you from the TV?"

"No."

"Oh."

"I'm from . . . er, *Hello!*" said Nico. "We're doing a feature on health clubs."

"Oh wow, Caitlin's going to be so chuffed! I mean, perhaps you'd better discuss this with Mrs Granger," suggested Kimmie. "To get her approval first."

"I'm kinda short of time . . ." The *last* thing Nico wanted to do was speak to Caitlin Granger. He gave Kimmie the benefit of his devastating smile. "I'm sure you'd be able to help me . . ."

Kimmie gave another furtive look around. Nico felt like banging his head on the desk. Any normal girl would kill to get her picture in *Hello!* It was hugely popular and well respected. Totally unlike him of course . . .

"Why do you want to know if someone got locked in the sauna?" asked Kimmie suspiciously. "I thought *Hello!* only wrote nice things about people?"

"We're branching out – to appeal to the common denominator. You know how the professional classes are always making complete asses of themselves."

Kimmie giggled. "You're right," she admitted. "Isabel

van der Straatan got trapped in there a couple of weeks ago. Silly tart was giving her boyfriend one in the gents' changing rooms. They were almost caught and so she thought she'd climb out onto the balcony and then back into the women's changing rooms. She made such a racket, Caitlin went to see what all the noise was about. Isabel hid in the sauna and got stuck."

"Isabel van der Straatan," repeated Nico, talking into his cellphone as though it was a tape-recorder. "How do you spell that?"

"Haven't a clue. But her family own Vanders – you know, the jewellery boutique up the road? They have some great stuff in there, really funky." She sighed. "Not that I can afford to buy any of course . . ."

Nico handed her the twenty-pound note. She looked at him meaningfully and he peeled another from his wallet.

"How did Miss van der Straatan manage to lock herself into the sauna? I thought those things didn't have locks? That they were communal?"

"Apparently a plastic wedge was jammed under the door and she couldn't get out. Personally I think she locked herself in for the attention."

This was a new one. "Why's that?"

"Not more than five minutes before, I'd seen her go out the main entrance, fully dressed. She must have doubled back, got changed into a swimsuit and somehow wedged the door."

"Are you sure it was her?"

"You can't miss that carrotty hair – and the snooty

way she has about her. I called 'good-bye', but she ignored me. Because she's got a rock-star boyfriend I suppose she thinks she's too good for the rest of us."

It was as though he'd strayed into *The Twilight Zone*. "How was Miss van der Straatan dressed?"

"She arrived in jeans and T-shirt, but left in a black trouser suit."

Nico stared at her. Did Isabel even own a suit? With the exception of parties, he'd only ever seen her in jeans or a denim skirt. "Are you *sure*?"

"Sure I'm sure."

"It couldn't have been someone else who resembled her?"

Kimmie seemed to think this was funny. "Not unless she has an identical twin sister!"

Chapter Twenty-seven

"We're here. Is she awake yet?"

"I don't think so." Someone prodded Danielle in the ribs. Her gasp was muffled by the folds of the blanket swathed around her head.

"No need to wake her up if she isn't."

Danielle forced herself to lie still, pretending to be asleep; that way she wouldn't have to communicate. It would give her time to gather her thoughts, work out an escape plan – and she *was* going to escape, of that she was certain. Who did these people think they were – that they could do this to *her*?

She was lying on the back seat of a car, possibly the same taxi, but she had no idea how long she'd been unconscious or, therefore, how far they had travelled. Despite the horrible, scratchy blanket over her head, she could hear a radio, softly playing pop music. Her kidnappers were silent and she could not hear other traffic – perhaps they were travelling through the forest?

Her hands were tied behind her back, the rope digging uncomfortably into her wrists. Her feet felt numb and, after surreptitiously trying to wriggle them, she realised there was more rope around her ankles. Bastards! Did they think she would attempt to jump from a speeding car?

As she lay there, silently fuming, she was quite sure she could feel the car slowing down. Her body rocked towards the edge of the seat – then, as the car manoeuvred around a sharp bend, someone caught hold of her waist, holding her in position. Oh, the indignity of it all!

She could hear the car's tyres scrunching across stones. The beach? Perhaps they were further along the coast and had not gone inland into the forest as she had thought. This was driving her crazy. Not being able to see, or to know where she was going, why they were doing to this to her. For money? Ha, that was a joke – Vanders was one step away from bankruptcy.

She had a nightmare vision of being bundled onto a boat and transported out of the country. "Calm, keep calm," she muttered under her breath.

The car stopped and the doors opened. Someone grabbed her ankles and attempted to drag her along the back seat, through one of the passenger doors. Danielle made herself as heavy as possible. She was damned if she was going to make it easy for them.

"Christ, she's a dead weight!"

Danielle felt a chill run through her. She recognised that voice, that soft drawling, American accent. Nico? No, not deep enough and there wasn't that familiar lilt that sounded as though he was laughing at a private joke.

"You're doing it all wrong," his partner was saying, with an accent that owed more to the Home Counties. "You should have pulled her out head first. You're making it difficult for yourself."

Danielle was inclined to agree, particularly when the American accidentally dropped her and her knees hit the bottom edge of the doorway. "*Sorry* – but I don't make a habit of this."

"I can see that."

"OK, you're the expert, you do it."

"Bugger that. Wake her up."

"Help yourself."

The Englishman swore under his breath and, grabbing Danielle around the waist, yanked her back. But he miscalculated her weight and she slithered through his arms, falling in a heap against his legs.

In the interests of self-preservation, Danielle decided to 'wake up'. "What happened?" she moaned. "Where am I?"

"There you go; she's awake. Better cut the rope around her ankles if you want her to walk."

"OK – but I'm confiscating those bloody shoes of hers."

The American held Danielle tightly against his chest while his friend cut the ropes from her knees and ankles and removed her high-heeled shoes. Danielle did not struggle. She had no wish to lose a slice of her leg.

They pulled the blanket from her head; she tried not to wince as it caught her hair, but she still couldn't see – she must have a blindfold over her eyes. It was a relief to be free of the stuffy blanket. She turned her head towards the breeze, cool and slightly damp against her cheeks, and took a breath deep into her lungs, feeling it pacify her – far more effective than any happy pills.

I'm doing very well, she told herself firmly. The secret to surviving this would be to not get hysterical and to resist the temptation to kick anyone in the balls – an action liable to result in a serious injury to herself. She had to stay relaxed, serene, let it all wash over her head . . .

"Can you walk?" the American asked her.

"I think so." Her legs felt stiff and they ached; her skin itched where the ropes had cut into her. Despite her resolutions, there was still one question she had to ask, that was burning into her consciousness so much she had to blurt it out. "Why are you doing this to me?"

"Shut up and walk!" The Englishman gave her a shove.

OK, learning curve. Next time keep her mouth *shut*.

"Take it easy," murmured his friend.

"This isn't a vicarage tea party. We're not friends. If anyone is to be making conversation, polite or otherwise, it'll be me. Do you understand?"

"Fine. Whatever."

Danielle said nothing.

As they walked away from the car, Danielle heard it start up and drive away. One gone, only two to go, she told herself.

Long wet spikes of grass, or weeds, brushed up against her ankles and she was sure could hear the faint sound of the sea. She was right! They were on the coast.

Despite her inner pep talk, with two men walking closely either side of her, hope of escape was looking rather slight. Besides, how could she expect to be rescued, if no one knew where she was? Would anyone miss her? Not Isabel, that was certain, or Jemma. She didn't see enough of Josh for him to realise she had disappeared. In fact, the only people she saw on a regular basis were the staff of Vanders and once they found she had vanished off the face of the earth they would probably throw a party.

As Isabel had taken great delight in pointing out, if she didn't go through life trampling all over people's sensibilities, she would have friends, a man to love her, a sister who cared if she lived or died.

The upshot was that, if she wanted to be rescued, everything depended on her. She had to leave a sign, drop something instantly recognisable as belonging to her, to show that she had been here.

But what? A piece of jewellery was the obvious choice – but she couldn't reach the jet brooch pinned to the lapel of her suit, and her rings were too small – they would fall in the grass and be lost forever. She was not wearing a bracelet – which left one thing – the gold and diamond watch her father had bought her for her birthday. It had the Vanders trademark, her name and the date of her birthday – and the inscription that kept coming back to haunt her: *Diamonds Are a Girl's Best Friend . . .*

But it was the last thing her father had given her before his death. There was no way she was going to part with it – it might never be found, or *worse,* be found by someone who would realise its value and never give it up.

Although if she did nothing it would be her that was never found – not until years later – in a shallow grave . . .

Scrap that last thought! Danielle felt the familiar swirl of fear knot up her stomach, the edge of nausea . . . no, she mustn't have a panic attack. Not here, not now. *Deep breaths – in, two, three; out, two, three . . .*

Before she could change her mind, Danielle caught her fingernail under the delicate fastening of her watch, flipped it up and felt the diamond bracelet slither from her wrist, brushing against the back of her thigh. She strained to hear it hit the ground, but there was nothing, the grass and mud dulling the sound so that it would be inaudible. Which was a *good* thing, she told herself firmly. It would mean her kidnappers would not notice what she had done.

The Englishman, however, had realised she was walking more slowly. He grabbed her arm. "If you try running off, I'll bloody shoot you!"

He shouted so close to her ear, Danielle felt herself cringe away.

"Don't forget, you're not a 'one-off'. If anything happens to you, we'll snatch your sister and get what we want from her."

Isabel? God, no . . .

"How can I run away?" she protested, and even to herself her voice sounded bitter. "You took my shoes!"

The sarcasm earned her a crack around the head. She staggered against the American, who pushed her upright. No sympathy there then.

"If you hadn't dug your *fucking* heels into me you would still have your *fucking* shoes!" the Englishman was bawling at her. "Jesus, those things ought to be classified as offensive weapons!"

"Quit it," murmured the American. "We're here now." He fumbled with a lock, there was the creak of a door and Danielle felt a hand against the small of her back encouraging her forward. "Look out for the steps!" he added – too late, as Danielle fell up the first one.

"Thanks!" The asperity came out before she could stop it. Well, she wasn't going to have a complete change of personality overnight. Danielle felt her way up the steps with her foot and realised she was walking through a doorway, entering a building, possibly a house, as she could feel bare boards beneath her feet. There was a short walk, a mere five or six strides, and then the American stopped her again.

"There's flight of stairs in front of you. I think there are fifteen steps . . . er, let's see . . . one . . . two . . . three . . ."

"We haven't got time for this," complained the

Englishman. "Start climbing, Danielle. You'll know when you reach the top."

Because they were going to push her off? Danielle began to climb. One flight, two flights, three . . . it was quite a tall building – a disused factory perhaps or a condemned block of flats – no, not flats, because the floor was wooden, not concrete.

Keeping her mind active, realised Danielle, was the only thing preventing her from going crazy. If she stopped to think about where she was, what she was doing, what was going to happen to her – she was going to go nuts.

A door was opened and she was pushed through. A large hand on her shoulder forced her down, so that she half-fell into a sitting position onto something soft. A chair? A settee? The ropes around her wrists were cut, but before she could massage them to get the circulation going, something cold and metallic was snapped around the left wrist. Handcuffs? Another click and she realised she was trapped, handcuffed to a fixed object beside her. There was the sound of the door closing, then silence. Danielle waited, then unable to bear it any longer, reached up and pulled the blindfold away from her eyes.

She was alone.

She appeared to be in some kind of storage room. There were no windows, or furniture, only the bed she was sitting on. It looked new so perhaps it had been bought especially for her. There was a bowl of fruit and a pile of magazines: *Marie-Clare, Tatler* – all the ones she liked reading; and a couple of books by her favourite authors. It was creepy. These men knew what she liked – they knew *her*.

Did that mean they'd be less likely to kill her? It was hard to tell. The American, who sounded so familiar it was driving her crazy, seemed kind, but the Englishman had a nasty streak. She put her free hand up to her forehead, where he had hit her. She couldn't feel any bump, or blood, but the skin was tender. If he was capable of hitting a woman, then surely he was capable of killing her? She had to get out of here – *but how*?

She looked around her prison, hoping for inspiration. Although someone had attempted to clean prior to her arrival, there were still cobwebs in the corners and trailing from the wooden beams above. Oak beams – that would signify an older building. And cobwebs would mean spiders . . .

Danielle nervously checked the area in her immediate vicinity, but it seemed clear of her little eight-legged friends. For the first time in what seemed like weeks, she actually found herself smiling. She had survived a kidnapping, had the very real threat of violence hanging over her head and all she was worried about were *spiders*?

It was then she noticed a small, square trapdoor. Escape! But it was about ten foot from the floor so she would need to stand on the bed – oh, and a hacksaw to get rid of the handcuff . . .

Bloody hell! She flopped back onto the pillows and wondered if she had the enthusiasm to peel an orange.

Gradually she became aware of low voices from the other side of the door, then the sound of the bolt being shot back. If they were going to kill her, she hoped they'd do it quickly. Her stomach churned. Would they stab her? Shoot her? Irrationally, she wondered what they'd do with her dead body. Bury it in the wood or take it out to sea and dump it?

Her hand closed over one of the oranges – although what did she think she was going to do with it? Throw it in someone's face and break their nose? Like the trick Isabel had pulled with the Cartier clock. Except her aim was not as good as Isabel's and, to be realistic about this, there was not a lot of damage one could inflict with a Jaffa.

She dropped the orange back into the bowl. The door opened and one of the men walked in. He was tall, gangly even, although his shoulders were slightly stooped as though embarrassed of his height. The black balaclava was menacing but strangely incongruous when worn with a smart suit. An expensive watch flashed diamonds on his wrist. Danielle felt her eyes drawn to it.

He tugged his cuff down.

"Too late, Max," she said quietly.

"*Shit*!"

"I gave you that watch last Christmas – and my heart too, I seem to remember. It seems so long ago – yet you still wear it. Why is that, Max? Is it some kind of trophy, like other men collect knickers – or can't Jemma afford to replace it with anything better – now that my father's dead and unable to support her in the manner to which she had become accustomed?"

He stared at her, uncertain. She thought he might pull off the balaclava, admit defeat, and let her go. *Please, please, please, let me go . . .*

"You took your blindfold off."

"No one told me not to!"

"Why do you think we're wearing these fucking balaclavas?"

"Fashion statement?" Now she knew it was Max, she felt she could relax. Max wouldn't hurt her. He might be a womanising bastard and a total creep, but he wasn't a murderer – she was sure of that.

He took two steps towards her, scooped the blindfold up off the floor and threw it at her. "Put it on!"

"No! You've got to let me go now. I know who you are."

"No – I've got to kill you – because you know who I am."

The idiot always did have a sick sense of humour. Only this time he wasn't laughing . . .

"I'm not going to prison, you stupid bitch! No way am I going to prison for *you*. So put the blindfold back on – do as you're told for once in your life – and quit arguing with me. You're so goddamn awkward. I *knew* we should have snatched Isabel."

"Look, if you wanted a pay rise, you only had to say –"

"Money? You think this is about *money*?"

"It's traditional! Kidnap the girl, ask the family for

money?" *Except Isabel wouldn't even know which bank we're with . . .* "How much do you want?"

"We *want* the diamond back."

"*Diamond*?" For a moment Danielle didn't understand what he meant. "The . . . the Ashlyn Diamond? That was *you*?"

"Isaac always swore you didn't know," Max's voice was cynical. "That you were innocent and weren't involved. Guess he lied about that as he lied about everything else."

"I'm not – I mean, I wasn't – I found the diamond in Dad's desk drawer when I was clearing out his office at the workshop. He'd made no effort to hide it. I thought it was rubbish until it hit the bin and went 'clonk'."

"In a *drawer*?" Max slammed his fist against the wall, startling her.

She began to feel frightened once more. When she had recognised him, she'd thought her troubles were over. Max had never been violent. Max would never hurt her – he wouldn't hurt anyone . . .

"If you knew how I searched Stortford House from top to bottom – I don't fucking believe it!"

"It was *you* who broke in and attacked Isabel?"

"I thought you'd all be at Jemma's party."

"You hit her!"

"It was her own fault for coming back early! I was frustrated! Have you any idea how much that diamond is worth? I've got a lot staked on it."

"Were you involved in those raids on the jewellery workshops? Were you and Dad working together? You must have a fortune stashed away. You said you don't want to go to prison – so why risk breaking into Stortford House for one lousy diamond, when you know we've got all that security because of the Tissot painting. Why not take the painting?"

"Because the painting is a *fake*, like everything else about Isaac. And the diamond? Because it's so famous, it could be worth a *hundred* million at the very least!"

As Danielle was too stunned by the revelation about the painting to interrupt, he carried on talking. "The haul was supposed to be split four ways. That was the deal. Except your father stole the Ashlyn Diamond without telling us. We didn't even know it was in the workshop. He must have casually slipped it into his pocket and the first we knew about it was when we read about it in the papers like everyone else. He double-crossed us."

"You killed him, didn't you? The car accident – only it wasn't an accident, it was a carefully staged hit. One of you ran him off the road – am I right? Then you watched as his car went up in flames and he died . . . you bastard!"

Instinctively Max took a step back, but Danielle was still chained to the headboard of the bed, forced to confront the man who killed her father and unable to do any more than chuck a bowl of fruit across the room in her frustration.

"Dad gave you every chance at Vanders, he thought you were great – someone who cared about the business as much as himself. He promoted you – he even wanted us to get married – and this is how you repay him? Fucking hell!" She sat abruptly down on the mattress. "First Jemma, then you – everyone sees him as this walking wallet – they take and take and he's too soft-hearted to realise he's being taken for a sap – "

"Your father wasn't a sap!" he interrupted. "He was no angel either. The raids – they were his idea. It was his gang, he got us together – and he planned everything. He wasn't the guy you thought he was, Dani, you're just gonna have to accept it."

"I do accept it – I knew the truth when I found the diamond. I'm not stupid! But he was my father and he didn't deserved to die like that. How could you *do* that to him?"

"He cheated us!"

"It sounds to me as though he did all the hard work – he had the most to risk if he was caught – he would have lost everything."

"You're condoning him?"

"I'm trying to understand him, what motivated him and why he had to die at the hands of the man he thought was a friend."

"He was a jewel thief, like the rest of us, motivated by greed. What is there to understand?"

"Vanders was doing – well, it was doing OK – we weren't poor – "

"You weren't as rich as he wanted you to be. Stortford House is rented; Vanders has been in trouble for years. Isaac was too weak to admit to failure. He kept on deluding himself – and you – that everything was coming up roses. The other guys called him 'the great pretender'. Nothing in his life was real."

"He could have admitted the truth. I would have understood."

"You think? If there's one thing I'm sure of, Isaac knew you and Isabel had him down for some kind of hero. How could he admit he was a fake?"

Danielle put her head in her hands. "So the fact that my father was a delusional jewel-thief is entirely my own fault?"

Max did not contradict her. He merely said, "Tell us where the diamond is, Danielle. Or we'll kill you too."

Chapter Twenty-eight

Isabel had a long soak in her own bath, dozens of candles spluttering around the room, aromatherapy oils scenting the air, a glass of chilled wine to relax her – and, if she was to be honest, prepare her for the inevitable fight with Danielle.

She didn't want to fight with Danielle; she never did; yet somehow it always happened. Where was the closeness between twins that the psychologists were always babbling about? Sometimes she could quite cheerfully stick a knife through her sister's ribcage – and she wasn't entirely sure she'd bother to bury her under the terrace – merely leave her body to rot where it fell, or to be picked over by the birds, or –

She took another gulp of wine as the theme from *Buffy* shattered the quiet air of the bathroom. Her mobile phone was frustratingly just out of her reach, so she was forced to scramble inelegantly out of the bath and snatch it up before it rang off.

The screen told her the caller was Danielle. "Hello?" she said nervously, wondering if she was about to be treated to an earful of abuse. "Danielle?"

"Isabel van der Straatan?"

Isabel had just pulled a pink fluffy towel off the heated radiator and begun to wind it around herself like a roman toga, when the voice on the other end – male and upper-class – brought up her short. She stared at the phone in confusion. The screen definitely said it was Danielle calling. She slapped it a couple of times. That would teach her to accept freebies from Taz. Maybe it only worked in Australia.

Except the caller knew her name . . .

"Yes . . ." she said hesitantly.

"We've got Danielle."

Isabel was still having trouble getting her head around the idea that there was a strange man using her sister's mobile phone. Had Dani been arrested again? Or was the simple truth that Danielle could no longer bring herself to speak to her – and had involved some poor guy to act as an intermediary?

"Why can't she speak to me herself?" Isabel demanded. "Put her on right now!"

"I don't think you understand." The voice was calm, emotionless. "We have your sister. Unless you do exactly as I say, we're going to kill her."

* * *

Nico was dreaming about bells. Wedding bells. He was standing by the altar at St Peter's Church. The organist started playing enthusiastically and, as all eyes turned towards the back of the church, Isabel made her entrance. She was wearing a horrible flouncy dress, straight out of *Gone With the Wind* and, instead of bridesmaids, was flanked by Patrick Kearney and Elton John, sporting pink leather suits and singing 'The Chapel of Love'.

Nico woke up in a sweaty panic. *Wedding*? Fuck, they had only slept together the once . . .

It was remarkable the tricks guilt could play on your subconscious, he decided, throwing back the duvet with shaking hands, before striding off towards the bathroom for a piss. He was halfway there when he realised the bells he had been dreaming about were, in reality, the ringing of his cellphone.

He scooped it up. "Isabel! Where the hell – "

"Have I called at a bad time?"

Patrick. "Christ, it's early."

"Some of us haven't been to bed yet."

Not for the first time did Nico wish he had a father like everyone else's. One with a normal job, who kept regular hours –

"I'm still waiting for Isabel's telephone number."

Who didn't keep trying to swipe his son's girlfriends. "Why?"

"Relax . . ."

Why did he get the feeling Patrick was having a huge joke at his expense?

"My intentions are honourable. I'm offering Isabel a

contract and I want her to meet with Sykes & Allen on Wednesday."

Nico felt the bottom drop out of his stomach. Natasha Sykes and Alicia Allen were the hottest songwriters in the UK – the twenty-first century's equivalent of Lennon & McCartney. If Patrick could persuade them to write for Isabel, she'd be guaranteed an international number one. Patrick must really think Isabel had something. He'd never approached Sykes & Allen to write a song for Aphrodite . . . Unless – was this some elaborate scheme to lure –

Nico firmly redirected his thoughts. The whole Emily thing had totally clouded his judgement. Isabel wasn't like her. Emily had known who he was right from the first and always hassled him to meet his family. He had assumed it was a security thing. In reality she wanted an introduction to his father. Nico hadn't even realised she *wanted* to be a singer. When they met, at a glitzy London nightclub over four years ago, she'd told him she was training to be a beautician.

"Nicolas?"

"I'm still here. I'm kinda . . . well, blown away is the expression I'm looking for. Sykes & Allen? How did you fix that?

Patrick chuckled. "Well, I once dated Natasha's mother it's true – but I can be charming when I put my mind to it. When I told the girls about Isabel, the plans I have for her career – "

"They haven't heard her sing. You don't have a demo or anything – "

"Who says I haven't?"

Nico felt cold all over. *Isabel had given Patrick a demo tape?*

"I recorded the karaoke night."

"That's underhand, even for you."

"It was above-board. We only recorded the acts signed to Trick Records – and er, Isabel. You must have practically tripped over the video camera, it was set up right inside the door."

He knew Patrick well enough to realise he was attempting to bluster his way out of a tight spot, but it wasn't worth falling out over. "We arrived late, you'd already started."

"Sky have asked me to produce a live concert on Christmas Eve. It was originally going to be Christmas Number Ones but, as I couldn't see Talisman performing 'There's No One Quite Like Grandma', we decided to broaden the appeal and go for songs with a Christmas theme. Talisman will be headlining, Aphrodite are signed up too. We've already cut an album; it'll be in the shops in December. It'll be great promotion for the label and with all the expense and stress I've suffered over The Lost Boys I'm in sore need of a lucky break."

Nico waited for Patrick to talk himself out. "You reckon Isabel has something special?"

"Are you *kidding*? That huge black voice coming out of a skinny white body? We're going to be wiping the floor with the opposition next year, I'm telling you."

Nico couldn't resist a bit of banter. "She hasn't signed with you yet."

"Has she had another offer?" There was a distinct note of panic in Patrick's voice.

"No, she hasn't had another offer. But maybe I ought to get her fixed up with a manager first – ensure you don't rip her off!"

"You're winding me up, right? OK, take her to see Sam Smith – "

"Sam Smith manages bubble-gum groups."

"Look, I don't give a flying fuck who you get to manage Isabel, just get her to the London office on Wednesday at twelve o'clock. If she stands up Sykes & Allen, after all I've done to put this meeting together – well, I'll be – "

"Stuck with The Lost Boys in boy-band hell?"

"Now don't go tempting providence!"

It was almost like old times, reflected Nico, replacing the cellphone on the bedside table. That easy camaraderie he had with Patrick – more like an elder brother than a father and then Emily had come between them . . .

Although he had never felt about Emily, the way he felt about Isabel. He loved watching her laugh, the perfect bow lips curving upwards until a cute dimple appeared in her cheek. He enjoyed provoking her too – seeing her slim dark brows draw together, her silver-grey eyes sparking furiously. But that distant expression, the desperately sad look in her eyes, when he knew she was thinking about her father – it really tore him up. He wanted to take her into his arms and banish the nightmares forever – slay the dragon, win the love of the princess . . .

Nico caught sight of his expression in the bathroom mirror and began to laugh.

Jeez – he *had* got it bad!

* * *

Danielle's fish tank was positioned right in the centre of a low, circular, marble-topped table – white of course, like everything else in her suite. Even the fish where white – or rather, an iridescent colour which changed as the scales caught the light. They were practically transparent too. As Isabel knelt beside the tank she could see their insides . . .

Isabel, if she had the inclination to keep a pet, would have chosen something more cute and cuddly. Danielle had always been a bit of a cold fish, so maybe they were perfect for her. After all, fish didn't need to go walkies, they didn't poop on the carpet – and they didn't need extravagant displays of love and affection to keep them loyal . . . Right up Dani's street.

Isabel felt a pang of remorse, remembering how she'd teased Danielle when Jemma had waltzed off with Max right under her nose. Or maybe 'goaded' was a better word and now Jemma had done exactly the same thing to her with Taz . . .and now she knew how it felt . . .

Isabel concentrated on the matter in hand. The bottom of the fish tank was lined with large clear crystals. It was an excellent place to hide a large clear diamond and certainly more secure than any safe. It only presented Isabel with one problem. How was she going to distinguish the real diamond from the fakes?

The fish, glimpsing her distorted reflection, swam as one towards her.

"Get out of the way," she muttered, rapping on the glass.

The fish, startled, fled to the furthest side of the tank.

Great, now she had guilt too. The poor little things wouldn't have been fed for ages.

"Look guys, I'm sorry," she mouthed through the glass – like fish could lip-read! "I'll feed you later, promise." She began to roll up her sleeves. "But right now I've got to –" She looked back at the crystals shimmering at the bottom. "Heck, they really do all look the same . . ."

The fish, more slowly this time, swam over to her side of the glass.

Isabel sighed. The only way around this was to empty the tank and check each crystal individually – which meant taking the fish out first – a real fun job – and smelly too, by the look of the slimy algae that had collected around the side of the glass.

There wasn't an alternative. If she didn't solve this problem, no one else was going to do it for her. And if she didn't get a move on, her sister was likely to wind up dead. That's what the kidnappers had promised. If they didn't get the Ashlyn Diamond back, they were going to kill her.

Isabel struck this last unpleasant thought from her mind and said, with a confidence she didn't feel: "Come on, fishes, you're taking a holiday."

She heaved the tank into her arms. She had underestimated how heavy it was. The sharp edges dug into the soft flesh of her arms and she could feel her palms start to slide down the cold glass. She tried to hitch it back into position, the water slopped from side to side. She glanced anxiously at the floor but, although there was water seeping through the floorboards, it didn't look as though she'd lost any fish.

Maybe it would be more practical to rest the tank on the floor and push it towards the bathroom. Then all she had to do was lift it high enough to tip it into the bath . . .

She wasn't quite sure how it happened. It could have been condensation on the glass, or perhaps her palms were sweaty; but, as she began to lower the tank, it slid from her hands and hit the stripped oak floor. Water, glass, crystals exploded in every direction. And the fish – the poor little fish were flapping helplessly amongst the sharp, jagged fragments.

"Oh no!" wailed Isabel, wondering which calamity she should deal with first. Dealing with a crisis was not her strong point. That was what Danielle had been there for. But while she stood here dithering about it, the fish were gasping their way into oblivion.

She had to pick them up – but they'd die without water – so she should run to the bathroom and fill the sink with water. *But what if they didn't like tap water?* What kind of fish were they? Didn't tropical fish require heated water? *But how hot?* And how could she reach the bath when the floor was littered with tiny shards of glass – *and she had bare feet.*

"Dani – "

Nico! She had got herself into such a state she hadn't heard the sitting-room door opening.

"I'm Isabel," she grumbled. Even after they had both slept with the guy he *still* couldn't tell them apart.

"I'm sorry – but this is Danielle's suite and I thought –"

"Nico, you've got to help me. I have to get the fish into water, so I need to run the bath, but there's glass all over the floor and I don't know if the water should be hot or cold. Or salt? Do you think they should be put into salt water? They're just going to die if I do nothing. Oh blast, I think this one's dead already!" And as she peered closer, at one of the larger fish lying motionless on the wreckage of its little crystal palace, she overbalanced.

Nico crunched across the glass and caught her.

"Watch out for the fish!" shrieked Isabel.

Nico raised an eyebrow, but was able to refrain from making any comment. He stepped carefully across the flapping fish, went into the bathroom, stuck the plug into the sink and filled it with water.

Isabel was still wringing her hands. "Do you think they'll be all right in tap water?"

"A whole lot better than they're gonna be on the floor!" Nico filled a jug with water and handed it back to her. "Use this to pick them up then we'll stick them into the sink."

Isabel took the mug from him and crouched down, gingerly picking up each tiny fish by its twitching tail and dropping it into the jug. Some were no longer moving, but she dropped them in anyway, hoping they would revive. She and Nico worked as quickly as possible until every fish was safe, albeit cowering at the bottom of the jug.

"Do you think they'll be all right?" she repeated. "They don't look happy."

Nico peered into the jug. "I guess they're in shock."

"Shall I give them some food?"

"Couldn't hurt."

"There's one small problem – I'm stranded here." She indicated her bare bleeding feet. "I can't walk over the glass."

Effortlessly Nico picked her up, crunching carelessly across the glass and crystals to the sitting-room. Isabel tried hard not to think about that priceless diamond that was somewhere underneath his size twelve shoes. As he lay her gently on the couch she saw that he was frowning.

"Your feet are bleeding."

She shuffled up against the scatter cushions, aware that a white leather couch was not the best place to be dripping blood. Particularly not *Danielle's* white couch. "I don't think it's anything much – it doesn't hurt. I'll go back to my room and dig out a couple of plasters and – "

"Don't move," he said grimly. "I'll get something to clean away the blood, then we can assess the damage."

Ordinarily his masterful attitude and Doctor Ross impression could have been quite a turn-on, but all Isabel could think of was how Danielle was going to kill her if she bled all over her precious sofa.

Except Danielle couldn't kill her if she was dead . . .

Isabel swallowed, feeling that familiar panic sweep over her, and she propped herself up on one arm, trying to see if she could spot the diamond glittering somewhere on the floor. Unfortunately at that moment Nico returned from the bathroom with one of Danielle's flannels and sat next to her, totally blocking her view, and began to gently dab at her feet, which were flecked with congealing blood.

Nico, she thought, in a flash of inspiration. He'd know what to do.

Except – she couldn't tell him . . . *"If you contact the police – we will kill your sister. If you tell any other person – we will kill your sister. If you dial back this number – we will kill your sister. Do you understand?"*

As she shivered, Nico glanced up at her face. "Is the water too cold?"

"Fine," she muttered, wishing he'd just hurry up and get it over with, so she could find this bloody diamond, save Danielle and put their lives back together.

"You'll be OK. I don't think you'll even need a plaster."

"Thanks."

"You're welcome." He slowly stretched out his hand to smooth her fringe from her eyes. "You know, you look kinda pale . . . do you feel OK?"

"Am I?" It must be the shock she was feeling over Danielle. She should take care to behave normally . . .

His fingers, still in contact with her skin, stroked

tenderly down her cheek to her mouth. Isabel's first reaction was to kiss him. But if she did that he'd never leave – and she still had to find the diamond . . .

He gently outlined her lips. "So, Isabel, do you think we have something here?"

Isabel regarded him blankly. Could he be a little less obscure? Maybe it was an American thing. Or maybe her brain wasn't firing on all cylinders. Why didn't he tell her he loved her? Then she could say it back.

A little voice inside her head reminded her that he couldn't possibly love her. He'd known her for little over a month and in that time he'd already slept with both Jemma and Danielle – callously dumping them when a better offer came up.

Perhaps her doubts were plastered all over her face because he bent to lightly touch her lips with his own before looking deep into her eyes and saying, "I love you."

Sure you do. Like you 'loved' Jemma and Danielle before me . . .

He smiled uncertainly. "You love me?"

"I . . . I . . ." *Why did he have to put her on the spot like this!*

He sat back and stared at her, disbelief flickering across those handsome features. "Or don't you?"

"Er, well, you see – "

The warmth in his eyes was replaced by a cold, hard look and abruptly he stood up. "Or are you like the rest? Only interested in me because I'm Patrick Kearney's son?"

"That isn't true! At least – "

"Don't lie to me, Isabel."

"I'm not! If you'd shut up and listen to me – "

He folded his arms and looked down at her, cold and forbidding and not exactly inviting confidences. "I'm listening!"

"It's too soon," she tried to keep her voice calm. "We're rushing things. I don't know you well enough –"

"You knew me well enough to leap into bed!"

She felt her face flush with colour. "That was different . . ."

"Yeah, you're an easy lay."

Wallop! She let him have it.

As she stared at him, seeing an imprint of her hand slowly begin glowing on his olive skin, she was utterly appalled by what she'd done. "Nico . . ."

"Save it," he said and abruptly turned for the door.

"Nico, please – I want us to be friends first and then –"

"You want us to be *friends*? Jesus, you are unbelievable!" He paused, one hand on the door. "Don't worry, you'll still get your contract. All you have to do is turn up at my father's London office at twelve o'clock on Wednesday and you have it made. Only don't expect me to be there to hold your hand."

The door swung shut behind him.

As Isabel sat back down on the settee, totally numb, she saw something glittering against the floorboards, half beneath the marble-topped table. She snatched it up, holding it up to the light, hardly daring to breath. A large, cushion-shaped, brilliant-cut diamond. *She'd found it* – despite the trauma. Her sister was safe.

Isabel turned it over in her hands. It was certainly beautiful – and had caused so much trouble – her father's death, her sister's kidnap, all this for one diamond. Personally she couldn't see the attraction. Sure, it was beautiful and maybe it did last forever – but it was cold and hard. She'd rather have love in her life – friends and lovers – than a whole vault filled with these ultimately worthless stones.

Her mobile telephone rang.

"Nico?"

"Sorry darling," said that same, hard-edged voice she had spoken to earlier. "This is business. Have you got it?"

Her fingers closed over the stone. "Yes," she said dully. "I've got it. And you're welcome to it. All I want is my sister back – "

"The ruined church at Port Rell. Wednesday. Twelve o'clock."

"What?"

"Bring the diamond." The line went dead.

Wednesday? Isabel slid the mobile phone into her pocket. But wasn't Wednesday the day she was supposed to be meeting Patrick? If she failed to show that was her career down the shoot as well as her love life.

Did she care?

Chapter Twenty-nine

Nico left Stortford House in such a rage he was hardly aware of what he was doing. As he ran down the steps to the drive, his coat streaming out behind him, he barged a security guard out of his way, barely apologising, before throwing himself into his car and tearing off down the drive. Instead of driving back to his London apartment (his first impulse), he took the road to the quay, abandoned his car in front of the bollards and headed straight for The Parson's Collar – the only bar in Calahurst.

As Nico was not a huge fan of alcohol (he considered he had quite enough vices already), he hadn't been here since his first visit to Calahurst – researching *One Rotten Apple*. The place didn't appear to have changed much. It was styled as a mocked-up church, with fake flagstone floors, pews for seats and what appeared to be an original stone font piled high with snacks. As it was early, there was only one barman, tall and gangly with a thatch of red hair, serving from a cut-down pulpit.

Nico ordered a double whisky, ignored the barman's attempt at polite conversation – why did the British always want to talk about the weather? – and stomped to the back of the bar where he could hide in the shadows and brood.

The number of empty glasses on the table had multiplied, and Nico was contemplating how much effort it would take to get up and buy another, when an additional shadow fell across the table.

"Hello, Nico."

He glanced up. Jemma. The dim light of the bar shone on her blonde highlights, giving her a halo effect, although no one would ever mistake her for an angel. Her breasts were straining at a tight pink T-shirt, which had the word 'Available' scrawled across. She didn't really need to advertise. Her sultry smile was already giving him the come on – although he was surprised to find she was having little effect on him. He preferred Isabel.

He was surely certifiable.

"Go on, you can do it," derided Jemma.

"Huh?"

"Say 'hello' back."

"Hello back," he grunted and took another slug of whisky.

Jemma ignored the frosty vibes and slid into the seat opposite, resting her chin on her hands and giving him the benefit of her smoky eyes. "Long time, no see," she said. "How was the trip to Bath?" Then, as that didn't get a response: "So, how *are* you?"

"I'm not up to chit-chat, Jemma. Sorry, but that's just the way I feel. Nothing personal."

"You've had a fight with Isabel?"

He didn't have to ask her how she knew. He always thought it one of life's little ironies that the telephone had not been invented by a woman. "News travels fast," he said. Aware he was being extremely boorish, he left the table and went to order another drink from the bar, without bothering to ask her if she wanted anything. Well, he hadn't asked her to sit down.

She was still there when he returned, playing with one of the tablemats. Couldn't the girl take a hint? He was sorely tempted to go and sit somewhere else, but that would have been churlish. He realised he was still wearing his trench coat and took it off, slinging it over a spare chair before sitting opposite her.

He decided he was going to have to be blunt. "I really want to be alone, you know?"

"If you wanted to be alone, you would be sitting at home, instead of drinking yourself into oblivion in public with 'fool for love' stamped across your forehead," replied Jemma calmly. She took out a packet of Marlboro and offered him one. They weren't his usual brand, but he took one just the same, and the light she offered.

Jemma blew a thin sliver of smoke towards the overhead lights. "So, what was the fight about?"

"You think I'm going to tell you?"

"Forget I'm a journalist – think of me as Isabel's best mate. Perhaps I can help? I'm good on relationships."

So he'd heard. Which was why he'd chosen her as his first 'hit'. "I don't think so," he said. "To a journalist, nothing is off the record – and I should know."

"You consider yourself a journalist rather than a biographer?"

"It's how I started out."

She leant forward, genuinely interested. "Did you ever work for a big national? One of the broadsheets?"

"Not in this country. After leaving college I had a job on *USA Today*, but it wasn't really my scene. I'm not a team player."

She seemed disappointed, leaning back in her chair and resuming her cigarette. It was like a nervous twitch, he thought, watching her body language carefully. But what had she got to be nervous about? Him hitting on her? Wasn't that what she wanted?

"Why choose biographies over fiction?" she was saying. "You could have closeted yourself away in a garret with only your computer for company – "

Her aimless prattle was getting seriously on his nerves. "Look, Jemma, I'm fine. Don't feel worried about leaving me on my own. OK, I've had a bust up with Isabel. I'm sure we'll sort it out and if we don't, well, that's life. I'm not gonna throw myself off the cliff at Port Rell."

"Let me know if you do," she grinned. "It'd make a great story."

"Scumbag Journalist Kills Himself After Row With Diamond Heiress?"

Jemma grimaced. "I can see why you failed to hack it in the newspapers. *Kearney's Son In Death Plunge* sounds better. Headlines have to be short and punchy, you know."

"Kearney's son," brooded Nico. "Ignore the fact that my books have sold hundreds of thousands, that I've won awards for my investigative reporting. When the chips are down I'll be remembered for eternity as 'Patrick Kearney's son'."

"What's so bad about that?"

"You want to go through life as Jemma Stortford, hot-shot journalist, or Lady Jemma, daughter of the Earl of Stortford – all ball-gowns and pearls and photos in *Country Life?* Wouldn't you rather be the one writing the headline? *Making* the headlines covering some groundbreaking news story?"

"I'm proud to be my father's daughter," she retorted, "and you should be proud to be your father's son. He's an idol to millions."

"I *am* proud of my father – but I don't want to spend my life – or my death for that matter! – in his shadow."

Jemma didn't reply to this. Instead she said, "This conversation is getting too heavy. Can I get you another drink?"

As Nico had barely touched his latest whisky he shook his head, and watched her progress to the bar. She certainly oozed sex appeal, he found himself thinking, realising every other man in the place was doing much the same thing. He wondered if she was still seeing Taz . . .

Jemma turned her head and looked back at him, catching him out. She gave him a wicked little smile. He smiled back before he could stop himself and then surprised the couple at the next table, who had him down for a melancholy drunk (the very worst sort) by unexpectedly laughing out loud. What a huge joke if, after bedding Jemma, Danielle and Isabel in search of the big story, he finished up with Jemma again. She was certainly his type. Little, blonde and sweet – a girl he could cherish and protect.

That was why he had failed to gel with Danielle. She had the traffic-stopping looks, but was tough enough to take care of herself. A princess who didn't need rescuing, who was quite capable of slaying a den full of dragons herself – with little more than a sharp tongue and a butt-kicking attitude to life. Isabel, however . . .

Except he was not going to think about Isabel.

He took another slug of alcohol and found himself choking on the raw alcohol. He did not usually drink whisky, only when stressed – which, on reflection, was the worst time to start. He had discovered a long time ago that it was impossible to work either inebriated or with a hangover and so stuck to smoking.

It dawned on him: why was he sitting in a bar at all? Jemma, damn her, was right. Getting legless in a room full of strangers was a form of attention-seeking self-pity. He should return to his little rented house, switch on his computer and work. Quit with the prevarication. Finish the book and return to London. After all, when he'd written about Paul de Havilland he'd never tried to seduce his daughter for insider information. What kind of sleazebag had he turned into?

By the time Jemma returned from the bar, with something white and fizzy in a wine glass, he was pulling on his coat.

"Are you going?" she asked in bewilderment.

"Yeah – work to do, sweetheart."

"We were having such a nice talk!"

"You mean, I talked – you listened. Sorry, guess I bored you to death."

"Not at all." She paused, looking up at him searchingly. "We never really talked before, did we? Just shagged. Perhaps that was our problem?"

She was talking as though they'd had a relationship, rather than a better than average one-night-stand. Was she deluding herself, or trying to delude him?

Guilt was starting to make serious inroads into his alcohol-fuddled brain. The temptation to clear his conscience and start with a clean slate was overriding all sensibilities . . .

"Jemma," he said, careful to look her straight in the eye, "there's something I've got to tell you. But not here." Because the couple at the next table had noticeably perked up when the word 'shagged' had made an appearance and he had an aversion to discussing his sex life in front of strangers. Besides, once Jemma found out the truth, it was likely to get violent.

Jemma cheered up, again misreading the situation. "My flat is just down the road. We could go there?"

"So is my house. Come back with me – for coffee. And I mean *coffee*," he smiled, so as to let her down gently, prepare her for the scene ahead. "I know how you Brits always misinterpret the word 'coffee' as 'sex'."

She grinned and jokingly punched his shoulder. "OK, 'coffee' it is. Let's go."

Nico left his car parked where it was. He had no desire to be picked up for drunk driving by his new friends from the local police station. So they walked along the quay, past the sailing club and up the hill. Although the sky was a brilliant blue and cloudless, the wind was brisk and cold, slapping the river up against the wall and sending icy spray right across the pavement. And again Nico found himself lending his sensible trench coat to a girl who had dressed for a beach holiday rather than the tail-end of an English fall.

Riverside Terrace was, as its name suggested, a row of eight redbrick terraced houses overlooking the river, built in the early 1800s for the Calahurst fisher folk. The occupants nowadays were mostly elderly – friendly, but they kept themselves very much to themselves. Their gardens were a beautiful tangle of roses, hydrangeas and fuchsias, as yet unblackened by frost, and the whole lane looked so pretty in the afternoon sunshine, Nico realised he would be sorry to leave. He was starting to think of the place as home.

"Nice house," said Jemma, pausing by the gate and

turning around to admire the outlook across the cliff road. "I've never been here before. Well, I've driven past it of course, but not actually stopped. What a glorious view you have, right across the river and you're not overlooked at the back either, because of the playing fields. They're the same playing fields behind my – hey, you can see my apartment from here!" She clutched at his arm and pointed down the hill. "Look, second house on the left, my apartment is the one with the window open, just below Taz's."

"Mmm," said Nico, busying himself by unlocking the front door. He was starting to think he might have made an error of judgement by inviting Jemma back here. All he had been thinking about was clearing his own conscience and how that would make him feel better. It hadn't occurred to him to think about how Jemma was going to take it – when she found out he'd broken into her apartment, then slept with her, not because he loved her, fancied her or even liked her very much. All because he had needed access to the close-knit van der Straatan family. The twins' twenty-fifth birthday party, where he could disappear into the crowd, had seemed the perfect way in.

As Nico walked down the passage towards the kitchen, gesturing for Jemma to take a seat in the lounge, he thought again what a total shit he was. So instead of switching on the kettle, he poured himself another drink from the dusty bottle of whisky he had found at the back of the cupboard, left behind by the last occupant.

He wasn't aware of how long he stood there, leaning against the worktop, sipping at his drink and staring out of the kitchen window at Jemma's apartment – until she appeared beside him.

"Hey, where's my coffee?"

Nico quickly turned, before she could see what was attracting his interest. The kitchen seemed to take a few seconds to catch up with his head.

She was looking disparagingly at the smeared glass in his hand. "Why are you drinking whisky? Have you got a cold? A couple of paracetamol is far more effective, you know. But don't drink them together or you'll OD!"

A *cold*? He was having trouble keeping up with her conversation. Isabel sometimes had that effect on him too. Leaping from one topic of conversation to another with barely a pause for breath.

Isabel . . .

He looked again at the glass in his hand. Fuck, now he knew he had drunk too much – he was becoming maudlin. He chucked the whisky down the sink and, before he could change his mind, tossed the contents of the bottle after it.

"Pooh!" Jemma wrinkled her nose at the strong fumes. "I think it was off – if it's possible for whisky to be off . . ." She switched the kettle on and then realised it was empty. "You haven't filled it with water," she grumbled. "Honestly, men!" She unplugged it and headed for the sink.

"Sorry." The words came out slurred, which didn't surprise him.

Jemma grinned. "How much have you had to drink? Are you going to feel it tomorrow!"

Nico grunted in agreement. It was about all he thought he could manage. He would have thought a brisk walk up the hill would have sobered him up – but it only appeared to have made him worse. Maybe this was not the time for confessions. He needed all his wits about him if he was going to be dealing with a woman scorned.

"Poor darling," Jemma patted his shoulder. "This thing with Isabel has really hit you hard. Let me make you a nice cup of coffee and sober you up." She rummaged through the cupboards, found the mustard and brown mugs and began spooning instant coffee into them. "I wondered what had happened to you. I'd been waiting for you in the sitting-room for ages – I thought you'd popped off to the loo!"

Her constant chattering was getting on his nerves. It was much easier to lean over the counter, rest his head on his hands and let her voice wash over him.

As a mug of black coffee materialised in front of him, Jemma jabbed at his shoulder with a bony finger. "Don't go to sleep on me! We don't want you choking on your own vomit."

"Thanks," he muttered, looking sideways at her. Again, the kitchen seemed to take its time catching up. "You know, I really don't feel so good. Perhaps, we could have this . . . conversation . . . some other time? I'll buy you a drink, lunch . . ." *Anything, just fuck off out of my house and let me crash out and forget today ever happened . . .*

The smile on her face appeared a little fixed. "Of course," she said. "I understand perfectly."

Which meant she didn't. He picked his coffee up, felt the nausea rise within him and put it back down again, slopping the steaming black liquid across the counter top. "I think I need to lie down," he muttered. "Can you let yourself out? Sorry."

His legs were shaking, and he managed to overshoot his bedroom several times, but eventually he groped his way to the bed and collapsed onto it. The room began to revolve around, spinning faster and faster, so he rolled onto his stomach, and dropped his left leg over the side, resting his foot on the floor and slowly everything came to a halt. It was a tip Taz had given him, after one particularly debauched night out in Bath.

Nico smiled at the memory – and promptly fell asleep.

Chapter Thirty

When Nico awoke, several hours later, he rolled over and found Jemma lying beneath the duvet beside him, snuggled down like a child. Her streaky coffee and cream hair was splayed messily over the pillow, revealing a high, rounded forehead; dark lashes curling over faintly freckled cheeks; a cute turned-up nose and pale pink lips, curving so temptingly it was a real effort not to kiss her to see if she was real.

Her eyes flicked open, making him start guiltily.

"Hello," she said, plainly amused by his discomfiture.

He drew back, widening the gap between them. "What are you doing here?"

"Sleeping." She pushed herself up on one elbow, the duvet slipping a little. Her shoulder, bare and brown, gleamed in the light from the street-lamps.

"This is my bed," he found himself saying stupidly.

She giggled. "You sound like one of the Three

Bears!" She put on a high, squeaky voice: "Someone's been sleeping in my bed and oh no, *they're still here*!"

He didn't find it funny and the fact that she was teasing him so blatantly strengthened his resolve. "I asked you to leave. Why hang around when you know I feel like shit?"

"Ooh, masterful!" She lent forward and dropped a kiss on his forehead. "Are you worried I'm going to take advantage of you?"

Goaded into retaliation, he flicked back the duvet, thinking she would call his bluff, scream and grab the sheets up around her ears. Instead, she remained perfectly still, lying provocatively back against the crumbled sheets, one hand beneath her head, causing her small breasts to jut upwards; the other, resting casually on her flat belly. She could have been posing for Renoir. He caught his breath.

She watched his reaction with a quiet satisfaction. "Do you like what you see?"

Nico struggled to regain the upper hand. He wanted to be the one in control. The way she was mocking him was stirring up a passion he didn't want to feel.

"Where are your clothes?" he demanded coldly, dropping the covers back over her.

"My clothes?" she feigned innocence. "Oh my gosh – I'm completely naked! How did that happen?"

"Quit trying to fool me we had sex – I'm fully dressed."

"Ah, but that's what the escape hatch is for." Her hand suddenly snaked from beneath the duvet, jerking down the zip on his jeans. "Handy, eh? And you thought it was for taking a piss . . ."

He slapped away her hand, irritably pulling up his zip and sat up against the pillows, hoping this would help him feel more in control of the situation. "For Christ's sake, Jemma! What's got into you?"

"I wish you would," she grumbled, flopping back against the pillows. "This born-again virgin act is getting tedious."

He didn't know how to handle her in this mood. "Look," he said, trying to keep his voice calm. "Please put your clothes on and leave. I can't see the point of continuing with this. I don't want to hurt your feelings, but neither do I want to make love to you. Can't you just go?"

She changed tack, staring up at him, eyes wide and hurt. "Don't you . . . find me attractive?"

English girls – so damn insecure! "Of course I do!"

"So what's the problem?"

"I'm not up to another one-night stand. I can't do it any more." That was the truth. It had taken some time it was true – but it seemed a conscience had finally kicked in.

For a moment Jemma was silent. He couldn't even hear her breathe. "It doesn't *have* to be a one-night stand . . . does it?"

In these circumstances, brutal honesty was the only option. "I can't offer anything else. I love Isabel."

"How do you know she loves you?"

A very pertinent question. "I guess I don't." Not that

it made any difference to the way he felt. Sadly, love was not always a two-way thing . . .

"No wonder you two are having problems with your relationship. Why not cut loose; she'll only get bored with you. Like she did with poor Taz. Did you know, she didn't even bother to phone him to wish him good luck before the Cardiff gig? Or even watch it on Sky."

Nico did not want to talk about Taz. He already had a major guilt thing going after moving in on the man's girlfriend. So he tried to get the conversation back to the point. Not for the first time did he wish he'd never invited Jemma back here. If they'd have gone to her apartment he could have achieved the same result and walked out at the end. Short of throwing her bodily out of his bedroom window, he was at a loss as to how to get her to leave.

Taking his silence for acquiescence, Jemma slid her fingers over his thigh. He immediately caught her hand and pulled it away.

"Sorry, Jemma," he said firmly. "I can't."

"I don't see why not. I don't mind sharing you. Isabel would never find out."

"Until you tell her."

"I wouldn't."

"Of course you would. One day you'll wake up and decide you can't live with your conscience any more and besides, Isabel 'really ought to know what a two-timing, double-crossing bastard' I am."

"I didn't tell her about Taz . . ."

Vaguely he remembered the old joke: *What part of 'no' don't you understand?* Was the only way to get rid of Jemma to make her hate him? The easy way to do that was to tell her how he'd used her to gain entry to the van der Straatan party. The reason he'd invited her round in the first place!

"I've got something to tell you," he said, before he could change his mind. "The night we met – well, we didn't actually *meet* – I broke into your apartment, got in beside you and waited for you to wake up."

She smiled uncertainly. "You're joking, right?"

"I watched you come home, roaring drunk. I watched you open your door by banging your fist against the side of the lock. Then I climbed through your hall window, the one you always leave open, let myself into your apartment and climbed into bed beside you."

"I don't believe you – "

"I set you up because I needed an invitation to the twins' party and I didn't have the time or the inclination to go through the girl meets boy chat-up routine. I couldn't take the chance that you might turn me down."

"But why *me*? Isabel's got loads of friends."

"One of the guys at the sailing club told me about you – a good-time girl who was always up for anything. How one morning you'd woken up in each other's arms, beneath the tarpaulin of the one of the Wayfarers, without a clue how you'd got there."

"James . . ." She was now staring at him in horror. "The *bastard*!"

"He told me how you have such a high turnover of friends you can hardly keep a track of them all – and that the only one who had stuck with you through everything was the rich Isabel van der Straatan – because she was the only girl in the village who hadn't had you move in on her boyfriend. Although apparently that hasn't stopped you throwing yourself at her wealthy father – "

This time he had gone too far. Jemma aimed a punch at his face; he saw it coming and turned his head away and the blow hit his shoulder instead. It was surprisingly painful. For a little thing she certainly packed a powerful punch.

"I've never slept with Isaac! Why won't anyone believe me?"

He had little sympathy for her. "Track record?"

She sniffed and looked defiant. "OK, I admit I wanted Max because he belonged to Danielle and I wanted to piss her off. She's such a bitch, doesn't know how lucky she is – living in her perfect little world, with her perfect career, her perfect blue-eyed boyfriend and her perfect stately home – which used to be mine! And, yes, I got a kick out of shagging Taz for much the same reason – but also because he was rich and famous. I can be as shallow as the next girl!" She laughed bitterly. "Isabel almost caught us recently. He had to run off and hide in the bathroom. Stupid girl – she used to treat him like shit. If it hadn't been me it would have been some groupie. These rock stars get it offered to them on a plate."

She paused for breath and glared up at him, shivering with fury. "*But* I never *ever* had sex with Isaac. He was like a father to me."

"You already have a father."

"Who died when I was fifteen! I know there's Josh, but he's not the father-figure type – he's not even the big-brother type! Bloody wimp! If only I had been born a boy, the house would have come to me. Josh is hopeless in business. All he's interested in is his wretched farm. I'd never have signed Stortford House over to Isaac. It was our birthright!"

"Excuse me? I think Isaac was pretty good to you. He got you the job with *The Calahurst Echo* when you were unable to get any of your children's books published. He paid for your apartment – "

Her mouth fell open in pure amazement. "How do you know all this?"

"Research, sweetheart. I'm a journalist – "

"You're an obsessed arsehole, that's what you are!"

Nico stuck valiantly to the point. "It poses the question, why would Isaac do all this for you? What was in it for him – if it wasn't sex?"

She shrugged. "Guilt – he'd made Josh and me homeless. Stortford House was our home and, I admit, at one point it looked as though Josh would have to sell it he had that big a debt. Then he and Isaac did a deal – that Isaac would *lease* the house instead – for his lifetime. It did seem odd, I admit – after all, it was a deal far more beneficial to Josh than to himself. I think he hoped that Josh and Danielle might get it together, that she'd become the next Countess of Stortford, keep it all in the family so to speak. But you know Danielle – she only cares about her bloody diamonds."

Jemma was crying again, the fight all gone from her – which made Nico feel a total shit – he'd said some pretty cruel things. But there was no taking them back. He passed Jemma the box of tissues that was on his side of the bed and she took a handful, burying her face in them. He waited, but her distress showed no sign of abating. Where did they go from here?

Reluctantly he put his arm around her, not wanting her to get the wrong idea, but as she carried on crying, he found himself drawing her closer. She snuffled into his shirt; it began to feel uncomfortably damp. He could feel her body shuddering against him, her skin, warm against his. This was in danger of getting out of control . . .

"Why are you such a bastard?" her voice muffled against his chest. "I thought you were so nice when I first met you. I couldn't believe my luck – it was like you'd dropped in from heaven or something."

"I'm sorry," he murmured against her hair. "I'm so sorry. It wasn't personal. I wanted to write a book; I thought I was doing research. I didn't mean for it to get out of hand. I guess I didn't think of you, Danielle and Isabel as real people – with feelings – you were just subjects in my book . . . Christ, I've been so arrogant!"

"You can say that again!"

Jemma said it with such feeling he found himself chuckling.

She pulled away slightly to look up at him. Even in the dim light from the street lamps outside, he could see her face was wet with tears, grey and black eye shadow smudged down her cheeks. She looked so vulnerable, so helpless; all he wanted to do was make it better. Without really meaning to, he lowered his head and gently kissed her cheek, tasting the salt of her tears on his lips.

She didn't kiss him back, neither did she push him away, just stared up her him with those huge grey eyes. In the dark he thought she looked a bit like Isabel. He smoothed her hair away from her eyes, tucking it behind her ear, then kissed her forehead, breathing her scent, hearing her gentle sigh, feeling her relax against him. Her body was silky and scented of roses. It felt good to touch her . . . He gently kissed her lips . . . He couldn't help himself.

What are you doing? his conscience screamed.

Maybe it was the alcohol, or unadulterated lust, or his way of striking back at Isabel after their row – but he slid one arm beneath Jemma, feeling her quiver delightedly. It was empowering to know his slightest touch could have that effect on her. He fumbled for her breast, feeling her hardened nipple brush against his hand, pinching it between his fingers. As she gasped, he crushed his lips against hers, pressing her back against the bed.

Her hands, cold, fumbled with the buttons of his shirt, but he couldn't wait that long and did it himself, tearing the fabric in his haste, impatient to feel her naked skin against his own.

She wasn't Isabel – but he was going to have to live with that – and his conscience the following morning. But she was soft and warm and he felt comforted. He wanted her and she needed him – and that made it all right.

Didn't it?

* * *

Isabel sat up in bed and gave up all pretence of trying to sleep.

She was going to have to talk to Nico. She had to explain about Danielle, the diamond, her feelings for him – get it all out in the open. It was the only way. The only difficulty she could perceive with this plan was that it was one o'clock in the morning . . .

She picked up her mobile phone and dialled Nico's number, but he'd switched his phone off. She lay back in the bed, in the dark, staring at the ceiling, then at the moonlight streaming in though the gap in the curtains. Another hour ticked past.

All she had to do was wait until daylight. How difficult was that? It wasn't long. She had to be patient . . .

Another thirty minutes . . .

She gave a grunt of irritation, flicked on the light and threw back the covers. She pulled on jeans and a thick polo-necked jumper, so she wouldn't have to search for a coat, and headed downstairs. The keys to all the cars were in a bowl on the hall table. Her own car was still at the garage; Danielle's Toyota was wherever she had left it. Which left her father's BMW next on the list. Isabel's hand hovered over the bowl. Could she drive her dead father's car? It was kind of creepy . . .

OK, Little Miss Conscience – walk the two miles to Nico's house . . .

She scooped up the keys and headed for the garage.

* * *

It was three o'clock in the morning when Isabel parked the BMW outside Nico's house. The lights were on, she noticed in surprise – the sitting-room and his bedroom upstairs. Perhaps he was working. She wasn't sure which he'd think was worse – being woken up at some ungodly hour or having her disturb his writing while he was desperately trying to meet a deadline?

So drive back home and forget all about it . . .

Slowly, forcing herself to every movement, Isabel got out of the car. She was about to cross over the road when Nico's bedroom window opened. Instinctively, she ducked behind the car.

Nico was leaning against the windowsill, his head in his hands. Isabel smiled – he looked as though he was about to jump! She raised her head and was just about to shout out some jokey comment like "Don't do it!" – when someone appeared beside him.

Jemma?

Talk about *Groundhog Day*! Isabel watched in disbelief as Jemma wrapped her arms around Nico, her cheek resting against his bare back. He turned to speak to her, taking her hands in his own and leading her away from the window. Back to bed?

Somehow Isabel found herself back in the car, inserting the key in the ignition, starting the engine. She looked back up at the window, but the curtains had been yanked shut and now she could see nothing.

The pure agony of seeing the man she loved, the man she had put all her trust and faith in, with another woman – with her friend – Jemma . . .

It was a betrayal twice over. While she had come to expect this kind of behaviour from Jemma – Nico? She had believed in him, he had been so kind, so loving; she thought she had found the person she wanted to spend the rest of her life with.

Isabel rested her head on the steering wheel and wept.

* * *

Nico held Jemma's hands in his and looked down at her, wondering how he was going to say what he wanted to say ("Sure, Jemma, the sex was great and everything, but now I've got it out of my system I know I'm madly in love with Isabel. So this is good-bye and hey, don't take it badly – we can still be friends!") – and whether he was likely to survive the experience.

Before he could speak, Jemma had pulled her hands away, had turned from him and was picking up her clothes from the floor. "It's OK," she said flatly. "I know what you're going to say. That it's been 'nice' and all that, but you don't really want me – you want Isabel.

I'm only a substitute. Don't feel you have to lie your way out of it, make promises you can't keep – because I understand. I've been there myself."

"I'm sorry."

She whirled round and glared at him, and briefly he saw the old feisty Jemma. "Stop apologising," she said forcefully, "or I really will get upset."

"Jemma, I have to know – "

She misjudged what he was about to say. "You don't have to worry that I'll tell Isabel about us. I wouldn't do that to her. Besides, she hasn't forgiven me for Taz. If she finds out I've been with you too . . . well, I might as well write my own obituary, punchy headlines and all."

Nico politely turned away as she dressed. He pulled on jeans and a fresh sweater. His Moschino shirt was shredded on the floor.

"I don't know why you're bothering to dress," she said. "I can see my own way out."

His head emerged from the neck of his sweater. "It doesn't have to be – "

"Like this? Don't go on a guilt trip on account of me. I can take rejection. The sex was fun. Perhaps we can do it again sometime. If not, so be it." She paused, one hand on the door, as though she wanted to say something else but lacked the courage. "I'll see you around," she said at last and left.

Nico watched the door close and sat on the bed. He glanced across at the clock on his bedside table – 3.15 a.m. – and felt stone cold sober. What to do now? He could go to sleep. He could work. He could walk after Jemma and apologise – look how well that went the last time. Or he could go get his car and drive back to Stortford House, demand to see Isabel and beg for forgiveness. At 3.15 a.m.?

Sure. Why not? He grinned to himself. We're talking about True Love here.

If he didn't think about making out with Jemma, he could pretend it had never happened.

* * *

As Nico walked down the hill to the quay, a white Toyota sped past going in the opposite direction. Nico turned his head and was startled to catch a flash of red hair. Danielle or Isabel? The inconvenience of dating identical twins!

Danielle drove a white Toyota, but why would she be heading off to Port Rell at this time of night. Was there a crisis at Vanders? Even Danielle wasn't that work-obsessed. However, Isabel's car had been written off in the crash . . . and she was not above borrowing her sister's if it suited her – now they were apparently friends again. But if it was Isabel driving . . . *where was she going*?

Maybe he wasn't the only one to have a secret lover . . .

Overwhelmed by a sudden rabid jealousy, Nico ran the last few yards to his car, unlocked the door, started the engine and jammed his foot onto the accelerator. The Bat Mobile shot up the hill, the tyres squealing in protest. Although he was only a few moments behind, by the time he passed his house she was out of sight. She could have gone turned right – through the forest and back to Stortford House, or alternatively driven straight ahead and on to Port Rell.

As he dithered, his cellphone began to ring. A glance at the screen told him the caller was Danielle. He was so surprised he dropped the damn thing. Why was Danielle ringing him? Unless the twins had had another row and she was worried about Isabel? He groped along the passenger seat trying to find his phone in the dark, but the damn thing appeared to have slid onto the floor. Should he leave it to ring? If he had to stop there was no way he was going to catch up with Isabel. Yet it could be important – and Danielle might know where she was going.

He pulled over onto the grass verge opposite Riverside Terrace, which overlooked the river. He left the engine running and his foot firmly wedged on the brake pedal, while he groped along the floor for his phone. He had just scooped it up as there was a terrific bang behind him and the Fiesta was jolted forwards.

What the hell was that?

Twisting in his seat he could see the white Toyota wedged up against his. Fuck it! Isabel must have seen Jemma leaving his house. It was *Fatal Attraction* all over again!

He had pulled on the handbrake, switched off the engine and was about to get out of the car to sort it out, when he was aware of the car behind going into reverse at high speed. He watched in disbelief. Was she drunk?

High on something? There was a squeal of rubber on gravel and the Toyota slammed into the back of him, shunting the Fiesta forward another couple of feet.

Nico felt the first twinge of panic. If his handbrake hadn't been on, he would have certainly gone over the cliff.

The Toyota was reversing, revving up its engine.

Nico quickly turned the key in his ignition, but before the engine could catch, the other car came at him again, slower this time, metal grinding against metal, literally forcing the Fiesta towards the cliff, inch by inch. Nico had the handbrake on and his foot on the brake pedal. He slid the gearbox into fourth, but none of it made any difference. The front of the car suddenly dipped as the front wheels slipped over the crumbling edge of the cliff.

There was no way he could stop this. He had to get out and get out fast. But as he fumbled with his seat belt, the ground slipped from beneath the car and he felt himself falling. He was thrown backwards in his seat and could see, with horrible clarity, the jagged rocks that littered the shoreline hurtling towards him. Instinctively, he threw his arms up to protect his head as the car smashed headfirst onto the rocks, slamming him into the steering column.

As the car bounced back onto its tyres he realised he was still alive, although there was an excruciating pain in his legs and he was pretty sure he had broken his nose; blood was spurting all over the place. He fumbled with his seat belt, but he didn't seem to be wearing it any more, so he looked for the door instead. But the sides of the car had been crumpled by the impact and were a mass of tangled black metal.

As though in a dream he could hear shouting. He turned his head and out of the darkness loomed a hooded figure. Without warning, something was swung at the side window, showering him in glass. Jesus – someone really wanted to kill him!

Hands were plucking at the broken glass, tearing it away, reaching out towards him. He tried to scramble away, but his leg was jammed beneath the steering column and every time he tried to pull it free he thought he would pass out from the pain.

"What the fuck do you want?" he moaned. "Why can't you leave me alone . . ."

Two arms lunged through the window, grabbing him around the chest, ignoring his screams of pain as his leg was wrenched around in the opposite direction to which it was intended to go, and heaving him through the window. There was a moment of agony, as the shards of glass still remaining in the window frame sliced through his flesh – followed by an explosion; a flash of pure white light.

Chapter Thirty-one

Danielle woke up. It was dark. She lay there for a moment, wondering what it was that had disturbed her. Then she heard it again; a crash from one of the rooms below, followed by cursing and drunken laughter.

"You scared the shit out of me," grumbled a voice. "I thought you were the Old Bill."

There was another dull thud. "Oh Christ! Damn stupid place to leave a wall." It was Max.

"You've been drinking!" accused his friend.

"Hark at the Rev Mother! I've only had a couple of beers."

"You could have been picked up for drunk-driving and then all our work would have been thrown away!"

"Well, gee, I'm sorry, but I needed it, OK? Have *you* ever seen a man burn to death? Hear him screaming for someone to save him? It takes more than a couple of beers to blot that out, I can tell you. You're like that damn van der Straatan. Get someone else to do all the really disgusting stuff, so you can keep your hands and your conscience clean!"

For a moment the other man was silent, then he asked softly, so softly Danielle had to strain to hear him, "You've done it then? He's dead?"

"As I've just shunted his car off a cliff? Yeah, what do you think!"

"He could have survived – "

"The car exploded on impact."

"Any witnesses?"

"None that I could see."

Pause. "It had to be done."

"Are you sure? Personally I reckon the guy was too busy getting his leg over anything in a skirt to be writing a damn book. But now – fuck me – every reporter and TV crew in the south of England is going to be camping on our doorstep tomorrow. You do know who he was? *Patrick Kearney's son!* And *you* don't want us drawing attention to ourselves!"

"We'll have left by the time the press turn up. It'll take time to identify the body. Anyway," he added, with more confidence, "you were driving Danielle's car and wearing a red wig. If anyone saw enough of you to give the police a description, they'll think it was Danielle who killed him."

"You'd better hope so. And, I'm telling you, I'm not doing anything like this again. Not for you, not for anyone. And certainly not for some stupid diamond."

If there was further conversation Danielle didn't hear it. She just made it to the bucket before she was violently sick. She had no idea how long she sat, hunched up on the floor. Time stood still. *Nico was dead.* The words echoed around and around in her head. *They'd killed him.* In the most horrible way possible . . .

Don't think about it, she told herself, rocking backwards and forwards, her hand clapped over her mouth so the men below couldn't hear her crying. *Don't think about it – you'll go crazy.*

All over a *diamond* . . .

She had to get out of here. She couldn't rely on Isabel to get her out. She loved her sister dearly, but the girl didn't have a thought in her head besides rock music and parties. Even if by some miracle – and it would have to be a bloody big miracle – Isabel did come through, there was *no* way Max and his friend would let her go. If Max was prepared to kill Nico and her father to ensure everything went his way, he wouldn't think twice about killing her.

* * *

At eight o'clock the following morning, Joshua, 12th Earl of Stortford, wandered dispiritedly through the gardens of Rell Manor. This afternoon he was due to exchange contracts with Elsa Tallant – the TV celebrity who was planning a complete renovation of the manor and devoting hours of prime time TV to the project.

After the hard work he had put in over the last few years to prevent the loss of the manor, it was soul-destroying to think someone else would succeed where he had failed.

For the past few weeks he had been unable to sleep properly and he found himself returning here again and again, torturing himself further with the thought of what might have been. If only his ancestors hadn't been so crap with money. If only the foot and mouth crisis hadn't happened . . . He hadn't lost any of his stock – but no one wanted to buy it from him either. When foreign meat was so cheap, who gave a toss about buying British?

He turned away from the manor, tugging his donkey jacket tighter around him as protection against the chill in the air. Winter was definitely on its way. Lewis, his black Labrador, snuffled hopefully along in the grass beside the path and soon fell behind.

Ironically, it was a lovely day for a walk. Although icy cold, the sky was a brilliant blue and the colour of the autumn trees glowed strikingly against its backdrop, the beech trees in particular burning like great Roman candles. As he walked back through the kitchen garden, startling a couple of rabbits tearing up great mouthfuls of dandelions, he grew depressed again. The sale of Rell Manor would boost his bank account for a few years, but what when it ran out? Farming was not the most stable business, but it was the only work he was trained for.

Then there was that other millstone around his neck – Stortford House. Renting it to Isaac van der Straatan had seemed a good idea – a regular income without losing the capital. Now Isaac was dead and Danielle was in financial trouble; if she gave up the lease the house would come back to him. How could he hope to keep it going? The plate literally ate money. Yet how could he bear to sell? The Stortford family had lived in the area since the time of Elizabeth I.

Although Josh's father had sold off parcels of lands to the local farmers, there was still a sizeable acreage of land attached to the estate. He supposed he could sell off a bit more. A neighbouring estate had sold for an absolute bomb last year – for upmarket housing. There was the rub – once the land was gone, it was gone forever.

It might not come to that, he told himself firmly, turning towards his Land Rover, parked just inside the gates. He glanced around for Lewis, who had a habit of wandering off. Sure enough, the dog was some distance back along the drive, having found something else of interest to sniff at. Josh hoped it wasn't fox doo-doo. If there was one thing Lewis absolutely hated, it was having a bath.

He whistled and Lewis obediently bounded towards him, something glittering in his mouth.

"What have you got, boy?" He caught hold of the dog's collar and, with the other hand, gripped his muzzle. "Drop!"

Lewis, indignant, tried to go into reverse, but Josh held his collar too firmly.

Clamping his legs round the dog's body, Josh tapped him smartly on his nose. "Drop!"

Lewis sulkily dropped and Josh quickly picked the object up.

"Ugh! Did you have to dribble all over it!"

Josh wiped away the saliva on his jeans and found he was holding a gold and diamond watch. Maybe their fortunes were looking up after all. Except it didn't look as though the watch had lain there for very long . . . He turned it over and found an inscription: *Diamonds Are A Girl's Best Friend . . .*

Danielle . . . ah well, at least it gave him an excuse to call on her.

Feeling happier, he dropped the watch into his pocket and whistled for Lewis.

Except Lewis had finally noticed the rabbits . . .

This was going to be one very long day.

* * *

Danielle felt as though her head was about to explode.

She was going to have to get out of here.

OK, so she was trapped in a derelict building with two murderers. The room she was lying in was locked from the outside and her left hand was chained to the headboard of a bed. Houdini she wasn't.

When she had first been kidnapped she had spent most of the first day trying to ease the cuff over her wrist, making it bruised and swollen in the process. She had long narrow hands, but they were not *that* small. So, if she couldn't slide it off her wrist, perhaps she could cut it off. *With what, exactly?*

OK, OK. Maybe she was approaching this from the wrong angle.

She couldn't take the cuff off her wrist – maybe she should try taking the other one off the bed . . .

She stood up, pulling the mattress back from the headboard to examine it more closely. She'd have to move the bed itself – but as it was on wheels that shouldn't be too tricky – although she was hampered by only having the use of one hand. She leant back against the wall, and pushed at the bed, squeezing herself between the resulting gap for more leverage. The bed moved a couple of feet away from the wall . . .

Danielle knelt beside the bed. Two large screws at the top and two more on the base fastened the headboard to the main part of the bed. The uppermost screw on the base appeared loose so she stuck her fingernail into the groove and twisted. The fingernail promptly snapped off.

She stared at her hands in despair. Because of the trauma of recent weeks, that had been her longest nail. What she *really* needed was a screwdriver (like Max was going to leave one lying around!) or – or a thin sharp edge! It would have to be fairly strong – strong enough to undo a screw . . . There were her rings – too wide . . . her brooch – too brittle . . . a coin!

Max had confiscated her handbag, but when she had paid for her ticket at the car park at Port Rell, she had *dropped the change into her trouser pocket . . .*

Danielle stuck her hands in her pockets and had a

quick turn out. Lip salve, a disintegrating tissue, a 5p and two 10ps. *Yes!*

She inserted one of the 10ps into the screw and slowly, carefully, turned it. The screw turned with it. Danielle paused, listening for any noise, which would warn her someone was coming up the stairs. Everything was quiet, so she set back to work. Gradually she saw the screw emerging from the metal tube holding the headboard in place, before it popped out, taking her by surprise. There was a bit of fumbling, but she was able to catch the screw before it hit the floor. Although large, it was unlikely it would make too much noise – but she didn't want to take the risk. This was the only chance she had to escape. If she blew it, she'd end up dead. It was as simple as that.

Hardly daring to believe it could be that easy, she inserted the coin into the groove of the other screw. This one was tighter. The coin didn't bend; it was too strong for that, but it was digging painfully into her fingers, until . . . yes, it moved too. As soon as the screw dropped into her waiting hand, one side of the headboard slid to the floor with a dull thud – she only had to slide the cuff down the tube and she was free!

Well, almost free. She looked up, at the little hatch set in the ceiling. Apart from the door, it was the only way out – she'd spent enough time gazing longingly at it over the last couple of days. But she needed something to stand on. The bed, obviously . . .

Now she had both hands free it was easy to push it across the wooden floor until it was positioned directly beneath the hatch.

She jumped onto the bed and reached upwards. The hatch was hinged on one side; on the other was a little catch. She flipped it back; the door dropped open, there was a blast of cold fresh air – and she could see the sky!

Danielle grabbed the sides of the hatch and attempted to pull herself up. But her weight was too heavy for her arms; she couldn't pull herself through the gap, only swing backwards and forwards ineffectively. How ridiculous!

"Damn and blast," she muttered, as she totally failed to get her elbow through the hatch and obtain leverage. That would teach her to not workout. Isabel would have found this a doddle.

The wooden frame around the hatch suddenly crumbled and she found herself falling backwards. She somersaulted off the bed and landed uncomfortably on her bottom. It brought tears to her eyes through pain and sheer frustration. She slammed her fists against the floorboards. It didn't matter how much noise she made now, she could already hear a man's heavy footsteps crashing up the stairs.

She tried to get her thoughts in order. In a matter of seconds, that door was going to open, Max or his friend would fly in and find her unchained, and that would be it. Basically, it was her or them.

She needed a weapon. The bucket! She seized hold of it and dived behind the door as it opened –

Wham! She let him have it. Not over the head, her aim was not that brilliant, but right in the face with all the strength she could muster.

Max screamed, staggering back against the wall, his arms going up to protect his head. It was tempting to crash the bucket over his head again, finish him off completely, but Danielle did not have much faith in her ability to come out the winner in a fight, so she ran through the open door, swiftly locking it behind her.

As she stood on the other side of the door she could not quite believe what she had done. She almost punched the air she was so happy. But Max, being a man, would not take ten seconds to smash his way through the door – and what of his friend – where was he?

Danielle made a dash for the staircase, expecting at any time for someone to grab her. She was almost down to the landing below when she began having a strange déjà-vu sensation. She slowed down, taking in the heavy oak panelling, the carved wooden banisters, broken in places . . . There was the master bedroom, beautiful carvings of flowers and animals of the forest –

She was in Rell Manor.

Danielle felt her legs weaken and caught hold of the doorframe for support. She had been in Rell Manor all this time? Josh hadn't had squatters. Her father's crooked friends had been using the house as their base.

"Danielle!" Max voice came from above, accompanied by some heavy thuds. "Let me out of here!"

Danielle had no time for conjecture. She ran on down the stairs, towards the kitchens and the back of the house. She had three options: to take the path across the kitchen gardens towards the cliff – except there was no way to get down the cliff to the beach. Or she could run around to the front of the house and the road, risking capture by Max's friend, who was presumably somewhere about. Then there were the woods, which she knew very well, because of all those romantic walks with Josh – too hard up to take her out on a proper date.

She could hear someone, probably Max, pounding down the staircase. Quickly she ran across the courtyard, her heels skidding on the cobblestones, through the undergrowth and beneath the ancient trees. She risked a glance behind her. Max, standing on the kitchen steps, had spotted her and was even now sprinting across the cobblestones.

The woodland path was uneven and overgrown. Brambles tore at her smart suit trousers. She had a plan – if she could remember the correct route to take. She might not be able to out-run Max, but she could certainly outsmart him. Except it had been years since she had walked through these woods and now one tree looked pretty much the same as another.

Then she saw it – a line of moss-covered stones, which anyone else might have mistaken for a natural rock formation. She hopped over them; there was a tiny grassy path, caused by either ramblers or rabbits. Another heap of stones in front of her, a couple of feet high – but she wasn't heading in that direction. Instead she took a left turning, forcing her way through the undergrowth until she came to a small clearing.

Her feet disappeared into the piles of leaves and she lost a shoe, but she didn't bother to retrieve it. Max was directly behind her, she could hear him crashing through the bushes, curse as he tripped over the little stone wall, hear his heavy breathing draw closer . . .

She moved cautiously forwards, until she had found that slight dip in the ground, the familiar glimpse of bare boards half-hidden beneath the leaves. She stopped, pressing one foot gingerly onto the rotting wood. There was a slight crack, a movement –

"Dani," Max was behind her now, gasping for breath. "Give it up! You know you can't outrun me. Let me take you back to the house."

Danielle took a long, careful stride forward, but the path had petered out. The trees had grown too thickly to pass between them. She turned slowly. Turning to face the man who had kidnapped her. The man who had once professed his undying love for her. The man who had murdered her father.

"You're going to kill me, aren't you?" she said.

"No, no, of course not!" Max's voice was unconvincing. "We've made a deal with Isabel. She found the diamond – it was right where you said it was. Now she's meeting my friend to hand it over. As soon as he's got it, he'll phone me and you'll be free."

"I don't believe you. It would be safer for you to kill me; bury me out here, where no one ever comes, where no one will ever find me."

Apart from Josh's dog, in about six months – if she was lucky. Lewis's sense of smell was not what it could have been.

"You've got it all wrong," said Max.

He took a step towards her, his arms outstretched as though he thought she might fling herself into them. Danielle found herself holding her breath.

"Dani, please! It's only for another couple of hours – until we have the diamond. Then you can go."

She said nothing, but let her shoulders sag and made a small movement towards him, then stopped abruptly.

Max, feeling his persuasion was working, took another cautious step. "Dani, I'd stake my life – "

CRACK!

One moment Max was standing amongst the leaves and long grass, the next the ground opened up and swallowed him whole.

Danielle couldn't believe it had actually worked. That she was safe. Her legs were shaking violently so she sat down, feeling the dew on the grass seep into her trousers. She'd done it! She was free!

"Danielle!"

Fuck, the bastard was still alive!

"Danielle!"

His voice was muffled but clear enough. She crawled towards the gaping hole in the ground and peered into the gloom, expecting to see Max bobbing about on some filthy water, but the brick-lined hole was filled with rubbish and he was sprawled on top of it.

"Help me, Dani, I think my leg is broken."

"Ding, dong, dell!" she said sarcastically. "Max has fallen down the well!"

"You knew it was here?"

"Oh yes! This was the gamekeeper's cottage – about

a hundred and fifty years ago, admittedly – hidden away in the forest, the best place to catch the poachers red-handed. There's nothing left now, of course, only a few bits of stone wall – and this well. Josh's father had it boarded up years ago after a child fell down it – in much the same way you did. But wood rots – and well, you're not a lightweight, are you, Max?"

"Danielle, I don't think you understand. My leg is broken. I'm trapped. I can't get out."

"Excellent," said Danielle, sitting back on her heels and standing up. "That was the idea."

"You can't leave me here! No one will ever find me!"

"Now don't go giving me ideas, Max!"

"Look," and his voice sounded increasingly desperate. "I'll give you money. I've still got my share from the robberies."

"How much?"

"Half a million?"

"What is that? Ten per cent?"

"OK, OK, I'll give you half, but it's not in cash – it's in jewellery and precious stones, not easy to get rid of on the open market – "

"Diamonds?"

"Yes!" Max's voice was eager. "You like diamonds, don't you?"

Danielle stood up. "You think that after murdering my father and Nico Kearney that you can give me a handful of diamonds and everything is going to be all right? What kind of unfeeling bitch do you think I am? You can bloody well rot for all I care." She began to walk away.

"Isabel's in danger!"

Danielle stopped, half-turned. *"What?"*

"She's meeting Flynn at the church on the cliff to hand over the diamond. She thinks she's going to get you back. Once he gets the diamond he's going to kill her."

"Flynn? Flynn is the one who has been helping you?" Of course, it made sense. Her father had recruited men he knew, men he thought he could trust. Max, Flynn and – who was the fourth? Simon, she supposed. Meek little Simon Castle.

Danielle felt a chill run through her at how easily she had been deceived for all these years . . . by men she trusted, who she thought loved her . . .

"Dani? Are you still there?"

Danielle walked away.

Chapter Thirty-two

Danielle ran back through the grounds of Rell Manor towards the road. She was halfway down the hill before she realised she hadn't got a plan – she just knew she had to get to the church before Isabel, to prevent her from meeting Flynn.

She had retrieved her lost shoe from the gamekeeper's garden, but heels were not intended for speed. It was only her sheer bloody-mindedness keeping her going – and terror that she would arrive too late to save Isabel. How had their father got them into this? What had he been *thinking*?

It was beginning to dawn on her that she couldn't do this alone. She was going to need help . . .

There was a line of thatched cottages to her right, huddled from the elements under a canopy of massive oak trees. Once they had been part of the original Rell

Manor estate, built at the same time. Now they were in private ownership – sold to meet the Stortford family's ever-spiralling debts.

Aware she looked like a total tramp, Danielle boldly pushed open the gate of the nearest, strode down the path and knocked forcefully on the door. It was opened almost immediately by a little old lady, blinking up at her through thick spectacles.

"Er, hello," said Danielle, pushing her hair out of her eyes in an effort to look respectable and not like some nut who had walked in off the street. She dislodged a shower of leaves and twigs. Oh great, the Worzel Gummage look. "I . . . um, know I look like a crazy person, but honestly, I'm not! I'm having a bit of a crisis and I really need to use your telephone."

The woman stared up at her.

"Please?"

"You're one of the van der Straatan girls."

"That's right." Danielle was surprised. "I didn't realise you – "

"Are you the nice one or the snooty one?"

Her scary reputation appeared to have preceded her. "Definitely the nice one!" She held out her hand and forced a smile to her lips. It was hard to behave 'normally' when so much was at stake. "The name's Isabel van der Straatan."

Finally the elderly woman relaxed, perhaps relieved that she wasn't about to be sold double-glazing or asked for a contribution to a charity she'd never heard of. "Ah, Isabel!" She took Danielle's hand in both of her own. "I've heard all about you from my grandson. It's lovely to meet you at last!"

Danielle had to hand it to her sister; she certainly got around.

"Would you like a cup of tea?" said the woman eagerly.

At that precise moment, there was nothing Danielle would like more than a stiff drink (and sod the tea!), but this was no time to be socialising. She smiled again. It became easier with practice. "Actually, I'm in a bit of a hurry. If I could use your telephone?" *There's an armed robber about to kill my sister . . .*

"Of course! Please come in!" The woman beamed and held the door wide open.

Danielle ducked through the low doorway and followed the woman into the cottage. The ceiling was so low, Danielle automatically bent her knees, fearing the top of her head was about to knock on one of the oak beams. The corridor had a definite slant towards the centre of the house and, about halfway down, the woman paused by a little occasional table with an old-fashioned telephone on it.

"Here you are, love," she said. "I'll go and put the kettle on. You look a bit peaky. Is it cold outside?"

Danielle nodded vaguely and, picking up the receiver, dialled the number of Isabel's mobile telephone. Unfortunately it was either switched off, or not picking up a signal. So she dialled the number of the local police station, asking for Detective Superintendent Hunter, the officer who had interviewed her after her arrest.

She was put through immediately. It didn't take her long to explain the events to date. He didn't interrupt, or ask her to clarify trivial details, for which she was grateful. In fact, he seemed to have a pretty good grasp of her situation – perhaps he'd figured out much of it himself; he didn't seem surprised when she told him about Max and Flynn.

"Don't worry, Miss van der Straatan, we'll send a car out to Port Rell church immediately. You stay where you are, lock the windows and doors and you'll be perfectly safe."

Stay? Like she was Lassie? Danielle felt indignant. After all she had been through – and he was treating her like a hysterical female!

"Mr Hunter," she began firmly, "My sister – "

"Will be safe in our hands. I'll go myself to Stortford House, see if I can cut her off before she gets to the church."

"But I'm only a few hundred yards away! I could get there myself in a matter of minutes – "

"I can't guarantee your safety, Miss van der Straatan. If you will please stay where you are, we'll keep you up to date. One of our officers will be with you directly. Now promise me, you won't go to the church by yourself? These men are dangerous. You could get seriously hurt."

"I promise," she muttered sulkily.

"I'll be in touch as soon as I have any news," he assured her and the line went dead.

Danielle stared at the phone with impotent frustration. She was supposed to wait here, drink tea and eat custard creams, like she was part of some knitting circle, while the gullible Isabel walked right into an armed ambush? Bollocks to that!

Danielle slammed the receiver back onto its cradle. She could hear the kettle boiling in the kitchen. (Honestly, what was it with little old ladies and tea?) She was about to storm straight out of the cottage when she noticed that the bedroom door opposite was wide open. There were clothes strewn across the floor, the smell of stale beer and cigarettes wafted out into the passage, and she could see CDs scattered over the dressing-table, of Talisman and Limp Bizkit. It must belong to the old lady's grandson – Isabel's 'friend'. Presumably he was at work; she hadn't seen any sign of him since she arrived.

Danielle was about to move on when she caught a glimpse of her reflection in the wardrobe mirror – her ragged burgundy suit, which was going straight in the bin when she got home; her dirt-streaked face; her hair, matted and tangled around her face like a cavewoman. My God, what a state! This dear old lady had actually let her into her house? It was more than Danielle would have done if faced with the same situation.

She noticed some jeans lying inside the door, as though their owner had recently stepped out of them and was struck by such an inspired idea, right out of the blue, it could have been divine intervention. It was brilliant, totally inspired! But she couldn't possibly pull it off! *Could she?*

Swiftly she stepped into the bedroom, closing the door behind her. She slipped off her filthy jacket and trousers, and stepped into the jeans, trying not to think about when they had been worn last – and by whom. They were about the right length, but much too large – she had to jack them in tightly over the waist to get them to fit. She pulled a Talisman T-shirt over her head and found a pair of disreputable trainers half hidden beneath the bed. Again, they were a couple of sizes too big, but she pulled the laces as tightly as they would go and decided they'd be fine. There was a relatively new-looking biker jacket hanging on the wardrobe door, which she slung around her shoulders. Then she took a deep breath and peered into the wardrobe mirror.

It was *spooky*. Apart from the bird's nest hair, it could have been Isabel's reflection starting anxiously back at her. For the first time in her life, Danielle found herself giving thanks that they were identical twins.

She picked up a comb and dragged it through her tangled hair, then cautiously opened the bedroom door to hear a voice from the kitchen enquiring, "Do you take milk and sugar?"

"Yes, please!" called back Danielle.

But by the time her hostess had loaded the tea things onto a tray, Danielle was long gone. The only sign that she had ever been there – torn, stained clothes abandoned on her grandson's bed and the front door open to the elements.

* * *

When Danielle arrived at the church it was deserted. There were no cars parked along the road either. Had she beaten Isabel here – or was she too late? Was Isabel's bloodied body lying inside? As Danielle walked cautiously down the path, she could see the heavy, metal-studded door was ajar. She gently pushed it open; just enough to peer inside – ready to bolt at the first indication of trouble. She wasn't that brave.

The church was deserted. There were no pews or furniture of any kind. The interior had been completely gutted, presumably to foil vandalism. Some of the stained-glass windows were already smashed, their pretty multi-coloured fragments nestling amongst the dried leaves littering the flagstones. There were some empty beer cans too, left over from Jemma's party, lined up on the tomb of the first Earl of Stortford.

One thing was certain. Neither Isabel nor Flynn were anywhere to be –

"Isabel!" A hand clapped her shoulder. "So glad you could make it!"

Danielle gave a little yelp of fear and whirled around. "Flynn! Bloody hell, you nearly gave me a heart attack!"

"Your enemies are always those whom you least expect," he agreed suavely. "Now, hand over the diamond, Isabel. I don't have time for gossip."

Of course, he was expecting her to give him the Ashlyn Diamond. In her haste to get here before her sister, she'd almost forgotten all about it. She decided to act the dumb female. If she stalled him for long enough, Superintendent Hunter and his band of merry men would roll up and catch Flynn right in the act. *But what if they failed to arrive?*

"Diamond?" she said, with what she hoped was a blank look on her face.

Flynn's easy smile turned nasty. "You have got it? Because if you're wasting my time Isabel, I swear – "

"Oh yes, I've got it," she assured him.

"So give it to me!"

"Where's Danielle? I'm not giving you anything until I know my sister is safe."

"Since when do you care about that selfish bitch?" sneered Flynn. "She's never done anything for you. It'd be better for you if she was dead – you wouldn't have to share that lovely money."

Danielle determinedly didn't think about what Isabel's response to that was likely to be and said instead, "No sister, no diamond."

Flynn sat on the edge of the tomb. "We'll have to wait a bit then. My friend is bringing her along."

Max? Flynn would be waiting forever for that to happen! Unless Flynn was talking about the fourth member of the gang – Simon?

Flynn was no longer between her and the door, but the distance was too far for her to be certain she could reach it before him. She had never been very sporty; a straight 'A' student, she'd never had much time for 'frivolities' as she saw it – and she was certainly starting to regret that.

Danielle also wished she still had her watch. How long did it take a police car to drive from Calahurst, lights blazing, sirens screaming? Perhaps if the Superintendent was deploying police marksmen, they had to come from further afield – possibly Norchester? Perhaps they were staking out the church at that very moment, hidden away in the surrounding trees – and she had walked straight in here and spoilt everything.

"Do you know what the time is?" she nervously asked Flynn.

"Got another appointment?" he derided, but flicked back the sleeve of his jacket all the same. "Twelve fifteen."

She must have made her phone call fifteen minutes ago. Where were the police? More to the point, *where the hell was Isabel*?

It occurred to Danielle that Isabel wasn't going to show up – that she had alienated her sister to such an extent that Isabel no longer cared what happened to her.

Danielle felt tears pricking her eyelids and blinked determinedly. All she had suffered over the last forty-eight hours and she had to pick *now* to break down? Isabel would turn up – eventually. She was always late. She'd even been late for her own birthday, for heaven's sake!

There were footsteps on the path outside and the door swung open, crashing against the wall.

"About bloody time!" grumbled Flynn, standing up.

Danielle moved nervously back against the wall, expecting the police to burst in, guns blazing. She hoped they wouldn't mistake her for one of the gang.

It was neither the police, nor Isabel who stood on the threshold, but a man casually attired in jeans and hooded fleece, a black balaclava pulled over his head. He wasn't very tall – so it couldn't be Simon – but what did it matter? He must be one of Flynn's jailbird friends.

"You've got the diamond?" he asked Flynn.

He sounded young – a teenager perhaps? The strange, almost growling way he spoke – it was as though he was trying to make himself sound tough.

"Isabel's got it," Flynn thumbed towards Danielle. "She wants to know if you've got her sister. If she's 'safe'."

"Oh yes, Danielle has been *well* taken care of."

They both laughed – assuming she was dead already, thought Danielle bitterly. Bastards. She was *glad* Max was lying in agony at the bottom of that well. She only wished these two were there with him.

"There you are," Flynn grinned at Danielle. "Everything has gone according to plan."

"Almost everything," added his friend, pulling something out of his pocket and pointing it towards Flynn.

It all transpired so quickly, it took a while for Danielle to realise what had happened. There was a loud explosion, the frightened cawing of the birds nesting in the rafters as they rose into the air as one, and suddenly Flynn's body was lying crumpled on the floor beside her.

Danielle stared at him in shock. He hadn't said a word, uttered so much as gurgle, but he was dead, she was certain of that. His pale blue eyes stared sightlessly at her; his mouth was curved into a slight moue of surprise, his features still perfect – on one side of his head . . . but the other . . . the other . . .

Danielle felt the bile rise in her throat and turned away, holding onto the wall behind her for support, staring up at the other man in absolute terror. There was a gun in his hand and now he was pointing it at her.

He walked slowly towards her, closing the distance between them, his arm out straight, barrel of the gun aimed directly at her head. "Don't even think about running," he said. "I'm a crap shot – so I can't guarantee a nice painless death like our friend Flynn here."

Danielle was in such shock she didn't think her legs could move even if she wanted to. So she watched him crouch beside Flynn's body, rolling him carelessly onto his back, before rifling through his pockets.

He wasn't paying her the slightest attention. Danielle glanced nervously towards the door. The route was clear. How many strides would she be able to take before she got a bullet in the back? Although, if she was going to die anyway, surely it was better to be killed taking the chance to escape?

"It's not here," said the man, standing up. He pressed the gun against Danielle's forehead. "So where's the diamond, Issy?"

Where are the fucking police? thought Danielle hysterically.

"Dani!"

Isabel was standing in the doorway, a huge grin on her face. "Are you OK? I've been so worried about you! Sorry I'm late," she added to the gunman. "You must think I'm terrible!"

The gunman glanced sideways at Danielle. "Wrong twin," he said softly in the same strange low growl. "Stupid, stupid me!"

"Bloody traffic!" Isabel was grumbling. "I had to go all the way into Norchester and out again. If you hadn't put an embargo on Dani's mobile phone I could have rung and let you know. So this is entirely your own fault, not mine. As long as we're clear on that?"

The gunman removed the gun from Danielle's temple and directed it at Isabel, who stared at him in surprise.

"What's the matter?" Her face crumpled in distress. "I've got the diamond, like you wanted . . ."

"Isabel!" screamed Danielle. "Run!"

Isabel didn't move. She had finally spotted Flynn's body, partly obscured by the tomb, his blood seeping across the flagstones in a large black pool.

Then she turned to flee.

As Danielle saw the gunman's finger move on the trigger, she grabbed hold of his arm, pulling it down. The bullet ricocheted harmlessly off a windowsill; the gun hit the ground and bounced off the side of the tomb.

Infuriated, the gunman punched Danielle in the face, but by the time he had scooped up his gun Isabel had gone.

"Bitch!" He fired again.

Danielle, staggering after the ferocious blow to her face, heard a loud bang and felt a sharp stabbing pain in her shoulder. She stumbled over the uneven flagstones and even as she did so, some primeval instinct told her to fall onto the ground, to lie motionless, to hold her breath.

There was a pause. Would he fire off another bullet into her body to be sure?

She heard him running lightly over the flagstones to the open door. When she dared to open her eyes again she was alone.

She tried to sit up, but was overwhelmed by nausea. She glanced down at her shoulder. There was a hole in the leather jacket. She slid it off and found an identical tear in the Talisman T-shirt, and dark red blood seeping from a wound underneath. She had no desire to investigate further, but knew she had to slow the bleeding. She looked around for suitable padding. A handkerchief perhaps – but the pockets of her borrowed clothes were empty.

She looked over to Flynn's motionless body. He did not seem the type of man to carry a handkerchief, but there was only one way to find out. She crawled towards him.

The contents of his pockets were sprawled over the floor; wallet, car keys, chewing gum, a compacted wodge of tissues . . . Danielle seized them, pressing them against her shoulder, watching the white paper turn crimson in a matter of minutes. So now what was she going to do? She didn't particularly care what happened to her. She hoped she'd been able to give Isabel a few extra minutes, give her the chance to get away, the chance to live . . .

Danielle leant back against the tomb. A delicious numbness was radiating out from her injured shoulder and she felt very tired. It was freezing; she realised she was shivering, shaking violently with the cold. Forlornly, she attempted to pull the leather jacket back over her shoulders with her one good arm.

Where were the police?

As she stared at the ground, not really taking in what she was seeing, trying to summon up the energy to stand up, to run to the door and yell for help, she realised there was a glint of something metallic, half hidden by Flynn's body.

Using every last reserve of strength, she leant forward and grabbed it.

It was her own mobile phone. Flynn must have taken it from her handbag. Honestly, the money he must have made from those diamond robberies and still he felt the need to steal her phone?

She keyed in 999 while she could still see straight.

"Which service do you require?" sang a voice into her ear.

"Police," mumbled Danielle. But the operator's words seemed to blur into each other. She couldn't understand what the woman was saying and she found she was shaking so much she couldn't even hold onto the phone . . .

It was far easier to let the phone slip through her fingers, to lean back against the wall, to close her eyes and go to sleep . . .

Chapter Thirty-three

As Isabel turned to flee she heard the retort of the gun. The bullet hit the windowsill to her right as she plunged into the porch. Then she heard another retort and a small cry. One glance back into the dark confines of the church and she could see Danielle lying motionless on the floor. Was she dead? Oh, God, she prayed, let her just be stunned or wounded! Every instinct urged her to go back to Danielle, but reason told her to run, to lure the gunman away from her helpless sister.

She stumbled through the porch and out into the churchyard. The bright sunlight and the tears in her eyes conspired to blur her vision. To cold-heartedly override her emotions in this way went against everything she believed in. But she must get away, get help.

A bullet, buzzing past like an angry bee, nicked the sleeve of her jacket, splintering the headstone in front of her.

She dived behind the nearest headstone, but knew she couldn't linger. The nearer to the gunman, the easier the target she made. She risked a glance back at the church. The gunman was walking casually towards her, his arm outstretched. There was the retort of a gun and *ping*! – another chunk of headstone turned to dust.

Isabel whimpered, tucking arms and legs as close to her body as possible. She could hear footsteps on the path – confident, relentless, closer by every moment. Her heart was thudding in her chest. He must be directly behind her. She waited for that final shot.

"Look," said the gunman, in a deep, husky voice. "We can stand here all day, while I take pot shots at you – or you could just hand over the diamond?"

"Why did you shoot my sister?" She took a couple of deep breaths, tried to steady her voice. "I brought you the diamond, I did everything you asked me to . . ."

"Danielle tried to trick us. She pretended to be you so she could keep the diamond."

Was that the reason? Isabel doubted it. The more likely scenario was that her sister had arrived at the church first to protect her – and the guilt she now felt was overwhelming. Danielle may have died to save her – and now she owed it to her to live.

"Will you hand over that bloody diamond – or shall I shoot you for it?" grumbled the gunman.

Isabel stared across the churchyard in front of her, hoping for inspiration. The last time she had been here, it had been the night of Jemma's party. In daylight the place didn't seem so spooky, and she could clearly see the break in the wall, about twenty feet away, to which Nico had led her as a shortcut to his car. But she couldn't run that way, towards the road; she would be too exposed.

To the left was the path that led through a small copse of trees to the top of the cliffs, heavily screened by gorse bushes and brambles. It was the only alternative. But she needed something to distract the gunman long enough to give her a headstart. Her attention was caught by some shards of clear glass, the remains of a broken bottle, glinting in the sunlight . . .

"Hey!" she shouted loudly, her voice echoing around the empty churchyard. "Do you want this diamond or what?"

The gunman watched in disbelief as a large, glittering object hurtled from behind the gravestone and landed in the long grass behind him.

"Fucking hell!"

It was her one chance and Isabel grabbed it; sprinting towards the wall, over the rubble, across a few metres of scrubland and into the comparative darkness of the trees. She wished she could see the look on his face when he realised his priceless diamond was, in reality, a lump of broken glass.

It was tempting to find a nice fat tree to hide behind and wait it out, but she couldn't risk being found. The small copse on the other side of the wall soon thinned out and she was hurrying along a well-worn path, between the dead gorse, right to the very edge of the cliff. In places there were painted warning signs, and rusting posts speared the crumbling soil, linked by ribbons of florescent orange tape.

The path declined sharply as it grew nearer to the village. On the beach below, she occasionally glimpsed some people: an elderly couple walking their dog; a younger man jogging along the sand; children looking for the shells and the fossils that littered the shoreline. They were all living out their lives in normality, blissfully unaware of the drama above their heads.

Isabel thought she could hear sirens in the distance. Were police cars racing to help her, or merely chasing another speeding tourist? She wasn't planning to be around long enough to find out. From the cursing she could hear behind, the gunman was slowly catching up.

As the path swung briefly inland, she caught sight of rooftops far below; the familiar grey slate of The Smuggler's Inn on the corner, La Dolce Vita right on the sand, the ramshackle but colourful beach huts stretching out along the water's edge. What was she going to do when she got there? There was no police station – the nearest one was in Calahurst.

Isabel remembered the children playing on the beach, the innocent people she was likely to meet along this popular path, and realised that while this had seemed such an excellent plan when under pressure in the churchyard, she hadn't really thought it through.

The path turned back on itself, causing her to stumble. A mass of soil and stones cascaded over the edge of the cliff and it was only by grabbing onto the branch of a stunted hawthorn tree that she prevented herself from joining it. She got a tighter grip on the tree, trying to slow her uneven breathing, her frantically scudding heart. She could see the sunlight glinting on the waters of the creek, the seagulls strutting over the mud banks where the anglers had been digging for bait earlier that morning.

One false move and she could have fallen to her death . . . one false move . . .

There was a rattle of stones behind her and she crawled into the undergrowth, edging towards the precipice in an effort not to be seen. It was too much to hope the gunman would pass right by her – but then, she had something else in mind entirely.

She hadn't long to wait. A matter of seconds and he crashed around the bend, losing his footing as she herself had done, and frantically reaching out for anything to break his fall. Isabel grabbed his ankle and down he went, rolling over and over. The gun was knocked out of his hand and over the cliff, but he was able to grab onto the nearest crop of brambles to halt his descent.

Furious that he hadn't fallen to his death as she had intended, Isabel threw herself on top of him, slamming his face back into the ground. "Not such the big tough guy without your gun, are you?"

He merely groaned as she hit him again, hardly putting up any kind of fight. He was several inches shorter than her and quite skinny – there was nothing to him. Feeling bolder by the minute, she rolled him onto his back and grabbed the top of the black woollen balaclava.

"Let's see what you look like under here, shall we?" she taunted. "Let's see why you're so ugly you have to wear one of these!" She triumphantly yanked it away, ripping out a hank of blond hair at the same time. "Jesus Christ! *Jemma*!"

Still holding the balaclava aloft, she stared incredulously at the person lying beneath her; at the choppy blonde hair, the silver-grey eyes . . . *Jemma*? *It couldn't be . . .*

Wham! Jemma had made a fist and swung a hard punch, hitting Isabel directly on the nose. A small bone crunched; a sharp, unexpected pain; warm blood spurted across her cheek and Isabel rolled away, hunching up against the trunk of the tree, holding her hand over her nose to try to stop the blood, feeling a sudden wave of nausea and an excruciating pain.

"Oh shit, oh shit, oh shit," she mumbled, as she took her hand away from her nose and saw the great pool of blood that had gathered there. There was a sensation of light-headedness too, which she recognised from the day of her car accident, and she concentrated on taking great gulps of fresh air through her mouth. This was not a convenient time to faint.

She was aware of Jemma struggling to sit up, hunting around for the gun, then realising it had gone over the cliff. What would she do now?

Isabel took her hand away from her nose again and wiped it on her jeans. She felt the bump of the diamond above her left thigh, digging into her skin. This was what it was all about. This was why her father had been killed, why Danielle had been shot. All because of one stupid diamond!

Isabel pressed her shoulder against the tree trunk, using it to lever herself up. Her foot slipped against the stony path, sending more shingle over the edge. It was so very close. The roots of the tree wove in and out of the compacted soil then jutted out into nothing, dried and withered, exposed to the elements.

She leant back against the tree, still feeling dizzy, trying to breathe deeply and evenly. There was a horrible metallic-tasting liquid in her mouth. She spat it out and found she was spitting blood.

"Well, that's attractive," commented Jemma, who was now standing, albeit hunched over, and panting hard, a mere couple of feet away.

"You don't look so great yourself."

Jemma had a large gash above her right eye and assorted grazes over her nose and chin.

Isabel pushed herself away from the tree to stand unaided, aware that her added height made her feel more confident. "You killed Danielle," she said flatly.

"That was the idea." Jemma did not even bother to deny it.

"I didn't realise you hated her that much?"

"You hate her too. Think of it as a favour."

If Isabel had had the strength, she would have punched Jemma right over the cliff. "Dani's my *sister*," she hissed. "Sure, we fight, but we love each other too!"

"You have a funny way of showing it."

"It's because Nico dumped you for her, isn't it? It was OK for you to pinch her boyfriends, but you couldn't bear it happening to you!"

"I don't give a stuff about Nico! The guy is a total sleazebag."

"That didn't stop you shagging him though!"

"You saw us?"

"I thought I was your friend. Even allowing for you being an evil psycho bitch, you don't *do* that kind of thing to your friends!"

"Evil psycho bitch!" Jemma was opening laughing now. "Oh, *do* grow up, Isabel!"

Furiously Isabel dug the diamond out of her pocket. "This is worth more to you than I am?"

"It means more to me than *anything*. With it, I can buy new friends, new lovers, even a new father seeing as the old one was so crap – "

"You father thought the world of you – "

"For goodness sake, I'm not the daughter of the Earl of Stortford! Everyone in Calahurst knows that." Jemma calmly brushed the loose soil from her jeans. "My father was Isaac van der Straatan."

"*What*?"

"How would you like to spend your entire life watching your father lavish all his love and money on your half-sisters and totally ignore you, because he didn't want to hurt *their* feelings, in case they realised what a complete arsehole he was?"

Feeling as though she'd been hit by a sledgehammer, Isabel could only shake her head in disbelief. "Why are you telling such lies?"

"Look me, Isabel! We have the same eyes – the same grey eyes as Isaac. I even have his blond hair – I'm the spitting image of him – and you've never noticed? Don't you remember the day you were locked in the sauna at Granger's Gym? I did that. I put on a suit, a long red wig and waltzed in there, pretending to be Danielle – to see if I could get away with it. I did – up to a point. I forgot Danielle's never worked out in her life. The receptionist thought I was you."

Isabel leant wearily against the tree. "Is that what this is all about? Gaining recognition?"

"No, it's about getting out of Calahurst – and the robberies were supposed to pay for that. Isaac had no money. He's been living on credit for years. He had the idea to rob his fellow jewellers. He knew them, he knew his way around their premises, the codes they used. He wasn't expecting to find the Ashlyn Diamond on that last raid, though. He put it in his pocket when the rest of us were concentrating on emptying the safe and the first I knew about it was the statement the police released to the press.

"He had cheated me, his own daughter, and it was then I realised I was living in fantasyland. Isaac would never acknowledge me, never love me as much as he loved you and Danielle. When Max and Flynn decided they'd had enough of his arrogance, it was fine by me.

I've learnt that everyone lets you down sooner or later – parents, friends, lovers – the only thing in life you can be certain of is money."

Isabel almost felt sorry for her. "You're so wrong, Jemma. If you had someone to love you – "

"Like your wonderful Nico?" scoffed Jemma. "Seducing him was so easy – a few tears, a trembling lower lip. Honestly, the man thinks he's Sir Galahad."

Isabel remembered the diamond still clenched in her fist. Slowly she uncurled her fingers, letting its many facets catch the sunlight. "And this was *your* Holy Grail?"

Jemma rolled her eyes. "Understatement!"

Isabel held the diamond between her finger and thumb, holding it higher in the air, so that it flashed rainbows of colour. "If I give you this diamond, everyone you have killed will have died for nothing. So take a long hard look at it, see how beautiful it is, think about how much money it's worth, remember the terrible things you have done to get it . . . now wave it goodbye, Jemma, because this is the closest you're ever going to get to it."

Isabel drew back her hand and threw the diamond high into the air.

"No! Give it to me!" Jemma made a grab for the diamond, lunging forward. Her fingers closed over the stone and for a moment triumph lit up her face. Then her arms began to flail, frantically whirling round as she tried to keep her balance. Her face registered shock, disbelief, fear . . . Then she was gone and Isabel could see nothing but blue sky and seagulls.

Isabel stared out towards the horizon, enjoying the warmth of the sun on her face, the breeze lifting her hair. Then she turned away and began to hurry back along the path.

(From The Calahurst Echo)

ASHLYN DIAMOND FOUND SAFE

by
ECHO STAFF REPORTER

The Ashlyn Diamond was found yesterday, abandoned on the beach at Port Rell. Police were forced to close off the area, to execute a fingertip search amongst the shingle. The gang behind the theft had attempted to dispose of the diamond after a spectacular clifftop chase by the local police, led by Detective Supt Sebastian Hunter (42).

Mr Hunter said last night, "It has taken many months of hard work to apprehend these dangerous men. We are thrilled to be able to return the Ashlyn Diamond to its rightful owner, Lady Alverstoke."

All four gang members have apparently been apprehended, although the police have only released the name of one of the men responsible, Jeremy Sweetham-Owen, also know as 'Flynn' who has already served an 18-month sentence in Ford Open prison for fraud.

For the thrilling story behind the recovery of the Ashlyn Diamond, turn to page 4.

ECHO REPORTER DIES IN FREAK ACCIDENT

by **ECHO** STAFF REPORTER

Lady Jemma Stortford (25), daughter of the 11th Earl of Stortford, and journalist with *The Calahurst Echo*, was killed yesterday in a freak climbing accident.

Lady Jemma had worked tirelessly on many of *The Echo's* top stories, and will be sadly missed.

Chapter Thirty Four

CHRISTMAS EVE

Josh Stortford drove his battered Land Rover towards the house he'd grown up in and wondered if he was about to make the biggest mistake of his life. Eight weeks had passed since his sister's tragic death and the country's press had circled Calahurst interminably, until only the prospect of another, more scandalous, story had finally lured them away. Throughout all the resultant madness, the huge iron gates of Stortford House had remained resolutely padlocked.

Josh, however, had a key.

He parked the Land Rover beside the house, expecting a light of some sort to flicker on as a sign of welcome, but Stortford House remained in darkness. He paused halfway up the steps. He had never realised how forbidding it could look. To him it had always been a place of joy and laughter, until that dark day when his father had died and his life had revolved in a downward spiral ever since.

He took the last two steps in one stride and jabbed at the doorbell with his index finger, leaning back against one of the Corinthian columns to wait for a reply, pulling his jacket around him as protection against the extreme cold. As his eyes became accustomed to the darkness, he could see his breath forming icy mist in front of him. He pressed the doorbell again. This time holding it down for a longer period of time. Even if she weren't in, he decided as he finally released the button, at least he would have tried.

The door suddenly opened, flooding the steps with soft amber lighting, and a young woman stood there, casually dressed in a navy sweater, an ankle-skimming denim skirt with bare feet poking out beneath. Here was a girl who needed looking after, he thought, feeling that familiar rush of love.

"Hello, Danielle," he said softly.

She didn't move; appeared rooted to the spot with shock. "You knew it was me?"

"The sling," he said, trying hard to sound casual. "It's a bit of a giveaway."

"My shoulder still aches sometimes." For a moment he thought she was going to tell him to get lost. Then she smiled weakly and said: "Do you want to come in?"

He would have preferred a little more enthusiasm but, there again, he was lucky not to get the door slammed in his face. "Thanks."

Someone had made an effort to brighten up the hall

with garlands of ivy looping around the walls and whole branches of holly arranged on the stone mantelpiece. He would have made some complimentary comment, but Danielle was already padding down the corridor to the rear of the house.

He paused. How long was it since he'd stood here? Ten years? Twelve? Although Isaac had frequently sent invitations to parties, receptions, even family dinners, each one had ended up in the bin. How could he return to the house he'd grown up in . . . the house he owned but could no longer afford to live in?

The shabby Victorian décor remained the same as it was in his father's and grandfather's day – the contract he'd got Isaac to sign had ensured that. Yet the atmosphere was different, even the scent – he remembered his father's citrus cologne, his mother's French perfume . . . He rubbed his eyes with the heel of his hand. Oh God, he couldn't do this . . .

With his eyes closed like a fool, he collided with the Christmas tree, showering himself in sharp little needles and sending a selection of baubles bouncing freely across the hall, smashing patterns of silver eggshell fragments against the grimy floor.

Christ; he stared up at the tree in awe. It was enormous. How on earth had Danielle got it through the door?

He was reminded of Christmases past; the delicate glass ornaments handed down from generation to generation, the practically threadbare tinsel, the potentially lethal pre-war fairy lights. His elderly father would wobble about on a lofty stepladder, determined to carry on the tradition of the head of the family in placing the gold star at the very top – and the staff, assembled for the occasion, would collectively hold their breath in case he fell. His mother would dutifully fix the beautiful porcelain fairy beneath the star and then he and Jemma would fight over who hung their favourite ornament – a little glass Father Christmas.

Where were the decorations now? In storage – or perhaps sold to meet the family debts when his father had died and nobody had cared much about Christmas for a long time. Which was pretty much how he felt now. Josh felt another wave of misery wash over him and told himself to concentrate on the good times. It was the only way to be certain that he was here for the right reasons.

Danielle was patiently waiting for him outside the sitting-room overlooking the garden. It had been his mother's favourite. The walls were still painted the same duck-egg blue she had chosen, although he didn't recognise the modern suite of a darker hue, grouped around the fireplace. The remainder of the furniture – dark Jacobean oak – was original, but there was a modern flat-screen television hung on the wall between two paintings of obscure maiden aunts. His father, he found himself thinking with a wry smile, had thought television an abomination and had refused to have one in the house.

Danielle politely asked if he wanted a drink. He shook his head, feeling his courage failing, and fumbled in his pockets until he found a crumpled manila envelope. "I brought you this," he said, placing it in her hands.

Surprised, and a little self-conscious, she tore it open. A glittering gold and diamond object fell into her open palm. "My watch! You found my watch! I thought I'd never see it again!" She fastened it around her wrist, holding it up to the light so that the diamonds sparkled, then flung her good arm around him and kissed his cheek. "Oh, this is the best Christmas present ever! Where did you find it?"

"At Rell Manor – "

"Really? That's where I lost it! I returned to search for it after I left the hospital, but the new owner has put up chain-link fencing and employed security guards. Luckily they're the same ones who used to work here, so they said they'd look out for it, but I didn't hold out much hope. Oh Josh," she kissed him again, "thank you!"

Josh, restraining the impulse to take her in his arms and kiss her back, decided not to tell her he'd found it weeks ago – and had been plucking up the courage to return it to her ever since.

"My father gave it to me," she was saying. "It was the last thing he gave me before he died. It means so much . . . I'm repeating myself, aren't I? Can I get you anything? Coffee? Something alcoholic?"

"Actually, I've got you another present here." From his other pocket he pulled out a thin green bottle. "Happy Christmas!"

"Thanks . . ." Danielle squinted doubtfully at the handwritten label. "Blackberry wine?"

He watched with amusement as realisation dawned and she forced an enthusiastic smile to her face.

"Did you make it yourself?" she asked.

"It's a new line for me. I thought it would appeal to the tourists. Sharon – the young lady who runs the market stall next to mine – has been so kind and helpful. She says that, at this time of year, you can write 'Christmas' on pretty much anything and it will sell."

"What does it taste like?"

'Blackberries', was the obvious answer, but he said instead: "Sweet – but drink it carefully. It's lethal!"

"It sounds wonderful. I need something to help get me into the Christmas spirit."

Perhaps giving alcohol to someone in her fragile state of mind was not the most brilliant of ideas. He watched as she scooped up a couple of wine glasses from the sideboard and then she tossed him a corkscrew.

"Open the bottle and let's try it out!"

He searched for a polite excuse. "I'm driving – "

"You can always stay the night. We've got enough rooms."

Did she really have no idea what hell that would be for him? Lying there knowing that she was sleeping only a few rooms away?

He eased out the cork and handed her the bottle to pour into the glasses. More to the point, *could* he sleep in this house? With all its ghosts of Christmases past?

"Where's Isabel?" he asked, attempting to strike the morbid thoughts from his mind.

"She drove up to Patrick Kearney's house in Bath this

morning." Danielle made herself comfortable in one of the large armchairs, curling her long bare legs beneath her.

Josh sat on the sofa. "Was she invited for Christmas?"

"Hell, no! She's not that chummy with him! She signed a recording contract with Trick Records a few weeks back and now she's going to be on TV." Danielle indicated the television up on the wall, which would have been blaring out some pop show on Sky One except the mute button was on. "It's a live Christmas show, broadcast from his castle. The chap must be mad," she added. "All those strangers, cluttering up his house on Christmas Eve."

Josh winced.

"Not you," she added hastily. "*You're* welcome here anytime. This is your house after all." She paused. "Is that why you've come? I'm sorry I haven't been able to pay this month's rent, but – "

"I appreciate you have other things on your mind . . ."

"Actually I have no money in my bank account. I'm going to have to terminate the tenancy agreement and find somewhere else to live. I've already sold my shares in Vanders to pay my father's debts, not that they're worth anything much now. The Board sacked me too, so I have no regular income – although Isabel, bless her, has offered to support me until I find something else –" she broke off with a bitter laugh. "A regular sob story, eh? How the mighty are fallen! My dead-beat sister financially supporting *me*! Although it's no more than I deserve. I was quite horrible and patronising towards her after our father died – "

"You saved her life."

She shrugged, her cheeks becoming slightly pink. "I didn't really do anything much . . ."

"You escaped from a locked room, brained a kidnapper with a metal bucket and chucked him down a well. Then you took a bullet in the shoulder to give Isabel time to get to safety. Impressive if you ask me."

"Josh, about Jemma – " She broke off, obviously embarrassed.

"It's all right, you can mention her name. Actually, it would be nice if someone did mention her name. Everyone is tiptoeing around me at the moment, not daring to say anything about her. No one even came to her funeral. People sent flowers – to say how sorry they were – but no one came . . ."

Danielle appeared to be carefully considering her next words. "Jemma told Isabel that she was Isaac's daughter . . ."

Josh hesitated, then wondered whom he was protecting, now all the leading players were dead. "It's been an open secret in our family since she was born," he admitted. "My father was so much older than my mother, so he knew it was inevitable that she would find love somewhere else. Although her affair with Isaac hurt him badly, he understood the reasons behind it and stood by her. It might have seemed odd to some people, I suppose, but it's the way my parents were. I think the big mistake was when they told Jemma the truth – I'm sure that led to the start of her problems. When my father died, and we had no money, she saw you and Isabel move into her house with Isaac – you had everything she wanted and that had once belonged to her."

Danielle seemed to understand. "Insult on top of injury . . ."

"Her sense of injustice must have festered away for years. I don't think it was a good idea for her to become so close to Isabel, but I didn't realise she had a sinister motive. She seemed to genuinely like Isabel, they had a lot in common – "

"I thought she was having an affair with my father! No wonder she always denied it so vehemently. Poor Jemma!"

"I'm not sure how she became involved in the robberies. I didn't know anything about it until the police called me to say she'd died. Perhaps it was because she would do anything to crave Isaac's love and attention. Perhaps she wanted excitement – she certainly wanted the great wealth we all thought Isaac possessed. I wish she had confided in me. I wish I could have been a better brother . . . I feel responsible –"

"Jemma acted of her own free will – and so did my father." Apart from a slight wobble to her voice, Danielle almost sounded her old, practical self. "Whatever happened they brought it on themselves. We have to grieve for what we have lost – and move on."

Easy for her to say. He'd lost his only remaining family . . . One moment he felt almost normal, could crack jokes with the best of them – the next, he felt like his whole world was coming apart. "It's going to take a long time."

He felt the settee dip as she sat next to him. "I think you were a bloody brilliant brother," she was saying. "A much better brother than I am a sister! You're always so kind to everyone, so thoughtful, and tolerant when people let you down. You're all the things I'm not – although I am trying," she added earnestly. "Isabel and I are getting along much better now. And it's not because she's now rich and I'm poor – " Danielle chuckled. "I suppose that's why we *are* getting along so well – I needed to learn a little humility!"

He didn't laugh, staring instead into his wineglass. He couldn't talk about Jemma to Danielle, not in the way he wanted to; she didn't understand. Perhaps one day . . . but right now . . .

As he took another swig of wine, the flickering of the TV screen caught his attention again. "So, Isabel is going to be a pop star?"

"Rock star," corrected Danielle, refilling his glass. "That's the mistake I made and got my head thoroughly chewed off. She's signed a five-album contract for an indecent amount of money. Bloody Isabel – she always ends up on top!"

"You're on your own for Christmas?"

"Perhaps. Isabel is supposed to be coming home, but I don't think it's going to happen. How can frozen pizza in front of the TV with your pain-in-the-arse sister compete with a never-ending party at a rock star's mansion?"

"Pizza?" Josh was surprised. He would have thought the ultra-organised Danielle would have had a five-course dinner planned. "Even I've got a turkey."

"With chestnut stuffing?" she asked wistfully.

"Well, actually, I haven't got around to stuffing it because the turkey – or Bernie as I call him – is still running around the yard – "

"Josh!"

He grinned. "I'm joking! I bought one from Tesco yesterday – plucked, basted and hygienically sealed in cellophane. You're welcome to come over for Christmas dinner – Isabel too, if she turns up."

Danielle was looking at him with something close to awe. "You're amazing . . ."

"I have an ulterior motive – I'd like your advice on a business deal! When I put Rell Manor on the market, Caitlin and Marc Granger, who own the gym on the quayside, approached me with an offer. They didn't have the money to buy Stortford House outright, but wanted me to come in on a partnership to turn it into a health spa. If you're serious on giving up this place, maybe they'd be interested in it – "

Danielle spluttered into her wineglass. "Are you *crazy*! Don't you remember what happened to the last hotel Caitlin Granger managed? It went up in flames! This place has so much potential. Executive flats, for example – you could live here yourself to keep an eye on things, or open it to the public. You're a real live Earl, for heaven's sake! People love that sort of thing. You could top up the income by staging rock concerts, obtain a licence for people to get married here – the opportunities are endless!"

Josh casually rested one arm along the settee behind her and assumed a helpless, anxious expression. "It all seems frightfully complicated . . . I don't know if I'm really up to that sort of thing . . ."

"Surely estate management is what you've been trained for all your life?"

"It doesn't mean to say I'm any good at it!"

"Perhaps I could help you?" she said earnestly. "Until I find a job. You wouldn't have to pay me – "

"Of course I would pay you! We ought to work out some kind of formal arrangement." He leant forward, closing the gap between them. "I've just had the most brilliant idea. You could become my business partner . . ."

Chapter Thirty-five

Isabel stared at herself in the dressing-room mirror. The thick, orange pancake, the shiny blue eye shadow, the cherry-pink lipstick. She looked as though she'd been mummified, circa 1979. Slowly she dipped her hand into a jar of cold cream and smeared it across her face.

Unfortunately, the make-up artist chose this moment to return to her side and let out a shriek. "What have you done? You've ruined all my work. Are you *crazy*?"

Isabel, now rubbing at the lipstick with a wodge of tissues, was making even more of a mess. "I can't go on national TV looking like this – I'm *orange*."

"But you have to have some colour – your skin's so white you look like death warmed up." The make-up artist scrabbled about in her case. "Here, if you just let me – "

Isabel seized one of the make-up brushes and waved it threateningly. "Touch me again and I'll sue for assault!"

The make-up artist backed nervously out of the door. "Stay here. I'll get someone. And, er, try to stay *calm* . . ."

Isabel emptied her bag and began to rummage through the debris for her own cosmetics, laying them out on the vanity unit, one by one. "Calm," she muttered, "got to keep calm."

With a trembling hand she cleansed, toned and moisturised. She blended foundation into her skin and deftly patted pressed power over it. Silver and black eyeliners combined to make her grey eyes enormous. Blusher gave her cheeks a healthy glow. She was concentrating so hard on achieving perfection, the terror gradually receded without her being aware of it.

As she finally finished, she stood up and pulled off the plastic pink cape she had been wearing and checked out her reflection. Her shiny pre-Raphaelite curls cascaded over her shoulders; her low-cut evening gown, sometimes purple, sometimes a deep, dark, crimson depending on the light – clung to every curving inch; an array of ethnic bangles dangled from each arm.

She grinned at her reflection. "Now that is more like it!"

There was a small monitor in the corner of the room, relaying the events from the banqueting hall. Aphrodite were on stage, singing 'Winter Wonderland' in angelic harmony. It was catchy. Isabel cheered up a fraction and began to dance along, admiring the way the bangles chinked at her wrists as she swung her arms about. She should try to be more cheerful. After all, it was supposed to be Christmas – joy to the world and goodwill to all men –

"Ouff!"

Lost in her own world, she hadn't heard the dressing-room door open – and had whirled straight into a tall male body, slamming one of her flailing hands right into his solar plexus, winding him. He doubled over in pain.

"Oh, God, I'm so sorry – " She bent down to look into his face, hoping it wasn't Patrick. This could be the shortest rock career in history.

"Nico!"

Nico leant against the dressing-table while he got his breath back, and rubbed his stomach with a pained expression. "I had this feeling you weren't gonna be pleased to see me, but I wasn't expecting to get beaten up!"

"What are you doing here?"

"I came to check how you were: nervous, excited, high on Imodium, etc."

"I'm f–fine," she said, even though she wasn't. The butterflies in her stomach appeared to have been joined by a herd of rampaging buffalo. "How . . . how about you? I heard about your accident . . ." Too self-conscious to meet his uncompromising gaze, she looked him up and down for any sign of permanent injury. He was looking as sexy as ever, dressed in his usual black, and the only legacy of the car crash appeared to be a livid scar across the bridge of his nose, now broader and slightly misshapen.

"I received your note," he said bluntly.

She felt her face flare. "Look, I didn't know about –"

He talked across her. "The one which went: 'Dear Nico, Sorry about your accident. I guess this is as good a time as any to let you know that our relationship isn't going anywhere; so don't bother to contact me because I don't want to see you again.'"

"I didn't *know* how serious the accident was! Not until later, when Danielle showed me the newspaper headline about the anglers rescuing you from your blazing car. When your father phoned, he made it sound as though you'd had a minor prang!"

"He didn't want to worry you. He thought you'd turn up at the hospital and he'd be able to explain in person." There was a wretched look about his face. "Why did you do it, Isabel? Why dump me that way? Don't you think it was kinda cruel? Didn't I deserve better than that? If you had any issues I'm sure we could have talked them through."

"I saw you," she said in a low voice. "That night I came round to your house to tell you everything – about the diamond, about Danielle's kidnap . . . I needed a friend, someone to confide in. And where were you? Shagging bloody Jemma!"

He winced. "Ah – I kind of guessed that was the reason."

"It was three o'clock in the morning – so don't try and kid me you were only having a friendly chat – just good friends and the rest of that crap."

"I behaved badly, I admit it. The sex didn't mean

anything, but I guess you're expecting me to say that? You know, we'd just had a fight, so I considered myself a free person. To sleep with Jemma was tacky, OK, but I made a mistake and I'm truly sorry."

"You're saying *I'm* to blame?"

"Of course not – but let's look at it another way. When you found Taz had been unfaithful to you, did you stick around? Talk it over? No, *you* left Calahurst with the next available man and had sex with him to get your own back."

"That's so not true! *You're* in the wrong, *you* screwed up – in more ways than one – and you want to blame *me* for your appalling behaviour?"

"I'm not apportioning any kind of blame. I'm suggesting you consider someone else's viewpoint for a change – "

"*Why*? *I'm* the one that gets hurt each time, *mine* is the heart that gets broken. No one seems to give a shit about *me*. Jemma was right. Diamonds *are* the only things in life that last forever."

He put his hand to his forehead. "Jesus, why am I bothering? Once you've made your mind up nothing can change it."

"That's right."

He glanced down, perhaps catching that slight break in her voice, the one she was doing her best to disguise.

"Isabel?"

"Look – " This time it came out as more of a sob. "Oh, fuck off and leave me alone, can't you? I was just getting over you and now you're back like a bloody boomerang. Why can't you accept it's over? You've got the material for your book; can't you leave me alone?"

"There is no book. I shelved it weeks ago. I made a complete ass of myself, I accept that. You know I would never deliberately hurt –

"You guys made it up?" Patrick stuck his head around the door. "Great work, Nicolas – we don't want to let this one get away. Gotta keep those millions in the family, eh?" And he playfully slapped Isabel's bottom before striding off down the corridor.

Nico attempted a joke to hide his exasperation. "My father the feminist."

Isabel didn't hear him. She had ducked past and run off down the corridor before he could stop her.

"Damn!" One of Nico's size-twelve feet connected with the side of the dressing-table, leaving a large, gaping hole.

From the dressing-room opposite, Taz stuck his head around the door, taking in the wrecked vanity unit and Nico standing beside it, clutching his head with both hands.

"Bad hair day?" he enquired blithely.

"I've really fucked up this time."

"Come and tell your Uncle Taz all about it." He waved a paper bag enticingly. "We've got jelly beans . . ."

Nico smiled despite himself. "You rock stars sure know how to live."

* * *

Isabel watched the remainder of the show from the

medieval banqueting hall, transformed for the night into a TV studio teaming with cameramen and production staff. The 'stars' were exhibiting typical diva-like behaviour and refusing to budge from their dressing-rooms until they were due on one of the three stages which had been set up with glittery winter backdrops. All except Isabel. She felt safer here. Even Nico wouldn't brazenly declare love for her in front of a room full of people.

Would he?

She was feeling twitchier by the minute, so when Taz walked silently up behind her she nearly jumped into the arms of the nearest cameraman.

"Sorry, babe. Guess I gave you a fright?"

"You shouldn't creep up on a girl like that. It could get you into trouble!"

"Never had complaints before," he replied cheerfully. "This is your big moment, eh? Gonna knock 'em dead?"

"I've got stage fright."

"Bollocks, you're not scared of anything. This is Taz, remember? You can't fool me."

"Well, I *am*!" Isabel felt miffed. Did he think she was faking it for the attention? "I'm bloody terrified. This is my first TV appearance. If I'm great I've got it made. If I'm crap, well, I'm going to be just another wannabe spending the rest of her life singing in pubs and living on benefits. I don't like being poor. I want to be rich again!"

"Get a grip, girl, you'll be fine." Taz pulled a small flask from his pocket and handed it to her. "Have a slug of this."

Neat whisky? Isabel hastily handed it back. "I'd rather have stage fright. If I drink any of that I'll fall off the stage." She caught sight of a monitor showing a young male singer putting in an immaculately polished performance and shivered. "Oh God, I know I'm going to dry up."

"You're miming to a backing track, babe; it's impossible."

"What if I start miming the wrong words?"

Taz thought this was utterly hilarious. "With your tits hanging out of that dress, do you think anyone is going to notice?"

Isabel leant one hand against the wall and started hyperventilating.

"You think this is bad? Wait 'til you're headlining at Wembley Arena!"

She snatched the hip-flask from him and took a hefty swig.

The Assistant Floor Manager walked up, blithely ignored the hip-flask, but confiscated Isabel's bangles. "They'll be picked up by the mikes," he explained brusquely. Then looked at her more closely, "Are you OK? You look *terrible!*" He grinned. "You got stage fright? Just remember, if you're going to chuck up, do it *off* camera."

Isabel whimpered and was about to take another slug of drink when Taz wrestled it off her.

"Bugger off, Matt," Taz waved him away. "She'll be OK."

"Sure she will," smirked Matt. "In exactly ten minutes."

"By then I'll have finished!" wailed Isabel.

Matt winked and strolled off

Taz gave her a hug. "Chill out babe, you know you're going to be fantastic. This is what you've wanted all your life; I know you're not going to blow it. And if you do, well, they'll switch to the adverts so it won't be some huge disaster, trust me."

"You're making me feel worse. You can't do tact, Taz, so I suggest you shut up and let me have my breakdown in peace."

"I was only trying to help."

He looked so downcast, and desperately attractive in his own pallid, scruffy musician way, that Isabel felt a sudden pang for what might have been. Taz was funny, kind – a bit scatterbrained and occasionally free with his favours – but he was basically a nice guy.

She wrapped her arms around his waist and hugged him back, his bony collarbone digging into her cheek. "Thanks, Taz. For everything."

He seemed surprised – and a little hopeful. "You . . . er, forgiven me then? For the . . . ah, Jemma thing?"

"There's no going back," she said firmly. "I don't do second chances. You're a loyal friend, but as a loyal boyfriend you're a dead loss."

"'Scuse me? Who went running off to Bath with Nico the moment my back was turned?"

As this was pretty much what Nico had been insinuating she blushed. "We'd split up! I could do what I liked!"

"A bit quick off the old starting-blocks though, eh, babe?"

Honestly, if she didn't know better, she'd think he'd been discussing her love life with Nico. "It wasn't like that . . ."

The smiled faded from his face. "You love him, don't you?"

She looked up at him, blinking to prevent the tears welling up in her eyes. "Sorry. I guess we can't choose who we fall in love with. Better sign me up to Assholes Anonymous."

A youth with the clipboard sidled up between them. "Isabel van der Straatan?"

"That's me." She felt like a condemned prisoner. "I'm on next, right?"

"Follow me."

"Good luck," called Taz, grinning as she turned to wave him goodbye – and tripped headlong over a power cable. "Break a leg, babe!"

* * *

Nico sat in Talisman's dressing-room, watching Isabel singing 'All I Want For Christmas Is You' (oh, irony!) on the monitor, grateful he didn't have to make polite conversation with Beano, the lead guitarist, who was sitting beside him, lovingly polishing up his Strat.

This was mainly because Beano *didn't* talk: Beano nodded his head along to an inaudible guitar riff; smoked filthy roll-ups and chomped endlessly on bags of jellybeans. He also had a discernible habit of staring right through anyone who attempted to strike up a conversation. But he didn't talk – unlike Carson who never stopped.

"Where's my fucking eyeliner," he was ranting. "I left it on the dressing-table and now it's fucking gone and I know one of you buggers has nicked it for a laugh. Well, you'll be laughing on the other side of your faces, 'cos I ain't fucking going on without it, no way." Carson, despite being brought up in a Melbourne suburb, was very proud of his cockney accent, which he'd gleaned from watching old Billy Idol interviews. "And if I don't go on, none of you bastards go on."

"Like we give a shit," grumbled the drummer, whose name was Russell. He chucked the TV remote at Carson. "Shut up, we're trying to hear the new girl."

"Eyeing up her tits more like. It's the only part of her that doesn't look like a scrawny, red-haired chicken. I thought Patrick had given up on that girl/boy band crap?"

Nico was contemplating smashing his fist into Carson's jaw, when Taz breezed through the door and plonked himself on the sofa, bouncing the others along. "Budge up guys! Make way for the seriously handsome rock star."

Nico glanced enquiringly at him.

"You're right," said Taz. "Isabel's seriously pissed with you."

"So that's it then."

"She also still loves you – God knows why, seeing as you behaved like a total shit."

Taz was wearing his trademark Artful Dodger grin, but there was a certain bleakness lurking in his eyes. Nico knew exactly how he felt. "Sorry."

"I should bloody think so – chatting up my bird the moment my ass was on a plane to LA." He sighed, his eyes sliding towards the image of Isabel on the little monitor. Even on 12 x 12 her star quality blasted out from the screen. "There's not much I can do about it. I had my chance – and I wasted it. As Isabel herself said, she doesn't do second chances." He looked back at Nico. "Except, I reckon, for you . . ."

Carson barged his bleached blond head between them. "Sorry to break up this little tête à tête," his voice dripped acid. "But have either of you love-sick puppies seen my *fucking eyeliner*?"

Nico nodded towards the dressing-table. "There's some mascara. Won't that do?"

Carson did not appreciate irony. "I'm the Son of fucking Satan. No way am I wearing fucking mascara."

"Oh bugger off, Carson." Taz, finally losing his patience, threw a punch at him. "I'm trying to give Nico some serious therapy here."

Carson staggered backwards and disappeared behind the couch.

"Get a load of that peace and quiet," said Russell.

Nico and Taz looked at each other, then over the back of the couch. Carson lay prostrate on the ground, eyes closed as though gently sleeping.

"Oops," said Taz, although he didn't appear too distressed.

"In ten minutes you've got a set to perform for a live TV show and your singer is out cold," reproved Nico. "Couldn't you look a little more panicky?"

"Guess it's going to be an instrumental . . . unless you want to take his place?"

"*What*?"

"Sing a soppy love song to Isabel and make a right tit of yourself. Chicks like that sort of thing."

"I can't sing!" protested Nico.

"You're Patrick Kearney's son. It's in the genes. Of course you can bloody sing!" Taz hesitated. "Can't you?"

* * *

Isabel finished her song. Instead of applause, there was only silence – very disconcerting – and all the attention switched to another of the three stages, where The Lost Boys were waiting to sing a hip-hop version of 'Frosty The Snowman', dressed in white suits and black shades.

Dejectedly, she hitched up her long gown and jumped off the dais she had been standing on, wondering whether to return to her dressing-room and phone Danielle for her verdict. Her relationship with her sister had recently reached an all-time high, but Danielle had never understood why anyone in their right mind would want to be a rock star. But who else could she talk to? She was desperate to share her excitement, before it faded away and she sank into that relentless, dark depression she had felt ever since she had caught Nico with Jemma.

There was Taz – but Talisman were on after The Lost Boys, so there was no time for conversation. Afterwards everyone would join them on stage for the finale, and then Talisman would go out on a bender to celebrate – and Carson certainly wouldn't want Taz's ex-girlfriend hanging around to cramp their style.

Isabel watched the largest stage being set up with Talisman's kit. She was careful not to get in the way, although no one seemed bothered by her presence. Taz, Russell and Beano climbed onto the stage from the opposite side; Taz caught sight of her, giving her the thumbs up.

As Matt wandered over with his clipboard, Isabel whispered: "Which song did Talisman get?"

"A nu-metal version of 'Here Comes Santa Claus'. Better get your earplugs ready."

He wasn't entirely joking. After a brisk "One, two, three, four," from Russell, they launched into an ear-splitting intro, which did not sound remotely like 'Here Comes Santa Claus'.

"Where the fuck's Carson?" Matt hissed into his microphone. "Patrick's going to kill me. I warned him that putting Talisman on at the end gave them a full forty-five minutes to get pissed and start a fight. God knows what they've done to Carson. Strung him up by his balls from the nearest Christmas tree?"

Isabel gently tapped his arm as she saw a man with short black hair race onto the stage and snatch up the microphone. He was wearing black trousers and a black shirt, and as he started singing, she saw him put his hand to his forehead to shield the blazing studio lights from his eyes, as though he was searching for someone.

"It's OK, he's here!" The relief on Matt's face was palpable. "The prat wanted to make an entrance to show off his new hairdo – oh *shit*! That's not Carson – it's Nicolas fucking Kearney! What the hell does he think he's *doing?* Is he *pissed*?"

As Nico's singing was truly terrible, it was a perfectly reasonable question to ask. Still searching his open-mouthed celebrity audience, he suddenly spotted her, standing below.

"This is for you, Isabel," he shouted, running over to her side of the stage, quite forgetting he had a microphone in his hand. The feedback made everyone cover their ears in pain.

"Sorry, folks!"

Now everyone was staring at Isabel. Great, she thought. They are all going to think I put him up to it.

"I *know* the backing tape isn't working," Matt was yelling above the din. "They're singing live! Cut to the bloody adverts. Whaddya mean, it's good TV? My spaniel can sing better than that!"

By now, everyone was clapping along encouragingly. One of the cameras panned back to film Isabel's reaction, and this time she couldn't run away because she had a Lost Boy standing right behind her, deliberately blocking her escape route, forcing her to listen to every bum note, every heartfelt word as Nico looked directly into her eyes and, doing his best David Cassidy impression, sang: *"I think I love you . . ."*

Love? Ha! If he truly loved her he wouldn't be humiliating her in public. Stamping on the Lost Boy's foot, Isabel forced her way through the crowd thronging the stage and was soon running down the corridor, bouncing off assorted TV folk until she reached the blissful sanctuary of the garden.

For a moment she paused, leaning back against the wall, trying to get her breath back and her frazzled emotions under control. What on earth did Nico think he was *doing*? Was he serious – or only having a laugh? Taz must have put him up to it, the rotten rat fink. It was exactly the sort of stunt he would have pulled himself.

It was too cold for al fresco introspection in a flimsy evening gown. So she started the trek back to the guest house in the dark, skidding on the frosty grass, hoping that the tears trickling down her face would not freeze on her cheeks.

As she approached the ruined hall that housed the swimming-pool, she heard a door slam behind her, then someone shout her name.

She began to run, but could now hear footsteps sprinting along behind her.

"Sweetheart," gasped a familiar American accent, "if you want me to catch you, you're going to have to slow down. My leg is still held together with pins. I can't run that fast."

The arrogance of the man!

Isabel turned in a blazing fury. "I don't actually *want* you to catch – "

"Ha, gotcha!" Two strong arms wound round her

body, pinioning her own to her sides, leaving her totally helpless against the onslaught of his mouth, which proceeded to kiss her so thoroughly she thought her head would start spinning like that girl from *The Exorcist*.

Then he suddenly stopped. She couldn't see his expression, but his hand was tenderly stroking the side of her face.

"Why are you crying?"

"I'm not crying! My eyes are . . . watering – because it's so cold out here." Which sounded perfectly reasonable – except she then spoilt it by adding: "You think I'm crying over you?"

"I wouldn't want you to be crying over me, Isabel, I'm not worth it."

As this was about to have been her next insult, Isabel was forced into silence while she tried to think up another one.

"Isabel, honey, I've grovelled, I've begged, I've even made an ass of myself in public. I guess I could probably walk across hot coals if you really wanted me to. If only you'd believe me when I say that I love you – "

"Like you loved Jemma, like you loved Danielle – "

"I used Jemma to get my story – I'm not proud of that. With Danielle it was different. I thought myself in love – but we weren't right for each other. *You* are the one I love. I'll do anything you want – "

"And say anything too – "

"If that's what it takes, yes! I don't want to lose you. You want proof? Ask me to make any commitment you like. I'll give up journalism, I'll move to Calahurst – I'll even move back in with my father if it means I can be close to you. I'll do whatever you want, whatever it takes because I need you, Isabel. I don't think I can go on without you."

Isabel was stunned into silence. He certainly sounded as though he meant it.

"I want you to marry me," he said firmly. "That way you won't be able to run away from me again. Not unless you get a damn good lawyer first – "

She felt herself weaken. "And take you for every penny you've got?"

His voice was unsteady. "Should I take that as a 'yes'?"

"It's a 'maybe'."

She felt his arms slide around her waist, drawing her closer and gave up the fight. "This is definitely your last chance. Any more extra-curricular shagging and you'll be in serious trouble."

"You'll be cutting off my balls?"

"With a blunt knife."

"Ouch!"

"We have a lot of talking to do," she added, "If we're going to make this work. All the serious relationship stuff, to ensure we're totally compatible before we do something we're going to regret. Maybe we should see a counsellor first – "

"Quite right. We have to decide on which celebrity magazine we can get to pay for the wedding and which designer we can get to supply the clothes for free – and

I know Taz and Patrick are going to be fighting over who gets to be best man – the loser will probably want counselling – very smart of you to think about that, Isabel. How big a rock do you want for your ring – "

"Cubic zirconia will do for me," she said breezily. "If you buy me a diamond you're likely to get it thrown back in your face."

"I thought all girls liked diamonds . . ."

"Not this one." Isabel slid her arms around his neck and pulled his lips back to hers. "Diamonds are pretty enough to look at – but it's a kiss from the man you love that lasts forever . . ."

THE END